So We Stay
HIDDEN

THE WEST HAVEN UNDEAD BOOK 2

So We Stay HIDDEN

4 Horsemen
Publications, Inc.

NICK SAVAGE

So We Stay Hidden
Copyright © 2023 Nick Savage. All rights reserved.

4 Horsemen
Publications, Inc.

4 Horsemen Publications, Inc.
1497 Main St. Suite 169
Dunedin, FL 34698
4horsemenpublications.com
info@4horsemenpublications.com

Cover by J. Kotick
Typesetting by Niki Tantillo
Editor: Blair Parke

Library of Congress Control Number: 2022948769

Paperback ISBN-13: 978-1-64450-699-8
Hardcover ISBN-13: 978-1-64450-859-6
Audiobook ISBN-13: 978-1-64450-701-8
Ebook ISBN-13: 978-1-64450-700-1

DEDICATION

*This is to everyone who believes in something
bigger than themselves.*

TABLE OF CONTENTS

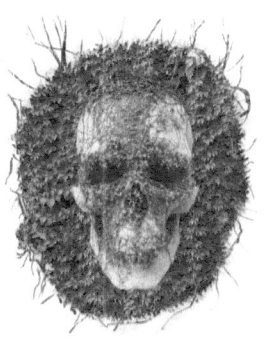

CHAPTER 1

"Celebrate now. It can all be taken away."
~V. Petrovsky~

An old jazz recording of "Chicago (That Toddlin' Town)" provides the perfect background music to their early dinner celebration as Ken and Tracy enjoy an appetizer of stuffed mushrooms in an upscale Italian restaurant.

The other customers seem equally jubilant this evening, perhaps also celebrating their own accomplishments with each other. Ken and Tracy look around at the tuxedoed staff swimming through the rows of tables and booth-lined walls, delivering food and drinks to happy, hungry people. The popping sound of a server opening a champagne bottle draws the couple's attention to a family a few tables down.

Ken turns back to see his wife breaking apart some bread. Tracy smiles at him, dipping the piece into a dish of olive oil sprinkled with a Parmesan/Romano mixture.

"Is this what the future is going to be? Days and evenings like this, all the time?" Tracy asks as she bites down on her oil-soaked bread.

Ken smiles back. He knows thoughts like that are naive, but he can't help but think she could be right. After all, if the prophecy is correct and their child is the one to bring together the Legends and the Normal world, then who would want to imagine it any differently? Ken gives a subtle nod as he thinks about a world without fear, a world where those who have had to hide for so long can feel free to be themselves—a world without prejudice.

"We can only hope," he responds. "Have you given any thought to names?"

She sits up a little straighter in her chair. "Yes. I think we need to honor those who passed before us. A way to remember where we come from, how far we've come, and where we still have to go. Also, a way to tell Scarlett she is as much our daughter as Connor is our son."

"So, you are thinking what, exactly?" Ken asks.

She bobs her head side to side. "I was thinking Hillary for a girl. And if it's a boy, Jimmy."

Ken stops and holds his wife's hands. "I think that is a beautiful idea. I love those names. Scarlett will feel especially honored if we name our child after one of her parents."

"She was your sister of sorts, too, Ken," Tracy reminds him.

"Of course, of course." Ken acknowledges his misplaced wording. "But I think she'll be very honored is all I'm saying."

CHAPTER 1

"I never understood why it says James on his tombstone. Everyone called him Jimmy," Tracy ponders aloud.

"His mother called him James; it's what he wanted in his will," Ken clarifies for his wife, while taking a bite of oil-soaked bread.

They look around the restaurant, soaking in each moment they can. From the feel of the slightly rough, overly starched tablecloth that gives this place its signature, polished look to the dark wood bar with writing etched into the glass behind it, everything tonight feels calm for the two of them. They feel a sense of peace knowing that this child Tracy carries is for the betterment of humanity. They see a group of young kids, all dressed in tuxedos and prom dresses, walk through the restaurant guided by the hostess. They find their seats at a table a few yards away from Ken and Tracy.

"Do you think the kids will have fun at prom?" Tracy asks.

Before Ken has a chance to answer, the waiter brings a large entree of Eggplant Parmesan to the table. A serving spoon is shoved under the food, its handle reflecting the light above them. The server sets it down and places an empty plate in front of each of them. He steps away while another server puts down a side order of potatoes Vesuvio.

"Anything else I can get for you right now?" the server's tone is a little more casual than the atmosphere otherwise alludes.

Tracy gently shakes her head at Ken, who looks to the server and says, "Just the check. Everything is perfect. Thank you."

The server nods and encourages them to enjoy their meal before leaving them to eat.

"I hope so," Ken says, returning to Tracy's yet unanswered question. "They need to have fun. The world is going to catch up with them soon enough."

"Why are we getting the check already?" Tracy inquires.

"Pictures. I know Vistrus will take some, but I want a few of our son. I want to see him out for this," Ken says.

"I heard Scarlett talking with Allison," Tracy starts. "Something happened while Jack was out with Connor. He's not going to prom tonight."

"Did Connor say what happened?" Ken asks.

"Not a word. I think with everything that is going on, the kids starting to find out and all, things aren't making much sense," Tracy offers up.

"I remember how hard it was. It's all so surreal at first that asking anyone about it seems impossible," Ken says. "They're going to let a junior attend senior prom without a date?"

Tracy chuckles. "She has a date. He's simply not going." She takes her fork and cuts through the Parmesan marinara sauce into the perfectly cooked eggplant. "This is amazing." She smiles.

Ken shovels a bite into his mouth. He lets it sit on his palate for a moment before nodding in agreement. "If they worked it out, then I say have fun."

"From what Allison told me, they planned to stop by his house first so he could have a dance with Scarlett before they head to the event," Tracy says, sipping a glass of water.

Ken looks at the table of prom kids having fun without a care in the world. "Can you believe Connor's graduating in a few days? I think we did pretty well with him."

Tracy looks at Ken, watching the kids. She knows what he is feeling—the emotions, high and low; the trials and tribulations of the past eighteen years all passing behind his eyes in a blurred wave, making him think that he has done something good with his son. A calm flows through him that, perhaps, he has not messed up his child, despite knowing the life Connor is finding out he has to lead. Tracy feels the same. She knows a chapter has closed, but she is not upset because she knows another is about to begin—the college years.

"We did well, honey. I can't believe that later tonight, our son will probably be dancing away one last school dance, not realizing everything he is about to leave behind." Tracy takes a deep breath, then sighs. "All good things. . ."

"I know. I know. I just want the best for him." Ken turns back to his wife and lowers his voice to an almost inaudible whisper, beyond a Normal's hearing capability. "Do you think we'll still need The Council and The Nation once our baby grows and the prophecy comes true?"

Tracy answers back in the same hushed tone, "I don't know. I'd like to think that even after everything settles, we will still have our own to look out for our particular needs."

"Imagine that, though; one day, we may have Councilman Connor Desalvo," Ken says with a full and proud smile.

As the server drops the check in the middle of the table, they laugh at the thought, breaking the almost silent mini-conversation.

"That would be nice," Tracy says as she finishes her serving of Eggplant Parmesan. "But first, we have to get him through college." She grabs the check and drops her credit card in the presenter.

Connor stares at himself in the bathroom mirror. His purposefully disheveled, sandy brown hair, held together with more pomade than a teenage boy should use, accompanies his clean, pressed tuxedo and vest, matching cufflinks, and a freshly shaved face, all part of the work he put in for one final, grandiose high-school event—Senior Prom.

He stares at himself, though, because he isn't sure why he should care about such things. His date, Allison, has seen him countless times. Rare are the days they don't see each other outside of school, so why this moment? Why one final exclamation point on a high-school career that is about to be gone to the annals of one's history? Or is that what it is about, one more night to live in the glory that is about to pass by as fast as it came? This one final night is to take a chance on something that has held him back. One more opportunity to bust a move on the dance floor with friends you may only see again at a reunion. One more night to live in this moment of life before it is gone forever. One more chance to do something great on the last page of this chapter of life.

He sighs an exhale of teenage apathy. He wants to be as excited as Allison and his cousin, Scarlett, are. He wants to be as enthusiastic as the rest of the students who have talked non-stop since the tickets went on sale three months ago. The whispers in the hallways of prom dresses, limousines, hotel parties, and more are all to symbolize leaving behind the four years called high school with a bang. He wants to be excited about tonight. He was excited about tonight. But as he stands, staring at himself in the mirror, all he can think is that tomorrow will be no different, that nothing will have changed. So, he forces out a smile that sends a jolt of fear, shocking his brain into ter-rifying thoughts. *What if everything changes? What if nothing is the same after tonight? Then what will he do?*

But his thoughts of doom and despair are saved by the laughter of his parents, Ken and Tracy, entering the front door after their dinner date.

"Connor!" Tracy calls out. "You almost ready? The limo will be here in a few minutes, and we want pictures!"

Connor shakes off the unnamed feeling and, in a moment of teenage awkwardness, snaps his fingers, points to his reflection, and winks. He shakes his head, realizing he is glad no one saw him do that, and runs downstairs.

He is greeted by his smiling parents, proud that their son cleans up so nicely. A tear wells up in Tracy's eyes.

"You look so handsome, Connor." She tugs on his collar in a vain attempt to straighten it out even more.

"You've grown into a man, son. If you ever doubted yourself, or our pride in you, you need not worry any longer," Ken says with a proud smile. Raising a pointed finger and shaking it, he says, "Hold on..." Disappearing into his home office, he calls out, "...your mom wants pictures!"

Connor rolls his eyes at the thought of taking solo pictures, but he knows every parent will be doing the same. Connor notices his mom's smile and the maternal look in her eyes. He sees someone who is both proud and worried, happy and concerned.

"Is everything okay, Mom? I can't tell if you're happy or about to cry," Connor asks.

She waves him off. "Everything is fine. I'm just so happy. Look at you." She smiles, holding in tears of joy.

Connor shakes his head at his mom. Ken comes around the corner, holding a Nikon D3400 DSLR.

"That's a heavy hitter for a few snapshots, huh, Dad?" Connor laughs.

"Nothing but the best for my family." His words escape through his smile. "Now give me a pose that says, 'Tonight's the night.'"

Connor stands straight, grabs the lapels of his tux coat, and smiles a sly smile. Ken snaps a picture of that pose and a few more as Connor switches up the look.

Tracy peers out the window. "The limo's here." She turns to Connor, who is finally starting to feel the hype of prom. "You ready?"

Connor nods as he checks his pockets for his phone and wallet. "All set. I love you, Mom."

"I love you, too, Connor," Tracy says, smiling.

Ken opens the door for his son. "Do you have the corsages?"

"Jack arranged to have them in the limo," Connor says, heading out the door. "Love you, Dad."

"Love you too, son. Have fun tonight." He and Tracy watch as their son disappears into the limo for one last hurrah.

They close the door behind them as the limo drives off around a corner.

Tracy grabs Ken's hand as he goes to lock the deadbolt. He stops and turns to her sliding his hands around her waist. "So now what?" she asks, biting her bottom lip.

"We relax. We have a nice, peaceful evening with no kids, no worries about The Nation, The Council, or anything. Just you, me, and a movie on TV," he says, watching the smile on her face grow.

They settle onto the couch with a bowl of buttered, air-popped popcorn and each a glass of cola as the DVD player closes the disc tray and loads up the movie's menu. Ken grabs the remote from the end table next to the couch and hits play, tossing popcorn in his mouth with his other hand. The light from the television is the only illumination in the room; even the curtains are drawn to keep the nighttime glare off the screen. The evening sky has grown dim as well, as if to watch the movie with them.

"Things have been so crazy lately. I'm glad we can spend some time together, just relaxing." Tracy snuggles into her husband.

He wraps his arm around her and gives her a loving squeeze. The couple sinks deeper into their seats as the romantic comedy starts playing the opening credits.

"It's been a bit much, and I'm sorry if I've not been the husband I should be," he offers up an unnecessary apology.

"My love, you have nothing to apologize about. It's been rough for everyone." She kisses him on the cheek. "Let's put all that aside and enjoy the movie."

They let their thoughts and worries slip away for the moment. A rare moment when a parent and spouse can enjoy the company of their betrothed without outside forces weighing on their minds—if only for a moment. But moments such as these bring sincere appreciation for the other person in the relationship. Pure moments like these, though, are fleeting as the sound of an unexpected doorbell interrupts their evening cinema.

Tracy looks at her husband, eating a handful of popcorn. "Do we answer the door or pretend we're not home?"

Ken chuckles. "We can wait. See if they go away."

Tracy presses her palms together, fingers pointed toward the sky. "Please make them go away."

The unwanted sound of the doorbell echoes once more.

"I think we should answer it." He stands up, sets his soda down after taking another sip, and heads to the door.

Tracy lifts her finger to the sky above. "One night wouldn't have killed ya."

Ken pulls back the blind just enough to peep out the front door window. All he sees is a head looking down at the ground and a police uniform. Next to the officer is a person in plain clothes looking back to the street; his blond hair faces Ken. All Ken can see is that this blond man holds a briefcase. Ken unlocks the deadbolt. "It's the police, babe."

Tracy gets up and pauses the movie. "Is everything all right?"

"I'm opening the door now," Ken replies. With caution, he opens the door. The officer in uniform lifts his head. The smile on his face belies the name on his badge: Espinoza.

"Hello," Officer Espinoza begins. "Ken and Tracy DeSalvo? Connor's parents?"

Tracy hurries her step and stops next to Ken. "Is everything all right, officer?" she asks with a hint of desperation. Experience has taught her that when news starts like this, it doesn't end well.

"May we come in?" Officer Espinoza inquires.

"Are you in?" Ken says in return.

The blond man, still peering toward the road, replies, "I am in a night, chilly and dark."

Tracy smiles. "The night may be chilly but not dark." A sense of relief overcomes the couple as they open the door for Officer Max Espinoza and the blond man. The momentary tenseness of the unexpected officers melts away.

Ken and Tracy both turn to let the men inside. Max enters and blocks the blond man from Ken's line of sight. The blond man steps inside but keeps his face turned away, surveying the decorations and furnishings of the residence, noticing a glass-topped coffee table in front of the leather couch. He looks past the dining room to the den patio beyond.

"I think it's best if you take a seat," Officer Espinoza says, gesturing to the couch.

The DeSalvos take a seat, and Tracy turns off the movie. The blond man enters the living room, proceeding past them to a dining room table on the other side while still hiding his face from Ken. The man sets his briefcase on the table and clicks the locks, slowly opening it.

"What's this all about, Officer?" Tracy tries to move the conversation along. "Is everything all right with Connor? Did he transition in public? Is he hurt?"

"We know," chimes in the blond man.

A chill runs through Tracy. An instinctual, adrenalized shot of fight or flight courses through her. But she doesn't know what to do.

"What did you say?" Tracy attempts to stall while she figures out her move.

"We know," the blond man says, again dropping a parchment from inside his briefcase.

Tracy and Ken's eyes go wide as they find themselves frozen, the headlight that is the falling parchment racing toward them, the deer in the road. Ken shakes off the fear as he feels the hair all over his body start to grow long. The pain of fast-growing fangs and thickening nails adds to his adrenaline. Thoughts flow through his head of his wife and unborn child and the harm that might come to them, maddening thoughts that cause him to huff with each breath. His arms shake with anger. But before Ken can make a move toward the blond man, Officer Espinoza has his gun trained point-blank at Tracy's head.

"What do you two know?" Tracy asks with deceptive innocence.

"What we know is of no consequence," the blond man says, turning around to finally face them. "It's what I know that is of much consequence." He holds up a syringe filled with a dark blue fluid.

The realization and terror of these unknown assailants intruding in Ken's home finalize his transition to werewolf as his irises shift from light brown to dark golden yellow.

"Please," Tracy cries out from her thinned lips and sunken eyes. "You know the response." Her nose is withered and veiny as her tightening skin scrunches up her cracking face. "You are in."

The blond man lets out a full-bellied laugh filled as much with disgust at what Tracy said as with amusement that he fooled her.

"I am in. Yes. But not The Nation. No. I am not part of some secret society filled with bottom-barrel scum," the blond man says, pressing the syringe up until a few drops of liquid seep out the top of the needle. "You..." he looks over at Ken "...Mr. DeSalvo, are a family man. Or at least people say. But I know you."

Ken's eyes fix on the needle and the dark blue liquid as it grips the metal, slowly working its way down. The liquid rolls until it hits the plastic body of the syringe, and Ken watches as the liquid falls to the ground—the first drop of ill intent.

"You don't know anything about me," Ken growls out.

The blond man takes a step closer to the couple, the menacing syringe drooling out its smiling point. "I know."

Ken laughs despite his disadvantageous position. "You think I am different from you because of the hair on my skin? Or the size of my teeth?"

"The better to eat me with, I'm sure," quips the blond man.

Ken looks at the officer, but his stare is not met. His gun and gaze are trained on Tracy for any sign of deception, watching for any movement that signals to him a need to squeeze the trigger of his well-maintained and polished gun. He sees Officer Espinoza's eyes, the mile-long stare that stops on Tracy. Ken knows that stare, the concentrated look of someone trained to kill, starting to question his path.

"To them, it's about the hair on your skin, the size of your teeth, and everything else that makes you the stuff of Legends," the blond man continues. "The DNA and RNA that causes your conditions," the blond man finishes while jabbing the needle into Ken's arm.

Ken stares at the blond man, unsure of what to say. The ever-growing feeling in his gut that everything is not, nor will be, all right has him glued in his spot. He cannot decide on what move he should make, if any.

CHAPTER 1

"You work for the city. You help make the laws. But what weighs on your mind, even after the laws have passed, is, were they the right laws? You can't help but doubt yourself," the blond man says, emptying half the syringe into Ken's arm. "You can't help but doubt every choice you've made for your family." He pulls the needle out of Ken's arm, still half full, and walks to Tracy. "Even now, you are wondering what you could have done differently to prevent this from happening. You are playing different choices in your head on how to get out of this alive. And each choice is halted by an outcome you wish to not see manifest. It is your nagging self-doubt that eats at everything you do. That is what I know."

The blond man jams the needle into Tracy's arm and empties the rest of the syringe before turning to Officer Espinoza. "You can lower your gun, Max. They aren't going anywhere."

"What did you give them?" Officer Espinoza inquires as he lowers his gun.

"It's something I've been working on. Similar to Rohypnol but tailored for Legends. He won't move. Neither will she," the blond man explains with an overconfident smile.

"Can't or won't?" the officer asks, taking small, cautious steps backward from the seated couple. His finger still rests on the trigger, ready to squeeze if need be.

"Does it matter? They are awake enough to respond and as docile as newborn kittens. This is what the drug does. Complete compliance." He pulls out a

15

rolled-up instrument belt and handheld analog voice recorder from the briefcase.

Ken and Tracy helplessly stare forward. They manage minimal movement in their necks, enough to turn to each other and see the desperation in their eyes as they sit, unable to move despite their imminent demise.

Officer Max Espinoza stares at the couple on the couch, looking at their monstrous features. Ken's ridged nose and fangs. His veiny muscles would make even the most hardcore anabolic steroid user jealous. The patches of thick fur covering his body. Max looks at Tracy and her withered nose, the sunken, thin lips that are cracked. Max studies her scarred skin and beady eyes, her thinned, wispy hair. He looks at her mouth as she tries to work up the will to speak and at her gums, the only teeth she has are her fangs.

But despite all the outward appearances that makes Max perceive the couple as monsters, he notices the despair in their eyes. The look in each of their eyes that shines love and humanity. The look that screams for self-preservation. The look in their eyes that searches for a way out of this situation. A look that, in Max, plants a seed of self-doubt.

Ken's eyes stay fixed on the blond man as he unrolls the black leather instrument belt in front of them. He sets the voice recorder on a coffee table and hits the record button.

"West Haven Patients KDS and TDS," the blond man begins as he rifles through his tools on the dining room table. "Complying injections have been administered."

A relaxing warmth starts in the back of Tracy's head and makes its way down her neck and spine, spreading outward as it travels. She looks at her husband, still seeing the scared husband desperately searching for ways out of this mess. He looks at her and sees a newfound determination in her eyes. She watches as the blond man picks through his belt. She sees Max's attention turn away as he watches the blond man, while Ken's eyes are fixed on his wife.

Tracy and Ken shift their attention to the front door as their ears pick up approaching footsteps. They sense a reserved casualness in their step. A step that wants to come across as casual, but a Legend can hear the subtle distinction that they are on guard. Tracy hears a rapid heartbeat accompanying the footsteps, stressed and ready to respond. She picks up the sound of the stranger outside, taking a deep breath to help calm down his heart rate a little.

A loud rap is heard on the door.

Officer Espinoza and the blond man turn their attention to the door.

The blond man turns to the others. "Is anyone expecting company?"

Officer Espinoza's stance grows shaky and more nervous. Tracy and Ken shake their heads as the blond man turns back to the table to cover his instruments. "I'll get the door."

Tracy glances at her husband and nods to the officer. The blond man steps away from the table he has commandeered and heads to the door. Tracy watches Officer Espinoza, whose eyes are still trained on the door. The blond man creaks the door open just a sliver.

"Help!" Tracy cries out from the couch.

The stranger, dressed in a police uniform, pushes his way into the house, knocking the blond man back a few feet and falling onto his knees. His gun already drawn, he points it at the blond man.

"Stay down!" the newly-arriving officer commands. The blond man motions to a chair at the table, gesturing the question of if he may sit. Without waiting for the new officer to respond, he pulls a chair out, nice and slow, taking a seat. Both the DeSalvos stay on the couch, unwilling or unable to move.

Tracy looks at the badge of the new officer and reads Smith.

Officer Espinoza points his gun toward the blond man as well. "They finally let you off of desk duty?" Espinoza says to Officer Smith.

"First day back on the beat," Smith responds. "What's going on?"

Tracy looks at the officer. "They're trying to kill us! Please help!"

Tracy sees the disgust, horror, confusion, and concern all mixed together on Smith's face as he lays his eyes upon her withered, gaunt body. Officer Smith takes a step back as he sees the massive muscles of the hair-covered, fang-touting Ken a couch cushion down. Tracy watches Officer Smith turn to Officer Espinoza and the blond man.

Ken looks at his wife, but she doesn't see him or the sad, resigned smile on his face that knows this may be their last moments together.

CHAPTER 1

"Max, what's going on here? What happened to them?" Officer Smith asks, aiming his gun back at the blond man.

Office Espinoza taps the barrel of his gun against his side, "So many things." Officer Espinoza looks at the bulletproof vest covering Officer Smith's torso. He takes quick note of his exposed neck, face, and arms.

Ken notices on Officer Espinoza's hands that the hair has grown a tad longer and darker than it was moments ago. Ken sees the subtle, translucent capillaries surfacing around the officer's eyes and trailing out from his nose like a bad case of sudden onset Rosacea. Ken opens his mouth to speak, but before a sound can be uttered, Officer Espinoza doubles over in pain.

A visceral scream emanates from deep within the bowels of the officer. Ken watches as Officer Espinoza looks at his hands as the dark, thickening hair overtakes them. Seeing this, the blond man grabs a syringe and walks over to Officer Espinoza, stabbing Espinoza in the arm and injecting the translucent substance into him.

Officer Smith stands speechless, waving his gun back and forth between the decrepit-looking DeSalvos still seated on the couch and his fellow officer.

"Will someone please explain what's going on here?!" Officer Smith yells.

The blond man takes the gun from Officer Espinoza and takes a deep breath. Ken watches as the hair and capillaries recede back into Espinoza's body. The blond man looks at Officer Smith. "We are about to make history. Too bad you can't be a part of it." He raises the gun at Officer Smith and shoots him in the forehead. As if he has just swatted a fly, the blond man hands the weapon back to Officer Espinoza and walks back to his tool belt.

As the newly deceased body of Officer Smith falls to the ground, Tracy seizes the opportunity and lunges at Espinoza. The officer turns and fires his gun but misses Tracy. The stray bullet rips through Ken's arm. He lets out a deafening roar in response.

A warm wave of relaxation washes over Ken. A feeling of all his muscles, starting from the back of his neck and flowing all the way down past his spine, overtakes him for a moment. He watches his beloved grapple with the mad officer for only a moment before the warm relaxation dissipates, and he feels his body freed from the chemical prison he was forced into.

The blond man grabs a scalpel from his belt and turns to Tracy and Max. Ken side-tackles the blond man causing the blade to fly from his hands and across the room. The two men tumble on the ground, trying to gain the advantage over the other. Ken listens to the racing heartbeats of those around him. The rapid pace of Office Espinoza, the eerie, almost calm beat of the blond man, and his wife's heart racing while she exchanges blows with the officer.

Ken finds the strength of the blond man rivals his own, an impressive feat for someone who is seemingly not in The Nation. The two stop tumbling as Ken pins down the blond man.

"Why can't you just leave us alone!?!" Ken growls out. A trail of drool drips down, landing on the blond man's cheek.

CHAPTER 1

The blond man takes a quick look around and spies Espinoza's gun within reach. He starts fighting against Ken with his right arm while reaching for the gun with his left.

Ken bends toward the blond man's neck, his fangs tingling with the will to live through this night. As Ken's teeth graze the surface, the blond man grabs the gun, jabs it into Ken's neck, and squeezes the trigger.

The deafening boom of the shot echoes through the living room. Ken falls to the side, grabbing his neck to try and stop the bleeding, but blood pours out from the matted hair on his neck, between his fingers, and past his palm.

Tracy turns toward the sound of the gunfire and screams a visceral scream. A scream that scratches her throat and lungs raw. A cry that, itself, claws its way out of her body.

The blond man, still holding the gun, leans into Ken. "Because you and your diseases are not welcome here or anywhere." He stops for a second to look at Tracy as she watches her dying husband. "Gods and beasts; that is what our world is made of. And clearly, you are the beasts. Nothing but lesser beings for us to clean up."

Tears flow from Ken's eyes, matting the hair around them. His will to live shines through his fading eyes.

Tracy jumps off Espinoza, pushing him to the floor. She lands next to her husband and holds him. Her attention turns to the blond man whose smile fades by the anger in her eyes that cuts through the room. He knows that hell hath no fury. And if there ever was a woman scorned, taking away the love of her life, the father of her children, and her best friend, is it.

She sets down her husband and lunges at the blond man. He raises his arm to shoot the gun, but she is too quick. He flies back into the coffee table, breaking it into pieces. The glass top shatters around him. She turns to Officer Espinoza, grabbing him with such blinding speed he doesn't have a moment to react. She throws him clear across the room into a curio cabinet and an end table next to it. He falls through the glass door and shelves, shattering the case and breaking every tchotchke it held. The lamp that sits on the end table rolls off onto the floor. She holds her stance for a moment as both men are trying to recover. She sees her husband on the couch, his eyes hold a vacant stare as the wound has stopped flowing.

A quick glance at Officer Espinoza to see he still lies motionless, her attention turns back to the blond man. She leans over him, teeth sneering through her broken face. Her thin and wispy hair hangs down, framing her rage. She grabs the blond man to lift him into the air but doesn't notice him grab the scalpel as she hoists him up. Her chest heaves with anger as she holds him over her head. As she leverages back to throw him, he swipes at her neck with the blade. In the sudden rush of pain, she drops the blonde man right on top of her.

She lies pinned beneath him while struggling to breathe and hold onto her life. The warmth of the blood gurgling out of her neck keeps her in the moment. She can no longer protect the child that is prophesied. She can no longer be the mother to Connor and Scarlett. Each time blood sprays from her neck and against the couch, she realizes that all the joy she felt for the future has faded. She watches with darkening eyes as the blond man stands up. Her strength is too weak to respond to the situation around her. She lies helpless, hoping the torture is done.

As her life slips away, Tracy is left with her thoughts. Thoughts and questions as to why they did this to her and Ken. Questions as to what this man has against them. They have done nothing wrong. She watches as this man who thinks of them as lesser beings has taken it upon himself to hold contempt prior to investigation. She keeps an eye on him as he surveys the carnage around him with a twisted look of displeasure on his face.

Max Espinoza, on the other hand, gets up and sways in place with a vile disgust shown on his contorted face. "This isn't what I signed on for," he says. "How am I going to explain this to the precinct? I can't justify any of this."

The blond man kicks the lamp into the hallway as he steps in front of Officer Espinoza, placing his hands on Max's shoulders to steady him. He gets Max's focus and looks into his eyes. "This is a war; this is for a better future; this is bigger than you and me."

"You said they were monsters. You told me that I could kill the monster inside me and be normal." Officer Espinoza falls back into his hysterics.

The blond man shakes Max. "Get yourself together. You are an officer of the law!"

Officer Espinoza slinks to the ground. The reality of the situation, the gravity of his actions, participation in this macabre evening, and previous events start to sink in.

Tracy's last glimmer of hope passes as the blond man throws a landscape painting above the couch onto the floor. Her slowed heart pounds a little harder as the blond man tears through the drywall to reveal two small vials, corked and housing a swirling, smokey substance. Her weak body tries to cry out to the blond man, to plead with him to leave the vials alone.

But there will be no salvation. The blond man opens the vials, and the smoke within them releases into the air. The smoke sinks but stays dense and connected, sinking to the ground. One of the clouds plumes as it travels to Ken, surrounding his face and retreating into his mouth and nose. As it dissipates, the glazed look in Ken's eyes goes white. Tracy watches as the final, proverbial nail in his coffin is hammered into place.

The other trail of smoke settles around Tracy. She tries to hear the world one last time. She tries to take in all she can before her leave from this life, but the smoke is suffocating. It, too, encircles her face as it seeps back inside her through her nose and mouth. But still, she holds onto what she can. She thinks of her son and memories of the holidays and family celebrations. She thinks of everything they had started to plan for the new addition to the family and what could have been. The flights of fancy of a world where Legends were not afraid to be who they are.

A world without fear of ignorance and the hysteria ignorance brings.

The blond man moves to the tool belt and starts rolling it up. "I didn't get any of the samples I needed! Everything here is ruined! I need my samples!"

"Why?" is all Max can muster up to say after coming to.

The blond man ties his belt up and takes an exaggerated step back to Max. He stops in front of him and looks down like a parent over a small child. "Because we can't make them like us if we don't know how to fix them."

Max just sits, shaking his head. "What if they aren't broken?"

The blond man squats down and points a skinny finger at Max. "Of course they are broken! Their diseases are proof of that!" He stands back up and strides to the door. "I am getting my samples from the Taylors. Let's go!"

Max turns his head to the blond man but doesn't stand up. He just watches as the arterial spray from Tracy's neck loses pressure and speed: her thinned lips cry out silent, vain pleas for help. He sees the humanity in her eyes while the lack of any in his accomplice.

"Fine," the blond man huffs. "Sit and wallow, but I have work to do. Remember, Max, the war isn't just beginning. Their kind has been waging it for many centuries. It's only now that we have a way to turn the tide. Get yourself together, soldier. Figure out whatever it is that is going through your mind and fix this mess. We need a soldier like you, and you'll need us."

"How should I fix this?" Max poses the question to the blond man.

"The same way you display a nice piece of art," the blond man says, tapping his temple, as if corpse mutilation should be second nature to Officer Espinoza. "Frame it," he adds with a wink.

The blond man exits the house, leaving Officer Espinoza to linger in the bloody aftermath. He looks around, trying to figure out how he can stage the situation to frame the DeSalvos. He sees the lifeless eyes and sneer locked on Ken's hair-covered face and gets an idea.   Tracy's dying eyes can't help but stare at Officer Espinoza as he reaches for a serrated folding knife he had tucked away on his belt. He bends down to the deceased cop and whispers a private apology in his dead ear. Tracy's eyes see Espinoza take the knife and begin to cut into Officer Smith's flesh. She hasn't the strength to turn away from what fate might await her, so she stares downward at the broken glass of the coffee table.

The world fades to black for Tracy. Her eyes try to hold onto this life as long as they can, but they succumb to the inevitable. The last thing she will ever see is a voice recorder lying in a puddle of blood, the little device that fell to the floor in the struggle. The record button is still pressed in, capturing the sound and fury of the events.

CHAPTER 2

T he mermaid tail of Scarlett's form-fitting red prom dress rustles in the slight breeze as she stands outside Jack's house, waiting for him to open the door. The darkened house looks more like a 1980s slasher film setting than the welcoming environment she knows it to be. Jack said to come by after prom to steal another dance. So here she is, but it appears she may be the only one.

She gives the door another hesitant knock. After a moment, she hears signs of life from inside: ambient rustling and approaching footsteps. She rasps on the door again, trying to catch the attention of whoever is still up. The knob starts to turn, but no voice calls out from inside. No curtains move to see who stands at their door.

Scarlett takes a cautious step back as the door creaks open a sliver. A cold shiver runs down her spine as if, inside, there is something far worse than a family sleeping.

"Jack? Is that you, baby?" she whispers.

The door doesn't open any wider. All Scarlett can hear is the sound of heavy breathing from just beyond.

"Scarlett," Jack huffs—his voice still distinctly his, only deeper and a little raspy.

"Yes, baby. It's me." A tremble of confusion in Scarlett's voice. "What's going on?"

"Call your uncle." His demand is soft but no less forceful.

Without hesitation, she pulls out her phone to dial, taking a step forward to enter his house. As she attempts to open the door, she is met with resistance.

"No!" Jack cries out. "You can't, well, you can't ... you can't come in. Just call your uncle. Call someone." His usual uptick and rising pitch he usually carries has settled down a few notches.

She tries unsuccessfully to open the door again, but Jack's strength proves too much. "Jack, I don't know what's going on here. I don't like it. I'm a little more than ... than unsettled."

"I can't, um, explain this to you," he starts but never finishes.

Each time her mind tries to search for reasons behind Jack's actions, every thought she thinks is cut short by the obscurity of the situation. However, one idea stops her dead in her tracks. A thought that has her starting to shake in a bone-deep fright that inside the house, everything is not all right.

"Are you safe?" she asks.

His heavy breathing calms down. His fingers wrap around the door to the outside, still holding it between himself and Scarlett. She sees his fingers and gasps: the long, thick claw-like nails, crude but sharp—the long hair covering his fingers in dense patches.

"Now, do you see? I need someone who knows," he says with a clear mind and even tone.

Scarlett pulls up her uncle's number on her phone and dials. "I'm calling him. Now please let me in."

Jack holds the door shut against her wishes.

"Jack!" she demands, stomping her foot.

"I have, um, no words ... for what you are going to, um, see," he says in his usual stutter, but still with an even tone.

Scarlett pushes gently on the door, shedding light on the darkness inside. Jack feels her push and helps the door open. She hangs up her phone.

"Voicemail. I'll try again," Scarlett says, surveying the gruesome aftermath. She sees the dead bodies as she re-dials her uncle's number. She stops dead in her tracks as the voicemail picks up again. Looking around at the carnage and chaos of recent past events— three dead bodies and the accompanying blood—the beep for the message sounds off. "Hey ... Uncle Ken ... please call me back ASAP," she starts with a slow release. "I don't ... I can't even explain. I'll try Aunt Tracy." She hangs up and swipes down to dial her aunt. Scarlett's gaze stays fixed on the horrible scene even as she tilts her body, attempting to turn to face Jack for the first time since entering the house. Her mind hasn't grasped the details of the scene, just the overall depth of it.

"Don't," he pleads, turning away from her. "You saw enough of me at the door."

She hesitates for a moment as the silence of the room surrounds them. Jack exhales a heavy breath, pushing the silence aside. He knows she won't look away much longer. "Slowly. It's not what you're used to. I can't ... be normal."

Scarlett makes the turn and lays her eyes on her beloved. The shadows cast by the moonlight peeking in through the curtains help hide the true nature of his form. Within the shadows, Scarlett can see his hulking silhouette, a far cry from his usual, lanky self. She sees long, patchy hair covering the unnaturally large muscles that adorn his chest. His face, too, is garnished in patches of thick, fur-like hair that seem to try and hide, or at least try to detract from, his thickset fangs. Varicose veins bulging through the surface of his skin (teasing an impending explosion) seem to connect the patches of hair together. She watches as each breath causes his chest to rise and swell, making his stature even more supernatural. Each exhale shrinks him down as if to sink through the floor.

"Who did this?" Scarlett asks, trying to absorb the gravity of the situation.

He takes another deep breath and holds it for a long moment, turning his stare to the dead blond man on the floor. His shredded throat lay in pieces around him, a garnish for a most macabre dish. The gaping hole where it once was taunts the teen who tore it open.

Scarlett moves her locked stare past the blond man and his missing throat to Jack's parents' bodies. She sees the plastic bag torn open but otherwise still wrapped around his mother's head. Jack's mother Lucretia's vacant stare from her cold body sends chills down Scarlett's spine. She sees Jack's father on the floor, face down in a pool of his own blood. The smell of copper dominates the room from the spilled life all around it, while the congealing blood reflects the dim light, illuminating the room enough to see the details best left unnoticed.

She lifts her phone to her ear, realizing the phone call she made to her aunt. She hears nothing and looks at the screen to see the call timer counting upward. "Where are you guys? We need you!" She hangs up, turning back to Jack.

"And you did that?" she says, gesturing to the blond man and his missing throat.

Jack nods, and his breathing picks up again. Scarlett takes cautious steps toward him. She reaches out and begins running her hand down his back, petting him. Scarlett stops for a moment, not realizing if her stroking him is to comfort him or because of the animal-like form he is in. No matter the reason, his breathing starts to slow as she does, so she continues.

"He's the man that, well, that kidnapped me ... and my parents," he says, wringing his hands. "He cut the power and ... and took down ... he ... he killed Dad. And Mom. He almost..." he trails off as his breathing quickens up again. Tears fall off his furry cheeks.

Scarlett can feel the tension in him tightening up again. She moves in a little closer and hugs him.

31

"Shh. We'll figure this out. We need to call someone. Someone who will answer. Someone who knows your ... predicament." She kisses a patch of skin on his face that peeks through chunks of blood-soaked hair.

His breathing stops for a moment. Scarlett continues to hold him. He slowly lets out a breath and takes in another to hold. She moves around to the front of his blood-stained face, cupping it in her hands. He looks her in the eyes, sees her fearless resolve in the situation, and drops his head to the ground in shame. Scarlett picks it right back up to meet her gaze. She holds his head, resting her forehead against his. Scarlett matches his breathing for a few breaths and guides him down to a much more reasonable rate of breathing. No words are spoken, only eyes connecting.

As Jack normalizes his breathing, his fangs begin to retract into his mouth. The hair that covers his face and body recedes, and after a few minutes of slow breathing, his body is again the Jack he sees in the mirror.

Scarlett releases his head from her hands and hugs him tight. Tears start streaming from his eyes as Jack relaxes in her arms.

"What did I do?" he cries out. "Why, Scarlett? Why?" he pleads as his tears moisten Scarlett's shoulder. "What am I going to do?"

Scarlett sits silently, unsure if his questions need answering or if he's talking out loud to the universe. She continues holding him, stroking the hair on his head.

"My mom! He killed my mom! I watched her die, Scarlett! I watched her die because..." Jack moves from her grip to look at her. "...because I couldn't do anything! I tried! I tried to save her! He tied me up! He tried to kill all of us, Scarlett!" He drops his head back into her.

She has no words that will help pacify him, no soothing maxims to provide relief. Even the fact that he killed the blond man seems like a small consolation at the moment. All she can do is keep petting his head and quietly try to calm him with soft "shhs."

"What am I going to do now?" He cries into her shoulder.

All Scarlett can think about now is the poor soul in her arms. Left without parents. Left without the parental wisdom to provide guidance in beyond difficult situations such as this. A boy who must now be a man from this day forward with no father to show him if his shaving techniques aren't quite proper and no mother to straighten his tie when he gets ready for graduation. No one to provide any sage advice when life throws a curveball. No more childhood. No more innocence. No more youthful naivety to fall back on when the real world seems overwhelming. All of this is stripped away right in front of his eyes. No sensor to block out the images so ingrained in his head, he will see them every time he closes his eyes.

Scarlett knows that—despite her presence there and the undying support he will have from Connor—he is truly alone right now.

She stops petting him for a moment to check her cell phone. Hoping for a text or a missed call, she is quickly disappointed by the lack of notifications on her home screen. No text, no missed call icon, no envelope to show a voicemail.

"I can't get a hold of anyone," Scarlett starts. "Should I call Mr. P?"

Jack calms his tears for a moment as he turns to Scarlett. "Who?"

"Mr. Petrovsky. Al's dad," she clarifies.

Jack nods his head before hanging it back down in grief. The weight of the moment is too much for him to hold it up.

CHAPTER 3

*"Rare are the moments
for which there are no words."*
~E. DeSalvo~

Connor flips the switch off for his bedroom light. Noticing the bloodstain smeared across the back of her prom dress, he holds his finger to his lips. Allison stands behind him, confused by his odd behavior moments after they shared a magical moment.

"What's going on?" Allison whispers, trying to figure out the peculiar situation.

He creaks open the door while shaking his head. "I don't know. Follow me."

Guided by the moonlight shining through the windows, they tiptoe out of his room and back down the hall toward the living room. The unfamiliar smell that overtook his senses on the way in tonight once again assaults him. He stops where Allison had been propped up against the wall earlier and examines what Allison can only guess is a streak of blood.

Allison turns to Connor, whispering, "That's not a good sign."

The overwhelming smell of copper now assaulting his nose tells Connor that Allison is right, even in the hallway's dark light. Connor finally realizes why the distinct smell that never faded while they shared her bedroom was so overwhelming.

The sight of blood causes Allison to stumble back a few feet. She realizes the sacred memories of what happened after taking off her prom dress will be forever tainted by the bloodstain on the back of it.

Connor sees a broken lamp lying on the floor. A lamp that, like the blood on the wall, doesn't belong there. The lamp that quietly sits on an end table in the living room has made its way here in the hallway—a sign that sends Connor's heart racing. A pounding he can now feel and hear inside his chest.

Connor and Allison cautiously turn the corner to peek into the living room, jaws hitting the floor at the bloodshed before them. The lost innocence of childhood naivety has been brushed aside and fire tested by the image forever branded into their minds. The bodies, the blood, the wrecked furniture, the hole in the wall behind where a painting once hung, the same piece of art now smashed on the floor, the smell of iron and sweat, and the painful presence that lingers, trying to reach for help are all still there. He hears the faint sound of an electronic device, a more subtle version of when a television is turned off, but the DVD player has been left on; almost imperceivable. But the DVD player and the television are both turned off.

The drying blood under Connor's feet as he rushes into the chaos from the night's earlier events leaves bloody prints with each step. He stops and crouches down next to his mother. Her eyes stare off into the void beyond. In the pale moonlight, her face seems more sunken and scarred. Even that, coupled with her thin, wispy hair, doesn't fully mask the familiar face of the mother he loves because the eyes never lie. He knows it's his mother, also recognizing her clothes, size, and strange familiarity of her unusual appearance to him. The faint smell of her usual perfume still lingers.

A surge of pain courses through Connor as he stares at his deceased mother. He can feel his skin crawl and his nails sting and burn. The taste of copper fills his mouth, and his eyes start to see the ultraviolet colors that were projected in class. He doesn't notice the patches of hair overtaking his arms and hands.

Allison gasps at the sight of the hairy beast lying next to his mother: the long, patchy body hair, the fangs frozen in a menacing grin, the massive muscles all lying motionless. Then she notices the hole in the shoulder where the right arm used to be, the torn flesh, sinew and muscle hanging out, as if in wait to hold something into place.

"Connor!" she screams out, unable to hold in the plethora of mixed emotions.

He turns to see her struggling to stand, fighting against an inevitable collapse to the ground, tears flowing down her cheeks, her eyes unable to look away from a torso and its severed head. The arms and legs have been severed. Connor sees the face of the dismembered body, and the memory of the first visit to the police station floods back into his mind. He knows this officer who was kind yet stern.

Connor rushes to Allison, and she reaches out to embrace him. Her gaze, no longer fixed on the butchered bodies, now looks upon his changed form, a form that haunted her in the shadows of the abandoned school now stretches out to comfort her.

"What's happening to you?!" she screams.

Connor looks at his arms and sees the wispy, long, patchy hair flowing like grotesque streamers in a macabre parade. He sees his typically short, chewed nails are grown thick, long, and nightmarish. The pain from the transition flows through him again. His body tries to adjust, but he collapses in front of her.

Allison pulls away from Connor, falling against a wall. She doesn't feel the transition happening to her. The pain washes through her in unnoticed waves, as the sight before her still overwhelms her senses. She doesn't feel her skin start to tighten or feel her nose begin to shrink or her lips thin out and disappear. She slides down, unable to move at the confusion from the sights in front of her. She holds her head in her hands from the splitting headache of the transition. In her mind, the pain must be from the intensity of it all. She doesn't feel the blood drip from her inside her mouth and down her chin. She doesn't notice any of this about herself, only the wretched scene before her.

Vistrus stands in the unsealed chambers surrounded by the serpentine-marbled stonework, a stoic stare upon his face. Tears well up in his eyes. He notices dust particles reflected in the lights from above, floating through the air, frenzied residents long at rest that are now disturbed. His mind imagines them frantic over the discovery he holds in his hand. The thick layers of dust still settled on the portrait betray the impossibility of the person drawn. The lifelike detail and remarkable accuracy, perhaps aged only a few years from the present, adds to the improbability of the charcoal portrait.

Even the sound of Beethoven's "Moonlight Sonata" emanating from his pocket can't pull him away from the sight before him. A thought in his mind pulls him out of his trance, the belief that the rest of The Council needs to know about this. But the frantic dust racing through the air whispers to him that the rest of The Council might already know. Maybe they didn't want him to know, or perhaps no one at all knows except for the last person to leave and seal the chamber. A portrait to be forgotten to the ages to hide who is shown from danger or from themselves. He thinks that this chamber might have never been meant to be found. He looks around at the perfectly architectured green-and-black marble walls, the way the walls slant back as they rise. He thinks this might be the inside of some Pandora's box.

His thoughts are once again tempted to distraction by the buzzing in his pants pocket and the accompanying sounds of "Moonlight Sonata." He succumbs to temptation and turns his attention to this phone, begging to be answered. Vistrus glances down and sees the number calling is not one programmed into his phone. Though it is a number that holds a ring of familiarity, he can't quite place where.

"Hello?" he asks the person on the other end. A female voice can be heard through the spotty reception in this underground chamber. A rising panic in her voice is losing a battle to stay calm.

He rolls up the parchment with the charcoal portrait and tucks it between his waistband for safekeeping. He steps past the white glove before second-guessing the possible importance of it, so he backsteps and pockets it.

"My reception is terrible. Hold on one moment," Vistrus says into the phone.

He closes up the chambers, hiding them from society once again. He jogs back down the hall to the museum vault. As the door concealing the room closes behind him, his cell reception clears up.

"Mr. P?! Mr. P?!" the panicked voice cries out on the other end. "Can you hear me? Mr. P, they're all dead!"

The sting of her last words stops him dead in his tracks. "Scarlett? Is that you?" he asks.

"Yes! Thank God you can hear me!" she says, starting to calm down once again.

"What is going on?" Vistrus's concern grows. "Did you say someone died?"

Her voice conveys a sound of relief now that she has a hold of someone. "Not just someone. We're at Jack's! I can't get a hold of Uncle Ken or Aunt Tracy. You need to get here. Now!"

He takes a deep breath, knowing full well the possible implication of everything that lies in front of the young kids. "Scarlett, listen to me. Stay where you are. Do not call anyone else, and wait there for me. I am going to get a hold of Ken and Tracy. We will be over."

"What do I do in the meantime? Should I clean up what I can? Or..." she asks, searching for a way to fill the time.

"No. Do not touch anything. Leave everything exactly as is. Look away and try to stay calm." Vistrus's words offer little solace for the young Scarlett.

"Please hurry, Mr. P." She hangs up the phone.

Exiting the museum with a determined step, he runs to his car. After buckling his belt, he hides the rolled parchment under his seat for safekeeping. He backs out of his spot and dials Ken's cell phone; it immediately goes to voicemail.

"It is Vistrus. Call me as soon as you get this. Utmost importance," he says, hanging up the phone.

He turns out of the museum parking lot, and his phone rings. He sees that it is from Ken's landline.

"That was quick," he starts, feeling a moment of relief that the call was returned so promptly.

"Um, hello?! Daddy! Please come to Connor's house!" His daughter's voice cries out in slurs of missing teeth on the other end. The sounds of Connor's sobbing can be heard in the background.

"Allison? Are you okay? What is going on?" he asks in a concerned, fatherly voice.

"Someone killed them, Daddy!" she cries into the phone.

"Killed who? Are you safe?" he asks, concern rising in his mind over the multiple calls.

"Something happened to Connor." She ignores her father's question. The hysterics pick up in her voice. "I think he's dying!"

"Make sure you are alone and lock the doors. I will be there in a few minutes!" Vistrus commands.

"Okay. I'll call the police…" Allison starts.

"No, do not do that!" her father interrupts. "I will take care of everything. Just stay safe. Keep Connor calm," he orders.

"Okay, Daddy," she forfeits.

"Allie, I love you," he offers up.

"Love you too, Dad." A calm starts to wash over her.

As soon as he hangs up the phone, his thoughts turn to the unborn child. Neither Ken nor Tracy are answering their phones, and his daughter called, saying that people have died. His mind races, wondering who could have known she was pregnant and also have known about the prophecy. He must check to see if the unborn is safe. He must find out why this happened.

The few minutes alone in his car seem like forever, knowing the kids sit near not just dead bodies but deceased loved ones. Vistrus knows he is somewhere on a list of those being hunted, but he doesn't know why. He doesn't know by whom. To him, right now, that doesn't matter. To him, the most important thing is protecting the kids. He knows they are all on the verge of adulthood, and technically his daughter is an adult, but they know so little, if any, about who they actually are.

Before his thoughts get too overwhelming, he pulls up to the DeSalvo's residence. From the outside, all seems peaceful. The front door is closed, and the screen door is latched. He knows, though, that inside, a nightmare scene awaits.

The calls from the kids and the unanswered calls to Ken are all fitting together like puzzle pieces. Vistrus realizes that the friends he's had for more decades than he'd ever admit to were taken from the world for reasons he can only imagine. He knows their deaths aren't the only deaths today and feels in the core of his being that the deaths of two Legendary families were no coincidence, not some random acts of violence sprung upon two families at the wrong place at the wrong time. No, this was deliberate, and he must stop it.

The eerie calm inside the house spreads outdoors as Vistrus knocks on the door to the DeSalvo residence. His ears pick up quiet footsteps tiptoeing to the door and sense the hesitation in the approach as the creeping feet stop just on the other side. He watches as a pair of pale eyes peek out from behind the door's curtain. Allison opens the door for her father.

The sight of his daughter makes him take a step back. Her confused reaction to his lets him know it wasn't as painful for her as it is for others.

"Are you okay, love?" he says, walking through the door, wasting no time shutting it behind him.

"A splitting headache out of nowhere. But Daddy, they're dead! I don't know what happened. They are all dead! Connor! Something happened to Connor," she cries.

A Legend as old as Vistrus has seen this before—a newly transitioned Legend not realizing what has transpired. His daughter's lack of pain (or inability to process the pain) is a gift. He'll have to help get her back to normal, but not until after he finds Connor. The sounds of him whimpering make for a quick hunt. Vistrus discovers Connor cowering with his knees against his chest ... a human dust ball in the corner.

"Both of you, I need you to take a deep breath. Slow and steady," Vistrus commands.

Connor's quick breathing doesn't change. "It hurts," he says.

Allison nods and follows his instructions.

"I know," Vistrus empathizes. "Slow, controlled breaths are the way through this. The way to help control it and put it away."

Connor looks to Vistrus, his eyes crying for help. Vistrus blocks Connor as he shifts his gaze to Allison for the first time since collapsing.

"Trust me," Vistrus whispers. "Breathe in," he says, taking a slow, deep breath. He holds it for three seconds, "And out." He slowly lets it out.

Connor follows suit on the second breath. All three repeat it a few times.

"Both of you continue taking deep breaths," he calmly says. "It is the best way to control it and keep it from hurting. To keep it from coming out."

Allison's skin quickly regains its youthful glow and softness. Her lips thicken out, and her nose fills back in, all unnoticed by her. "My headache's gone."

Connor takes a few more breaths as the excess hair starts to recede. His nails begin to crumble off to the ground. Even his vision returns to normal.

"Keep breathing slowly. It will help," Vistrus says as he stands up. He surveys the scene, noticing the hole in the wall. "They will not be happy about this," he notes to himself.

Vistrus stands, trying to be stoic and authoritative now that he has a moment to see the massacre. The tears in his eyes betray his need to stay detached at the moment. The loss in front of him proves a bit too much for even one as aged as himself. He looks at the slain Tracy and sees her stomach is untouched. The unborn child has died inside of her; the prophecy has died. A wave of sadness engulfs him. The loss is too much to bear, causing his knees to shake—a weakening foundation that has held him for all these years. But even in the sadness, there is a touch of relief. It's a strange, dark solace in knowing that whoever did this doesn't seem to know about the prophecy.

"Connor," Vistrus begins, "I need to take care of this, but you cannot be here. We need to go."

Connor turns his tear-soaked face to Vistrus. "I can't leave. I need to be with my parents."

Vistrus gives a subtle nod of understanding. "You will get a chance to see them again," Vistrus starts. "And when you do, it will be in a less…" he gestures around the room to the blood and debris. "But we must go. I have to leave, and you both need to come."

"Dad! What do you mean 'you have to leave'?" Allison scorns.

"I have much to explain to you two but not *just* you two," he says, stretching out a hand that helps Connor to his feet.

Vistrus and Allison assist Connor as they exit the house. The feet below him provide wobbly support in these uncertain times.

Once outside, and after Connor and Allison are in the car, Vistrus pulls out his cell phone. Standing a few feet from the driver's door, he dials a number, keeping an eye on the young adults inside the car. After a few rings, a female voice picks up on the other end. "Eleanor," he starts. "I am so sorry to have to tell you this. Ken and Tracy have been…" He lets the sentence trail off in a rare moment when he is at a loss for words. "Yes, we will need to clean it up."

"Is a revival possible?" Dying hope and desperation in her frail voice.

He shakes his head while watching his daughter. "I do not think so. I could not find the 21-gram vials, but we can try. We will need to clean the Taylors' house afterward. Someone is coming after us. We need to find out who and why, so we can stop them."

"Are you saying what I think you're saying, Vistrus?" Eleanor asks, worry seeping out in each word.

"We are being hunted and must stop them before they kill us all." Vistrus's stoicism returns.

Eleanor hangs up on Vistrus, allowing him to enter his car.

Not long after they pull away from the house, they arrive at the darkened Taylor residence. Vistrus turns off his car to see Scarlett popping her head in and out of the front window.

"Stay here. I will be back," Vistrus commands to the teens.

"Why are we at Jack's?" Connor asks.

Vistrus takes a deep breath. "There is more going on tonight than I can explain without the others."

"Why is it so dark?" Allison asks.

"I will explain in due time. I have to go inside now," Vistrus says, stepping out of the car.

Allison and Connor stare at each other in an unspoken acknowledgment that what happened at his house may have happened here. Neither teen wants to say it for fear of making it true. They both know, though, that speaking it won't make it true if it already occurred. So, they stare into each other's eyes. Neither teen wants to talk at all; a thick, suffocating silence fills the car. The images flashing in their minds of his house are still too much to process and too hard to talk about. The two stare into each other's eyes, trying to find an oasis of serenity, a calmness that does not exist within themselves at the moment. Neither of them is sure if they will ever actually know peace again.

The rap of Sylvia's knuckles against the stained wood door wades through the running water of the shower. Brianna sits curled on the shower floor as the water attempts to wash away the monster she thought was too hideous to look at in the mirror. The dark, unlit bathroom provides her only cover against having to look at the withered and rotting features that have become her.

"Honey, you've been in that bathroom for hours! You can't hide in there forever!" Sylvia's voice has turned from the earlier derision to motherly concern.

Brianna lifts her head from between her knees. The darkness hides her sagging skin. "I can't! Just leave me alone!"

"Bri, the water can't even be warm anymore! You can't seriously want to sit in a cold shower!" Sylvia's shouting more not out of actual anger or frustration but so her daughter can hear her over the water.

"I don't want anyone to see me! It's not ... right!" Brianna responds before burying her head back into her knees.

An idea starts to form in Sylvia's mind, an idea that this is no longer about the prom dress. That the stress from prom and, perhaps, her actions have triggered a change—a change that was just a matter of time at this point.

Sylvia reaches above the door frame to grab the lock-out key. She wiggles it in the tiny hole and lets herself into the bathroom after replacing the tool. The sight of blood and teeth in the sink confirms her suspicions. Sylvia takes a seat on the toilet lid, staring at the drawn shower curtain.

Brianna looks at her mother with fear-filled eyes, begging and pleading for help. At this moment, though, there is not much her mother can do for her. Brianna must get through this on her own.

"This must be a very confusing moment in your life," Sylvia starts. "Finding these things out about yourself is hard."

Brianna sits on the floor, crying and staring at her mother. "What's happening to me?"

"When some children reach a certain age, their bodies go through changes. Sometimes it starts with hair growing in unusual places. Other times, like when I started going through my changes, it was rough patches of skin that would flake off."

"I don't understand," Brianna pleads.

"Before now, Bri, your body was in a rested state. As you reached your teen years, your body started producing new hormones," Sylvia explains.

Brianna's face contorts as her confusion grows. "This can't be some puberty side effect they fail to mention in school, Mother."

Sylvia bobs her head side to side. "It's a bit more complicated than that." She pauses while searching for her words. "There are those of us who have what is technically classified as an auto-immune response. One that causes great changes. They tend to manifest around the mid to end of puberty or early adulthood."

"I don't get it," Brianna cries out.

"Think of your situation as a bad skin condition rearing its head." Sylvia keeps her explanation plain.

"A skin condition? You call this a condition!" Brianna roars, pointing to her teeth lying in the sink.

"Bri, my darling, you are becoming so much more than you know. I wish there was an easy way to explain this where you would understand and be okay." Sylvia's answer less than satisfies her daughter.

"Please try then, Mother," Bri pleads.

Sylvia rubs her eyes. As she lowers her hand, the whites of her eyes have gone a mixture of greys and red-browns. "We are part of something called The Nation. We live in secret among Normals, and have for longer than you can imagine. No one in The Nation speaks of their condition in outsider presence or even if the possibility of Normals being present exists. They don't understand. And because they don't understand, they fear us. Fear of what they can't, or refuse to, understand leads to suspicion and hatred. So, we stay hidden."

Bri hears her mother's words as her eyes lock on her mom. She is unsure of what to think about her mom's discolored scleras.

"So, what do I do? Who do I tell?" Bri asks, shifting to lean against the shower wall.

"Most important to understand, you offer the information to no one. You tell no one. Do you understand?" Sylvia commands.

Bri shakes her head but stays silent.

"If you are ever asked these three words, 'Are you in?' you answer as follows, 'I am in true, whate'er befall.' And only answer if you feel comfortable doing so. Now you say it," Sylvia tells her daughter.

Brianna looks a little less confused but no less scared of the current situation. "I am in true. Whatever free falls."

Sylvia takes a deep breath. She knows getting angry will not make this any less painless. "Whate'er befall. *Not* whatever free falls. Don't pronounce the v, and befall is one word. Try it again."

"I am in true. Whate'er befall," Brianna says.

Sylvia smiles. "Those words are your ticket in, so to speak. Always remember those words."

"But how do I return to normal and not look like a zombie?" Bri continues crying.

"You are not a zombie. Zombies do not exist. Zombies are brainless, cannibalistic creatures created to entertain the masses. You are so much more.

"Returning to normal, however, takes time but calming down is the key. Focusing on your breathing, clearing your mind. There's a world more to you than I can explain here," Sylvia offers.

"So, what do I do?" Brianna's breathing starts to slow, but her mind continues racing.

"Take it one day at a time," Sylvia says, attempting consolation.

Brianna is caught thinking about her newfound state—her old, withered skin, the teeth in the sink, her sunken features. All things she was working so hard to prevent in old age hit her at a young age. Her mind isn't even thinking that this could be something special. All she is thinking about is her looks and how disgusted she feels about herself.

The four high schoolers are all seated on the couch in Petrovsky's den. The uncomfortable silence surrounding them is so dense and malleable that they dare not move. They stare straight ahead, unable to look at anyone else, all knowing they feel the same awkwardness of not knowing how they will react or be reacted to. The secret is out, and they know there is more to them than they thought they knew. But how much more is the question.

The wainscotted walls are lit by four recessed lights above. Vistrus stands, pacing back and forth, as he tries to figure out how and where to start. His shadow follows behind him like a plucky sidekick, ready to repeat every important phrase spoken. The teens' heads stay unmoved as they track him with their eyes. Each one's heart races with nervous anticipation of the inevitable speech.

Unfortunately, even with the added time given by all four taking showers to clean up, Vistrus's thoughts still haven't fully formed on how to explain all of this. There's a part of him that would be bluntly honest—if his daughter wasn't seated in front of him. There's the part of him that knows his paternal side is clouding his ability to reason this out and explain. No matter the situation, he must stay strong and well-spoken.

"You are all vampires and werewolves, for lack of better words. While some—and sometimes myself—within our societies will call us that, we are not." He stops pacing. "We are what we call Legendary." Not the gentlest way to break the news.

Jack lets out a sigh of relief. The dense silence has been broken with news that is old to him. "I know. My parents…" his words sting him. "I was told while I was, um, in the hospital. They all know," his thumbs pointed to his friends.

"Yeah, Dad. We figured something was up when I knew you were lying about the parchment. You said it was a delivery for the museum, but it was the one Connor found," Allison says, half self-satisfied in her looming despair.

Connor turns to Jack. "Is it always this painful?"

Jack nods. "Well, at first, it's the worst. It has gotten a little easier, I guess, but the pain, uh, will always be there. I think."

Vistrus takes a step toward them. "He is not wrong. The pain never fully subsides. You adjust." He eyes his daughter. "Some are lucky enough to barely feel the breadth of the pain. It centralizes as chest pain or migraines."

Allison stares at her father, oblivious to her transition. "So, if the boys are both wolves or werewolves or whatever, who's a vampire? You said we were vampires."

Scarlett, Connor, and Jack all turn their attention to Allison. While Allison seems lost in the moment, the other three have made a reasonable assumption that Vistrus is referring to the females among them.

"I think he means you and Scarlett, my love." Connor pats her knee.

"At the very least, I mean my daughter," Vistrus confirms.

Allison turns to her father with a shocked stare. The thoughts of all the negative stigmas associated with vampires flash through her mind. The idea of being something that is so misunderstood, even by herself, is a harsh new reality ... if Vistrus is correct.

"How could I be? I haven't transformed," she blurts out. "I'm not some monster."

"Transitioned, dear," Vistrus corrects. "We do not say transformed. We say transitioned. And no one here is a monster."

"Yeah, Al, we don't transform. We're not alien robots," quips Scarlett.

"Whatever," Allison says with a wave of her hand. "I haven't done anything yet."

"Yes, you have, dear. You just did not realize it." Vistrus keeps his voice soft. He steps toward her, in case the need for a fatherly gesture arises.

"What do you mean?" she says as the thoughts of knowing nothing about this side of herself move her further into uncomfortable territory.

Scarlett, Connor, and Jack all watch her as they see the panic growing on her face. A visible shaking overtakes her body. Connor reaches out and puts his arm around her, sliding closer to her.

"When you answered the door earlier, you were in your full vampiric form. You did not realize it," Vistrus's voice takes on a comforting tone.

"Nope. No way. Nah-ah. Not me," Allison denies, slinking down into the couch and trying to disappear into Connor's arms.

Scarlett sheepishly raises her hand. All heads turn to her, each giving a curious look as to why she did that.

"Yes, Scarlett?" Vistrus calls on her.

"Was I changed too and didn't realize?" she asks, unsure of things at this moment.

Vistrus's head shakes a little bit. "No. I am not sure about you. Your ... unique situation has left us wondering which you might be."

"Jack's parents are..." Vistrus pauses, knowing that the tense of his verb was wrong and the delicateness of the fresh wound. "...vampires, but Jack is not. At least one of his grandparents was a werewolf. Scarlett's lineage was not fully established before their passing."

"It's all genetics, Mr. P. We know," Connor interjects. "We figured that out already."

"You may have read about it somewhere, but living it is another story. One that will be harder to deal with. Something that Jack here already knows." He looks at each of the teens, making sure he has their full attention. "The hardest part is that we are no different from people without our conditions. We are not supernatural. Nor are we above them. We are them. But Normals do not accept us as easily. It is why we have The Nation. It is why 'Are you in' will become the most crucial phrase you know. But more important is that you must live your life as you have been up until now. Nothing can change."

"But everything has changed," Connor blurts out in a fit of well-placed anger. "How can things be normal again? My parents are dead! I find out I'm some monster from a horror story, and you want us to act like nothing's wrong?!"

"Partly. You can mourn and grieve your loss all you need. That is a normal response to this sort of situation," Vistrus starts.

"Thanks for your permission," Connor snaps back.

Vistrus clears his throat as a gentle warning. "The grief, the loss, the pain everyone is feeling, everyone eventually feels. The only thing that cannot affect you is how you act and deal with the newfound knowledge that you are what you are."

"But how?" Scarlett asks.

"With my help. I will be here for all of you," Vistrus responds.

"That's great for the others, but I don't even know what I am," Scarlett mumbles.

CHAPTER 4

"The sleeping mind tries to understand
what the waking mind cannot."
~V. Petrovsky~

Allison stands in the middle of an unfamiliar forest filled with lush, green trees and tall grass. A silent windstorm whips the tree branches around in a wild tantrum. She surveys her surroundings, noticing the absence of any forest creatures ... land or air.

The sound of shoveling breaks the eerie silence. Even the powerful storm lightning above makes no sound. She looks in the direction of the shoveling sound to see a flickering light ahead. She darts from tree to tree for cover from the storm and whatever lies ahead, but her steps between are lost in her mind, as if she were transported to each tree without the need for footsteps. She stops close enough to the source to see four people digging two holes. There are giant piles of dirt next to the gravediggers, behind which lay two mangled and torn bodies. Their features are too distorted to recognize, but there is an air of familiarity to the corpses.

Allison looks at a ditch digger and sees the face of her father. Vistrus looks in her direction and holds a finger to his lips. "Shh. Everything will be all right." He looks back toward the bodies. "On a long enough timeline…" He references one of Allison's favorite movies.

A sense of serenity floods her body as he says his words. In her mind, she knows that these are not words that should pacify her but, spoken by him, they do.

She looks at another digger and sees Sylvia shoveling away. As if an appendage, a wisp of her long, curly hair holds a martini glass filled with a sour apple martini. She looks at Allison and smiles. Sylvia's hair tips the glass to her lips for a sip of her cocktail.

The other two diggers' identities are obscured by shadows from the trees above. They do not lift their heads to the girl. Both of them stop digging and jam their shovels into one of the piles of dirt. As they each drag a body from behind the mounds, moonlight glints off one of the people's hands. Allison notices the wrinkled skin and fragile-looking nature of the hand, a hand that appears too old and weak to be doing such heavy lifting.

The torn and bloodied bodies are pulled around, and the familiarity strikes Allison; they are Ken and Tracy DeSalvo. Both deceased are gently placed into the grave. Vistrus and Sylvia start throwing the dirt on top of them like a primitive burial. The obscured duo both reach into a pouch that adorns their belts and pull out two small vials. The glass of the jar is swirled with iridescent colors that brilliantly shine in the soft moonlight. Allison sees various shades of purples, pinks, oranges, and whites all changing in the vial, as it moves around in the hand of the stranger.

The mysterious figures each hold a vial over the graves as they are being filled with dirt. They open them and wait a moment. The shoveling stops, and the bottles are pulled back toward them. They look into the vials for something that they expected to find. Allison watches as the look on her father's face goes from hope to sadness and despair, a look she has never seen on her father before.

Vistrus turns to her with tears in his eyes. "They are truly gone, my child. We cannot help them anymore."

He turns back to the bodies. The forest around Allison starts expanding outward, moving the scene further and further away from her at an ever-increasing rate. She closes her eyes as the sight of it all is too much to take in, the entirety of which is accompanied by a high-pitched, grating noise. BEHH-BEHH-BEHH. BEHH-BEHH-BEHH. After a moment, the motion stops, but the sound is still there. BEHH-BEHH-BEHH. She opens her eyes to find herself in her bedroom with the annoying sound of her alarm clock poking at her eardrums.

Allison slams her hand against the clock to turn it off, knocking it to the floor. She waves it off for later and grabs her dream journal. She knows the routine— write while it is still fresh, every detail remembered, though she feels there is more to this dream than she can figure out in a sleepy state of mind. Perhaps her time at the funerals today will help her figure out what they all mean.

Sylvia opens her eyes, struggling to adjust to the bright light and fresh from sleep as the sun breaks through the window blinds. The sounds of music and rushing water carry down the hall—a sure sign Brianna has begun her morning beauty ritual.

As she gets out of bed, she hears, beneath the sounds of music and water, the thin metal frame of the front screen door slam shut. She stops as she hears the sounds of an unknown person trying to hush the settling door.

She sneaks to her bedroom door with no time to change out of her nightgown. She needs to figure out who is sneaking into her house and why.

As she peers out into the hallway, Brianna starts singing soulfully, yet loudly, in the shower. A song her mom can't place at the moment, but something about a boy and lost love. But at the moment, that doesn't matter. What does matter is Sylvia keeps her daughter safe. The lack of anyone announcing their entrance makes Sylvia feel quite unsafe and fearful for her daughter. No one is in the hallway yet.

She creeps out into the hall to try and sneak a look at the intruder, but the hallway is empty. It isn't until she can see the way to the living room that she spies the intruder's foot disappearing into the next room.

CHAPTER 4

She speeds up her stealthy walk to surprise whoever her unwanted guest is. At the living room entrance, she finds no one there. But the living room connects to the kitchen. And in the kitchen, she hears the sounds of someone trying to be quiet.

Now she knows someone is in her house while her daughter is vulnerable, and they have access to her knives.

She sneaks into her kitchen as the intruder enters the stairs leading to her basement. At least it's farther from Brianna, who is blissfully unaware as she continues wailing out the song in the shower.

Sylvia stops at the top of the stairs that lead down. The basement light has been turned on, a clue that he can't see in the dark. A sign that he is most likely not Legendary. But the warning flag only raises further questions in her mind—one of which is, who breaks into a house in the morning hours?

She listens but doesn't hear any detectable movement, so she descends the stairs. Her basement is an adult den—a bar built into the adjacent corner, an 8-foot billiards table in the middle, and a couch off to the far side that faces a television framed in various movie formats, from laserdisc and VHS to DVD and Blu-ray. Even a dartboard hangs on the wall, though to use it, one would have to stand on the opposite side of the pool table, making simultaneous use of both either very dangerous or unavailable.

But she doesn't see the intruder. Can her mind have been playing tricks? She steps into the basement and starts looking around. She tries to listen, but while enhanced above a Normal, a Fairy's hearing is not as improved as others like vampires and werewolves.

She steals a quick look behind the bar, but no one is there. As she turns to check the rest of the basement, she is greeted with a fist to the head.

"Why?" This is all Sylvia can say as she falls to the floor and finally gets a look at the intruder—a man wearing a black, full-face ski mask and blue hospital scrubs.

The man laughs as he jumps on top of her. His laugh sounds like a cross between a bad Ray Liotta impersonator and a poor man's Mark Hamill's Joker. Something about it is both sad and frightening, causing Sylvia's instincts to kick in. Instantly, her skin thickens into grey-brown bark. Her hair twists and becomes almost vine-like. Her eye color fades to a grey throughout the pupil and sclera.

The man starts to land a few blows on her body and face. Sylvia lays beneath that man as her thick skin shields her from harm. The attacker's hands begin to bleed as they strike against her bark-covered skin, only taking around a dozen blows for the man to stop and stretch his bleeding hands. Sylvia takes this opportunity to shove the man off herself.

"Why are you doing this?" Desperation covers Sylvia's words.

The man looks down at his torn, bleeding knuckles. "Because we know."

Sylvia stands up from the ground, staring at him. Staring at the man who might be responsible for the parchment that started the stir in their quiet community.

The man tries rubbing his hands to soothe them, but they are too raw and sensitive. He turns and runs up the stairs.

As Sylvia follows after him, her daughter's singing becomes more audible with each step up the stairs.

The intruder does not pursue Brianna, however. "See you soon," he warns, running straight for the door and outside.

Sylvia stops shy of the door and transitions back to her Normal state. A full-body quiver overtakes her for a second as things calm down. She watches as the intruder runs down the street and out of sight.

The sound of Brianna's sad, soulful singing comes to an end as her shower shuts off. Sylvia stands at the door to her house, wondering why what they know seems so dangerous. She wonders who else might be involved in this "we" part of we know, if perhaps this was a one-time event or if he'll be back. If he comes back, will he go after her daughter?

She thinks about calling the police for a moment, but she also knows her Normal face, unbloodied and only bruised, would not justify the drips of blood on her basement floor. Too many questions could be raised, and she would not want to potentially endanger her daughter any more than she might already be.

The wind whips through the cemetery, a welcoming gesture by nature to call her children home. The morning sun shines down on the tombstones, grave markers, and mausoleums as a universal acknowledgment of the deceased's passing.

The family and numerous friends of the deceased, all of whom are dressed in black, gather around the four graves, standing solemn in their remorse. The four caskets sit on their platform, waiting to be lowered to their final resting places.

Connor and Jack each stand in front of their parents' caskets, their heads bowed in respect. Both young men are hesitant to look up, afraid that tears might start to flow that will never stop.

Allison stands next to her father, whose black suit attire for today isn't too far removed from his everyday wear. Both of them are a few steps behind Connor. This tiny observation plants a seed in Allison's mind that perhaps her father isn't just a fan of black but is in some perpetual state of mourning.

On the opposite side of the caskets from Connor and Jack is Eleanor DeSalvo, the matriarch and eldest of the DeSalvo women. She is the biological grandmother to Connor and has been a mother figure to countless more over the years. As she looks out over the crowd to the people in attendance, her sun-lit face reflects the tears that run down her cheeks. She watches as her grandson mourns the loss of her only blood child, his father, as well as his mother. She looks at an elderly gentleman whose thick, white hair has been fighting a long battle against his receding hairline. Though his age may be more than it seems, his piercing blue eyes melt away the years. His round nose and high cheekbones give him the illusion of a thin-looking Santa Claus. They look at each other for a moment and smile sad smiles before she looks a few tombstones over to her granddaughter, Scarlett. She sits leaning against her mother's headstone, watching the funeral from the comfort of her mother's arms. She holds back the tears that well in her eyes as she listens to the wisdom of her elder.

"It is truly a sad day," Eleanor begins. "We mourn the loss of four souls, four souls that were paired in love. A love that spawned a child for each couple." She stops and again turns her attention to the young men standing vigil. "Words cannot express my sorrow for you both right now." She turns back out to the crowd. "What makes it especially hard for me is that Ken was my son ... and in so, Tracy, my daughter. But that doesn't dull the loss I feel for James and Lucretia. They were members. They were one of us. Like all of us, they were in."

Allison shoots a look that is met by Scarlett. The idea of everyone around them being these Legends, as they were told, is a bit more than unnerving to both the girls. In a time of loss and a time when they are told these impossible things about themselves, the idea of being anything but ordinary is not one either of them wants to entertain.

"We ... we," Eleanor starts to get choked up. She stops for a moment to collect herself. "We say goodbye today…" Again, she stops to control the torrent of emotions flooding through her. "…for they are finally at rest. As one day, eventually, so too shall we."

Scarlett hears soft footsteps behind her. She turns to see a figure whose face is covered in a black veil and hidden from sight.

"Scarlett," Brianna's hoarse voice whispers from beneath. "I'm so sorry for your loss." She shifts her stance around, fidgeting.

Scarlett stares at the cloth hiding the face. "Veils are traditionally for the widow. Why are you wearing one?"

Brianna shuffles her feet, uncomfortable with the question. "We need to talk. Something has happened, and I don't know how to explain it."

Scarlett's instinct tells her that this unexplainable situation Brianna feels somehow compelled to tell her about is more understandable to her than Bri knows.

"Are you in?" Scarlett whispers.

Brianna's body freezes. Her shifting comes to a standstill, and her shuffling feet rest, not moving for a moment. Even her breathing seems to have halted. "What?" she sheepishly asks. "What did you say?"

Scarlett once again whispers, "Are you in?"

Brianna leans in toward Scarlett. The black veil still conceals her face from the outside. The funeral crowd close by, unaware of the conversation, says their final respects to the deceased. Even Allison is staring off in another direction. Connor and Jack are still looking, heads tilted down at their parents' caskets. Brianna moves a tad closer to make the distance between her and Scarlett a little past comfortable and into "too close" territory.

Brianna takes a deep breath and speaks hesitantly, "I am in true. What … e'er … befall."

Scarlett gives her a puzzled look. "I don't know what that means. Is that how you respond?"

A slight chuckle escapes Brianna's veil. "It's what my mom told me to say if I was ever asked. No idea what it means."

"What did she tell you?" Scarlett inquires.

"She thinks I'm something supernatural or special or something because I have a skin rash. My mom has fallen off her rocker. She gave me this whole speech. It was bizarre." Brianna's feet begin shifting uncomfortably again.

"So, that's what's up with the veil?" Scarlett points.

Brianna turns away from Scarlett toward the caskets as they begin lowering into the ground. "Yeah. Little skin rash, like I said," she lies. "Should clear up soon. I hope," Brianna says to delude herself as much as to make an excuse for Scarlett.

"All of this is just so weird," Scarlett notes.

"Weird and unusual, to put it mildly," Brianna confirms.

Allison makes her way to Scarlett and notices Brianna. "Bri? What are you doing?"

"She's got a rash," Scarlett answers.

"Who cares?" Allison lifts Bri's veil away from her face. She quickly drops it upon seeing the sagging, wrinkled skin, discolored eyes, and sunken features.

"Whoa!" Allison starts with an unsuppressed chuckle. "Karma really can be a…"

"Stop, Al," Scarlett interrupts.

Allison crosses her arms, huffing.

"Haven't you returned to normal or whatever we're supposed to call it?" Scarlett asks.

Brianna shakes her head. "It's just a rash. I'm gonna go to the doctor to get some ointment."

Allison circles her hand at Bri. "It's going to take a lot more than ointment to clear that up."

Bri turns to Scarlett. "I was just hoping we could talk. It's why I came over here, to see if we could find a time."

"Why would we want to talk to you? You made it clear when you ghosted us back freshman year that we're not cool enough anymore," Allison retorts.

Brianna hangs her head and nods to the girls. Her veil blows in the wind as she turns away. "Sorry, I just wanted to say my condolences. I'm very sorry for your loss." She walks away, leaving Allison and Scarlett behind.

"Seriously, Al? You can't be nice even at a funeral?" Scarlett scorns.

Allison shrugs. "I thought I was being nice. Sorry, Lil' Lett." They stare at the graves as the crowd retreats to their cars. "Hey, and Scar…" Scarlett turns to Allison. "I'm sorry."

"Thank you, Al."

"So, what do we do now?"

Scarlett looks to the cemetery before her. "Like your dad said, we keep living like nothing's changed."

"Except everything has," Allison mutters.

CHAPTER 5

Graduation Day

"This isn't the end of the road.
You're just a little farther down than before."
~E. DeSalvo~

Proud family members fill the football bleachers with excitement as the clear skies and slight breeze provide a perfect and beautiful setting for graduation. The field is filled with rows of folding chairs quickly being filled in by students finding the last assigned seat they will sit in for their high school careers. The stage constructed for the ceremony takes up the 15 to 20-yard line of the visitor's end on the football field.

Scarlett and Allison sit in the first row of bleachers, looking out at where they will be in a year. They try to imagine what it will feel like to be in a graduate's shoes—the excitement and anticipation of the day. Scarlett wonders if she'll be nervous about making the long walk down the aisle for her diploma or if the excitement of graduation will wash away any nerves.

The only grandmother Scarlett has ever known, Eleanor, sits next to them. The same elderly gentleman from the funeral sits next to her. The families around them all talk about their child's accomplishments and the pride they feel. For Scarlett and her family, the feeling of loss still prevails.

Connor sits in an aisle seat only a few rows from the stage; Jack sits next to him. They both stare at each other, smiles on their faces, but Connor struggles to maintain his.

"Dude, it's okay to smile. You, well, made it," Jack says, trying to pacify Connor's guilt.

"It doesn't feel right—being happy. I wish our parents were here," Connor replies, looking around the field.

"Me too, bro. Me too," Jack starts. "And if they were, they'd be happy, right?"

"Yeah," Connor admits.

"And, uh, they'd want us to be happy too, right?" Jack continues.

"Yeah, of course." Connor starts to smile again.

"Then be happy. It doesn't mean you've forgotten about your parents or, or, that they aren't in your thoughts. It means ... despite everything, you've made it," Jack finishes.

A genuine smile breaks across Connor's face. Perhaps the first to do so since his parents' murder.

"You, uh, know what has to happen now?" Jack's voice is a bit shaky.

"What, my friend?" Connor asks back.

"Max." His one-word answer is in a tone more serious than Connor has ever heard before. No hesitation. No stammer or stutter in his tone. Solid and confident.

"Slow down one moment, killer. You had no choice on the other guy. He was going to ... well," Connor tries to counter.

"And how long do you think it'll be before someone else like Max pays us a visit?" Jack rebuttals, the confidence in his voice still solid.

Connor leans in to whisper to Jack. "If the two of us kill Max, who's only one man, we will literally be adding to the total number of murderers in West Haven."

Sylvia Waldgrave, adorned in full faculty graduation attire, walks up to Connor and Jack. Daylight casts a shadow on her face, but even in the shadow, a poorly concealed black eye stands out like a sore thumb. She rests her hand on Connor's shoulder. "Be proud of yourselves, boys. I know your parents would be. I certainly am, if that's any consolation. I hope it is," she rambles.

"Thanks, Ms. Waldgrave," the boys reply in unison. They toss each other a glance in reference to her rapid-fire speech.

"Are you sure you're ready for your speech, Mr. DeSalvo? I hope you're ready since it's time. So, I guess the question was more rhetorical than not," Sylvia shoots off at Connor.

He shakes his head while taking a deep breath, trying not to stare at her bruised eye.

"Then follow me," she says, gesturing for him to rise.

He stands up and straightens his graduation robe. He high-fives Jack and starts following Sylvia.

As they walk to the stage, he leans close for quiet conversation. "You feeling okay, Ms. Waldgrave? You seem a bit edgy," he inquires.

She slows down her walk a little but marches on. She takes a deep breath and calms herself before speaking. "Just dealing with something. Don't we all, though, at some point, deal with things?"

That said, Connor takes his cue of silence and makes his way to the graduation stage. He pulls out a few index cards from inside his robe. Connor stops at the podium and glances at his notes. His heart pounds in his chest while looking over the graduating class of close to 800, feeling each beat as if his heart is going to explode. His ears pick up the quiet conversation of the students, each whispering something different; some of the following parties and gifts from their parents, others of college and future plans. But he hears Allison whisper to him, "You got this, love." And he smiles. He turns to his paramour, seated a good twenty yards down, calming his heart. He smiles at her, and she smiles back.

He taps the microphone in front of him to test it. The double thump through the speakers lets him know the ceremony is ready to start.

"Class of 2018, what can I say?" Connor pauses and glances at his notes. He holds them up to the audience. "I have these cards. Ideas of what I wanted to say. Things that made sense when they asked me to speak." He lowers his cards back down and shakes his head. "This year has been hard on all of us in various ways. For those that know what happened to mine and Jack's family, you don't need to be told; for those that don't, I'm sure the whispers around school aren't too far off. But our struggles don't invalidate yours. Your struggles are yours and must be dealt with as we deal with ours." Connor stops to squint his eyes and keep the tears that have formed from falling.

He takes a deep breath to collect himself. "They say high school is a trial of sorts. I think everything we go through is a trial of sorts. Everything we do defines us for better or worse. But high school was not a trial unto itself. As I was starting my freshman year, my grandmother told me, 'High school isn't a chapter in your life. You can't revisit it by turning a page backward. High school is a one-way road. It will be in front of you for a much shorter time than it will be in your rearview mirror. So, as you drive forward with your eyes on the road, watching out for obstacles to avoid, don't forget to glance back on all you've done and where you've been.'" He looks out at his smiling grandmother. "I hope I didn't mess that up too bad, Grams." He smiles with a small laugh.

From the audience, Eleanor nods in affirmation of his story.

Connor looks back to the crowd. "We will find out more about ourselves moving forward than we ever knew or will know by always looking back. From young freshmen with eager eyes looking to conquer an overwhelming new school, to the jaded eyes we had by the last week just waiting for it to all be over, there are countless memories between. Some great and unforgettable; some horrendous that we'll spend years trying to forget. But good or bad, those memories are ours. They helped shape us into who we *have* become and possibly who we *will* become. So look to your left and your right. See the faces that we spent four years with. See the faces of who we are. And while our memories are here, we must move forward to bigger, better things that these halls have helped prepare us for."

He stops, and a smile crosses his face. "So, class of 2018. What else can I say? I say we did it! Congratulations, and thank you for this honor."

The end of his speech is met with a standing ovation. A sure sign that, paired with the bright skies, the rest of the ceremony will go off without a hitch. Names are called off, and diplomas are handed out in the usual pomp and circumstance of commencement symbolism. The mostly soft claps of families proud of their graduates follow each name.

As the students throw their hats into the air against the staff's wishes, Connor can't help but have his thoughts turn to his parents, the two people he wants at this occasion more than anyone else. But before he can wallow too long in his mind, Scarlett grabs him for a big hug.

"Great speech, Con," Scarlett grins.

"Thanks," he responds. Turning to Eleanor, he asks, "What did you think, Grams?"

She nods with a melancholy smile. "Perfect, young man." She says, handing him a card.

"Where's Gramps? Wasn't he with you?" Connor says, searching the crowd.

Eleanor looks past the crowd. "He had to run off, but he wanted me to tell you he is very proud of you."

Connor smiles a little as he opens the card. A humorously sappy *congratulations grad* card has a handwritten message to accompany it.

Young man, you are in. No one can ever take that away from you. As The Law Of The Wolf dictates, you are "in because of his age and his cunning." Know this always. As they may be in as well "because of his gripe and his paw."

Connor finishes reading the seemingly sense-less scribbles, knowing there is more to it that he is missing. He looks at his grandmother with an upturned eyebrow.

"Words to live by in your shoes," she responds as he closes the card. "Don't be scared of whatever happens next. How we hold ourselves in the face of adversity determines how the rest of the world sees us."

Allison saunters up, holding a sauerkraut covered bratwurst in in a bun. "Happy to be done with all this?" she asks through a bite of her brat.

"Where did you get that? I'm starving." He motions to her brat, assuming her question was rhetorical.

She points to a long line at the football field con-cession stand, and seeing its length, offers up her brat. "Here, have a couple bites."

He swipes it from her and devours half the brat in two bites before handing it back. He looks past his family and waves his hand in the air. "Jack!"

Jack turns and makes his way to them. "What a day, huh?!" He looks at everyone. His gaze passes Scarlett and lands on Connor.

"Go, enjoy the spoils of the past four years! I'll call you later, bro!" Connor says as Scarlett approaches and wraps her arms around Jack.

Connor spies Coach in the crowd, talking with a parent of a graduate. "Give me one moment, Grams."

Eleanor sees his coach and gives Connor a nod.

"Hey, Coach!" Connor shouts as he weaves through the crowd.

"Mr. DeSalvo, congratulations!" Coach greets him.

"Thanks. Rough year, huh?" Connor jests.

"One hell of a way to go out." Coach laughs.

"Again, thanks." Connor sounds more mature than he has before.

"No, I meant for me." Coach playfully jabs at Connor's celebratory day.

"What do you mean, 'for you'?" Connor inquires.

"I mean, you aren't the only one moving onto bigger things. I'm proud of you. How you held strong to your convictions, even though everyone around you thought you were going off the deep end," Coach starts.

"I kinda did, Coach," Connor interjects.

"Doesn't matter. You graduated with a full scholarship. You rescued your friend," Coach continues.

"Wasn't just me. It was me and my cousin and Allison," Connor humbly corrects.

"And still so humble. I can't wait to hear about what you do next." Coach punctuates sincerity into his words.

"Look me up on Facebook," Connor pauses, looking past the bricks and mortar to the halls and classrooms he's leaving behind. "So, where you headed off to next?"

"Heading out west. Got offered a job as head of the athletics department at a school in Arizona," Coach says, smiling.

"That's wonderful. Congrats to you!" Connor gives a pride-filled slap on the arm of his superior.

A parent walks up, interrupting the conversation to talk with Coach, though Connor doesn't mind. He knows that all good things must end, and in his mind, there couldn't be a better way to end their relationship.

As he walks back to his family and paramour, Mrs. Hsu cuts in front of him. "Congratulations, Mr. DeSalvo. You've graduated, which leaves the big question. What's next?"

"College ball. Hey, I wanted to apologize..." Connor starts.

"No need," she interrupts. "In the end, you handled it well. The road doesn't apologize for its bumps. Neither should you." Mrs. Hsu smiles and turns away.

Connor goes to continue back to his family but stops; he remembers something she asked him as he was leaving her office. He turns and whispers below the noise of the crowd. "Mrs. Hsu, if you can hear me."

She slows down as if to turn around but does not.

"To answer the question you asked in your office. Yes..." Connor realizes the words he seeks are written on the card in his hand. He opens it and continues talking in hopes she hears him. "I am in because of his age and his cunning."

He watches as Mrs. Hsu turns back around and smiles at him. She doesn't say anything more—only smiling before turning back to the crowd. Now he is left wondering if she heard him as though she, herself, is also in, or if her turning back around was a suspicious coincidence.

He watches the families around him as they celebrate the joyous occasion, returning to his family and Allison. Looking around the crowd, he has a nagging curiosity that wants to know who else is in. He wants to know how many others are out there. Is it a small, isolated portion of this town or every town? Is it this entire town, with a few exceptions for those who aren't in? All these questions start running through his mind, questions he knows he'll need answers to at some point. They are questions that never would have crossed his mind had it not been for the past year's events. But they are there now, floating around in his head like buzzing flies demanding attention. If these questions are in his mind, he knows they will be in the girls' minds as well, if they aren't there already.

While the class of 2018 cheerfully graduates from the past four years, Vistrus stands outside the remains of North Haven High.

Unlike the teens on their rescue mission, Vistrus doesn't feel the need to hide in shadows or worry about being detected. The silence around him tells him there is nothing to fear. Even his acute hearing identifies nothing beyond the sounds of an old building further settling, birds landing in trees, and other critters crawling around.

Vistrus makes his way to where they found Jack. He knows that the excitement of finding them alive meant not thinking about the equipment or where it may have come from. It was a joyous mistake that he hopes he'll be able to redeem by finding clues to where the tools came from and possibly finding a lead as to who is behind this.

The door is open that leads to the hallway and then to the room used for the unspeakable acts. He stops and turns his ear toward the hall. He listens intently, not wanting any surprises. Nothing.

He makes his way down the hallway and stops outside the door to where the Taylors were found. Again, he listens. He waits. Still nothing. No sound of monitors beeping or even the hum of a fluorescent bulb.

Vistrus opens the door and flips the light switch. Empty. The machines and beds were taken and presumably entered into evidence down at the police station. The West Haven police station is off limits to anyone in The Nation since discovering that at least one policeman is involved. He looks around the room and the rubble of what remains. The place that once was used for theater, then torture, has been all but destroyed. The acoustic ceiling tiles and framework have been torn apart and discarded over the floor. The table in the middle of the room has been overturned, and the legs are bent and broken. Even the paint on the walls is scratched, and the drywall rots away. Mold grows on the concrete behind the damaged plasterboards.

For a moment, his mind tries to fill in the gruesome details of the events that unfolded here. He tries to play out scenarios that flipped the tables and brought down the ceiling, but it is too much. The sadness of the possibilities and the people involved push him back to the present.

He begins rummaging through the ruins, looking for something, anything that might be a clue to how to move forward. He sifts through the debris for anything that forgives their oversight in finding clues from the joy they felt finding them alive because, if something is found now, they will have a voice in their deaths.

His hopes quickly wane as he finds nothing but wet acoustic tiles, metal frameworks, rodents (both dead and alive), and papers so wet and torn that they are useless.

After a good half hour of fruitlessly rummaging, he turns to leave, disdain having set in. He stops in the doorway to the room, scans it one last time, and is about to turn off the light when something catches his eye. Something that looks out of place, even in this pile of useless garbage, so he halts.

He lets go of the switch and makes his way to the center of the room, keeping his eye on the mystery piece that shines in the light's reflection. Under a section of broken ceiling tile, pinned under the overturned table, he finds a short length of tubing. Nothing printed on it. His heart drops.

Even as his heart drops, his eagerness for the search renews. He turns the overturned table upright, or at least as upright as it can go, an action he now thinks he should not have overlooked before.

Underneath where the table had lain, he sees more tubing, trash, and a plastic bag. He lifts the plastic bag, shaking off the debris. He finds the cardboard topper is still hanging on by a staple, a bag that once held the tubing he found a piece of. Distribution information is printed on the stapled-on topper, but nothing that will clue the Council to which hospital it came from. He turns it over, scouring it for any sign of a clue, and finds one. Off in the corner, faded and almost gone forever, the faded remnants of a stamp: WHG ICU.

Now he has something more than the hospital it came from. He has a ward. Now, he has to figure out how this new information can be useful and utilize it.

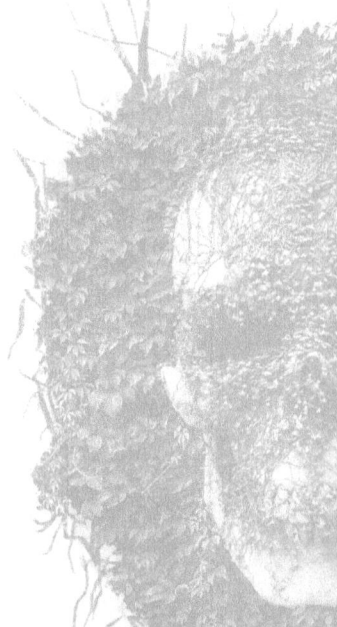

CHAPTER 6

"Do something.
Big things start small.
So, do something."
~K. DeSalvo~

Vistrus sits at the same corner table he sat at with Tracy in the greasy spoon of a restaurant. Across from him now sits Eleanor DeSalvo, resting calmly as he describes in hushed tones the blood and carnage of the scenes.

While the two talk in tones that only some Legends can hear, Eleanor takes deep breaths with each piece of new information she hears. She knew from the day it happened that they were gone, that her child and his betrothed were taken from this earth. The devil is in the details, though, and these details sting with the force of a million venomous scorpions.

"And that is when I noticed the child," he says with sadness in his voice. "Her stomach was still whole. Untouched."

"I was at the funeral home. I know these things," she says matter-of-factly. "Why do you feel the need to relay details of their demise to me? No one needs to relive these emotions."

"Forgive me, Eleanor. I," he pauses, searching for his words, "am at a loss. The man who must always know what to do and say is at a loss. I honestly cannot remember such a time."

"How old are you now, Vistrus?" Eleanor asks.

"Actual or normal?" Vistrus asks for clarification.

"Actual," Eleanor replies.

Vistrus takes a sip of a half-empty water glass sitting in front of him. As he is about to answer her question, a server walks up to them with food in her hands. She places the plates down.

"Anything else?" she asks.

They both shake their heads no.

"Thank you," Eleanor responds.

The server nods. "Enjoy."

"320, give or take a few years." Vistrus keeps his tone plain.

"That is a long time to always be Johnny-on-the-spot with words and actions. I bet dollars-to-donuts that more than once before, you have been in these same shoes." Eleanor's words pacify him for the moment.

They each take a bite of their food and enjoy the beginning of their meal.

"I guess what I have been trying to get at is, what about the prophecy?" Vistrus asks with concern. "How will we ever be able to reveal our existence without resistance? How will people ever stop believing the negative tales that are our myths if there is no prophecy?"

Eleanor smiles. She finishes chewing a bite of her salad and sips her creamed decaf coffee. "Three hundred and twenty years old and still asking questions like a teenager. Young man, in all those years, has any marginalized group of people ever been met without resistance? Were whole cultures not killed off simply for not believing in the same gods or for having darker skin? Were cancer patients not once shunned because the cancer was thought to be contagious? Same with HIV when people thought it was transmitted by touch or cough."

"What are you saying?" Vistrus half demands.

"I am saying you are old enough to know some things never change. The prophecy will have a way of working itself out. Whatever genetics are supposed to be changed by the prophecy, or whatever fantastic event is supposed to, somehow, make everyone tolerant isn't going to happen overnight," Eleanor says before taking another bite of her Caesar salad.

"So, what is the point of the prophecy? To give us all false hope?" he says as his anger swells.

Eleanor lets out a small chuckle. "No, my dear. Whatever its medium is, is still unclear. There is no event grand enough to end everyone's struggle. Struggling is part of life. It's not a fun part of life, but it's a part of it. People will always believe false tales of those who are different than themselves. Especially if the falsehoods strengthen the party that hears it."

Vistrus takes a deep breath before attempting to interject, but Eleanor puts up a finger to stop him from interrupting.

"But despite all that, we must love each other. Life isn't about eliminating struggle, misery, and negativity. If we did that, we would have no basis to compare our happiness. Life is about minimizing the bad so that the good can shine brighter.

"Until the prophecy is revealed, we must ask ourselves this question, 'Is the action I am about to take going to make the world a better place for every living creature?'" She ends with a smile on her face.

"You have literally told me nothing about the prophecy! Nothing of what we need to do about it," Vistrus growls before heaving his chest in frustration.

"Calm yourself. All in good time," Eleanor says, standing up from the table. "Until then, keep doing what you are doing. Everything will make sense."

Vistrus watches in frustration as a seemingly uncaring Eleanor walks toward the bathroom, abruptly ending the conversation. Vistrus takes the solitary moment to ponder what it all could mean. He considers the why of his centuries and the meaning of it all—wondering how it will all make sense.

"So, a free tutoring program for those who can't afford a paid tutor? That's what you're proposing? That's a very noble cause, Ms. McAllister. A cause that should be given its due consideration. So due consideration, it shall get," Ms. Waldgrave confirms.

Scarlett sits at a student's desk across the teacher's desk from Ms. Waldgrave, a notebook and pen open in front of her. "Yes," Scarlett says, trying not to stare at Ms. Waldgrave's fading black eye. "A way to provide subsidized help for those who need a little extra academic boost."

"When you say subsidized, do you mean that the tutors will somehow receive compensation for their time?" Ms. Waldgrave clarifies.

"Yes. That is the hope behind this program. A benefit for those who need the help and a part-time job for those who need the money and are able to tutor properly," Scarlett answers. "You see if each department... Is everything okay with your eye?" She changes the subject.

Ms. Waldgrave brings her hand to her eye and softly touches the healing bruise. "Not a very appropriate question to ask a lady. Also, not a teacher. Not appropriate at all. But as someone I know outside of the school, I shall not hold it against you."

"Sorry, Ms. Waldgrave," Scarlett bows her head.

"As I mentioned, I'll forgive you, but yes, my eye is fine," she says, pausing for a moment. "Late night a while ago. Must've been more fun than I remember. Which is also something, as a teacher, I shouldn't be saying to a student, but then again, I knew your family."

Scarlett hears Ms. Waldgrave's words, though they sound more like searching for excuses than the truth.

"How's Bri?" Scarlett asks, fishing for something that will give her a clue.

"She's fine. Just taking it easy this summer." Ms. Waldgrave keeps things simple. "I like the idea, but department budgets are tight. And tight budgets don't have a lot of room for subsidized funding." She gets back on the subject.

"Budgets are always tight. But this is for a good cause on both ends. The future of America is in our hands," Scarlett objects.

Ms. Waldgrave smiles and shakes her head. "Your uncle taught you well. He was very proud of who you are becoming." She realizes the sting her words may have had. "I'm sorry I said that. I wasn't trying to bring up sensitive subjects. Just trying to put a smile on your face."

Scarlett lowers her head as the moment has taken a sobering turn for her. The few weeks since their passing has been a constant reminder of what is missing. This moment is just another for her. "It's all right, Ms. Waldgrave. Thank you. That means a lot," Scarlett whispers, still bowing her head.

"Let me get through summer school classes and talk with the department heads. I think we can work something out. Even on a trial basis," Ms. Waldgrave adds for encouragement.

Scarlett lifts her head. "Thank you so much, Ms. Waldgrave. I already have a kid who is asking for help."

"Who is this eager soul? Someone with great potential, I hope," Ms. Waldgrave asks.

"His name is Duncan. He wants some help with math," Scarlett responds.

"Duncan Elias? I know him. Please be careful with this program, young lady. You don't want the wrong element taking advantage of your generous nature." Ms. Waldgrave uses choice words. "Between you and I, and I'm only saying this in light of recent events, some kids are trouble."

Scarlett waves off her teacher's caution. "He seems okay. Just marches to his own drummer."

Ms. Waldgrave stands up, prompting Scarlett to do the same. She steps toward Scarlett. "Anyway it goes, starting with a student now would show great initiative while we work out the details of the program. Understand? I think you understand."

"Of course. Thank you so much!" Scarlett says with a bounce in her step as she starts to the door.

Before Scarlett reaches it, Ms. Waldgrave stops her. "Scarlett, why do you want to do this, besides the reasons already given?"

Scarlett furrows her brow. "I want to leave something behind. A legacy. I always felt like I should be doing something more. Perhaps this is my something more."

The teacher doesn't say anything in return. She only smiles and nods before looking down at the papers on her desk.

Scarlett leaves her first meeting to get her program off the ground, filled with a sense of accomplishment and confidence that this will come to fruition. She knows that this was not the way she felt she would go about doing this. In the end, Scarlett really did want to win student council president. But she knows that a legacy can be left by anyone, not just those in political positions. Of the many things Uncle Ken taught her, that was a big one. Hopefully, when her program starts, it will continue for many years. Or, as the thought progresses in her mind, the program will turn into something more.

Scarlett only wishes her aunt and uncle were alive to share the news with, but she will always have Allison.

Connor stands in his living room, organizing everything that moved around during the incident and subsequent quick rebuild. However, the recent events are still fresh in his mind. He looks around at the house, cleaned and somewhat straightened since that fateful night, but the images will forever stay burned into his memory. Everywhere he looks, he sees blood and bodies—even with the newly laid carpet, furniture replaced, and the walls repaired. He looks around and knows this torment is what Jack feels every moment he is in his home. He turns to his grandmother, who sits in a thrift store rocking chair nearby.

"This isn't a place you have to be. You and Scarlett should come stay with us," Eleanor says in a quiet, gentle, maternal voice.

Connor shakes his head as he wipes down the dining room table. "This is *my* home. If I leave, then the bad guys win. I won't be pushed out because someone apparently doesn't like who we are."

Eleanor smiles at the maturity of her grandchild. "I understand. I'm not saying move in forever. Just for awhile while you heal."

Connor stops and thinks. He looks around while images flash in front of his eyes. He can still smell the faint, lingering scent of iron in spilled blood. "Once, when I was only a few years into playing ball, I got hit in the side of my jaw with a fastball."

Eleanor nods. "I remember. You were only a year or two out of tee-ball."

"Yeah, it wasn't a very fast pitch comparatively, but I was much smaller," he continues. "It hurt, and I had a bruise on my face for a few weeks. But I couldn't just walk away from the pain and the bruise. It hurt to eat, to brush my teeth, to talk. Everything hurt because there was a hairline fracture. There was no cast to put on it, nothing they could do. It just needed time to heal; this is no different. I can't just leave the parts behind that need healing because of convenience. Scarlett needs this as much as I do." He turns back to his cleaning.

Eleanor sits silently, listening because she understands his need. She is no stranger to loss and the process that accompanies it. She, like any parent, wants to protect those she loves as long as she can.

"One summer vacation is all I have left here, and then I'm off to college. I want to be here as long as I can. That way, when I come back, things may have a tinge of normalcy to them. Or at least as normal as things will be from here forward. But it's mine to deal with," he finishes, realizing that he may have come across angrier than he intended. "Sorry if that sounded mean."

Eleanor chuckles. "Your parents were so proud of you. They still would be. I know I am. Just know that you don't have to go it alone. Your grandfather and I are here for you anytime you need."

"I know, Grams. I know," he says in a much calmer voice. He turns to a shelf of knickknacks and sees a voice recorder—an object unfamiliar to him in an otherwise overly familiar house.

The front door opens to the sounds of Scarlett and Allison giggling—a pleasant sound that breaks the tension in the room. The girls stop when they see Scarlett's grandmother.

"Girls, how are you today?" Eleanor greets them.

"Getting ready to go to work, Grandma," Scarlett answers. "How you doin'?"

Eleanor smiles in response. "Just talking with Connor."

Allison strides to Connor and plants a kiss on his forehead. "I gotta work too tonight. Stop by if you want."

Just as fast as the girls entered the room, they disappear into Scarlett's bedroom.

Eleanor turns to Connor. "You really do like her, don't you?"

He nods his head as he looks in the direction of the girls. "She is ... something. I don't know what I'm going to do when I leave for college."

"What do you mean?" she nudges.

"I've never done anything long distance before. Never had to. Hell, I've never had a serious relationship before." Connor moves the voice recorder to wipe the shelf. He notices dried blood caked on the speaker slats and between the buttons.

"Serious? I didn't know things were serious." Eleanor adjusts in her chair.

"I mean, as serious as I guess they can be for now. Honestly, I'm not sure what I'm doing," Connor says with a bit of a smile.

"But you like her? Yes?"

"So much. She's amazing on so many levels." His smile grows.

Eleanor stands up from her chair. A spryness in her movements belies her apparent age—a fluidity that belongs to someone much younger. It's a trait more noticed by Connor in light of his newfound family history.

"Hey, Grams."

She turns back to her grandchild. "Yes, dear?"

"I know it's generally not proper to ask, but…" He stops, unsure if he should have even started.

Her expression turns to one of curiosity and wonder.

"…how old *are* you?" he finishes, utterly aware of how awkward that sounds.

She lets out a tiny laugh. "Old enough, my child. Old enough." With that, she turns back around. She turns the handle to the front door and begins to open it.

"But," he continues, "you are in, though? Right?"

She shuts the door and gives Connor a gentle look. "Some questions are best asked when privacy is most absolutely known."

He nods in understanding.

CHAPTER 6

"And it's always, 'Are you in?' no matter what would seem proper," she informs her grandchild.

"Are you in?" he asks with proper wording.

She smiles, and a look washes over her face. A comfort is apparent in her eyes that lends to happier times. "Before I answer, you must know that when someone responds, it is responded to in confidence. Never to be shared unless they are the ones that share it. Even if everyone in a room has heard everyone else respond, it is still to be taken as such a confidence not to be spoken of. Understand?" she replies.

"Yes. I think so," he answers with an unsteadiness in his voice. While he understands the words that she spoke, the idea of such secrecies within his own family seems a little profound. "I think I will understand more as I learn more about myself and us."

Her smile relaxes a bit. "I am in each lovely thing." With that, she turns around and exits the house.

He ponders aloud, "What the hell does that mean?"

He looks back to the voice recorder he can't recall seeing before. He looks at the buttons caked shut with blood and the cassette inside. He tries to press play, but the dried blood has soaked in and killed the device.

His thoughts immediately turn to the melancholy yearning of being able to hear his father talk about whatever it was he used this device for—perhaps to discuss laws and legislation. Not the most exciting subject, but to listen to him speak one more time would mean the world to Connor.

Then another idea hits; his mother may have used this for therapy—a method for her to be able to transcribe later what was said at the moment. It could be a way to hear his mother speak again.

The thought of hearing either parent speak again, a way to stay connected to them, sends a momentary panic through him. He takes the batteries out and pockets the tiny machine, not wanting to accidentally erase anything.

Scarlett stands behind the podium-style host stand at her restaurant job. The unusually slow Monday night has many staff begging to go home and the hosts twiddling their thumbs. A summer night during the week can sometimes be busy, but tonight it is anything but. The few tables occupied by guests are all camping out, as if they have nothing to do with the rest of their night. The televisions in the bar play old sporting event highlights; it's as if nothing is happening at all tonight.

The doors open, causing Scarlett to look up from scrolling Facebook on her phone. She shoves it into the host stand and smiles at Sylvia and Brianna, dressed very incognito in sunglasses, a hat, and a decorative scarf on this relatively comfortable 76° night.

"Welcome to Manic Mondays! How are we this evening?!" Scarlett says in her best host voice.

"We're good, Scarlett. Celebrating her *eighteenth* birthday tonight!" Sylvia says with a bit too much enthusiasm, causing Brianna to stare at the floor in embarrassment.

"That's right, it is," Scarlett remembers after years of not celebrating with her. "Happy birthday, Bri!"

"Thanks," Bri responds, trying to sink her head into her torso.

Scarlett grabs two menus and silverware and waves for them to follow. "Right this way." She turns to walk them to their table. "How have you been, Bri? I see the..." she gestures to her own face, "...is calming down a lot."

"Yeah, thanks. So *not* how I wanted to spend my summer," Bri says, as if the whole Legendary thing is more of an inconvenience than anything else.

"Here we are." Scarlett seats them at a four-person booth.

Sylvia and Brianna slide to opposite sides of the booth. "Thanks," says Sylvia.

"My pleasure," Scarlett says before turning back to Bri. "I know this whole thing hasn't been the easiest. We're all commandeering the wall for the fireworks this year. Join us if you want."

Brianna forces out a smile. "I'll think about it."

Sylvia gives a smile that silently apologizes for her daughter's manners.

"Enjoy your meal! And happy birthday! I'll be sure to let your server know!" Scarlett turns around and returns to the host stand.

She leaves the Waldgraves alone to enjoy their meal in private, only tending to a handful more guests until her shift ends.

CHAPTER 7

*"The world judges with its eyes and ears
long before its heart and mind."*
~E. DeSalvo~

The overcast sky sheds its tears upon the world outside. Inside though, an excited Scarlett waits for her first student needing to be tutored. She looks around the classroom, which is a temporary home for her passion project, and keeps her fingers crossed that Ms. Waldgrave can make things happen on her end.

No time to ponder on such things anymore as a reluctant Duncan strolls through the door. He squeegees the rainwater off his shaved head with his hand. Beads of water fall off his well-worn and hand-decorated leather jacket. The cuffs of his torn jeans are wet from his walk inside.

Without any pomp or circumstance, he enters the room without so much as a greeting, plops down at a desk, and pulls the pen out from behind his ear. He currently uses the metal clip once attached to the pen as a chew toy.

Scarlett turns her desk to face him. As she settles into the seat, she finds that Duncan has slumped into a comfortable, slacker position of nonchalantness.

"So, Duncan," she begins.

"That's me," he interrupts.

She forces a smile as she tries to understand why he signed up for this tutoring yet seems so apathetic to being here.

"In your application, it said you needed general academic help. Can you elaborate on that?" Scarlett tries to bring an air of professionalism to her program.

He pulls the metal chew toy from his mouth and starts fidgeting with it. "Yeah, I was told that if I don't pass my classes, I don't graduate. So's I gotta pass 'cause I want to get the hell outta here," Duncan so eloquently states.

"Okay, well, that's a start. What areas are you most struggling with?" Scarlett asks, pulling teeth.

Duncan pulls out an overly polished chrome chain from his shirt and starts twirling it. "I'm not so good at math. I have some trouble with the sciences. Like, pretty much any subject that isn't gym or history; those I'm solid in."

"Do you like sports?" Scarlett asks, searching for a relatable topic.

He shakes his head. "Nuh, bruh. Just good at them. They're fun, I guess. Why?"

"Just trying to find common ground," Scarlett responds. "Why don't you get comfortable? Take off your jacket. Stay a while."

Duncan looks her up and down a few times as if she has an ulterior motive. After deciding she is okay, he takes off his jacket to reveal a red-and-white plaid button-up opened to a Run DMC shirt underneath.

"You said you were good at history. Why do you think that is?" Scarlett attempts to move things forward.

He drops his chain and looks down at his desk. He uses the metal pen clip he was chewing on to start scratching up the desktop.

"I don't think the teacher's…" Scarlett starts to say.

Duncan interrupts her with a stabbing stare. He pauses to let the look sink in before continuing his desk art.

They both sit in silence for a moment as she waits for him to say something. Duncan continues to carve what appears to be a carefully detailed tree into the top of the desk. After a few moments of work on the tree, he looks up.

"The variables that come together to make history what it was. But I don't need help with that." He pauses. "Art's good and all. Not science or math textbooks, ya know. They don't make sense. This whole institution of learning don't teach us anything." He starts to feel comfortable and turns back to carving the desktop.

Scarlett sits, intrigued by his thoughts. "Can you elaborate on that?"

He straightens up a bit but still carves away on the desk. "They don't teach us nothing. No ability to think for ourselves. All they care about is their test scores and making themselves look good, even if it means sacrificing our futures by not teaching us the skills we need to succeed in life. Life isn't about filling in a bubble with a number two; it's about being able to balance a checkbook, or cook a healthy meal, or even what goes into a healthy meal. We need to know how to change a tire, change oil, make a resume—basic life needs that they never teach. Nothing. It's all about what parts of history they want to teach while leaving out the rest. Never the "why" behind the events.

"It's all about the math skills that, sure, we need, but they don't tell you how you will need them or how they will relate to the everyday. So why should we care? If the adults can't teach us how all this relates to the real world, then how do they expect a bunch of teenagers to figure it out?"

He stops carving and catches his breath. He looks at Scarlett, who wears an ear-to-ear smile.

"What? Why are you smiling?" He puts himself on guard. "I'm not dumb; I just don't get it. Like, I see the puzzle pieces, just not how they all fit."

She shakes her head. "It's not that you don't want to learn. It's the way they teach that makes no sense. That's something I can help with."

Duncan shivers for a moment and gets a bit uncomfortable, returning to carve his desk. "Look, I got a question for you. I know we had a class together, and I saw you around the halls."

"Yeah, I saw you around too," Scarlett responds, urging him on.

"I saw you talk with this girl sometimes."

Scarlett laughs. "Oh, Allison?! What about her?"

Duncan shakes his head. "Not Allison. The other girl. Blonde, really pretty."

"Do you mean Brianna? What about ... oh?" Scarlett realizes his intentions. "She's not the nicest person most of the time."

He finishes his carving as a look washes over his face that sits in judgment of Scarlett's judgment of Brianna. "People say that about me sometimes. I'm not asking for a setup. Just a mention of my name. Something that puts me on her radar, even just a blip. I can do the rest."

Scarlett tries not to smile. She finds his reservations a bit contrary to his outward rebellion. "I'm not sure you're her type, but I'll say something."

"You've nothing to lose by giving it a shot, and who knows what you have to gain." He smirks.

"It's her mom you'll have more trouble with," Scarlett warns.

"Her mom?" He raises a brow. "I can handle her."

"Ms. Waldgrave? I don't know. I'm not one for gossip, but have you seen her? Looks like she got into a scuffle," she responds, as if it should be common knowledge.

"Hmm. Wonder what happened," he mutters.

"I asked her, and her excuse seemed pretty flimsy," she continues the gossip; while it might not be academia, he's letting his guard down. "Lying about a black eye seems pretty shady."

"Yeah, it does. She could be coverin' for someone. Or she doesn't remember," Duncan says with a suspicious look in his eye toward Scarlett. "Or she's scared to come forward."

"Like I said, I don't normally gossip, but it was bad. Thought you'd be able to appreciate that," Scarlett says, trying to loosen him up a bit more.

"Not sure why you'd think that." He holds his gaze at Scarlett, who is sitting like a deer in headlights.

He laughs after an awkward moment. "It's all good. Who doesn't like to hear that a teacher got a shiner for some strange reason." His words add to the uncomfortableness that Scarlett started. "I'll worry about Ms. Waldgrave. I can make a strong impression. You just put in a good word." He tries to end the uncomfortableness of the situation.

"Thank you for helping me with this program." She returns the thanks.

"Hey, man, I just gotta get outta this place. So, if that deserves thanks…" Duncan half-smiles.

"Then whaddya say we do this?" She taps on her textbooks.

He nods and points to his carving. A detailed tree in full bloom with a rope swing attached to a branch. The bark of the tree has the texture and look of actual bark. Even the leaves have a realistic look to them.

"This is what has meaning." Duncan looks down at his work. "No matter how lost someone feels or outta place, they can always find some refuge in art. Know what I mean?"

The weight of his words hits Scarlett, and she wonders if he could be in, if he is somehow hinting at that or if he is just, perhaps, a soul in need of direction.

"Are you in?" she asks, opening her science textbook.

He looks at her, clearly unfamiliar with the phrase. "Yeah, I'm in this. You help me get outta high school on time, and I'll help you." He straightens himself up for the road ahead.

Scarlett nods, knowing he isn't in The Nation, and straightens herself as well for the road to travel with him.

Vistrus takes an extended lunch break from his duties at the museum to determine who at West Haven General's Intensive Care Unit might be plotting against the town's Legends.

Before driving to the main inpatient building, he visits the primary care facility. Vistrus, Sylvia, and any member of The Nation that has come to transition in West Haven use Dr. Wong, their go-to guy for all their specialized needs.

He has hopes for the venture, but if the slight drizzle and gloomy clouds above are any indications of what lies ahead, then this might not have been the best use of his time.

The automatic doors open, signaling the nurse seated at the reception desk to look up from her paperwork as he approaches.

"Hello. How may I help you?" The nurse forces a smile.

"Is Dr. Wong in today? I need to speak with him." The sounding authority in his voice is not lost on her.

"He left a few minutes ago to do his rounds at the main building," she says, looking down at the appointment book. "If you'd like to make an appointment. . ." She looks up to pencil in a date and time, but Vistrus is already out the door.

He hops in his car and drives across the parking lot, main road, and into the main parking structure. Shortly after, he finds himself once again at a reception desk.

"I need you to page Dr. Wong. It is urgent," Vistrus says to the elderly desk clerk.

As the old lady lifts the phone with a frail hand to page the doctor, Nurse Practitioner Scott steadily approaches with a slight limp, an outstretched arm, and an ear-to-ear smile.

"I'll handle this, Gladys," Scott says. "I remember you! I heard on the news about what happened to your buddy. That's so sad."

"Where can I find him?" Vistrus says, cutting down Scott's smile with a razor-sharp tone.

"He's left already. He said something about an emergency trip somewhere. I don't know; it's all bizarre." Scott pulls a fleur-de-lis chain pendant from under his shirt and starts twirling it.

Vistrus takes note of the old, mostly healed scrapes on Scott's hand.

Scott continues, "To be honest, he seemed very twitchy. Paranoid. Very unsure in his movements. I tried to ask if anything was wrong, but he ignored me. Like I wasn't there."

Vistrus listens with suspicion in his mind that this guy's story seems a little too out of character for the doctor, but there have been documented stories of such things happening: Elisa Lam, Emma Fillipoff, and Diane Schuler, to name a few. All of these incidents were preceded by tragic events.

"It had me a little nervous at first, but he just left," Scott says with the smile returning.

Vistrus tosses him an unsure look. "Last we met, you did not have a limp. Is everything all right?"

Scott's smile instantly fades. Even his friendly demeanor shifts. "Ever ride a motorcycle before? Dress for the slide, not for the ride. I should've listened." He pauses for a moment. "Now, if there's nothing else about Dr. Wong, I have patients to attend to."

Vistrus watches as Scott turns and limps away.

"One more question," Vistrus starts.

Scott turns back to Vistrus with a feigned smile.

"Have you ever been to North Haven High?" Vistrus finishes his inquiry.

Scott's face drops. A dead-serious look replaces everything that came before this moment. Vistrus hears the racing and pounding of Scott's heart. The thumping is so intense that Vistrus realizes Scott knows something. He listens as Scott takes a slow, deep breath through his nose, exhaling the same way.

"No," Scott says. "That school closed down before my time. How old do you think I am?"

With that, Scott turns and continues walking. Vistrus is left in the hospital lobby, having gained little to no ground in finding Dr. Wong or who might be behind the conspiracy against West Haven's Legendary residents.

The stadium is packed once again, though this time the football field is empty. Outside the bleachers stand even more will-be-spectators of the area's largest and best pyrotechnics display—the Maine West Haven High Independence Day fireworks show.

The freshman soccer field between the stadium and the main road, which runs along the school, is filled with families camped out picnic-style, while the far side past the stadium is blocked off for the pyrotechnics. Even the sidewalks along the main road are filled with standing-room-only crowds. Across the main street sits a dark brown brick wall that displays the entrance to a townhouse community. The 10-foot wall makes an ideal vantage point for the teenagers sitting on top; this is where Jack and Scarlett sit hand in hand. Allison sits between Scarlett and Connor with her flask tucked under her leg.

The crowds around them are all too engaged in their own conversations to pay mind to what the teens are talking about. Still, they keep a watchful eye out for anyone whose ears might be listening.

"I still say he's next." Defiance frost Jack's words.

Scarlett looks around with a guilty conscience. "Not so loud. But even if we all agree, how would we ... go about accomplishing this?"

"We already know where he lives. We make it happen there." Allison swigs from her flask as if the plan is that obvious.

"I don't think so. We need to find out what 51 knows. We need to handle this properly," Connor adds.

"Fifty-one?" Scarlett is a bit confused.

Connor points to where an officer wears his badge. "Fifty-one."

Scarlett taps her temple. "Gotcha."

Connor pulls the recorder out of his pocket. "Oh, Allison, I found this cassette thingy; I think it was one of my parents. I have the tapes, and I think they are good, but the recorder is broken. I need a usable one. I think I can hear my parents' voices again. Well, one of them, at least."

Allison leans forward. "Mini cassettes, ya said? Cause if it's cassettes, I think I can get you one."

Connor nods. "Cassettes. Thanks."

"Don't futz with it until I find you a new one. And especially don't touch the red button. That can erase the tape if it winds up working somehow," Allison warns.

Jack raises his hand.

"Yes, Jack," Allison calls on him.

"We, uh, well, back to the matter at hand. We still need a plan of ... of attack," Jack points out. "Information gathered and all."

"He's not wrong," Connor confirms. "And if we aren't planning the surprise at his home, then we might need more than just us."

Scarlett, staring out into the crowd, sees the leather-clad Duncan and a group of his misfit friends scanning the scene while smoking cigarettes and passing a flask around. Duncan looks up to Scarlett, exhaling a drag of his cigarette. He gives her a smiling nod.

Scarlett smiles back and gives a nervous wave. She turns to her friends. "I know we have to keep everything we've learned a secret, but what if we had help?"

"What the hell does that mean?" Allison bluntly asks while taking another swig.

"Well, what if I know someone who knows people, and all of us have a mutual enemy?" She stops and waits to see if everyone else is on the same page.

They all give half-nods, indicating a mutually confused understanding.

"We need him dealt with because of his actions against our families. This other group doesn't like him simply for his profession's profiling of youth. What if we came together in a mutual, even if concealed, understanding for a chain of events?" Scarlett lays out.

"We still need more info on what's going on at a root level," Connor reminds.

"That's fine. I mean, when the time comes," Scarlett clarifies.

A voice from the base of the wall calls up to them. "You get a chance ta talk to her for me?"

They all look down at a bald-headed Duncan, the epitome of a wrongfully profiled youth with misdirected anger.

Scarlett turns to her friends with a Cheshire smile on her face. "This is what I mean by people." She looks down at Duncan. "Haven't seen her in a while. I don't think she'd miss tonight, though."

Duncan huffs out of disappointment and looks around at the wall. "How the hell d'you get up there?"

Scarlett makes a grand motion to the back side of the wall. "There's room if you wanna."

Duncan turns before glancing back at Scarlett, nodding towards his friends. "I think they need me over there."

Scarlett nods in understanding as Duncan heads back to his friends.

"Talk to who, Scar?" Allison probes, taking another swig.

"Part of the deal for helping me with my tutoring program. He helps me, I help him," Scarlett responds, avoiding a direct answer.

Not letting sleeping dogs lie, Connor chimes in, "That wasn't an answer."

"I know," Scarlett says, laughing.

They drop the subject for the time being and sit for a while, chatting about other aspects of life, love, and teenage existentialism, waiting for the evening sky to darken. Brianna approaches the group, and her appearance has returned to normal from her Legendary form. Her skin, however, is still sort of blotchy that even foundation has trouble covering up. The dark circles under her eyes make them more sunken, telling of a trying summer so far, while her smaller and meeker smile replaces her typically oversized and gilded one.

Allison and Connor don't seem to notice Brianna as they are lip-locked between sips from the flask. Scarlett motions Bri around the wall to the backside so she can climb up.

Brianna sits quietly next to Scarlett without any fanfare or backhanded compliments, unsure of what to say.

"Thanks." Bri voices her sincerity, as if Scarlett is doing her some sort of favor.

"Yup," Scarlett replies. "So, I know you've had a hard summer."

Bri nods in agreement.

"How about a little interesting news?" Scarlett continues.

"What's that?" A nervousness underlies Bri's voice.

"Don't make it obvious, but see that kid over there?" Scarlett attempts a discreet motion to Duncan and his friends.

"Which one?" Bri looks out to the sea of people awaiting the fireworks.

"The bald one talking with the police," Scarlett says, not narrowing down the crowd as she points to four of them, all bald or buzzed about twenty yards away across the street.

"There's three of them," Bri replies. "What's going on?"

"A kid asked about you," Scarlett starts.

"From *that* crowd?" Bri is half-disgusted, half-intrigued.

"Yes, from *that* crowd. Duncan actually seems to have some intelligent thoughts about things," Scarlett carries on.

"Why were you talking to *him*?" Bri asks, as if even Scarlett is too good for the likes of him.

Duncan turns around and sees Scarlett and Bri talking, occasionally glancing in his direction.

"I assume it's the one who keeps looking this way like a pound puppy wanting to be taken home?" An air of snottiness drips off Brianna's comments.

"His name is Duncan," Allison snaps back, stopping her lip-locking with Connor. "At least I assume that's who you are talking about."

Allison takes a big swig from her flask as Duncan turns to them again, causing the policeman to see her. She tries to hide it under her leg, but the cop is already shaking his head at her.

He heads her way with determination in his step, holding his pointed finger in the air at the young Petrovsky.

Allison sits, a deer frozen in headlights.

Duncan sees the confrontation about to go down and jogs on over. He snakes through the crowd and ducks behind the wall as the officer approaches them.

"Young lady, I saw what you were doing. Come down from there," the officer commands.

Connor feels a tap on his lower back. He and Allison turn to see Duncan motioning for the flask.

"Jump down from the front; don't go the back way," the officer continues.

Allison turns back to him. "But I don't know if I can get down that way." She starts lifting herself as if to jump, giving Duncan enough concealed reach to grab the flask. "I just can't do it from this side." She lowers herself back down.

The officer smiles at her attempts to be slick. "Where's the flask?"

"What flask?" Allison bats her eyelashes.

"The flask I saw you drinking from a moment ago," he snaps back.

She shrugs and turns her palms up. "I don't have a flask. Are you sure the sun wasn't in your eyes?"

"I'm sure. Now get down here, or I'll arrest you for resisting an officer of the law," he snaps.

With that, Duncan steps out from behind the wall holding the flask. "Seriously, officer, you just can't stay away from me; it's my flask."

The officer's eyes shoot daggers at Duncan. "I don't know how you got here from way over there, but fine. You want this on you? Then come here."

Duncan looks up at Brianna with a devilishly charming smile as he hands the officer the flask. "Hey, Brianna. What's up?"

The officer smells alcohol and pockets the flask. He turns Duncan around and handcuffs him.

Brianna has a confused yet delighted smile on her face. She doesn't quite understand why Duncan is doing this for Allison, but she finds it charming. "Hey, you." She smiles back.

The officer starts to haul Duncan away, so he turns back to Brianna. "Call me."

Bri blushes and smiles an uncomfortably excited smile.

"So that was Duncan," Scarlett quips.

"A fascinating first impression," Bri responds, as the fireworks start to illuminate the Fourth of July night sky.

CHAPTER 8

"Even those discriminated against discriminate.
It's a fundamental flaw of human nature."
~K. DeSalvo~

B rianna stands in front of her bathroom mirror, staring at the new blotchy patches across her face. She presses and pulls on her skin, inspecting every square inch—as if all of this is a sudden onset of a very mild case of vitiligo. Her teenage eyes try to find the source of what she considers a fatal imperfection.

"I don't understand this, Mother! I take such good care of my skin!" Brianna pouts.

"It's not you, my dear." Sylvia shakes a metal martini shaker. "It's genetics. You are and always will be a beautiful woman." She shakes her head at her words, as if she knows they are not the right words to say, but nothing else will calm her daughter.

"But consumer products are more powerful than genetics! That's what the commercials say!" Bri shouts back as she starts dabbing on concealer.

"That's what the commercials want you to believe, but it's not true," she responds, pouring her freshly shaken martini into her already garnished glass.

She smiles as the light green alcohol fills her glass, the destemmed cherry at the bottom dancing around as the appletini settles around it. She lifts it to her lips and takes a savored sip.

Bri mutters, "Well, they should be stronger. At least then I'd know all my time spent in here wasn't wasted."

Brianna continues applying foundation, satisfactorily concealing what she deems less-than-desirable skin variations.

Sylvia sways up to the bathroom door, martini in hand. "Where you headed tonight that you're putting on a nice face?"

"Meeting up with a few friends. Hoping to run into a new boy that Scarlett introduced me to, kinda," she says.

"I saw Scarlett not too terribly long ago. I am helping her set up her tutoring program. She took on one rough kid to prove the program works. I told her that she should be careful. But kids these days don't listen to us anymore. I tell ya, Brianna; this kid she is tutoring, Duncan, nothing but trouble. If she starts hanging out with him, stay away from her. I disapprove of the likes of him." Sylvia has wandered into her own little world by the time she stops her soliloquy.

Brianna finishes applying her lipstick as she stares at her mother. She doesn't want to lie to her but also doesn't want her mother to make all her decisions for her as well. Duncan didn't seem so bad the first time they met.

Brianna sees her mom drinking and doesn't want to feel the sting of her palm against her face.

"What's so wrong with this Duncan kid?" Brianna casually inquires.

"Just the wrong element. All shaved head, leather jacket, ripped jeans, and flannel. Once, before he shaved his head, he had a mohawk. Always listening to that music. Gangster rap, or whatever they call it nowadays, and that black metal. Just not a good person. He never does his work. Well, he did in my class, but I hear the teachers talk. You are better off steering clear of that one." She gulps down the rest of her martini.

Brianna finishes putting on her face, caps her mascara, and turns to her mother. "Mom, is everything okay?"

Sylvia snaps back to the moment. "Yeah. Why, dear?"

"You seem ... I don't know. Distracted? Or maybe ... edgy? On edge," Bri says, taking a half-step back.

Sylvia smiles, looking down at her empty martini. "I know. I know. There's so much I need to tell you still. Things around here have been a bit ... unsettling for me lately. Not that it's anything *you* need to worry about. It's just something on my end that I need to take care of once I find out how."

"What's going on? What do you *need* to tell me? Is this something I can help you with? Is there something I can do?" Brianna shoots off, picking up her mother's newfound rapid-fire speech. She takes a half step toward her mother and attempts to make eye contact.

Sylvia lifts her head to meet Brianna's eyes. "My eye. I didn't get this," she points to her black eye, "by going out for drinks with friends."

"You told me you got it falling off a chair," Bri corrects her mother.

Sylvia lets out a laugh that's more like a huff. "That's right. A chair. Either way. You know our conditions?"

"My skin condition?" Bri says, pulling out a tube of cream and rubbing it over her arms and neck.

"You'll need to come to terms with this. You are what is called, in our society, an Undying. It goes far beyond a *skin condition*," Sylvia starts.

"So? What's my *Undying* thing have to do with your black eye?" Bri questions.

"Come sit with me," Sylvia says, turning around to the living room.

Brianna follows her and sits next to her mother on the couch.

"People don't always accept what they don't understand," Sylvia starts.

"I know." Bri's response remains calm, though the impatience of uncertainty bubbles below the surface.

"Well, sometimes when people don't understand something or when they fear something, they try to kill it. Like when someone is afraid of spiders. Instead of putting it outside, they kill it." Sylvia keeps eye contact with her daughter.

Brianna's face still contorts in confusion, not quite grasping where her mother is taking this.

"When people don't understand other people, or when they falsely believe they don't have common goals, they try to get rid of them," Sylvia continues.

"Is this some Israel versus Palestine thing we're gonna have a powwow about?" Bri asks as she starts catching on.

"Good comparison, but that's not the only example either. What I'm talking about is genocide," Sylvia says.

Brianna puts up a hand as she stands back up. "Ma, I'm all for waxing intellectual about history, but I gotta get ready."

"I'm serious, young lady. This is important." Sylvia follows her back to the bathroom.

Bri's impatience finally come to a boil. "Whatever, Mom. People will judge us without knowing. It's the way of the world; it's what society does. It sucks. This sucks. I didn't ask for this. No one asks for any of this. But it's life. I'll deal with people not liking me. Try being popular. You'll find out how many people actually don't like you," Brianna spouts off, working up her anxiety again.

"No one ever wants it or asks for it. It is just the way things are. And we all learn to deal with it. That is what I am trying to teach you, how to deal." Sylvia attempts to calm her daughter.

"So how do we deal with this then? I'm so lost right now in this conversation. You went from telling me about your black eye to telling me I'm not dying and part of some society and Israel." Brianna swipes her cheekbones with blush.

Sylvia takes a deep breath. "One, you're Undying, not 'not dying.' This society you are a part of— The Nation…"

Bri interrupts, "Yeah. Don't tell anyone, even if you think they might be in it. Blah, blah." Her bratty, defiant tone overshadows the reminder that she already knows this.

Sylvia grabs the makeup brush from her daughter's hand. "Do you think that is everything you need to know in life? There's always more. Never think there isn't more or that you are done learning. You are never done."

Brianna stares at the makeup brush. "Then what, Mother? What is this all about?"

"I've been attacked. I've kept you safe and always will. But there may come a day when you are not safe. When I can't keep you safe. If you don't understand yourself—what you are capable of—then you won't be able to defend yourself as best you can."

Brianna's annoyance has turned to concern. She stops staring at the makeup brush in her mother's hand and looks into her mother's sad eyes.

"So, what then? What do we do? What do I do? Why now, Mom? Why are you telling me this now?" Bri begins to shake as her breathing starts to quicken. Sylvia notices Brianna's skin blotches appearing through her foundation.

Sylvia looks at her daughter and holds her gaze for a moment, trying to quell her budding hysteria.

"What do we do? We live. We go on living our lives. No one needs to know about our conditions. Never call them diseases. They are no one's business but our own. As I said, tell no one. You continue living your life. Do the things you enjoy. Study, watch TV, send snaps to your friends, read books. Nothing has changed except that you know a little more about yourself than you did before prom. The Council will worry about how to deal with the situation." Sylvia lays it all out for her daughter.

Brianna waves her hands in the air. "Hold up. What's The Council?"

Sylvia smiles. "They're a government for our people. A group of Legends that run our community, deal with the day-to-day, and how to stay integrated with the Normal society while hidden at the same time."

"What are Legends?" Bri raises her brow.

Sylvia lets out a slight huff of amusement at her own oversight. "We are Legends. You, I, everyone in The Nation. We are called so because of the history and mythology behind our abilities."

Brianna shakes her head. "This is heavy stuff, Mom."

"So it is. But I told you because I wanted to be honest and let you know things are being done about it," Sylvia continues.

"Now I just go hang out with my friends?" Bri returns to doing her makeup. Anger lingers in her glances at her mother.

"What else would you do?" Sylvia offers in response, leaving her daughter alone to finish her routine before heading out for the night.

Some generic pop-punk band graces the stage of The Attic. In their usual spot, Scarlett, Connor, Allison, and Jack are all comfy on the far-back couch, surveying their haunt one last time together before school starts.

"This is a bit mellow even for a birthday, Lil' Lett," observes Allison.

"What did you expect? A kegger?" quips Scarlett.

"Something along those lines, yeah." Allison slips a new flask out from the back of her jeans.

Connor shakes his head while smiling. "I thought you were laying off that for a while."

"Cutting back." Allison winks.

"6:30 a.m. seems a bit early for a move, Connor," Jack says, changing the subject.

"It is," Connor sighs. "But college is over two hours away, and I have to check in by 9:30 for move-in."

"Classes start in a week, right?" Allison asks.

"A week from Monday. They were spouting something about us acclimating to our new environments before classes start or something. Basically, it just gives us time to meet people and explore the area. Learn the campus layout," Connor explains.

Allison turns to Jack. "What about you?"

Jack shakes his head. "After everything that has, well, happened, I decided to stay home. The scholarships I got offered weren't as good, as helpful. I can't afford it. Let's end this subject. Don't want to, well, ruin your birthday, Scarlett."

Scarlett puts a comforting hand on Jack's knee as she shifts her attention from the band back to her friends. "It's okay, love. You're fine. It's gonna be a long day tomorrow. We don't have to celebrate my birthday, as much as I appreciate it," Scarlett adds.

"It's your birthday. Of course, we're celebrating, or at the very least, hanging out at our usual spot. Plus, what else do we have to do?" Connor replies.

Allison pulls out a mini-cassette voice recorder from her pocket. She starts going over the device functionality, but he stops her.

"Hey, we might be a digital generation, but I know how to hit play, stop, pause, and all the other fun buttons," Connor assures.

She playfully throws up her hands. "Just makin' sure."

"Thanks, baby." Connor turns to Scarlett. "On second thought, Scarlett..." He stands up, turning to leave.

"I could come with you ... if you need," Allison offers up as she starts to stand. "If it's cool with Scar."

"Wait a second, you two," Scarlett interrupts. "This is our last shindig together before school starts. You can't leave now."

Connor holds up the tape recorder and shakes it at her. "I love you all, but the tapes might be the only way to hear my parents' voices again."

"Fine." Scarlett feigns a pout. Pointing to Allison, she adds, "But she stays."

Allison sits back down.

"It's cool, Con. I can look after everyone," Jack tosses in his two cents.

"Thanks, bro." Connor turns back to Allison. "Thank you, my love." Connor gives Allison a very appreciative kiss.

Before heading out, he turns back to everyone. "I love you all, and we will do this again. I just..." he looks to the recorder, "...this."

Connor turns around to the door again, then immediately swings back to the group.

"You're still coming tomorrow? Right?" Connor asks Allison, unsure of her intentions.

"Of course, I'll be there with Red Bull and Monster." Allison smiles.

Connor turns back to the door and takes a few steps before turning back and leaning down to give Scarlett a big hug, "Happy birthday, cuz."

Scarlett shakes her head. "Thanks, Con. Now go."

Scarlett eyes Brianna as she walks through the doors. She turns to Allison, who has not seen Bri yet. "Be nice, Al." Scarlett waves to Brianna.

Allison turns to Scarlett. "Nice about ... oh." She sees Scarlett waving at Bri; the answer to her question is making her way toward them.

"She asked if she could come out with us," Scarlett sums up as Brianna approaches. "Just be nice."

Allison puts on a fake smile and points to it with both hands. "Aren't I always?"

Scarlett turns to Brianna as she stops in front of them. "Cop a squat, Bri."

Brianna looks around, exuding a nervous demeanor. "Is he here?"

"Not yet. He'll show. Said he'd be here when I tutored him earlier," Scarlett answers.

Brianna sees her usual clique holding drinks at the side of the dance floor. They sway with the music. One of the girls sees Brianna and turns to her friends. They point in her direction and laugh. The girl who first made eye contact taps the other girl on her arm and starts walking toward Bri with a determined step.

As the girls make their final approach, the adjunct leader puts out her arms to stop the rest and plants her front foot firmly in place, directly in front of Brianna.

"You've been hiding from everyone all summer. What's your deal, Bri?" The snide lead girl asks. "Are you going mental?"

"I was sick for a while. Couldn't really talk to anyone." Bri keeps her reply dry.

"Sure you're not still ill? Sitting here with these..." spouts the leader as she gestures to Jack, Scarlett, and Allison.

Brianna stares at her false friends as she shifts her look to Scarlett. Scarlett gives her a slight nod of encouragement.

Brianna looks back to her popular crowd. "They're not as bad as you'd think, girls."

Scarlett gives Allison a look that screams, "at least she's trying to be nice." And Allison knows it. However, she doesn't want to admit that Brianna might not be the big bad wolf she makes her out to be.

"If you got a chance to know them..." Brianna continues.

Before she can finish her sentence, the lead girl cuts her off. "The fact that you took time to talk to them shows how far you've sunk. Are you actually staying here, or are you coming with us?"

Brianna takes a deep breath as she contemplates the rest of her high school career in a few seconds. "I'm meeting someone," Brianna replies, avoiding a direct answer to the question.

"Radio silence all summer, and your first outing isn't even with us. It's with them?" Disgust drips off the leader's words. She turns to the group behind her. "Oh, how the mighty have fallen, girls."

The rest of the girls laugh at Brianna's expense.

As if from out of nowhere, Duncan speaks, "At least she is mighty. What do you all have? The ability ta be told what ta do, what you should think, and how ta act? Followin' each other around like sheep and lost puppy dogs, beggin' for the love and approval of an abusive master. When ya finally do the terrifyin' act of thinkin' on your own, you'll find yourself loathsome of the existence you've led and, worse yet, disgusted and repulsed at what ya see in the mirror. I just hope you're strong enough to make it out the other side alive."

Brianna and Scarlett, with smiles on their faces, look up at Duncan, who approached them sometime in the encounter. Allison sits, pondering the words just spoken, an almost melancholy look on her face.

The entitled, superior look on the girls' faces all wash away as his words sink in. They turn away, trying to save what little pride they have left.

A smug smile on Duncan as he waves them off with a bent wrist. After the mean girls are far enough away to end any potential drama, Duncan turns to his new friends, putting his hands in his pockets.

"Sup?" he says to the group.

"Just destroying my high school career," Brianna replies.

"High school's overrated. Screw those girls," Duncan says with a laugh.

Allison shakes her head and smiles. "Have a seat."

While Allison is the first to take jabs at Brianna, there was something sweet in Duncan's defense of her that made Allison wish she had said something to those girls first.

He nods and sits between Brianna and Scarlett. Duncan scans Jack, Scarlett, and Allison with quick eye contact and an acknowledging smile. In the end, his attention is concentrated on Brianna.

"So, I was thinking," Duncan begins before giving pause. "You seem interestin', and I'd like to talk. Maybe grab a movie, then coffee or dinner. That way, we at least have the movie to talk about, ya know?"

Brianna gives an unsure smile that doesn't go unnoticed by Duncan.

"Or not. No pressure," Duncan amends his proposal.

"I'd like that. It's just," Brianna starts, then stops.

"I understand. I'm not your type or whatever. Ya haven't even seen my art yet." Duncan starts to go on the defensive.

Brianna shakes her head. "Stop, Duncan. It's not you; it's my mom. She … she listens to the whispers of the other teachers."

"What the hell does that mean?" Duncan asks, now clearly getting offended.

Allison, who, much like Scarlett and Jack, has been eavesdropping on their conversation since it started, chimes in, "It means her mother's a bitch."

"What did I say, Al?" Scarlett scolds.

"What? That was as nice as I could say it," Allison defends.

"My mom's not a bitch," Brianna snaps back. "Well, not all the time. But, come to think of it, she is being hypocritical. But what it means is that she said I couldn't hang out with you."

Duncan raises a brow. "Why would she say that? Then why did you show up here?"

"I don't know why she said that. I'm here because I wanted to see you. See what this mystery is about," Brianna says, withholding the truth of the conversation she had earlier tonight.

Duncan stands up, still caught up on the prohibition of Bri's mother. "Well, that's cool. If she doesn't want ya hanging out with me, then I shouldn't be here. The hypocrisy of the situation and all. I wouldn't want to give your mother any more fuel for her misguided fire." He turns to Scarlett. "Sorry to cause trouble for you and your friends. Scarlett, thanks for gettin' me through summer school."

"You passed both your classes?" Scarlett asks with a hope-filled voice.

"You shoulda seen the teacher's faces when I passed." He smiles. "Made it worth all the sessions."

"Glad to hear it. It's been my pleasure," Scarlett adds.

"See you next session?" Duncan asks as he starts to turn away.

"Of course, Duncan. Tomorrow night." Scarlett smiles.

"Dude, screw that. Sit. Brianna can go," Allison chimes in. "She has friends she has to go grovel to."

Duncan shakes his head as he walks away. He raises his hand into the air. "I gotta take care of things. See you at school." He stops and turns around. A mischievous smile crosses his face as he looks back at Brianna. "Maybe your mom will change her mind, B." He turns back around and walks off.

Jack pipes up, "So this night is fun, huh?"

"Real birthday blast," Allison confirms. "Sorry I didn't plan anything better."

"No worries, Al. At least the music isn't terrible." Scarlett finds a silver lining.

"Sorry, guys," Brianna says.

"It's cool," Jack consoles.

"No, it's not," Allison jabs.

"Allison!" Scarlett squeaks out as if surprised.

"Don't 'Allison' me, Scar," Allison defends. "It's our last night together before school starts. One last night and you use your birthday as an excuse to invite someone along who hasn't given two craps about us in years because what, Duncan wants to hopefully stick his tongue down her throat?"

"One, I didn't use my birthday as an excuse. It's nothing more than coincidence. Two, it's not like that, Al," Scarlett defends.

"Then what is it like? Cause I can't find one good reason she needs to be here." Allison pulls out a water bottle from the couch seats and takes a swig.

"Having more?!" Scarlett calls out Allison's drinking.

"Betty White up, Scarlett," Allison says, taking another swig. She offers it to Scarlett, who gives in to peer pressure and takes a small swig.

Brianna sits there, unsure if adding in her thoughts would help or hinder the tension right now.

"So?" Allison reminds Scarlett.

"She just blew up her entire junior high and high school legacy to try and make amends with us. The least you can do is be civil," Scarlett finishes.

"Actually, no. *She* walked away from being friends with us. *She's* said nothing but backhanded compliments and condescension since that day. *She* made her bed. You just want to lie in it with her. I'm not going to make it that simple. Maybe she needs to walk a lonesome road awhile." Allison realizes she might be talking about someone else in that last sentence.

"Maybe I should go." Brianna starts to stand up.

Allison jumps up. "No. You stay. I gotta take a walk. Happy birthday, Little 'Lett." Allison walks away, thinking about her reaction. The mixed feelings she possesses about someone she outwardly cries so much hate for confounds her in ways more so than when she first thought about Connor. Allison looks back at her friends and Brianna sitting in awkward silence, staring at the band. But even in their silence, she doesn't feel like Scarlett is the one who betrayed the group. Allison doesn't even feel Brianna is wholly to blame. Her confusion runs much deeper than she understands.

CHAPTER 9

*"It's all those little things we
don't think about that kill us."*
~S. Waldgrave~

The drive to the Waldgrave residence isn't quite long enough to figure out everything that weighs on Duncan's mind. How will he convince Sylvia that he isn't a bad seed? How will he explain that he knows where they live, having never been to their house? To him, the simple answer of Facebook photos of their home, mixed with what he's heard at school, gave him a street name and home to look for isn't nearly as creepy as it sounds. He knows, though, that the answer won't seem nearly as innocent; that aside, what will he say? Doesn't matter now. He sits outside the house from the Facebook photos.

He shuts off the car and the headlights. As he exits the car, he sees the house curtains yank closed. The fabric of the curtains sways for a moment in a violent wave-like fashion. Then, as quickly as it was pulled shut, the curtain and curtain rod fall to the floor.

CHAPTER 9

The light inside shines bright, illuminating the profile of a hulking figure. Duncan stops in his tracks and stands in the middle of the street, staring at the towering figure in the window. Before he can get a good look, the creature appears to pounce on something out of view.

In his teenage curiosity, Duncan runs to the window to try and sneak a better look. He crouches down below the sill, his back to the wall, and takes a few deep breaths as the numerous thoughts of what he could have seen all race through his mind. After calming himself, he lifts himself up and peaks through the window.

On the floor, he sees something his mind cannot fully comprehend. He thinks that the window might be obscuring his sight or that he might not be seeing what he is seeing. But an instinctual feeling that says to run whispers to him that he sees what his eyes tell his brain; on the floor is a human-like creature who seems to be covered in something resembling tree bark and hair that has been overgrown with Spanish moss. The eyes of the being are thoroughly grey, except for the wide pupils that call out for help in such a human-like, emotion-filled way that Duncan's heart skips a beat. The creature that kneels over the tree creature is large and overly muscular. Duncan sees that under what appears to be thin layers of long fur covering the skin are varicose veins all over the arms and back. Thick claws protrude from, what Duncan can only assume to be, hands and swipe at the bark-like covering on the face of the pinned creature.

The speed and violence of the acts freeze Duncan like a deer in headlights. He watches, frozen in horror and disbelief, as the furry beast claws away at the living tree. Pieces of bark chip off with each strike, not seeming to affect the creature.

Duncan's mind tries to sort out what his eyes see from what must be true of the situation. His brain searches for cosplay scenarios where this would make sense. Perhaps some live-action role-play that is a bit too realistic for his outside observation to realize is just a game.

The tree-like figure on the bottom unsuccessfully attempts to push the attacker off. A voice that rings familiar to Duncan cries out, "Why do you keep doing this to me?!"

Though he can't be positive in all the commotion, Duncan thinks the voice he hears is Mrs. Waldgrave's.

The attacker pauses for a moment, a pause that indicates something, but what that something is the tree-like figure can't put a finger on. The break, however, is just long enough for her to strike back. A blow against the side of the head stuns her attacker, and she rolls him off her.

As the bark-covered person crawls out from under the beast, her grey eyes look in Duncan's direction for a split second. At that moment, their eyes lock; at least Duncan thinks their eyes meet. This most human of interactions causes him to jerk his head forward, hitting the window. The beast shakes off the blow from the bark-covered person and looks toward the window for the source of the noise.

Under the lights of the room, Duncan sees fangs glisten. Instinct takes over as Duncan runs full speed to his car. All notions of making Sylvia change her mind about him are gone, as he must deal with the impossible and unreal situation he thinks he just witnessed.

As Duncan speeds away, he sees a much more human-like figure rush out of the house and into the street. His foot refuses to lessen on the gas as he speeds through a stop sign and into the night.

Now he has to sort out what he saw from what his mind thinks it saw and determine if there is any difference between the two.

Connor closes the door to his bedroom for privacy; it's a habit ingrained in him from years of growing up and not wanting anyone to hear whatever it was he was doing in his room alone. He keeps the door closed and sits on his bed. He plays around with the tape recorder that Allison gave him and practices for a few moments, making sure he doesn't erase the sound of one of his parents.

Once he is comfortable, he reaches to his desk for the one he found in his living room. He can feel his heart start to race in his chest. Tears well up in his eyes at the thought of hearing at least one of his parents' voices one more time.

It's a small thing that people tend not to think about—the sound of someone's voice, remembering how it sounds and if the tone of the voice remembered is accurate to how it sounds in person. If it is, how long will that memory last before it starts to warp and fade until the memory of a memory is all that remains? Then the sound of their actual voice is replaced with what someone's mind thinks it once sounded like.

For Connor, he will have these tapes. He will always have the sound of his father talking about legislation or his mother talking with a patient. Whichever parent this recorder belonged to will always be with him. All he has to do is rewind the tape and push play.

He does.

As the tape begins, his heart races faster and faster, waiting for a familiar voice to sound. The voice that speaks first into the recorder is one unfamiliar to Connor. "West Haven patients KDS and TDS."

Connor hears rifling and shifting in the background of the tape. "Complying injections have been administered."

Connor continues to listen as the voice moves away from the microphone. The shuffling, shifting sounds in the background carry on. His ears momentarily pick up the faint sounds of a woman whimpering, while continuing to hear something else shift and move about.

Connor knows this tape is not a city council session; no talks of new laws and legislation will be heard. He knows this might be somehow related to his mother's work, but the voice ... it is not hers.

The background shuffling and whimpers continue even as the unfamiliar voice goes silent.

He pauses the tape and grabs a pen and a left-over notebook from his high school classes—one with plenty of blank pages for him to transcribe the recordings into. He rewinds the tapes and starts over, this time jotting down what he clearly hears.

West Haven patients, KDS? TDS? Complying injections.

As the voice fades again, leaving just the noises in the background, Connor realizes the patients' initials, the double capital in his last name, that the bloodied voice recorder wasn't his parents; it belongs to whoever killed his parents.

After a few moments of background noise, a hard knock is heard. To Connor, it sounds like a knock on the door. It is the faint sounds of the doorknob being turned and the latch opening.

Connor struggles to hear what is going on, keeping his ear tilted to the speaker.

"Help!" Connor hears his mother's voice cry out.

Tears form in his eyes as he envisions the events that played out, the events he hears on the tape.

Connor hears a commanding voice yell, "Stay down!" followed by the sound of a chair being pulled out.

"They finally let you off desk duty?" Connor hears this, and anger swells inside him. It's a voice that has taunted him before, a voice that taunted him at the tuxedo shop—Officer Espinoza. The tears start flowing because Connor knows the outcome. He knows what he is listening to. He can't stop it, helpless to turn back time and save them. Helpless to do anything but listen as his parents are about to be killed.

"First day back on the beat," the voice responds. "What's going on?" Connor knows. He knows that this voice he hears is the third body he discovered.

Connor again hears his mother cry out, "They're trying to kill us! Please help!" A heaviness in his chest starts tightening its grip. With each breath, it is harder and harder to take in the air around him.

"Max, what's going on here? What happened to them?"

"So many things." Connor hears Espinoza speak again. Again, a construed lie to conceal what he is about to do. His fear has him paralyzed on his bed, stomach-churning; he can't even hit stop on the player. Connor can't get off the proverbial tracks as the train races toward him. He watches, knowing he'll be smashed. He just hopes he can survive.

A loud, inaudible scream blows through the speaker—a cry so pained that tears cascade down Connor's cheeks in a torrent. Hysterical tears mix with the snot running out his nose, but he can't wipe any of it away, still paralyzed by the sounds coming from the tape.

"Will someone please explain what's going on here?!" Words that pull Connor back into the moment, it's a chance at knowing the why behind the what of the events. Perhaps it's the why behind everything happening to him, his family, and Jack's family.

The unfamiliar voice from the start of the tape speaks again, "We are about to make history. Too bad you can't be a part of it."

A loud, unmistakable gunshot echoes out, followed by the thud of a body hitting the floor.

Connor's heart races and pounds. The queasy feeling in his stomach sinks deeper and deeper. Nausea builds up at the thought of what is being played actually transpiring in the other room. The idea enters into his head that he is unsure of who was just shot. Did he just hear one of his parents die or the stranger? Guilt sets in that he hopes it was just the stranger. A pang of guilt because he places the value of his own parents' lives above a stranger's life, even though they all ended up the same way.

The following minutes are filled with screams, smacks, thuds, whacks, and other chaotic, messy, and macabre noises.

"Why can't you just leave us alone!" Connor hears his father plead.

"Dad!" Connor yells out of surprise, not as if his father will respond.

After a few more moments of struggle, Connor is jolted by another booming gunshot. The silence that falls is thick but brief.

"Because you and your diseases are not welcome here or anywhere. Gods and beasts. That is what our world is made of. And clearly, you are the beasts. Nothing but lesser beings for us to clean up."

The ambient, convoluted noises of movement flood Connor's ears as the struggle ends. He cannot take anymore, as his stomach tries not to reveal what it holds. The wells of his tears have dried up for the moment. His mouth is covered in a layer of snot that seeped out through his hysterics. He cannot go on. Not now.

Now, Connor is left to think that while he was at prom, having what he thought was the time of his life, his parents were losing their lives. He can't help but think about what he was thinking that night. The joyous memories he should have had. That his first time together with Allison, now and forever, will be overshadowed by the noises he heard on the tape—the voices crying out for help.

Vistrus sits at his piano, playing Beethoven's "Moonlight Sonata" in a slowed, flowing style. His take on the music adds to the Gothic undertones of the piece. The lights in the house are off, save the one table lamp next to the piano that illuminates the framed portrait of his deceased wife, Inessa.

He stares at her, remembering the reasons he still loves her, wishing for another moment with her before she was taken from him. His thoughts of her and the joy they shared throughout their century together bring a sad smile to his face.

As he savors the moment of reminiscence, Allison comes through the door and heads straight to the bathroom.

"Hey, Dad," she says, starting to gargle mouthwash.

Vistrus slows his playing to a halt. "How was your night, dear?"

She spits and walks back into the living room. "It was okay." She sees her father at the piano. "Thinking of Ma?"

"I wish you could remember her." A wistfulness coats his words.

Allison sees her father's pain and takes a seat on the couch. "You could always tell me something about her. You never like to talk, but you really loved her."

He smiles at her maturity. He looks at the picture and then back to his daughter, who is the spitting image of her mother.

"The first thing you should know is that she loved you very much," he says with a proud smile. "You were her world. We waited longer than you can imagine to have you."

"What did she do?" Allison asks, trying to keep her father talking.

"She worked for my museum. But we met while working at a different museum back home in Russia."

"That's so cute. You met at work. What did Mom do there?" Allison continues moving the story along.

Vistrus smiles. "Inessa was a curator. But then she was offered a job overseas, so we lived in New York for a while before being offered a better position in West Haven."

"What was she like? Was she a ... like you?" Allison pauses, unsure of how to properly ask the question.

"Like us, you mean?" He lets a little laugh escape him. "Yes. She was. It was why she jumped on the chance to move here when the position opened up.

There is a large concentration of Legends in this town. At least compared to others." He trails off his thoughts. "But your mother. She was something. A smile that lit up a room. The sway in her walk commanded attention ... when she wanted it."

Allison smiles. "It's so nice to hear about her. If she was like ... us, did she have dreams like I do?"

Her father's smile fades. "I do not like lying. Despite what children think, parents do not relish being untruthful to them." He scrunches his face at some internal thought. "She did. And they were, much like yours seem to be—very realistic. At first, they were thought of as a gift. Perhaps they could have been."

Allison pipes up, "If she got help, I bet. Someone to guide her and interpret them."

Her father again gives a sad smile. "No, my dear. That is where things started to go bad. In the end, my beloved Inessa became ill."

Allison crashes back into her seat. "Ill? I don't understand."

Vistrus thinks for a moment while holding a longing gaze at the picture. He turns back to his daughter with a downtrodden expression.

"She had vivid dreams that started sometime after we moved here. She was fine at first but said she needed help after a while. There was no reason back then to think it would be adverse."

Allison starts to realize there are deeper reasons for his resistance.

"We were here, in West Haven, for a long time. Everything seemed to be going well. Then the dreams started. Once she started seeing a therapist for them, she began to decline," he explains.

"How old was I? I don't remember any of this," Allison says, looking around the darkened room.

Even the wind outside, with its constant, subtle sounds, doesn't disturb the tangible silence that fills the room with haunting eeriness between their words as Allison learns more about her mother.

"No more than a year and a half; it was quick. At first, the doctors looked at it as some sort of ... post-partum condition. The tests, though, the tests showed nothing. Then she changed," he continues.

"Changed?" Allison says, scooching toward the edge of her seat.

Vistrus stands from the piano and moves to his red chair. He sits and grabs a cigar from his humidor. The five-pointed star with the equal sign in the middle, all surrounded by a circle engraved into its top, catches his attention. He's seen it every day for countless years, but something about it and the conversation he is having grabs hold of him for a moment. He looks back at his daughter as he lights his cigar.

"She started talking to herself. Not in the way that everybody does once in a while. She would have whispered conversations with no one." He puffs the cigar.

Allison starts to paint a very different picture in her mind of her mother, an image far removed from the caring wife and mother whose days were filled with love and laughter.

"As I said, Inessa's decline was rapid. Once the conversations started with herself, she would say cryptic things to me. Things that did not make sense," Vistrus continues.

Allison's teenage curiosity gets the best of her. "Like what?"

Her father gives her a hard stare that says questions like that are not appropriate. But his gaze relaxes as he knows he can't hide the truth from her forever. "She would talk to me about these two things. Always these two things. Nonsense things."

"What things?" Allison nudges him along.

"Faoi Dhó Duine and The Mind," Vistrus says with a tight face. "Always as if they were real, and I should know what she was talking about."

"What's free dough dinner?" Allison asks.

Vistrus takes a puff of his cigar and exhales a big cloud of smoke. "Faoi Dhó Duine. She pronounced it like fay gho din-ya, almost like a lisp. She never said what it was. She never said much. Just ramblings about Faoi Dhó Duine. What scared me is that most of the time, when your mother mentioned Faoi Dhó Duine, she would appear very lucid."

"What about The Mind?" Allison further inquires.

"No idea," Vistrus shakes his head. "When she talked about it, she made it seem like both the organ and a place. I just never understood."

"Did she keep dream journals like you told me to keep?" Allison further asks.

He lets out a puff of smoke. "She did. She wrote incessantly."

"What did they say about Faoi Dhó Duine or The Mind?" Allison continues.

Vistrus gestures his cigar toward his daughter. "I have never read them. They were hers; they were private."

"But you still have them?" Allison asks.

Vistrus nods.

"While I appreciate the respect of boundaries that you don't read mine or hers while she was alive, I don't think she'd mind so much now," Allison states.

"They were her private thoughts. Hers for herself. I could not breach our trust." However, Vistrus is unsure of his conviction.

"Dad," she says with a dramatic pause, "the dead don't care."

He smiles as he puffs his cigar. "But I do."

Allison offers sage words. "Whatever answers her diaries may hold for you, they won't do you any good collecting dust."

Vistrus leans back in his chair as his daughter's words resonate in his ears. He starts to wonder if perhaps she is right, that "the dead don't care." Maybe, he should read them. See what her thoughts were as she started to decline. Is that a wound he is willing to reopen and relive? All thoughts to ponder while the cigar smoke encircles his head.

Allison stands up and kisses her father on the forehead, breaking the ring of smoke and his concentration. "I have a stupid early day tomorrow. I gotta hit the hay." As she walks away, she turns back to her father. "If not her diaries, there's always Google. That has the answers to everything." She laughs and walks to her bedroom.

Vistrus lets out a small huff of a laugh as he sinks back into his thoughts. His mind wanders towards his wife's diaries, Google, and the possibilities of answers.

Brianna pulls up to her house after her lukewarm reception from her old friends and the cold shoulder of her current ones. Not the best night out for a teenager, but the night is over. She pulls into the driveway and turns off the car. Through the light of the window, she sees her mother straightening up, an odd activity at this hour. Thoughts of intoxication and the feel of her mother's hand against her face creep into her mind. No matter, she must go inside.

Her mother greets her daughter with a friendly smile that tries to hide the fresh bruises and scratches on her face.

"What happened, Ma?" Brianna cries out in concern over the apparent mishap. Her breathing starts to quicken as she works herself up.

Sylvia finishes putting the curtain and curtain rod back on its bracket and closes them shut. "An unwelcome visitor. Nothing that can't be taken care of. Well, nothing that won't be taken care of, I should say. I said I would keep you safe."

Brianna's thoughts turn to the earlier events of the night, the moment when she told Duncan "no" and his leaving. The frustration she saw in him, she didn't think would lead to this. But the evidence is there in her mind. All she has to do is confirm it.

Brianna's thoughts make her more anxious. The idea of having some budding feelings or attraction to someone who may have done this does not sit well with her. The circumstances she connects to this event race through her mind as a shooting pain starts coursing through her face and jaw.

"Do you know who did this to you?" Brianna asks as her anxiety heightens, causing the skin to loosen around her hands and eyes.

"It doesn't matter if I know or not." Sylvia doesn't notice the beginning of her daughter's transition.

"Like hell, it doesn't!" Brianna interrupts. "We need to get him arrested. Call the police! Isn't that what they are there for? To serve and protect?" Brianna finishes in a frenzy, as a couple of teeth tumble out her mouth.

Her mother takes a deep breath, taking note of Brianna's teeth in the sink. Sylvia touches the scratches on her face. "The police won't do anything. They wouldn't even know what to do. Try telling one of them your story. Show him your Legendary form." Sylvia moves toward her daughter and gently touches her transitioned face. "See how they react? The disgust. The fear. The lies they tell others because of their ignorance. The hate they spread *because* of their unfounded fear. It's easier to hate and live in ignorance than to learn the truth and love. Reporting an incident like this is the last thing I'd do."

"Well, what if we tell them something simpler?" Brianna slurs through the missing teeth and pooling blood in her mouth. "Like a home intruder that you somehow fended off." Brianna runs to the kitchen and spits the blood into the sink. The taste of it adds to her anxiety and quickens her transition. "Please help, Mommy," Brianna desperately cries.

Sylvia shakes her head at her daughter's naivety, rubbing Brianna's back as she hunches over the sink, spitting out blood. "There's so much you don't under-stand because you've just begun discovering this. And this is something that's on me. I should have eased you into it. Told you when you were younger. Done something different. Now it's all being thrown at you, and I can't stop it. But slow, deep breaths help. Always keep that in mind."

Sylvia thinks for a moment to collect herself. "To call it a simple home intrusion when it was something more is lying to the police and, in essence, filing a false police report. To give a name..." Sylvia sees the look her daughter's turned head is piercing her with, "...assuming I know it, would put that person in a spot he doesn't need to be in. And put us in a spot we don't *want* to be in." Sylvia continues rubbing her daugh-ter's back. "Take a deep breath. Slow and deep. Hold it for a moment." After a few breaths, Sylvia continues, "He's troubled enough. The things he's going through. Most important above any of what I just said is if I tell the police, there will be evidence technicians here, and they will collect DNA. DNA that will tell the Normals about us. That's not good. That is something we most certainly don't want."

Brianna spits out a mixture of saliva mixed with a bit of blood. She wipes her face, which is scrunched in confusion. "I don't understand. Don't we have people we can tell? People who know about whatever it is that's so secret that can look into it?"

"Take a seat, dear." Sylvia takes a seat at her kitchen table and pushes out the chair next to her. The bruises on her face still surfacing as they talk. "Yes, we have people who we can tell, and I shall. I will tell them; you can be assured of that. But we deal with things differently than Normals because we have to. We only have ourselves. We don't have anyone else. And, like everyone else on the planet, we have those within our kind who don't care for us. In the past, when our kind tried to live peacefully among Normals, bad things happened. Fears are stoked, lies are spread, people are hurt and killed, and we retreat. All because of our genetics. Because we are different on the outside."

Brianna shifts uncomfortably in her chair. The pain of her transition subsides as the weight of her mother's words sets in. The realization of a life less uncomplicated and far less ordinary begins to grip her. She takes a deep breath, trying to absorb the situation.

"But here's what you need to know now, why we don't want some guy in here swabbing everything for DNA. As with every Legendary condition, yours is a combination of many rare and uncommon genetic disorders that have combined in a very unique way," Sylvia begins.

Brianna lets out a small smile for the first time since opening the door to her house this evening. "Unique is good."

"While all the different disorders that make up what we have come to call Undying are chronic, their

145

symptoms are acute. We call this your Legendary state. When your symptoms are quiet, that is your Normal state. Until recently, you have only lived in your Normal state," Sylvia starts to explain in a much calmer and more collected voice than her recent self.

"So, what genetic diseases make this thing up?" Brianna asks.

"As with all Legends, genetic rickets somehow keeps you in a Normal state. Or, at the very least, it allows the transitions. The rest of the Undying condition is a mix of progeria, Ehlers-Danlos, Werner syndrome, syndrome x, Rothmund–Thomson syndrome, HGH deficiency, and, as with all female Legends, Turner syndrome. I'm missing a few, I'm sure, but that's the general makeup," Sylvia says, as if listing off groceries to be purchased.

"Hold on, Mom. What do all those mean? I can't even repeat half of them; they sound so complicated," Brianna says, trying to keep herself calm.

"All it means is that when you stress out, like now, this happens," Sylvia gestures to her daughter's appearance. "You are still you, and that has not changed. No amount of genetics can change that. Find others like you. Undying, Fairies, any Legend. They are your ear to bend. They will be your rock as you will be theirs." She looks at her daughter, who is reverting back to Normal but starting to work herself up again. "Take a deep breath. Remember to breathe deeply."

Brianna sits in the kitchen chair, watching and wondering why her mother has begun making herself two martinis; that is not something her mother does.

But Sylvia shakes up the tin and pours a full martini in one glass and half of one in another. She carries both back to the table, extending the half-full one to her underage daughter.

"You're not leaving again tonight. I am here for you. Drink this slowly. It will help calm you down," Sylvia informs her as she takes a sip of her martini.

Brianna takes the martini and looks at it, unsure if she should take a sip. After all, her mother doesn't hold her alcohol too well, so Bri doesn't want to go down that road. On the other hand, she needs to calm down, and half a martini is more medicinal than recreational. She looks up at her mother, who gives a slight go-ahead nod. Brianna takes another deep breath before sipping her half martini.

Allison creeps down the hallway from her bedroom to her father's study. The shadows cast on the walls from outside make the safe walk far more ominous. She slowly shuts the door to the study, carefully turning the doorknob so the latch makes no sound. She does not want to alert her father.

Allison has never really given her father's library much thought as to what it might hold. Her mind knows of the thick-spined books that fill the shelves but not of their contents or titles.

She turns on the light and starts filling in the missing pieces of information her brain has yet to know. Titles ranging from Russian history and culture to books on the Moors and their invasions throughout the Middle Ages fill a few of the first shelves. She continues past a section, spanning floor to ceiling, that appears to be books on museums, artifacts, and antiquities. She keeps scrolling the titles until she comes to the shelf that houses her mother's diaries.

Allison has never read the diaries, but after her talk with her father tonight, she should have expected books on dreams and their meaning to be close by. She sees books titled *Dreams: The Talking Subconscious* and *In Dreams, I Walk With You.* A few other books of similar titles sit next to those two.

She pulls them all down and opens their pages. She skims the books, looking for answers or some kind of guiding hand to help her understand why she dreams what she dreams and why it is all happening.

The books, however, do not seem to be her friend. They all point to the greater good of life and the internal conflict her subconscious is trying to sort out. The symbolism of flowers and birds defining what she is thinking, the idea of bird-like flight, and its relation to being free all seem to be a bunch of malarkey to her. None of what she is reading seems to touch on her experience or what she feels.

She continues through the books for another hour or so, hoping her initial experience will change. Allison keeps her fingers crossed that a phrase or meaning will strike a chord with her and help her understand. But nothing.

Her time for the night passes with nothing to show except the sleep she has now missed out on, sleep that will be sorely missed as she helps Connor move into his dorm.

Scarlett stands in the dark hallway of her house. The only light illuminating it creeps out from under Connor's bedroom door. From the hall, Scarlett can hear the click of the voice recorder as Connor starts and stops the playback. She knocks on the door.

"Come in," Connor replies.

She opens the door to the usual sight of his messy room. He sits on his bed with dripping wet hair from having taken a shower after listening to the tapes. The voice recorder, notebook, and pen lay next to him on the bed.

"Earlier night than I expected," Connor observes.

"It's just a birthday." Her meek smile covers her true feelings. "I'm sure I'll have plenty more."

"I think that's a safe bet. You'll be okay when I'm gone?"

She nods an unsure yes. "It'll be a little quiet, but I'll be fine. Plus, Grams isn't too far, and I'll still have Al."

"You'll still have me. Just a text or call away." Connor smiles.

"I know. It's just going to be a weird senior year. I can feel it." She bashfully kicks the floor. "You showered?"

"Yeah. Just felt the need." Connor turns his stare to the notebook. "Something about this coming year just feels strange."

"It sure does. Making any progress?" She gestures to the notebooks.

Connor shakes his head. "It's hard. I'll get to it at school, I'm sure." He turns to the wall; looking her in the eye while lying is not something he enjoys doing.

"You look tired," Scarlett observes. "I'll let you get some rest before the move."

Connor steals a quick glance at his phone. "Yeah, I'll barely get five hours at this point."

Scarlett gets up, turns off the lights, and shuts the door. The school year is about to begin.

CHAPTER 10

"Just because one door closes
doesn't mean another one is going to open.
Life is not that convenient."
~I. Petrovsky~

The school parking lot in the early morning hours before the first day is filled with a mix of bright-eyed, bushy-tailed, and overly tired, not-ready-for-classes-yet students. Scarlett and Allison fall somewhere in between as they lean against Vistrus's BMW, watching the clouds float by above them.

"It was really nice of your dad to let you use his car for school," Scarlett says while looking skyward.

Allison keeps her eyes on the sky. "Not like he had much choice considering the still recent events."

"Still, it was nice," Scarlett amends Allison's statement.

"Sure," Allison adds, as if it's something that Scarlett need not have said.

After a few moments of quiet reverie while looking toward the heavens, Scarlett turns to Allison. Miming a microphone in hand, she asks her, "First day of our senior year. What big plans do you have in store?"

Allison, doing her best news segment passerby, states, "Well, Scar, you see, we plan on avenging each of our boyfriends' parents. So, you see, it should be a pretty exciting year."

Scarlett pulls the microphone back to her. "And how do you plan on doing that?"

Scarlett moves the mimed mic back to Al. "While the details are uncertain, we do know it involves one teacher and a police officer. We are still working out the details and. . ." Allison stops talking as she spots Brianna in the flow of students making their way inside.

Bri is dressed to the nines in a sky blue and cream-colored, low-cut dress that stops at her knees. Her perfect hair is styled in an updo with loose curls, and her makeup is flawlessly applied to match her outfit.

Scarlett sees Allison staring at Bri; however, she also notices the look on Allison's face is not of disgust but something that hints at admiration, perhaps, though Scarlett can't pinpoint the emotion.

"You okay?" Scarlett asks, nudging Allison.

"Just … wow," Allison says to herself.

Standing right next to Allison, Scarlett hears the quiet response. "Wow? Not ick or die or get a disease or something to that effect?"

Allison turns to Scarlett. "Perhaps you're right. I could have been nicer to her on your birthday."

Scarlett puts her hand to Allison's forehead. "You feeling okay, Al? It sounded like you said something that can be construed as nice."

Allison sees Brianna in the distance, as she is approached by Duncan. The look that Allison reads off Brianna appears mixed, as if Bri is both happy to see him and apprehensive at the same time.

"I'm fine." She turns to Scarlett. "I think." She turns back to watching Brianna and Duncan. "Look at them. Two kids from opposite sides of the tracks. It's so…"

"Nice to see two people talking and seeing where things go instead of passing uninformed judgment?" Scarlett adds in a roundabout way to keep Allison grounded.

"I was gonna say cliché, but we'll go with yours." Allison laughs.

They watch as the apprehension washes away from Brianna's face and turns into a smile. Duncan leans in and whispers something into her ear that causes her to pull back for a minute. Both Allison and Scarlett know the look; it is a look that says, "Think quick and make it something he'll believe." After a quick second, Brianna says something back in what appears to be a hushed tone from her leaning toward him. Duncan seems to buy whatever Bri is selling and smiles. His hand reaches forward and grazes her hand in a hesitant attempt to hold it. Before their fingers get a chance to interlock, he pulls away before she can reject him. Brianna looks around the parking lot in some final surveillance of the scene before motioning for Duncan to follow her.

They start to walk toward the building as Allison shouts, "Bri!"

Bri and Duncan turn around to see a surprised Scarlett staring at Allison.

"What are you doing?" Scarlett asks.

"Not really sure," Allison responds, as she waves Brianna and Duncan to walk their direction.

"This first day of senior year has really gotten under your skin," Scarlett observes.

"Something has, I can tell ya that," Al responds.

"'Something has, I can tell ya that?' Are you an old-timey reporter?" Scarlett jokes.

"Shut it, Scar," she gets out before Duncan and Bri are close enough to hear. She turns to them. "Two days, and your mom has seen the light?"

"God no," Brianna replies. "We've been texting. He told me all about the fight he saw when he went to talk to my mom. He didn't know about her back-to-school costume party," Bri finishes with a leading tone.

Allison is utterly oblivious to the subtext and tone. "Your mom has a back-to-school costume party? That's odd."

Brianna's tone gets even more leading. "Yes, Allison, it's creatures-of-the-night-themed."

Scarlett jumps in. "Al, vampires, werewolves, you remember?"

Allison finally catches on. "How easily I forget sometimes." She turns to Duncan while bobbing her head. "I can be a little slow."

Duncan replies, "It's cool. Scared the cool right outta me. The costumes were so real. Really great work."

"Art teachers and all," Bri says, trying to shut down the conversation.

"You look nice today," Allison says to Brianna. "Is this some back-to-school thing or an attempt to kiss up to your old clique?"

"There it is," Brianna says.

"There what is?" Allison responds.

"I apologize. I will forever look back at my first three high school yearbooks knowing how fake my friends were. I'm trying, Allison. At least you could do the same," Brianna scolds.

"What? That's not what I meant," Allison defends. "It was just a question. But I mean, you look good. I'm impressed. I'm just saying, welcome back."

"Welcome back?" Bri and Scarlett ask simultaneously, both shocked.

Allison looks at Scarlett and then at Bri. "I don't know how long my nice will last. So, yeah, welcome. Look, I gotta get inside anyway." Allison turns to Scarlett. "We'll catch up after first."

Scarlett nods. "For sure."

Allison separates from the group and makes her way inside. Scarlett, Brianna, and Duncan stand next to Allison's borrowed car.

"She's a little off today. Not sure what's gotten into her," Scarlett says in Allison's defense.

"You don't have to make excuses for her. I'm pos' you didn't for me," Brianna says.

"Actually, I did. But hey, she's being nice. So, there's that," Scarlett says, putting Bri in her place. She turns to Duncan. "You ready for this year?"

"Hell yeah. Thanks to you," Duncan smiles.

They all start walking toward the school together.

"How wild do you think this year is going to be?" Duncan asks.

"I think wild might be accurate," Scarlett replies, thinking about its context.

"I think this year's gonna be so fetch," Bri adds.

"Didn't happen then, won't happen now, Bri," Scarlett says.

"But it was such a good movie," Bri pouts.

"Yes, it was. Now let it die," Scarlett demands.

Bri is obstinate. "Fine. But it will happen. Whatever. We need a word for this year."

"Take that up with Al. She's still trying to make 'Betty White up' a thing," Scarlett says with a hint of sarcasm.

Duncan laughs. "I remember."

Scarlett shakes her head at his amusement.

"Good morning, Scarlett!" Sylvia greets Scarlett as she walks into the classroom. "How are you doing today?"

Sylvia halts her writing and turns her attention to Scarlett. She lays her pencil on top of the notebook.

"Hoping to have a quick chat before I have to run to class. But like most of us, I'm tired. Forgot how early school is. Excited to be back, though." Scarlett weaves between the desks and stops in front of Ms. Waldgrave's desk.

"Senior year. Big women on campus. So on and so forth. It should be a good year for you," Sylvia touts.

"Hopefully, and hopefully, you can help make it even better," Scarlett hints as she glances down at the writing on Sylvia's desk.

Sylvia turns to the chalkboard, oblivious to Scarlett's little spying moment. Sylvia scribbles bullet points for today's classes on the board, "So, you've alluded to. How can I help with that?"

"With good news about the program. My pilot student passed his classes, and, as I mentioned before, investing a little in our children who are the future says a lot about the school," Scarlett reiterates.

Sylvia continues scribbling. "Yes. I know. I have talked with the board and presented your program to them. They think it is a great idea…" she stops and turns to Scarlett, "…but you already helped a student pass his courses for free. They think it should be a volunteer program." She flips a page in her notebook to glance at her lecture points before leaving the initial page open.

"That's crap, Ms. Waldgrave, and you know it. You were the one who said, 'take initiative,' so I did. Now they want to use that against me. You even said that I had a good idea. A win-win."

"They aren't against the win-win. The administration likes the idea of a win-win, but they need a win-win-win." Sylvia turns back to the board.

"But if they are volunteer tutors, then the caliber of tutors will lower, as will the final outcome of the tutoring sessions. The idea of some sort of income for the tutors was to be able to select more qualified tutors. They are proposing a lose-lose; that's the exact opposite of a win-win," Scarlett sounds more like a teenager throwing a tantrum than a young adult trying to win a losing fight. She lowers her head and stares at the teacher's desk.

The notebook has a flow chart, the center of which are the words "The Nation" circled, and branching out around it are five other circles: Tennyson Society, Coleridge Society, Poe Society, Kipling Society, and Frye Society. From those little dashes are drawn from each, but most stop there. Before Scarlett can see what's circled besides Poe and Tennyson, Sylvia turns around, causing Scarlett to look up. Sylvia gives Scarlett a suspicious eye as she closes the notebook.

"You are missing what the administration is asking. They like the ability to draw a higher caliber tutor. They like having a more efficient tutoring program in place. What they don't like is taking money that can be spent on other things, or worse, taking away money from other things. Right now, in their minds, it's a win-win-lose. You need to think of a way to turn that last part into a win." Sylvia puts the notebook in the center drawer of her desk and locks it.

Scarlett's eyes grow big. "Credit."

"Credit?"

"Credit."

"For whom?" Sylvia takes a seat.

"For the tutor. Elective credit. If they need to take a course, why not be in charge of one that teaches the skills to teach while helping those in need of learning?" Scarlett smiles.

"That sounds like a win-win-win." Sylvia smiles back.

"Thanks."

"What do we call it? If it's going to be a functioning program, it needs a name," Sylvia throws out there.

"That's why I actually stopped by today. I need to leave an impression on this school. Something that says I was here and not just passing through," Scarlett offers up, a little more sheepish than she wanted to sound.

"Okay?" Sylvia raises a brow.

"McAllister's Learning … Society," she finishes with pride.

Sylvia scrunches her lips together in thought for a moment before speaking. "I think we might have something there. We will work out the details of recruiting tutors and exactly how much elective credit once the board approves this offer."

Scarlett gets a little bounce in her step as she starts swinging her hips in joy. "Thank you, Ms. Waldgrave! Have a great day!"

And with that, she skips out of the room.

Scarlett turns a corner to a hallway where Allison saunters so Scarlett can catch up. Scarlett takes a few skipping steps and slows to keep pace with Allison.

"How's your first day been?" Scarlett starts.

"Okay. I got Abramowitz for algebra; that man is such a hardass,' Allison says, frustrated.

"You'll be fine. I had him freshman year. Pay attention and follow his lead. He just wants to make sure you learn. He's not one for being the popular teacher," Scarlett informs her.

Allison looks at Scarlett while they continue walking. "That was very ... specific? Or ... distinct."

"He literally told me those words. Well, something akin to that one day after class. He's not as evil as people think," Scarlett sums up.

"Oh, so I heard this joke in first period," Allison starts. "I thought it was right up your alley."

"Shoot," Scarlett encourages.

"What's the difference between a ... crap. Hold on. Now I lost it." Allison struggles to remember.

"Not the best delivery," Scarlett jabs.

Allison thinks for a few steps.

"Okay, yeah, what's the difference between a whale and a Bic® lighter?" Allison doubts her memory.

A smile crosses Scarlett's face as she tries not to laugh. "What?"

"One's really big, and the other's ... nope. That's not right. Let me think," Allison says, frustrated.

"You have part of your punch line in the joke," Scarlett informs her. "Next time, instead of a whale and a Bic®, go with a hippo and a Zippo®."

Allison pipes up, waving an excited finger at Scarlett. "That's it! Damn. How did I forget that?!"

"It's okay, Allison. I like your version," Scarlett comforts. "So, I think my tutoring thing might actually pan out. Not quite student council president, but it's something."

They turn the corner to the cafeteria and immediately, and unintentionally, make eye contact with biology teacher and soccer coach, Linda Espinoza, seated on a chair overlooking the overflowing lunch line in the hall. Linda smiles at them, but there is something in her smile that makes the girls uncomfortable. A hint of superiority and condescension shouldn't be in a teacher's smile.

Linda waves the girls over. Scarlett and Allison exchange a glance as they walk to the teacher.

"Yes, Mrs. E?" Scarlett says, as they stop a few feet away from her.

"You're Mr. DeSalvo's cousin? Correct?" Linda asks, already knowing the answer.

"Yes. Is everything okay?" Scarlett continues.

"Will I be seeing you in my class this year? Your cousin and his friend excelled, so I assume you will, too," Linda says with an evenness to her tone that gives the girls an unsettling tingle down their spines.

"We have a pretty full schedule, but maybe second semester," Scarlett says.

"Not me." Allison beams with a smile. "I've fulfilled my science requirements. Done with that stuff."

A crooked smile crosses Linda's face. "But science always has so much to teach, as the people who study it always have so much to give in return."

Allison takes a deep breath and sees Scarlett's feet shifting back and forth. "Is there anything more we can help you with?" Allison asks.

"Nope. Just seeing if I'd be seeing you in my classroom." Linda's casual reply does nothing to calm the girls.

"I've heard what happens to your students," Allison quips under her breath.

"What was that, young lady? I couldn't hear you," Linda snaps at her.

"Nothing. I'm sure we will see each other around. We have a full year left," Allison says with a restrained voice.

As the girls start to walk away, Linda pipes up again, "I had a young man in my class last year who always hung around with your cousin. His name is Jack, I believe."

The two girls stop dead in their tracks but do not turn to face Linda. The anger coursing through Allison causes her migraine to flare up.

"How are he and his family doing since the whole ordeal?" The subtle tones of joy betray the pleasure she tries to hide in her words.

Allison clenches her teeth as the migraine spreads and transforms into a shooting pain in the center of her face.

Scarlett's eyes well up with tears as she tries to hold them back. "You didn't see the aftermath. No one with a soul could have done such a thing to another living creature."

Linda Espinoza lets out a huff of amusement. "Must have been a greatly terrible sight to see."

Allison clenches her fists and whispers, "All in due time."

Scarlett turns to Allison and sees her begin to transition. Allison's nose begins to narrow and starts to recede. Blood starts to drip from the corner of her mouth. Trying to stop the transition, Scarlett grabs Allison's hand and gives it a firm squeeze.

Scarlett remembers how she got Jack to calm down and hopes it will work on her best friend. "Breathe." Scarlett takes a deep breath with Allison. "Just take slow, deep breaths."

Scarlett walks away with Allison in tow. Each of them takes slow, deep breaths as they walk.

By the time they make it into the lunch line, Allison's nose has returned to normal. Her migraine and shooting pain have waned, and the drip of blood has been wiped away while the rest she swallowed.

Once in line, the girls stop and smile at the always silent lunch lady whose name tag reads December. She slowly piles scoops of what is being passed off as beans and rice onto their trays.

A soft, soothing, feminine voice enters Allison's head. *"Actions taken in haste yield unseen consequences."*

Allison sees no one as she looks around for the source of the voice, save December. Allison fixes her gaze on the lunch lady as the words continue.

"This is a long battle. Not one that will be won with words in a high school hallway," the voice advises. *"And definitely not by exposing yourself. Become who you are first. Retribution has no time limit."*

Allison parts her lips to say something to December but stops as she hands Allison her tray.

"Thank you," Allison says as she takes her tray before continuing down the lunch line.

The voice rings in her mind once more. "*You're welcome.*"

The words bring Allison to a halt. She turns back to December, who is plopping the food into Scarlett's tray. December turns to Allison and nods. Allison waits as Scarlett gets her food, and both head into the cafeteria for sustenance.

The girls plop down at their usual spots from the past three years. They bite into their food, still uncomfortable from the encounter with Mrs. Espinoza.

"Do you ever get the feeling…" Allison begins. "Nevermind."

Scarlett looks up from her food. "What? We've come a long way to not finish our thoughts. Are you calmed down? You started to change, or transform or transition, or whatever we call it, back there."

"Yeah. No. I'm not playing into everyone's delusion that my friends and their families are being killed because vampires are real. See, I'm fine. She just got me so mad."

Scarlett squints her eyes at her friend's denial. She sits for a moment contemplating if they should continue this conversation about Allison's true nature or not but comes to the conclusion that the school cafeteria is not the place.

"So? Getting a feeling?"

Allison shifts her scrunched lips while searching for the right words to say. "It's more than a feeling. Have you ever had a conversation in your head?"

"Like, do I play out how a future uncomfortable conversation will be?" Scarlett asks for clarification before sipping her chocolate milk.

"No. But yes, everyone has those. I think," Allison responds through a bite of her beans and rice. "I mean, like a voice will enter my thoughts. A voice, not my own, and no one I know."

Scarlett stops eating and stares at Allison. Half-chewed food in Scarlett's mouth waits for permission to continue being chewed, but only after the thought is complete.

"In the lunch line just now, I heard a woman tell me not to be hasty. Then when I said thank you for lunch, the same voice said, 'You're welcome,'" Allison specifies.

Scarlett goes back to chewing the food in her mouth. "Yes!" she exclaims as a bit of beans fall out. She extends a hand to catch it.

"That looked delicious," Allison quips.

"It looked the same as it did on our trays," Scarlett jokes back.

They both laugh at the grotesqueness of her accuracy.

Scarlett turns back to their conversation. "I swear to the gods that the silent janitor talks to me somehow."

Allison's eyes light up. "And this isn't the first time I've heard the same voice when near the lunch lady."

"Do you think this has something to do with our ... special circumstances?" Scarlett says, carefully avoiding certain words.

"I'm still in the mindset that you are all playing with crazy on that. No one in their right mind would want to be a ... one of those. Certainly not me," Allison responds.

"Al, it's not a question of wanting it or not. It's something we are born with. I don't think there's a person on earth who asks for the troubles they face for the circumstances they can't control. But they deal. Just as we do," Scarlett whispers back.

Allison sits in quiet defeat for a moment. She knows that Scarlett holds some truth in her words.

"I just wish there was another way," Allison says, still defeated.

"Don't we all," Scarlett gets out in between bites. "As far as the voices in our minds, let's just keep that between us for a while. I don't think your dad will take too kindly to us hearing voices, ya know."

"You're right. What we need is a plan," Allison urges.

"A plan for what?" Scarlett asks as she shifts in her seat.

"Taking them down. We can't just sit back saying we need a plan. We actually have to make the plan," Allison says, anger creeping back into her voice.

CHAPTER 11

*"Change the way you look at things.
You might be surprised at what you find."*
~I. Petrovsky~

Scarlett and Allison relax in Scarlett's living room as the television drones in the background, with the nightly news taking over whatever rerun they are half-watching as they talk. Cans of mostly empty soda surround a day-old box of delivery pizza sitting on the coffee table in front of them.

Allison stares at the mess as they talk. "The idea is simple. Well, at least in theory. Here." Allison leans into the soda cans and starts rearranging them.

Allison looks around for a pen but doesn't find one. So instead, she grabs a can and dents in the side. "This is the door." She places the can in the center of the side closest to her. On the side of the box that faces her, where she placed the can, she tears two different slits. "These are the windows leading to the basement." She grabs four cans and places two at each window and a fifth can behind the box."

Scarlett reaches out for the fifth can and taps it. "Who's this? I assume the other four are me, you, Jack, and Connor. So, who's this?"

Allison smiles. "Duncan. He said he'd be down for some anti-authoritarian disruption."

Scarlett sits more upright. "So, we really are going to drag him into a mess he isn't a part of simply because he has issues with authority figures?"

"Basically," Allison snaps her reply.

"But what if we change and he sees it? Then what?" Scarlett proposes.

Allison taps her temple a few times. "That's why we leave him outside."

"Have you ever stayed put when told so? No. No one has. What makes you think he won't wander from his post if he hears a commotion from inside?" Scarlett rebuttals.

Allison leans back onto the couch. "Even if he does, he seems like he'd be cool enough to not freak out and tell anyone."

"You barely know him. What makes you think that?" Scarlett asks.

"He has good taste in women," Allison replies before she has time to think.

"What?" Scarlett responds, confused.

"I mean..." her mind races to cover what she blurted out, "...he's giving Bri a chance, and so are we. Maybe there's more to him than we can assume."

"Oh," Scarlett says with a hint of dejection, "I thought maybe you were saying you thought she was attractive."

"I can see how she is. I mean, she has a classic, All-American beauty that people long for," Allison responds.

"And you?" Scarlett interjects.

"And me what?" Allison asks.

"Are you longing for it?" Scarlett shoots back.

Allison's face turns a bright red as a smile crosses her face that she tries unsuccessfully to squash. "What?! No! Don't be stupid!"

Scarlett throws her hands up. "Woah. Just saying. Connor's at school. People grow, self-discovery, and all."

"God, no. Not Brianna. Can we get back to the break-in?" Allison switches back to the subject at hand.

"Sure, so Duncan outback to what? Keep watch?" Scarlett inquires.

"Yeah, and any of his crew he trusts." Allison places scraps around Duncan's soda can, little papers indicating his crew.

"You really are missing the point of a secret society," Scarlett jabs.

"Well, maybe it's time it's not so secret," Allison states with feigned confidence.

"Not our place to make that decision. Not now," Scarlett says.

"Why not?" Allison shoots back.

"What?" Scarlett is a little shocked by her response.

"Why isn't it our place? Are we not the ones supposedly affected by this? Are we not the ones who are hiding from the rest of the world?" Allison says rhetorically.

"Fine," Scarlett concedes, "go outside right now and shout to the sky that you are a vampire."

Allison is a bit taken aback by Scarlett's acceptance. "Huh?"

Scarlett stands up, grabs Allison's hand, and starts pulling her up. "Come on. Get up, and let's do this."

Allison follows Scarlett to the door, albeit a bit confused by what Scarlett demands.

Scarlett opens the door to the evening sky and breezy air. She drags Allison to the street and motions for Allison to make her declaration.

"Come on, Al. Let's do this," Scarlett urges.

Allison stands there for a moment, looking around at the empty streets. She sees a few houses up and down the block with lights shining through the windows and one lonely person walking away from their direction.

"Say it. Come on out of the supernatural closet," Scarlett insists.

Allison takes a deep breath and tilts her head toward the sky before shouting, "I am a vampire." She whispers, as if making some self-denied admission about herself.

Scarlett shakes her head. "Louder. Shout it for all the world to hear."

Allison turns her gaze at Scarlett. "You know this is pointless, right?"

"And why is that?"

Allison gestures around. "Because vampires don't exist. This is all a bunch of shanongins, and it's not real. None of this is."

Scarlett shakes her head. "First, it's shenanigans. Not shanongins. Second, why do you think this is all fake? Like we are all playing some elaborate joke on you? People are dead because of this."

Allison sees the anger growing in Scarlett's expression. She lets go of Scarlett's pronunciation lesson and resigns to the position she got herself into this evening. She takes a giant deep breath, puffing out her chest. She makes fists and straightens her arms downward. "I am a vampire!" Loud and clear, she shouts. She feels like her voice carries for miles.

The lone figure walking the road stops and partially turns back to the girls. "No, you're not! The world is!"

The sarcasm in his voice carries back to the two girls. The lone figure continues his walk as if nothing about her declaration could possibly be factual.

The tone in the stranger's voice hits a nerve in Allison. If all of this is true and she can scream it to the mountaintops, as it were, and have the only person around not believe her, then who would without proof? And, if the evidence she gave frightened them, how would they react? How would they treat her when they see her Legendary form? Could they see anything but her Legendary form? Could they see past her outward appearance to what lies beneath?

All those questions come to her mind as her declaration goes unnoticed. Though it's not the questions that send the hairs on the back of her neck standing up; it is the answers to those questions and all the possibilities she thinks of that make her quickly realize she is glad the lone stranger did not believe her.

The girls walk back inside in defeat of Allison's moment, a moment she does not wish to revisit in any fashion anytime soon.

Inside the house, Scarlett sits back on the couch and in front of the pizza-box-turned-battle-plans. "So what, are we breaking in through the basement again?"

"No. Two of us are. The other two will knock at the front door as if nothing is wrong. When Linda answers, we force ourselves in. Overtake her from both sides." Allison smiles.

"What if she's stronger than us? Or has a gun?" Scarlett proposes.

Scarlett's phone pings. She looks down to see a text message from Jack.

[Jack: Headin' to the carnival now. See you soon.]

"Crap," Scarlett exclaims as she hops up.

"Everything okay?" Allison also stands up.

"I *totally* forgot about our plans tonight." She makes her way to the door.

"You and Jack?"

"Yeah. West Haven's fall carnival. We missed last year. Jack wanted to make sure he made it this year." Scarlett starts putting on her shoes. "Come on."

"Sure he doesn't want it to be a date thingy?" Allison tries to be polite.

"You're fine. Let's go."

Allison is already to the door and slipping on her eternally tied Converse All-Stars as she eyes the television.

"Wait!" Allison cries out. "Take a look." She points to the television.

The newscaster is playing the old, blurred-out footage of the teens breaking into Max and Linda's home. Scarlett takes a few exaggerated steps back to the couch and grabs the remote, turning up the volume.

"...still no leads, but the police are offering up a reward of $10,000 for any information leading to the arrest of the unknown suspects.

"The renewed efforts come in light of the recent spike in crime in the community. If you have seen the suspects or have any information, please call the tip line at the number below. 847-555-2178.

"In other news…"

Scarlett turns off the television as the image changes to a picture of a dog.

"At least they still have nothing," Scarlett sighs in relief.

"If they don't by now, I'm confident they won't ever," Allison says, as wheels turn in her head. "Which gives me an idea."

"What?" Scarlett says as they step outside and lock the door.

"We can use that number to call the police and create a distraction while we all do our thing," she says with a sly smile.

"So, in addition to our first B&E that we intend to repeat, we can add premeditated assault *and* making a false report?" Scarlett spurts off.

"Are we crazy doing all this?" The reality of the situation starts to hit Allison.

"More than a little. It's what the boys want; it's what I want. They were my family too," Scarlett starts. "I just wish there was another way."

They get into her car and drive off.

The ringing bells, ambient conversations, the machinery of the rides, countless flashing and static neon lights, cooking funnel cakes and turkey legs, and overfilled port-a-potties of the carnival assault their senses as the two girls meet up with Jack.

"Jack!" Scarlett calls out after he pops a balloon with a dart.

The carny hands Jack a small stuffed animal sloth. He turns and extends it out to Scarlett. She grabs it and gives it a welcoming hug before leaning in to kiss Jack.

"Sorry we took so long. A news clip caught our attention." Scarlett kisses him again.

"No worries. I just got here, uh, a few moments ago," Jack replies, causing the carny to chuckle. Jack gives a stink eye to the carny. "Well, a few attempts ago on, well, a few of his games. I wanted to win you something."

"And I love it!" Scarlett reassures him, squeezing her new stuffed sloth.

"You have to name him," Jack says.

"Name him?" Scarlett raises a brow, slightly confused.

Allison pipes up. "He needs a name; it's not a hard concept. Jack won him for you. Now you name him."

"Can't I just name him Sloth?" Scarlett proposes.

"Like naming a dog Dog, or a cat Cat, or from that old movie?" Allison asks.

"Yeah, from *The Goonies*," Scarlett confirms.

"No, you can't name an animal after itself, its species. Even if it's the name of, of a character from a movie," Jack says, denying her choice of name.

Scarlett thinks for a moment as they start to walk past a funnel cake stand.

"What about Loves Chunk?" Scarlett says.

"Loves Chunk?" Allison asks, not getting the reference.

"In the movie, Sloth loves Chunk. He says so himself. He's a sloth..." she holds him out like a child, "...so he can be Loves Chunk."

Jack shakes his head, smiling and laughing. "I like it."

"Punny, Lil' Lett, but I like it too," Allison says. "Oh, I brought some tickets, bought some, brought bought, whatever. I buyed some tickets so we can do some rides."

"Purchased would have also been an acceptable word choice," Scarlett adds to Allison's list.

"Betty White up, Scarlett. I'm making up new word forms," Allison defends.

Scarlett shakes her head, laughing at her friend.

Allison gets in line for the Zipper, a thrill ride that spins the caged car as you go around an oblong, vertical track. Allison hands some tickets to Scarlett and Jack. As they step up, Allison realizes that each car only holds two people.

"I'll go solo. You two enjoy." Allison steps behind them so they can ride together.

The carny lowers the lap bar as Scarlett and Jack can get in the car. After securing them in place and shutting the cage, he flips a switch, causing the ride to slowly spin upward.

"So, Al and I were talking about *our* plans. We think we've come up with a pretty straightforward idea," Scarlett begins.

The sounds of a large bell close by dings loudly to tell everyone around that someone has won something. Jack cringes at the sound of the bell, his ears overly sensitive to the noise.

Allison's cage is shut, and the ride starts to speed up. Their cars spin on their axis while the ride spins on a separate axis. They watch the world go by in blurred motions.

Jack looks to Scarlett. "Babe, I've been," he pauses before a stutter to catch his thoughts, "thinking about that too. So much we haven't thought through. So much we still have to think about." Jack's tone no longer shares the same near-homicidal excitement as Scarlett's.

"No. We thought through all of it. We know that for whatever reason, we don't show up on cameras," Scarlett starts.

Jack interrupts her. "Wh ... Who doesn't show up on video cameras? Uh, all of us? Or, uh, one of us? Just some? Why video cameras? Why now? All video cameras or, or just that one?"

"That's easy enough to test out," she defends.

"But Mr. P told us, well, it's autoimmune, which means stress-induced," he says as his voice ticks upward. "So, what if when we test, we aren't, we aren't stressed enough? How do we know that it'll work if we aren't, or whoever of us blurs the camera, isn't stressed or activated or stress-activated or whatever it is?" Jack returns the rebuttal.

"What are you saying, Jack?" Scarlett asks, her eyes squinting at the man before her.

The ride slows down, and they stop at the top. Jack looks around at the passersby below, eating cotton candy and popcorn and sipping their 80-ounce sodas and beer. He watches as young couples stroll hand in hand, holding prizes and trophies from the midway. Jack listens to the screams of people enjoying the carnival rides. As the ride resumes and the car again spins on its axis, Jack looks back at his girlfriend.

"I have no family left. I'm 18 years old and have no family, immediate or, or otherwise, left. No aunts or uncles anymore. No cousins waiting for me around the holidays. I have you. I have miss drinks-a-lot over there." He tries to point back to Allison. As they spin, they spy her taking a sip of something she didn't have before. "I have Connor. We ... we have this," he points around to the lights, rides, and the entirety of the carnival. "I don't want to waste it on some, some half-baked revenge plot begging to go wrong. I don't want to take an eye for an eye for an eye."

Something in Jack's words, the passion, the clarity, perhaps some yet-to-be-pinpointed aspect has Scarlett's heart fluttering hard. Hard enough that Scarlett can feel it pounding away in her chest at a million miles an hour. She tries to calm herself but cannot.

"So, you don't want to get the people who killed your family? Are you backing out? Do they not deserve justice? Retribution?" Scarlett's words do anything but calm her racing heart.

"Of course. Of course, I want justice. Don't ever question that about me," Jack states with piercing words. "But we were told that it would be taken care of. And I, I have to trust that. I don't want my life turning into uh, well, some tale of vengeance."

The ride again stops. This time Scarlett and Jack's car points backward toward the ground, and Allison's car is in front of them for the moment. Scarlett is looking everywhere but at him. She looks over at Allison, whose twisted torso is snapping pictures of something in the sky above Scarlett and Jack. Scarlett tries to look at Jack but shakes her head and looks away.

"You can't just wuss out now with some moral high ground. We know who killed your parents and who's behind it all. If we don't stand up for what we know is right, then aren't we culpable too?" Scarlett starts. An itch crawls over her skin. She scratches it, reliving the itching sensation.

"Yeah. And I killed the guy or, or at least one of the guys. I'm culpable in my own way. Don't ever forget that. And I don't … I don't want to kill any more people. I don't want that weighing down on me. You don't know. You don't know what it's like and, and trust me, you don't want to know. It's not something that sits on your back like a lightweight silk shirt. It presses down. It digs into your soul, fogging out the peripheral of your mind. It slows time and movement. It makes the world uh, uh, a darker shade of grey for having to live with that. It turns every eye that looks at you into judging eyes 'cause, well, while you know they don't know what you did, in the back of your mind, you feel they do know what you did. They know but are too afraid to say anything, too afraid that they might be next if they push the wrong buttons. And that's not what it's about," Jack says, tears rolling down his cheeks.

The ride starts for a moment and stops again with Jack and Scarlett stuck at the top. They look down to the ride operator below as he lets on more riders.

"We've only known about ourselves or our true selves, or whatever you wanna call it, for a relatively short time, and already, already, we are changing. Becoming these people who, who a few years ago would never have entertained the idea of doing something like this. I don't want us to do this because I don't like who we are becoming. I don't want to look back years from now and think about what I could have been if, if I hadn't become who I turned out to be," Jack continues.

Scarlett's furrowed brow and big, slow breaths relax as she realizes he is not sympathizing with his parents' murder but trying to deal with his experience. She hugs him tight and gently whispers in his ear, "It's okay," as she holds her man. "We aren't becoming anything but ourselves. Stay true to you," Scarlett offers in reassurance. "If you don't want to go through with this, then you don't have to. I'm sure Allison and Connor will understand."

He takes a deep breath and looks around him. "Despite the death that surrounds us, love, we are becoming something more. Becoming more, more than just human. So do we use that for our own ends or for something greater?"

From in the car behind them, Allison sees them hugging. She lifts a little in her seat and puts her hands around her mouth. "Look at you two! Getting all cozy on the wheel! Don't do anything I wouldn't do!" Allison jokes to her friends, unaware of their conversation.

Scarlett turns her head to Allison and gives her a smile while shaking her head. "Shut it, you perv!"

Scarlett's itching has completely subsided as her heart finally calms down.

Scarlett turns back to Jack. "When this is done, what do you say you try and win me another prize?"

He pulls away and wipes the tears from his face and eyes. He nods his head and smiles a little. "I'd like that."

They disembark from the ride and wait for Allison, her face still buried in her phone as she exits.

"Got something really cool on there?" Scarlett nods to her phone.

Allison looks at them both, then back to her phone. "So, I was trying to shoot the sky before."

"I noticed. What the hell had you so needing to snap a picture while riding the Zipper?" Scarlett inquires.

"I was trying to get pictures of the carnival for Facebook, but then the moon was surrounded by clouds…" Allison trails off.

"Must be a great picture there, Alli," Jack upticks.

Allison waves them to her phone. "No. You need to see what you look like."

Scarlett and Jack stand on either side of Allison and stare at the picture.

"It's blurred," Scarlett notes.

"It's digital," Jack notes.

"So?" Allison asks.

"Analog pictures, audio, video can, well, blur for many reasons. Digital, uh, doesn't," Jack informs Allison.

"So, it was probably just something in the lens." Scarlett waves off the blur.

Allison points to the rest of the picture. "Yeah. Something that only blurred you and Jack."

Allison swipes through the few other snapshots from that moment. All of them are blurred where Scarlett and Jack should be.

"Okay, that's weird." Scarlett takes Allison's phone.

She snaps a selfie. Normal. No blur to her or the surroundings. She snaps a picture of Jack and another of Allison. Both normal. She photographs herself again. Normal.

"What the hell were you two talking about back there?" Allison asks, as she takes back her phone and puts it away.

CHAPTER 12

Vistrus sits at his museum office desk. The white glare from his computer screen opened to a Google search is the only thing that illuminates the room. A cup of coffee that was once hot sits half-drunk next to him. The early morning daylight has yet to break the horizon.

The time of day is of no concern to him. He knows he has to find something pertaining to the chamber—something about the old council and something that may lead to the prophecy. His months of repeated Google searches for anything about the West Haven council only result in the city council's past and present, revealing nothing about the elusive Nation his kind has worked so hard to keep hidden. He is not terribly surprised by this, as The Nation is a secret society, and having search results readily available would undermine the secrecy of it all. But he knows there must be something buried somewhere that can clue him into why that chamber was built.

Then a light bulb goes off in his mind. He has spent his time since finding the old chamber searching for, what he considers, the most relevant keywords—the words that are too ordinary to yield anything but ordinary results. He needs to search for the unordinary or extraordinary—the supernatural and paranormal. Stories that would read as fake, speculation, unconfirmed encounters, or anything but legitimate. Stories that read like something out of an old tabloid magazine.

Legends are anything but paranormal or supernatural, but now he finds himself sitting at a computer typing in keywords like a teenager about to go down a YouTube rabbit hole. Now to see how far that hole leads.

West Haven, IL, ghost stories. He hits enter. The search results are more numerous than expected but, of course, are littered with results that are far from what is needed. He searches through the first ten pages, quickly losing hope as the results read about generic folklore and haunted houses long since torn down or rebuilt.

He changes the search results from page hits to images, hoping the visuals will strike something for him. Again though, the first few pages are images of old houses, some of which aren't even from West Haven, and other homes that are not from Illinois. Additional photos are of Bigfoot, and some are too blurry to lend credibility.

After a few more pages, he notices some images have similar backgrounds, but the subjects of the photos are different. So, he clicks on the thumbnails, all but one of which lead to an old, defunct webpage. The other leads to a YouTube countdown video of the ten most paranormal places in the midwestern United States.

The defunct page is what has him intrigued. There are three pictures, all of which are slightly blurry and in low light, but he still has an unnerving feeling tingling through him. One of the photographs, through the slight pixelation, looks like it should be him in his Legendary form. But the clothes he is wearing are unfamiliar to him. They look like street clothes, casual and unassuming. But the other two pictures, one appears to be a werewolf who is also wearing the same clothes. The third is no different, though this person's face is turned away from the camera. There are only two words above the row of pictures— *Possible shapeshifter.*

Vistrus knows that is impossible. Outside of the autoimmune response that causes the change into their Legendary form, there are no shapeshifters. Nothing could cause such an unnatural thing to happen, no condition that could cause multiple, different transitions within the same individual. In all his centuries, he's never encountered such a thing. Only heard about them in fables.

Then again, he has been alive for a long time. Perhaps these pictures are of him from some old men's club he's long since forgotten about. But something lingers, something that he knows will require more research on his end.

Allison and Scarlett sit in the empty hallways of Maine West Haven. The lights overhead cast a bright glow opposite the dim light of the early morning outside. Their books spread out in front of them as they catch up on homework. Scarlett writes in a notebook as Allison skims pages while talking on her cell phone.

"I'm glad we are finally able to talk. I know they keep you busy between baseball and classes," Allison says, trying to convince herself she's okay with the distance. "I just miss you."

"I miss you too, babe. I'm sorry we haven't really talked; it's been stupid busy. I've been meaning to call you back." Connor sounds slightly distracted.

Scarlett pauses to listen in on the conversation.

"Baseball is still going okay?" Allison asks. "Wait, I'm gonna put you on speaker. Your cousin's right here."

Allison touches the screen to put the phone on speaker. She sets it down between herself and Scarlett.

"Okay, sorry. So yeah, how's baseball?" Allison repeats.

On the speaker, he continues, "Good. I think. Sorry about any background noise. I'm getting ready for my day."

"It's okay. We can hear you just fine," Scarlett assures. "What exactly is 'good, you think?'"

"I'm not sure. The team has a few dissidents who aren't exactly grasping the idea of team spirit and family." He makes some background noise.

"How is that unusual?" Allison asks.

"I mean, it's not, I guess. I think we were just tighter-knit in high school than here. But then, this isn't high school anymore. I don't know. Something seems off, but it is probably just me," Connor concludes.

"Classes?" Scarlett continues her line of questioning.

"Good. Classes are different on this level. There's a lot more room for talking about the subject instead of just listening. The classroom atmosphere is different. You can feel the intellectualism as you walk in the room. Very strange. How's our house?" He changes the subject.

"It's fine. We haven't let it go to the flies yet. Grams comes by once a week and helps clean it up. You coming home for Halloween this weekend? You still haven't given us an answer," Scarlett reminds him.

"Halloween is next Wednesday," Connor corrects her.

"Yeah, but the party's *this* weekend," Allison reminds him.

"Honestly, I'm still not sure. The team might be doing this retreat thing. Though even that's not verified yet." Connor makes excuses.

"But you missed Homecoming; It was supposed to be our last one together." Allison pouts.

"I know. I know. I'm sorry. College is not like high school. How was Homecoming?" He changes subjects again.

"I'm sure it was great. I saw pictures from people who went." Allison's pouting turns to scorn.

"You could have gone. I'm not mandatory," Connor defends himself.

"It's not about you being mandatory. I wanted you to be there. I wanted you to want to be there. I wanted it to be special in that final homecoming way, but whatever. I understand that college is important. So? Halloween?" Allison tries to placate her attitude.

"As I said, I don't know. Things here happen at a moment's notice. They expect you to have a free and open schedule for it all. It's not as fun as you'd think." Annoyance grows in his voice.

"Well, it's a week away. I'd like to see you," Allison says with a hint of smoke. "You know, all of you."

Scarlett throws her hands up in the air. "I'm right here. Don't want to hear this."

Allison turns to her friend. "It's been a while."

"Crap! I gotta run, but I'll let you know." He hurries up the closing to their conversation.

"Love you," Allison responds.

"Bye, Con," Scarlett slips in as they both hang up.

"Good to talk to you too, Scarlett. Sorry I've been MIA … Oh, it's cool, Connor. I understand things get busy." Scarlett mocks a conversation with herself.

"He didn't say he loves me." Allison slumps, dejected.

"What did you say?" Scarlett comes back to reality a moment too late for Allison.

"He didn't say, 'I love you,'" Allison repeats.

"I'm sure he didn't mean anything by it. Like he said, he's been busy," Scarlett assures her.

"But that was our first actual phone conversation since he left for college, and he didn't say he loves me. I guess it really isn't high school for him anymore." Allison digs her anxiety deeper.

"You at least text, though. That's something." Scarlett searches for support.

"Barely. He's probably met some girl. Some college girl who doesn't look like she's 12 years old with her big, sexy librarian glasses. Someone who is super intellectual and makes him forget all about me over here. I can see it now. She approached him asking for a 'study buddy' for some class she didn't even need help in. Then they meet up. . ." Allison spins her story.

"Stop right there," Scarlett interrupts. "There's no way he'd do anything like that."

"I also thought he'd be home for, well, homecoming," Allison interjects.

"He loves you. Besides, you two have known each other far too long for him to want to stray and for you to say anything like that."

"Then why didn't he say it? Why haven't we talked? Why hasn't he come home?" Allison begs.

"Because it's been a while since you've talked on the phone. Because as much as we'd like to think college is the same as high school, it's different. Connor's busy. And he hasn't been home because a four-hour drive isn't a weekly thing to make," Scarlett tries to reassure. She takes a deep breath, hoping her next words are more than that. "I'm sure the thought was there," Scarlett assures.

"I don't know what to do," Allison admits.

"Give him his space. It's not a 'let him go' thing. It's a trust thing. Give him his space. He'll come back when he can. Push him though, and he'll be more anxious than excited about coming back," Scarlett advises.

Allison looks up and down the halls for any signs of life but doesn't see any. She pulls out her flask from her backpack and takes an extended sip. Putting it back and leaning her head against a locker, she stares at the overhead fluorescent lights.

"I just really miss him. This is way harder than I thought it would be," Allison resigns.

"I know. It's been weird at home. How many high schoolers live alone? Ya know?" Scarlett admits.

"It's gotta be weird for him too. He's far from home and surrounded by people who are supposed to be a team, but no one really knows each other. How is camaraderie supposed to establish itself amongst strangers?" Allison says.

"Camaraderie and establish? Big words, Al," Scarlett says, surprised at the vocabulary.

"Hey, I can say big words when I need." Allison smiles, all proud.

Scarlett chuckles, shaking her head. "Big words like those make you sound like a sexy, big-glasses-wearing librarian-type."

They both chuckle for a moment as Allison's paranoia subsides.

"Who knows?" An idea sparks in Scarlett's head. "What if he's embarrassed?"

Allison shakes her head. "I need a little more."

"I hate to think of my cousin this way, but I mean, I guess it could happen to us, too," Scarlett stalls.

Allison twirls her finger. "Where ya going, Scar?"

"What if when he gets excited," Scarlett pauses for a split second, "he starts, ya know…" She makes awkward body and hand gestures.

Allison cocks her head to the side. "Orgasming?"

"Ew, no!" Scarlett laughs. "Changing."

Allison's face drops. "Oh. That would definitely scare off any potential librarian girls."

"But we didn't transition when we first did it," Allison says.

"Yeah, but neither of you had transitioned before then, either."

"Whatever his reason is, it's wearing me down." Allison shrugs before turning to Scarlett with a light-bulb-look in her eye. "Here's one for you. You don't have to live alone."

Scarlett upturns her left eyebrow. "Yeah, I do. We already told Grams we weren't moving in with her and Gramps."

"Nope. Not what I mean. What if I move in with you?" Allison offers up.

"So you go from thinking he's cheating to wanting to move into his place in like two minutes?" Scarlett asks, confused.

"Yeah. So?" Allison defends. "One's a thought about him, and the other's about you. Well, I don't mean permanently. Just while he's at school, so you have some company."

Scarlett smiles. "If you can get your father to say yes, then I'm in."

CHAPTER 12

"Uh, I'm eighteen. My daddy legally can't tell me no anymore." Allison's petulance shines through.

Scarlett laughs at her friend. "Yeah. Go tell Daddy that and see how he reacts."

CHAPTER 13

Halloween Party

"Never trust what your senses can't detect.
Also, never trust most of what your senses can."
~J. Taylor~

Allison opens her eyes as adrenaline shoots through her veins. She looks all around, confused by her unfamiliar surroundings of a pitch-black sky and trees.

A sense of panic fills her thoughts as she can't remember how she got here. The dirt under her back is sparse with grass and even more sparse with signs of life. No insects crawl on her skin. No birds in the trees singing the night's lonely song. Just a soft breeze that whispers for her to follow.

She presses her hands against the forest floor to stand but is weighed down. She looks to her lap and sees Scarlett draped across her, covered in blood, with her lifeless eyes staring at the vast void of nothing.

In a panic, Allison crawls out from under her best friend's body. No sound emanates from her lungs as she cries to the sky above. She tries again. Again, no sound. She silently weeps while examining Scarlett for the cause of the massive blood loss. Even as she crawled out from under Scarlett, no sounds passed her ears. No rustling of the grass and leaves. No pounding of limbs against the dirt. Nothing. Not even the sound of her blood rushing through her ears or the hum of electronics that slowly drain electricity. No noise from the wind that blows by.

She hastily looks over her friend but finds no wounds. No gashes, cuts, or slices. No holes from bullets. Just blood. But the noiseless wind sends whispers through her mind to follow.

So, she stands, abandoning her deceased friend, and begins to step in the direction of the wind. A few steps past Scarlett, the wind stops and changes direction. It starts up again but blows down toward Scarlett. Allison looks back and sees Scarlett's clothes blowing about. She takes a few cautious steps back and bends down toward her friend. The wind whips in excited fury. Allison lifts her friend over her shoulder as though weight is not an issue.

She follows the wind through the trees into the dark forest and stops at a clearing. There is a haunting familiarity with this clearing, as if Allison has been here before. While the whole of the area is new to her, she looks around, unable to shake the feeling that it is not as new to her as it feels.

She notices a hole has been dug in the center of the clearing, a hole that extends down about six feet.

The dirt around the hole is piled up with a shovel sticking out of it. The wind blows to make sure there is no confusion, even though she feels like she knows what must be done. It whips past Allison, Scarlett still on her shoulder, and down into the hole.

Allison walks to the hole's edge and peers down to its bottom. No coffin awaits the dead teenager. No podium from which someone will speak a long-dreaded eulogy. No folding chairs for elderly guests or hearse in the background. It is only Allison, Scarlett, the wind, a shovel, and a hole.

She takes Scarlett off her shoulder and places her at the edge of the hole. She lets go of Scarlett and watches as her body tumbles six feet till it hits the ground below.

As Scarlett's body hits the ground, a loud horn blows, a horn that sounds deep and bellows out into the night forest.

Allison knows now that she is stuck in a dream. She must wake up to find out what that horn is: an alarm clock, a car horn, or possibly her ringing phone. She must wake up from this place to save her from having to bury her best friend. She can't wake up, though she must. The wind blows stronger as the horn blasts again.

Shovel in hand, Allison begins to throw dirt on top of her life-long friend. With each shovel full of dirt, the horn blares again, deafening and touching every nerve of her body. But Allison can't wake. She must shovel on for the wind commands it. As she shovels more and more, the wind picks up, shaking Allison's tiny frame, but her feet remain steadfast. She keeps piling dirt to fill in the grave. The wind flings her body back and forth while her feet stay rooted on the ground, looking like a drunken hula dancer on a car dashboard. The horn blares over and over against the silent backdrop of her dream.

As Allison shovels the last bit of misplaced dirt on top of her friend, a voice sounds in her mind. *Nothing lasts forever.* Her eyes open. She sees her father standing over her and hears the alarm clock diligently calling for her. Then she notices the time: 7:45 a.m.

"I could not wake you. Gave me quite the scare." Her father leans over her with a nervous smile on his face, concern starting to wash away.

The drowsiness from Allison's sleep fades as she realizes she is finally awake. "Yeah. Sorry. Intense dream. Hand me my journal."

"Your dreams have become more severe." Vistrus hands her journal to her. "Write it down before you forget."

She opens to the next available entry. "I don't think that'll happen anytime soon."

"You need to get ready for school. You are already late," Vistrus chides.

"I know. Right after I finish this." Allison starts scribbling away.

Vistrus nods, leaving her to her diary, shutting the door behind him.

The excitement of all the movies released in 2018 made the theme to this year's Maine West Haven High's annual Halloween party pretty much a gimme: superheroes.

The decorations are a throwback to children's birthday parties—streamers that spell out various heroes, mylar balloons plastered with images of the different characters, and even a slew of butter-cream-frosted cakes for each main alter-ego.

Allison and Scarlett hang out by the food table, nibbling on finger foods. Each girl has a white T-shirt with Sharpie scrawled across it. Allison's says, *"I'm* Batgirl," while Scarlett's says, "I'm whoever you want me to be."

They watch as a few boys in costume read their shirts, smile, and whisper to each other as they pass by.

"I still think your shirt gives the wrong impression," Allison notes.

"I don't do the whole superhero thing. So, whoever everyone thinks I should be is who I am," Scarlett tries to clarify.

"Oh, I know what you were going for. It's just that it comes across a little less superhero hipster and a little more ... camgirl." Allison tries to make her understand.

"What's a camgirl?" Scarlett asks.

Allison shakes her head, unsure how to explain this concept to her, but she is saved by the bell, so to speak, as Brianna, dressed in her best Black Widow outfit, shows up with Duncan, who is dressed as Blade.

Allison's attention is immediately drawn to Bri in her black, skin-tight outfit, showing off every curve and leaving little to nothing to the imagination. Allison can't help but stare at the girl who spent so many years making her life miserable and wonder if it was her conflict within that made her miserable.

She watches as they scan the crowd until they spot them. Duncan waves at Scarlett, and Brianna waves at both of them.

Allison stares as Duncan says something to Bri, and they head in their direction.

"I don't think that means what you think it means," Duncan says to Scarlett, gesturing to her shirt.

"So I've been told," Scarlett says. "What's a camgirl?"

Duncan laughs at the question, unsure of where it came from.

"One more time," Duncan says.

"Tell her never mind, and let's move away from that," Allison pleads.

"Fine by me," Bri chimes in. "Nice costumes. Superhero super hipster. I approve."

"Wouldn't think these would get your stamp of approval, but thanks. It was more about not wanting to put together a good costume than anything else," Scarlett says.

Duncan notices Allison staring at Brianna's curves with an unintentional smile on her face.

"So, Allison, no Connor tonight?" Duncan asks.

She breaks her stare and moves her attention to him but doesn't answer immediately.

"We're not talking about him right now. Sensitive subject," Scarlett offers up.

"Apologies," says Duncan. He leans in and whispers to Allison, "Looks like you found something to distract you, though."

Allison turns to him with a shocked look of disbelief. "I have no idea what you're talking about."

The genuine look on her face makes Duncan think maybe she hasn't come to terms with her, to him at least, obvious feelings and orientation. He also knows this pot might not be the best to stir.

"Perhaps, I was wrong. Again, apologies. She does look beautiful, though, no?" Duncan nods his head toward Bri.

Allison looks at him and smiles but doesn't say anything. She gives him a slight nod to confirm.

Scarlett looks at her group and around at the event. She sees the rest of the crowd all standing around in their costumes, comparing details and quality; all she sees, however, is what will be left behind. Her last high school Halloween party. The last time she knows she'll be with her friends. She sees it already ending, as Connor isn't here.

"Where's Jack?" Brianna asks.

Allison and Scarlett let out a laugh.

"He should be here soon if he can get his costume in his car," Scarlett says with a laugh.

Allison points to a giant green hand poking through the front door, one big enough that it needed its own seat in the car.

"Speak of the devil, and he shall arrive," Allison says.

As he gets one hand through, the overly large head pokes through the doors, followed by the rest of his costume. After making it through the double doors into the room, he stands tall at over ten feet, a height that is still too small for the costume proportions.

The group laughs at the marvel of his costume while other attendees are stunned at the entrance of their former teammate and classmate.

"Is he on stilts in that thing?" Brianna asks, both amazed and thinking he's a bigger dork than she thought.

"He's been working on this since they announced the theme," Scarlett says with pride.

Duncan's eyes are big with excitement for the cosplay. "Where did he get stilts? I need some of those!"

"I guess back in the day, his dad used to do drywall," Scarlett says. "He found them while cleaning his house after ... everything."

"I heard. I heard," Duncan says. "Did they ever find the guy?"

"Funny you should ask," Allison says to him.

Jack lumbers over to the group. "Hey, guys! What do you, uh, think?" In his excitement, the uptick in his voice has returned full force.

"I think it's not quite big enough," Scarlett quips.

"I know. I wanted it to be, well, bigger, much bigger, but I had to, uh, fit it into my car," he says through an opening in his gigantic head mask.

"Love the get-up," Duncan inserts.

"You drove like that?!" Brianna asks, a bit aghast at the thought.

"No, no. I had to strap a lot of it to my roof," he laughs. "I got dressed, put it on, in the parking lot."

The group laughs at his dedication to the event.

Allison taps Duncan on the shoulder and motions for him to follow.

"Where ya going, Dunc's?" Bri asks with an inquisitive tone.

He shrugs his shoulders. "Allison wants to talk. I'm sure it's nothing."

Allison and Duncan find a quiet spot to talk but still within eyesight of their friends. The high volume of the music and the surrounding crowd's involvement in their conversations give them the privacy Allison is looking for.

"What's up?" Duncan asks, holding the grip to his vampire-slaying throwing stars attached to his belt.

"Okay, remember a while back we asked you about helping out on something?" Allison tries to jog his memory.

"I don't think you could have been any vaguer with that," Duncan jabs.

"It was on the…" Allison starts.

Duncan is quick to interrupt. "Oh no. I remember. I was just making a statement about your ludicrously vague reference."

"Well, look who is being all verbiose," Allison tries to quip back.

"I think you mean verbose," Duncan corrects.

"Whatever." She resigns from the playful fight.

"So, what about it all?" Duncan asks, anticipation starting to drip from his chin.

"You know what happened to Connor's parents and Jack's parents, right?" Allison starts.

"Yeah, of course." He looks around the room, starting to feel this conversation might better belong in a back alley than here.

Allison checks her surroundings as well to make sure no ears are tuned in. "We know who did it."

"Wait?! What!" Duncan loses his quiet cool.

A few faces from the crowd turn toward them. Almost as if the music should stop, everything should freeze, and all eyes on Duncan. Except, it's only about five people, no one froze, and the music still plays. Allison looks at the faces staring at them.

Allison turns to the staring crowd. "He just found out you can use Doritos to make nachos," she shouts, killing off outside interest in their conversation.

The bystanders turn back to their conversations, dancing as the music plays.

"I never actually thought of that. I think I must try it soon," Duncan thinks out loud.

"Seriously, though." Allison gives him a friendly slug on the arm.

"Seriously," he continues in a hushed voice, "if you know, why haven't the police done anything?"

"It's far more complicated than that. Details of which I'm not allowed to get into. But here's the rub, bub. It involves a police officer and a teacher in our school." She watches his eyes widen.

"Oh, please tell me it's not Mr. Eubank. That guy's the only one who ever listened to what I had to say," Duncan begs.

"No. It's not Mr. Eubank. I can't tell you who it is just yet. This is something we all were planning, but now Jack wants to let sleeping dogs lie, and Connor is off at college, ignoring the world back home. I think it's something that needs to be done. Justice. Ya, know?" Allison fills him in on the vague details.

"Okay. So, we take down a teacher and a cop. Sounds like a suicide mission, but nothing like a little anti-authoritarian establishmentism to shape the rest of my life," he says with a hint of a smile.

"It sounds good even though I have no idea what any of that means. I'm working out the details of the ... plan. But you can't tell anyone. Heard?" Allison asks, as her eyes pierce him with the seriousness of the situation.

His smile fades as he grasps the seriousness of the subject. "Heard."

"So," Allison starts, "are you in?"

He nods his head, "Yeah, I'm in."

Allison knows that he is not in The Nation, though he is in on the plan. He has the joy of being a Normal boy. This means she now has to protect their secret from him, all while keeping him involved. A notion enters her head that perhaps she should have led with that question before telling him of their mission. An idea that possibly getting a Normal involved wasn't the best idea in the first place. But then again, an outside ally is always a good thing to have on your team.

As they return to their friends, Brianna catches Allison's eye. Allison notices Brianna's bold red lipstick on lips begging to be kissed, and for a fraction of a second, Allison wants to be begged. Brianna notices Allison's stare.

"What? You look like you're about to make some snide comment about my costume. Is there something you'd like to say?" Brianna goes on the defense before any words are thrown as punches.

Allison is taken aback by her accusation and shakes her head. Her words elude her as she tries to say something back. Finally, Allison responds below the volume of music, "No. It's just that ... I think your lipstick looks really good on you."

Brianna takes a step closer to Allison. "What?! That sounded like you might have been nice."

Allison smiles. "I said, I like your lipstick. It's a nice color."

"Thanks! It's called MisRed. Sorry if I was a little unhinged," Brianna offers up.

Allison slides a half step closer. "It's a little new to me."

"What? Being nice?" Brianna jokes.

"Being friends again," Allison admits.

Brianna moves to whisper in her ear, "Well, if it helps, it's weird on my end too. If you need to take a jab from time to time for comfort's sake, I'll understand."

Allison leans in to whisper back as she smells Brianna's perfume, a scent that anytime she smelled in the past sent waves of anger down her spine, but tonight it seems a little more pleasant. The emotions that start running through Allison's mind carry a sting through her temples, a pain that is as sudden onset as her newfound feelings. The taste of copper slowly creeps into her mouth.

"Same here. I wouldn't want the world to think everything is all hunky-dory. Might cause an end to all things as we know it," Allison offers back as a drip of blood slips out of her mouth.

Brianna looks at Allison. She sees her eyes slowly begin to sink in. Veins in her face begin to rise to the surface in a varicose fashion.

"Are you okay?" Brianna asks. "I think you are starting to transform or transition or whatever."

Allison shakes her head and laughs. "Just a bad migraine and apparently a bloody nose. I can taste it."

Brianna turns to Scarlett, who is engaged in conversation with Jack.

"Hey! Scarlett! She needs help!" Brianna is quick to get their attention with a tug.

Scarlett and Jack move in to cover their friend.

Jack steps by her side. "You're, well, uh, transitioning, Allison. You feeling okay?"

Allison takes a step away from him. Her transition is slow but noticeable to the group of Legends. The blood dripping from her mouth starts falling to the floor below.

Scarlett steps toward her and speaks softly to her. "Hey, Al. You need to calm down. You can't do this here."

Allison looks up at her group of friends. "I'm not this thing! This! It isn't real!"

She pushes her way through her friends and rushes out the front door. Jack's gargantuan costume halts his pursuit before he can even start to follow after her. Scarlett motions to Jack.

"I got this! Stay here!" Scarlett says as she runs off.

Duncan looks to Brianna. "Is everything okay?"

Jack takes the floor to answer. "She gets these bad, well you saw, nose bleeds. The loss of blood can make her ... lightheaded." His voice upticks as he searches for words. "If she loses too much blood, she, she, she gets disoriented, and her face looks ... what's the word ... goat, um, gout. No, gaunt! Not fun!"

"Damn, I never knew." Duncan shakes his head.

Scarlett enters back inside and walks back to her friends. The rest of the crowd seems no worse for the wear. No real spectators seemed to notice what was transpiring. Or, Scarlett observes, they just didn't care enough to pay attention. Either way, Scarlett puts that in the win column for the moment.

"By the time I caught up, she was already pulling away. Fast little bugger," Scarlett accounts for her re-emergence.

"So, what do we do?" Jack asks, trying in vain to sit down in his oversized costume.

"Enjoy the night. Home is probably the safest place for her right now," Scarlett offers up, as she grabs a drink from the punch bowl.

Allison runs into her house and past her father, who is already asleep in his bedroom. The dried blood around the corner of her mouth is cracked and flaking. While the bleeding has stopped, she is still in Legendary form.

She bolts the bathroom door shut and turns on the light. She looks into the mirror and jumps back in disgust, dropping her phone to the floor. Tears well up in her eyes as she falls to the floor.

"This isn't happening," she cries into her hands. "They aren't real! I'm a girl. Just a normal girl."

She continues weeping into her hands. She feels her rigid veins against her fingers. The blood coursing through them is a reminder that she is, in fact, not an ordinary girl.

She stands up, eyes closed, and faces the mirror. She stands for a few moments, just breathing, trying with each inhale to control herself, to control her emotions. As she gets her breathing under control, she starts to open her left eye just enough to see her reflection in the mirror. She takes control and slows down her breath as it quickens again. She continues opening her left eye, keeping her right eye closed in fear that if both eyes see the same thing, it will become real to her. It will be cemented in stone, never to be undone. A reality she is unsure she is ready to face.

Through her open eye, the first thing she notices is her hair, much thinner than before. Her scalp is visible through the wispy strands. Even the texture seems different at the moment. She is unsure if it is changed or if her senses are messing with her.

She sees her nose, slightly withered at her young age. It is thin and streaked with tiny red veins that loop under and into her nostrils.

She looks at her lips, already on the thin side, now thinner, almost disappearing altogether into her face.

CHAPTER 13

The only signs she has lips are the cracks from the chapped skin around her mouth.

She touches the veins that protrude from her head and face that look like she's been injecting anabolic steroids for decades. She notices their translucent nature. Not purple like standard varicose veins. She watches the blood flowing through them. She presses down on one to see how squishy it is but is met with more resistance than she thought, as if evolution has formed a protective barrier to keep the veins from easily rupturing.

She smiles into the mirror to finally check out the source of the copper taste. As she does, she notices her teeth are shifted as fangs come in through the gaps that have been made. She touches them and knocks a tooth out. A gentle touch sent what was clinging on over the edge and into the bathroom sink. She is even more careful as she checks all her teeth, all of which are loose. Even her gum line has reshaped itself to accommodate the new fangs.

Again, tears start running down her cheeks. She finally opens her other eye and knows she cannot run from the truth. She has conceded that this unfamiliar image that reflects back in the mirror is a complete stranger to her. A form that, in her mind, cannot be accepted by her. It is that thought that sends the salty tears streaming. If she cannot accept how she looks, how will people who don't know what she is? How can people who don't look like her accept her? She's already had her fair share of discrimination and prejudice, but nothing that will prepare her for what lies ahead.

She picks up her phone and starts scrolling for a name—any name that can understand and listen. A name of someone who cares and won't judge. Connor.

She calls him and knows he hasn't been the best of boyfriends since college started, but he's still her Connor, she hopes.

It rings once. The thoughts race through Allison's mind of what she'll say when he answers.

It rings twice. She knows it takes a moment for Connor to get to his phone. But why?

It rings thrice. Now Allison's thoughts shift from when to if Connor's going to answer, still wondering why he isn't picking up.

It rings four times. Perhaps he is on a "no phones allowed" retreat. Or a girl has captured his interest. What has happened to her Connor?

The voicemail picks up. A greeting she dreaded to hear. It beeps☐the universal sign to leave a message. She doesn't know what to say. She just cries into the phone, but no words come to mind. If nothing else, he'll call her back. At the very least, he'll call her back. She hangs up, unable to form the words she wants to say.

Her mother. A simple thought that sends her out of the bathroom and into her father's study. She's never read her mother's diaries. Journals are a private matter, but her mother hasn't been alive for many years. She had told her father to look inside, that, perhaps, the diaries could hold some sort of solace for him. She hopes tonight they hold some kind of solace for her.

She knows exactly where they are kept in the study. But the study was never really a place she gave much thought to. She looks at the rows of books that line the in-wall shelving units. Units that adorn the two long sidewalls of the study. Details she had never paid much attention to before now. The diaries are still in the forefront of her mind, but she is taking in these familiar surroundings in a new light. She is stopping to smell the roses for once, so to speak, and scans a section of the wall filled with notebooks and handwritten tombs. Notes by himself and others on dealings with the museum. Sketches of display setups and floor plans.

She moves on.

It is time she opens her mother's thoughts scribed in journals long ago, all in hopes of answering some question Allison herself can't put into words. She sees her mother's diaries next to the dream books she had read before. The assortment has no printing to suggest it is an old Reader's Digest condensed book or hardcover that lost its sleeve. These diaries have inch-and-a-half spines, are leather-bound, and are deep brown-red in color. The cracked and wrinkled leather lends an ominous feel to the books. In a row of five, these are what Allison hopes has some sort of answer or can provide guidance in these trying times. It is the type of book that Allison would journal in if she had found these in some souvenir shop, except that Allison knows these were not purchased in some tchotchke shop. These are probably the only five that exist. Handmade by some artisan back when the word meant quality, handmade goods by a guy in a leather apron slaving away next to a hot furnace and whose hands were sweating under some heavy gloves.

She reaches out a withered hand. Her nails, cracked and yellow on boney fingers, grab the middle book. She knows her mother started going insane and wants to know what was written before then, a need to understand what Inessa thought and what others must have missed. Allison needs to see that she is not headed down the same path.

She opens the leather-bound cover and starts with the first entry of this volume.

Allison reads the date of the entry: *March 25, 2000.*

"I wasn't even two months old yet," Allison mumbles.

She remembers her father saying that this was about the time all her episodes started.

> The dream was strange. More real than others before. I could feel the environment. A new experience for me.

For Allison, the experience is something she is now familiar with. Allison can't help but wonder if she is headed down the same path as her mother.

A sound in her ears rings out a high-pitched tone for a moment. Then all the noise becomes distant. Not faded or low in volume, just far, like a carnival that can be clearly heard from blocks away. Except she doesn't hear a carnival. She hears breathing and pounding. A thumping. Thump-thump. Thump-thump. She notices two sets of thumps. One much closer than the other.

She quickly spins around to find the source of the thumping. No one is there. She eyes a closed closet door next to the room's entrance, perhaps from in there. The thump-thump does not get louder, only faster as she creeps to the closed door. She opens the door as the thump-thump turns into a constant thumping.

Empty. Except for the locked cabinets that house museum work.

She looks down and sees her chest pounding in sync with the loud thumps. Her heart. She hears her heartbeat. But the other thump-thump is slow and steady. Her hearing has attuned to her surroundings. She listens to the wind outside as it wisps through the trees. The nocturnal animals scurry about scavenging for food. She realizes the other thump is her father's.

It is a realization that sends a calm through her. She knows the source of what she hears. Now she can use that as she stalks her father's study.

She turns her attention back to the diary. The entries continue for a few pages talking about her dreams' realism and tactile sensations. It isn't for another twenty entries that something grabs Allison's attention.

June 6, 2000

He was so real. A man shrouded in shadow and mystery, yet I could feel his breath as he looked down on me from beneath his hooded face. His menacing stare blank behind the shadow, yet I know it was for me. His deep, slow breaths ... heavy. He wants me gone.

That entry strikes a chord with Allison. She has dreamt of him as well. He was in the woods when they performed whatever ritual that was over both Jack and Connor's parents. He was there. Only this man could have such a menacing presence. The same ominous tingle of not being wanted. The instinctual feeling of needing to protect yourself.

Allison stops reading, as she is not really sure what else she is looking for. She knows she's looking for something that will help her understand. Something that will help with her dreams—a way to cope and deal. A hint toward therapy. Therapy. The word her dad's been oddly avoiding since she asked. Allison knows her mother was in counseling. Hopefully, Inessa wrote about it.

She skims ahead, looking for words that signal therapy, psychiatrist, social worker, or whatever catches her attention. Her skimming techniques pay off. Another 15 pages or so in, she sees the word—therapist.

There was no couch to lie on but sitting in his chair was comfortable. It felt good to talk about my dreams. What they could possibly mean about my situation. Who the mysterious figure could be. This new therapist might just be what I needed.

Allison scans through a few pages of entries, noticing that each gets a little more cryptic and paranoid.

13. It's a game of chess. How to tell my love? I can't. What to do? Who is the Faoi Dhó Duine? The Faoi Dhó Duine is the key.

As the entries continue, Allison starts to work herself into a more anxious state. Her breathing starts to pick back up. She catches it right away, taking control. Her ears pick up on distant movement; her father is awake. She tilts her head to the window and sees the sun start to rise. She has been reading longer than she realized.

She puts the diary back on the shelf. As she moves away, her shirt snags the book next to where she placed the journal. She is too distracted evading her father to notice it fall to the floor. She doesn't see it fall, and if she heard it, she ignores it as well. What she also doesn't see, lying open on the floor, is the heading on each page—*The Adeirrig* on one page and *The Clochnawa* atop the other.

Allison creeps down the hall and into her bedroom. She closes her bedroom door as Vistrus opens his, apparently none the wiser to his daughter's inquiries into her mother's past.

While Vistrus might be blissfully ignorant of his daughter's prying, thinking she is asleep, Allison is anything but. Her wide eyes stare up at the ceiling, watching the shadows cast from swaying tree branches out her window. She watches the shadows twist and turn into ever-changing shapes, the monsters in her head manifesting on her ceiling. She tries to close her eyes, but all she can see is the reflection of herself from earlier. She stares upward, and the bottom of her vision sees her hands clutching the blanket by her chin. She sees the veins and sunken features; they have diminished a bit. A slight return to normalcy, but she feels far from normal anymore.

She can't help but wonder if this is what her mother felt, if this is what all Legends experience when they first discover their true self. The shame, guilt, and disgust of her appearance. *Do all Legends feel this way?* She is overtaken by the immediate propulsion to the hypothetical future events where she is ridiculed, tormented, attacked, or worse, all because of who she is.

Tears fall down the side of her face and into her ears, despite keeping her breathing calm. As the tears fill up the outside curves of her ears, they overflow onto the pillow beneath her head. For a girl who has always felt a little abnormal because of her childlike looks, she has never felt less ordinary than tonight. The one night a year when ghosts, ghouls, goblins, and all varieties of hideous creatures come out to play, she feels unworthy—dirty and unclean.

She stares at the ceiling, wondering if her disgust and growing self-loathing have anything to do with the Halloween celebration not being on Halloween but a few days early.

It doesn't matter right now. Now all Allison needs is to feel less, more comfortably numb. She reaches into her nightstand, shifts her diary to the side, and pulls out a flask. The frightened girl takes a swig, followed by a long, deep breath. She tells herself, *This is normal. Hell, all high schoolers drink. I just prefer to do it alone.* She takes another swig and a deep breath after swallowing. *It relaxes me, and it's just for medicinal purposes, so it's okay.* One more swig, and she puts it back and covers it with her diary. *Now I'm calm. A little makes it all better.* It only takes another moment or two for the warmth of her picked poison to wash over her.

She knows her worries about feeling like a misfit seem foolish, but given the newfound circumstances, she is not sure what to think about anything anymore. So, she stares upward, warm from the alcohol, waiting for sleep.

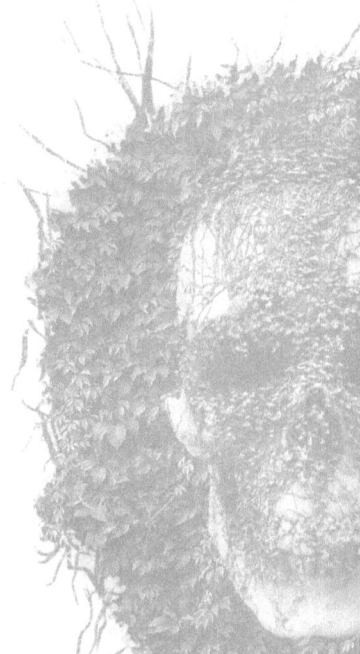

CHAPTER 14

"There are reasons we stay hidden."
~E. DeSalvo~

Sundays at the record store are always a toss-up of being super busy or completely dead. After last night's Halloween fiasco, Allison was hoping for a busy night that would force her to take her mind off things. No such luck.

Two hours into her shift, only three people have walked into the store. Not a great way to keep her mind off things. Even Scarlett has yet to return her text messages.

Allison has her face buried in some phone game while sitting in the back employees-only room next to the Metal Haus section. A while has passed since anyone has been in, so she learns to enjoy the silence and the calm.

The alert of a text message distracts Allison. She swipes down to see who sent it. Connor. A little butterfly floats through her tummy as she opens the text to see what he has to say.

[Connor: Sorry I couldn't make it. My psych prof decided to make us write a ten-page essay by next week on some BS. How was it?]

Allison's butterfly has dropped and died. She tenses up as a growing frustration overcomes her. She goes to the work fridge and grabs her flask, chugging down a good bit.

She starts typing back, emboldened by her liquid courage.

[Allison: Great. Good times, as usual. Thanks for the heads-up on not being able to make it.]

An alert rings out.

[Connor: I already told you that I might not. Didn't realize I had to tell you again.]

The fury in her fingers as she types back tests the strength of the device.

[Allison: Might not means might yes … whatever. I hope your Halloween weekend was fun.]

[Connor: Was what it was. I wish you weren't so angry.] Connor tries to douse the fury.

Allison laughs out loud at his comment.

[Allison: Have you ever talked to a female before? Saying crap like that is not going to make anything better. What happened to the Connor I fell in love with?]

She walks back to the fridge and takes another swig of her flask. As she shuts the door, her phone starts ringing.

"That's what it takes to get you to call?" she answers with a piercing shot.

"I'm right here. Things aren't exactly wine and roses over here." His response remains calm in another attempt to soothe Allison.

"Well, how would I know! It's not like you ever call. I get a text here and there. And yeah, for the most part, they're pleasant enough, but nothing real. Nothing of substance!" she says as her frustration swells.

"What do you want me to say?" Connor pleads.

She listens for a moment, trying to discern anything she can from the background noise on the other end of the phone. She hears nothing and tries to hone in like she can when she transitioned, but nothing stands out.

"Well?" Connor asks again.

"I want you to tell me that you don't want to date someone in high school. That the distance is too much for you," Allison starts.

Before she can continue, Connor interrupts. "Is that what you want? Is the distance too much for you?"

"No. It's not the four hours; it's the emotional distance. Tell me there's someone else. That some college girl has swept you off your feet, and you've been avoiding *this*. Give me something because anything is better than what I've been given since you left." Her words are passionate and fierce but also a little slurred from hitting the flask.

"I'm sorry. There's no other girl. No other anyone. Just me trying to make this college thing … trying to balance college and us," he admits in a rare moment of vulnerability.

"Well, you suck at balance, Connor DeSalvo!" Allison shoots back.

"I just wanted to say, 'Happy Halloween,' and I miss you. I … I just can't do this. I love you," escape Connor's lips before hanging up the phone.

Allison drops her phone onto the table and starts to cry. There is a part of her that whispers to her that her reaction to the distance and his absence is for nothing. The whisper tells her that he loves her. Though for every whisper, there is another, more profound whisper that tells her, "No. He isn't there anymore. He's moved on." It is those deeper whispers that send her back to paranoia, back to her flask.

She knows she did nothing to help her cause right now, but she is lost.

"Al? What happened?" Scarlett's genuine concern is overshadowed by her sudden appearance in the store.

Allison jumps up, startled by Scarlett's appearance. "Jesus, Scarlett!" She hastily tries to wipe away the tears from her eyes, as if nothing was wrong, "It's nothing, just allergies, I guess."

"Allergies, Al?" Scarlett dismisses. "Do you always yell at your allergies?"

"Did you, like, beam yourself over here, like in *Star Trek*? I didn't know we could do that." Allison wipes away more tears.

Scarlett chuckles. "No. I walked through the front door like everyone else in the world."

"Oh. I didn't hear the door-noiser thingy." Allison changes the subject.

"Maybe it's 'cause you were yelling at your allergies," Scarlett jests. "And it's called a chime."

Allison approaches Scarlett and wraps her arms around her for a good hug. Scarlett reciprocates, and they hold each other for a few moments.

"Must be some pretty bad allergies to get you all up in arms," Scarlett whispers.

Allison pulls back and wipes away the last of her tears.

"I got your text earlier. Thought I'd stop by." Scarlett takes a seat in the employees-only area. "See how you're doing after last night."

Allison takes a step and loses her balance. She starts stumbling forward but catches herself on the table before any real damage is done. She plops down on a chair next to Scarlett.

"Connor took me out for my birthday this year," Allison says, laying her head on the table.

"Yeah … in February … when your birthday is. Dinner date, if I recall?" Scarlett is unsure of where this is headed.

"Yeah. Yeah. But it was something we talked about. About vampires. About Jack. We were just talking. But it was nice." She lifts her head a bit before the weight of it makes her drop back to the table.

"Okay?" Scarlett nudges.

"He said being a vampire would be cool. I said it would be lonely," Allison attempts to clarify.

Allison looks around the room and out toward the store to see if anyone has entered without her noticing. All seems quiet. She lays her head back down.

"I just didn't realize how lonely," Allison finally admits.

"I'm here for you, Al. Always have been, always will be," Scarlett assures.

"Sure." Allison lifts her head and sits up. "But you never changed. You never experienced 'the change'." Allison air quotes the last two words.

Scarlett's face scrunches up and does matching air quotes. "I'm pretty sure 'the change' is menopause, not being a vampire."

"Whatever. We can't say the 'L' word in public," Allison defends.

Scarlett grimaces a little. "The 'L' word is lesbian. So…"

"So whatever, you know what I mean." Allison slouches into her seat, "You still haven't done any *change*. So, you can't relate. Not really. And the two that have, Jack and Connor, well…"

"Well, what?" Scarlett urges. "You have to finish the thought if you want to condemn them."

"Jack is moving on. He doesn't want to do anything about his parents and hasn't said a word about being what we are, and Connor is off in Wis-con-sin doing whatever he's doing in college," Allison huffs out.

"Have you tried talking to your father?" Scarlett asks.

"Yeah. But Dad's afraid I'll end up all crazy like my mom," Allison rattles off.

"What are you talking about?" Scarlett asks.

Allison sits up in her chair. "Learned a few things recently. I'll explain later, but what it comes down to is he's no help either. I have no one to talk to who can actually understand this."

"If you really need to talk, there's always Bri," Scarlett offers through hesitant words.

Allison breaks out laughing. Scarlett tries to resist but is infected with laughter.

"Oh please," Allison chuckles. "Could you imagine us talking about something that real?"

"Just a thought. I could always see if Grams knows someone," Scarlett offers.

"What? Like a supernatural support group? Vampires Anonymous?! What a riot that would be! What a name." Allison mocks a conversation,

"Be home late tonight, honey. I gotta stop by VA later." A fleeting notion escapes her mind. "The VA?" Allison's laughter calms down a bit. "Maybe I should go see that counselor lady at school. Something's gotta be better than nothing, right?"

"If you need. But, Allison, I'm here for you whenever." Scarlett stands up to give her a hug. She is about to relay the meaning of the VA to Al, but the door chime interrupts their moment.

A customer walks up to the cash register and knocks on the counter to try and grab someone's attention.

"Coming! I guess I gotta do some work," Allison relents to Scarlett.

"You do you. I'll be right here all night," Scarlett smiles.

Sylvia stands in her kitchen, mixing an appletini when she hears her front door slowly creak open.

"You're home early, dear. Thought you'd be out much later," Sylvia says.

The footsteps grow closer to her as the door closes. Sylvia turns to greet her daughter, only to be surprised by the same masked intruder from the summer.

"Sorry I took so long," he says, swinging a tire iron.

Before the iron connects with her face, she transitions to full Legendary form. The bark-like covering on her skin shields the blow. She drops the martini glass. It shatters, sending apple vodka-flavored shards of glass flying across her kitchen floor. The impact knocks her back against her counter but not down to the ground.

The intruder swings again. This time she blocks his arm with her left. She uses her right arm to land a punch straight to his throat.

He drops the tire iron as he falls to the floor, gasping for air.

"Why me?" Sylvia towers over him. Her vine-like hair and grey eyes pierce his soul. Her bark-like skin shifts between her Legendary and Normal state. Her emotions remain in control but are unsure of what she needs to stay safe.

"They said..." he gets out while gasping for air, "...I could be ... like you." He continues gasping for air. "All I had ... to do ... is kill ... you."

She steps on his chest to keep him on the ground. "Take a deep breath," she advises.

"Can't... with you ... on me," he manages to get out.

"Then I'll be quick," she starts. "Who are they?"

His eyes start to tear up. His lips are turning pale. The rest of his face is concealed by his mask.

"You … know," he spits out.

"The same people who killed the others?" she asks as she squats closer to him, still keeping one foot on his chest.

He only nods "yes." His pale lips start showing hints of blue. Tiny red veins start to form in his bulging eyes.

"They're playing you; it's not like the books. You don't become one of us. You're born one of us. You're either in or you're not. And you are not." Sylvia steps off the masked man's chest.

"Please … I'm … sorry … Don't … kill…" he starts.

His gasps for air become more shallow as his eyes bulge more and his lips turn a deeper blue. She sits him upright and plants a hard smack on his back. "I'm not going to kill you. We aren't killers."

Color returns to the intruder's lips as air rushes into his lungs. While Sylvia helps him stand up, his shirt shifts, revealing a fleur-de-lis tattoo on the back of his neck.

"Invade my home again, or even attempt to harm anyone else, and I will kill you. Do you understand?" Sylvia says as her grey eyes stare into his, imposing their will.

He nods before running off. Sylvia is left to clean up the mess before her daughter comes home for the night.

CHAPTER 15

"And some are excellent reasons."

~I. Petrovsky~

The 10x10 square foot office is well-lit but not overpowering. The neutral walls of the school office scream unoriginal, exemplifying that there's no need for personality in the educational system. The chairs are still that borderline uncomfortable that they forever will be, but sturdy enough not to need replacing.

Mrs. Hsu sits behind her desk, pen in hand, hovering over a yellow legal pad waiting for something to write.

Allison sits in the chair, unsure of what she is doing there. She keeps shifting her focus between the unmoving eyes of the social worker and the ever-ticking hands of the clock.

"Maybe this was a bad idea," Allison says, finally breaking the silence.

Mrs. Hsu puts down her pen. "Maybe it was."

Allison shifts in her chair. Not the response she was expecting.

Mrs. Hsu continues, "Perhaps it wasn't. Something happened that pushed you to come here. After all that has happened to you, something else happened that, in your mind, was the final straw."

Allison continues to fidget and shift. Her eyes are now focusing on the clock and the surrounding shelves filled with books, but she won't look at Mrs. Hsu.

"There's no final straw. No camel's toe to break," Allison blurts out.

Mrs. Hsu holds back a smile from Allison's faux pas. "The expression is 'straw that broke the camel's back.' No toe."

"Whatever. There's nothing; it's not one thing. Like, I know there are books on dreams and how to interpret them. They just bug me," Allison lets out.

"What bugs you?" Mrs. Hsu asks, jotting down notes on her pad. "The dreams or the books?"

"The dreams. Well, the books seem really cheesy, so I guess both. I've skimmed those books. They all have either specific definitions for things that you dream about, which is ridiculous, or they tell you it's all open to interpretation, which is then pointless to write about in broadness," Allison continues. "Sorry. I don't know. I'm just wasting your time. I'll leave."

Allison starts to stand up.

Mrs. Hsu puts down her pen. "My time is yours. You are not wasting it. It's why I took this position. To be here for students like you who need someone to talk to."

Allison freezes but doesn't sit back down.

226

The social worker continues, "You said you've skimmed the books. Did anything seem helpful?"

Allison hesitates before sitting back down. "No. Outside of general interpretations, the books seemed like they were trying to tell me what I was thinking and who I am based on what my mind decides to think about at night."

"And you don't like that?" Mrs. Hsu asks.

"Like what?" Allison asks back.

"Being told who you are and what you are thinking," Mrs. Hsu clears up.

"No. It's stupid. One night I'm dreaming about sodas and ice cream in my bedroom while watching reruns of *SpongeBob*, and no book is going to psychotically analyze that, but I have a few dreams that seem much more significant, and, all of a sudden, these books are digging into my soul and subconscious. Screw that," Allison responds. "Sorry I said, 'screw,' I guess."

Mrs. Hsu lets out a small chuckle. "There's no need to apologize about saying words in here. We are all adults. No one is going to psychoanalyze you here."

"I've been going through some stuff while my boyfriend hasn't exactly been competing for boyfriend of the year. Ya know?" Allison continues her torrent of thoughts.

Mrs. Hsu jots down a few notes on the pad.

"Let's put a pin in the boyfriend for a moment and tell me what this stuff is you've been going through." Mrs. Hsu tries to guide her in a direction.

"I can't really explain it. I mean, I can, but it's hard," Allison starts, slowing her pace a bit.

"Take your time. This is for you. It's not a race," the social worker states, as she jots more notes on her pad.

"Ever since Connor's parents died, things haven't been the same. It's like we're all finding out all this stuff about ourselves, and it feels lonely," Allison begins. She sinks into the chair as the weight lifts off her chest. "I tried talking to my dad, but he says I need to deal with things on my own. Then he tells me my mother went nuts after starting therapy, so I shouldn't do it. But here I am. So if I go nuts, he was right. And she did. I read her diaries. Talking about crazy things and chess and some Faoi Dhó Duine. I don't know. I just want … I don't know what I want."

Allison has worked herself back up but kept the migraines at bay. No shooting pains. No sinking nose or thinning lips. Just Allison as a Normal. No hints to Mrs. Hsu that she might be something more.

"And sometimes you find things out about yourself that you didn't know were there. And it changes everything," Allison continues.

"Care to elaborate?" Mrs. Hsu tip toes around being too probative.

Allison shuts down for a moment. Her mouth unmoving as any words fail to form in her head that would make any sense.

Mrs. Hsu waits patiently for Allison to say the words, whatever they may be, that will help her move forward with whatever it is that has her so angry and determined to self-destruct.

Allison raises a brow as a thought in her head strikes her. "It's feelings. Or at least the way I feel about the things that are happening. It's also other things. Like, okay, my mom died when I was a baby, well toddler, I think, whatever, I was young. So, she never got the chance to have 'the talk' with me about what happens when we hit our teens or preteens."

Mrs. Hsu nods. "I'm following. Go on."

"Okay, so, and men don't really think about such things, so my father never had 'the talk' with me either. And when it finally happened, it was scary. Magical and eye-opening in a weird movie-moment way because I wasn't entirely sure what was going on. Either way, it wasn't normal."

"I get the metaphor. What are you relating it to?" Mrs. Hsu probes.

"I might be small, but I have discovered I am stronger than I look … by a lot. And I know what happened to both Connor and Jack's parents isn't finished," Allison says, hoping she doesn't have to elaborate into much detail.

Mrs. Hsu puts up a hand to stop Allison from talking. She glances at the clock, knowing their time is running out for today. She looks back at the young Petrovsky.

"I think I know where you are going with this. Before you say anything that requires me to take action, I have two things to say. One, be careful where you tread. There is far more to the world than you can begin to comprehend," Mrs. Hsu starts.

Allison nods in agreement. "I think I may have an idea. Things have gotten strange for me recently."

She pauses for a moment, waiting for the social worker to continue. She doesn't.

Allison takes a deep breath. "What's the second thing? You said you had two things to say."

"Yes, I did." Mrs. Hsu starts back up. "The second is, well, more of a question."

"And that is?" Allison starts to get nervous. "I don't do any hard drugs or anything."

"Why would you think I was going to ask that? You have given me no indication you do," Mrs. Hsu questions.

"I don't know? Always the guilty conscience, I guess," Allison admits.

"It's okay. The question is … Are you in?" Mrs. Hsu pauses, not breaking eye contact but not demanding it from Allison either.

Allison freezes, shocked by the question. She recognizes the three words; though, at this moment, they make no sense, as if this person asking shouldn't know the fact those three words can be combined to form such an important question.

But important the question is, and all questions wait for an answer. And here, the question waits for Allison to respond. Her brain can't recall the words, the phrase that needs to be said so Mrs. Hsu knows she is, in fact, in The Nation. Though Allison is still unsure what it is and why she is in it.

The randomness of having genes that make her part of something bigger doesn't make sense. Allison can't see the rhyme or reason behind it. She doesn't grasp the logic of her situation and, therefore, still can't comprehend that it is happening to her. But this moment, right here, those three words spoken by the social worker tell Allison that, in fact, yes, she is part of The Nation. Yes, she is part of something bigger than her; and all of it is because of happenstance, nothing more.

So how does she answer?

The bell rings.

Mrs. Hsu hesitantly reaches into her desk, hoping it gives Allison time to answer. But no words are spoken. Allison sits, frozen in her chair. Mrs. Hsu pulls out a pad of hall passes. "This was good. First sessions can be hard, and you did very well."

She scribbles on the hall pass and tears it off the pad. "Anytime you need to talk, I am here."

"You won't tell anyone?" Allison asks.

"Everything you tell me is confidential. As long as you don't pose a threat or are going to harm yourself or others, nothing will leave this room," Mrs. Hsu answers, handing Allison the hall pass. "Take all the time you need to collect yourself."

Scarlett, Brianna, and Duncan hide in the courtyard during their lunch period. They endure the brisk breeze and chilled air while tucked away in a safe corner, kept even colder by the building's shadow. A few yards away, a group of five die-hard hacky sack kids attempts to maintain a session for more than three hits. While two players have actual talent, the others are there more for fun and social interaction than the sport itself. All five of them, however, are wringing their hands as they blow into them for warmth.

"Where's Allison?" Duncan stands behind Brianna, wrapping his arms around her waist to help keep her warm.

"Elephant and a rhino. She has fourth free, so she's usually here already," Scarlett smirks while looking around for her.

"Elephant and a rhino? Clever," Duncan hints of sarcasm.

"Thanks. I guess," Scarlett says, as Allison appears from inside the building.

Allison watches the ground as she walks to the group.

"Scar, I think Mrs. Hsu is in..." Allison looks up to see Duncan standing behind Brianna, "sane. Just insane."

Scarlett shakes her head at Allison's close call.

"I dunno. I've seen her before, and she was pretty chill. She said she likes my art," Duncan adds.

"Yeah, that's 'cause you're a talented artist," Scarlett notes. She looks at Bri. "Got to see him carve ... a piece of wood."

He nods his head at her compliment.

Allison checks the bottom of her shoes but finds nothing unusual. "Yeah, but how many teachers, counselors, school employees, or whoever have said someone is good, talented, whatever but then gives no actual, real feedback? How many kids are falsely believing they are talented musicians, singers, artists, writers, whatever because some teacher said they were, but in reality, all they show is potential and promise?

They *will* be good, great, whatever, but aren't there yet. Or worse, they are just okay with no potential to become great. Like they just don't have it in them. But because of the authority figure's lack of real, honest feedback, they continue down some dream for something that is out of reach because instead of being gently honest with us, all they do is tell us we're wonderful and shit."

"Two things, Al." Scarlett holds up two fingers. "One, why do you keep looking down and checking the bottom of your shoes, and two, you okay? That speech was a pretty long walk."

Allison laughs it off. "Yeah. I thought I stepped in gum or something. Eh, I guess it was nothing."

"And the *Good Will Hunting*-style rant?" Duncan asks.

"What's *Good Will Hunting*?" Allison replies.

"Great movie. We'll all watch it sometime." He chuckles.

"I don't know. I think Mrs. Hsu got under my skin a bit. Why are we out in the freezing cold anyway?" She surveys the courtyard and the clear sky above. "What's going on with you all?" She turns back to her group of friends. "Still sneaking around behind your mother's back, I see."

Brianna and Duncan both give bobbing nods.

"She just doesn't understand," Bri speaks up.

"No, she just wants the best for her daughter, and, apparently, I'm not it." Duncan tightens his grip around his girl.

Brianna turns her head and gives Duncan a deep kiss, a kiss too deep for school grounds.

"Uh-hmm," a throat clears from behind the group.

They all turn to see Ms. Waldgrave standing cross-armed and tapping her foot.

"Young lady, what do you think you are doing? Can you explain yourself? I think you should," Ms. Waldgrave scorns.

"I thought I was kissing, but I must've been doing it wrong if you had to ask," Bri jokes.

"Not funny, Bri. Not funny at all, and definitely not the place to be so," Ms. Waldgrave strikes back. "You are going to be in so much trouble tonight."

"I apologize. I don't mean any disrespect," Duncan starts.

"Not meaning disrespect doesn't mean you aren't being disrespectful. Making out with a girl on school grounds, and my daughter, nonetheless," Ms. Waldgrave snaps back.

"He knows," Scarlett interjects, seeing the unease on his face, "that's why he said he doesn't *mean* any."

Ms. Waldgrave turns to Scarlett, shifting the way the light hits her face, exposing a skillfully concealed bruise that Scarlett sees hidden under concealer and foundation.

Scarlett steps toward Ms. Waldgrave, who looks at her with caution, unsure of why she has not only stepped to her but stepped so close.

Duncan, Bri, and Allison all watch with anticipation to see what she does.

Scarlett leans in and whispers to Ms. Waldgrave, "I still see those bruises. You've been covering them throughout the year."

Ms. Waldgrave takes a step back. "That is none of your business! And completely inappropriate, young lady!"

Scarlett steps back and turns to walk away. "Let's take a walk, Ms. Waldgrave."

Confused by Scarlett's audacity, Ms. Waldgrave follows Scarlett to a spot surrounded by bushes, giving them a little more privacy.

"Mind what you say, young lady," Ms. Waldgrave warns. "You have things that are happening. I wouldn't want your behavior in this to put a stop to those things."

Scarlett shifts her eyes to make sure none of the others are watching.

"Don't threaten my program; it's unbecoming," Scarlett strikes back.

"Is that why you pulled me over here? To tell me not to threaten you? It would have been more effective in front of your friends. Always threaten with a friendly witness around," Ms. Waldgrave jabs back.

"No. I walked over here to tell you I know," Scarlett says in a hushed tone.

"What did you say?" Ms. Waldgrave stands shocked and bewildered at Scarlett's presumption, as well as terrified at Scarlett's choice of words.

Scarlett takes another look around. "I said, I know who did that to you."

"You don't know what you're talking about." Ms. Waldgrave plays dumb.

Scarlett takes a deep breath to calm her frustration. She looks the teacher square in the eye, making sure no one breaks contact.

"Are you in?" Scarlett asks.

Ms. Waldgrave's jaw drops open, unsure of what to think at such a question from someone her age and her child's friend.

"What?" Ms. Waldgrave makes sure she heard what she heard.

"You heard me, Mrs. Waldgrave," Scarlett responds.

Both ladies look around their immediate surroundings. Through the space between the leaves and branches, the rest of the group laughs about whatever was just said but, more importantly, not listening. Nor are any of the other students in the courtyard, no prying ears or eyes to catch their conversation.

Ms. Waldgrave turns back to Scarlett. "I am in as they put out the starlight."

Scarlett stands, not knowing how to respond, especially since she is unsure what type of Legend, if any, she may be. Ms. Waldgrave notices the lack of a ready reply but doesn't press the issue.

"That's a poetic response," Scarlett replies.

"It's Poe," Ms. Waldgrave starts.

And in that instance, Scarlett's mind flashes back to the notebook that was on Ms. Waldgrave's desk. Poe Society and the others as well ... if only she could remember those names.

"Why are you asking me this?" Ms. Waldgrave ponders to Scarlett.

"Because the same people who killed Connor's parents, *my* aunt and uncle, *and* Jack's parents are doing this to you," Scarlett tells her. "And a teacher is involved."

Ms. Waldgrave grabs Scarlett's arm and pulls them even closer to the brick wall.

"This is not the time nor the place to make such declarations," Ms. Waldgrave says in angry whispers.

Scarlett looks at Ms. Waldgrave's hand, gripping her arm until Sylvia lets go. She turns to the teacher and responds in harsh whispers as well.

"I know. But what I'm saying is we have plans. And while Duncan is not *in*, he's in. He cares for your daughter."

Ms. Waldgrave looks at her child as her lips move, telling some story. She turns back to Scarlett.

"He might care for her. And I hope he does. But I have seen him skulking around outside my house. I've chased him off, but he doesn't know I know it was him. And as for the other issue. Be careful where you tread. We have people who will take care of those things," Ms. Waldgrave says.

"Yeah. The Nation. They're doing a bang-up job too. The cop, the teacher, they're both still alive. The only reason the blond man is dead is because of Jack. Did you know that?" Scarlett lays it out on the table for her.

A look of confusion mixed with concern washes over Ms. Waldgrave's face. No words flow forth as she opens her mouth to speak. She closes her lips to pick her next words, but they never come.

Scarlett turns to walk away, knowing that Sylvia is not as informed as she was hoping.

"Scarlett," Ms. Waldgrave calls out to stop her. "I just don't trust him."

Scarlett turns back to her. "But your daughter does. So, even if you're right, trust her. She'll never learn otherwise."

Ms. Waldgrave smiles and huffs in amusement. "When did you get so smart?"

Scarlett grins and returns to her friends.

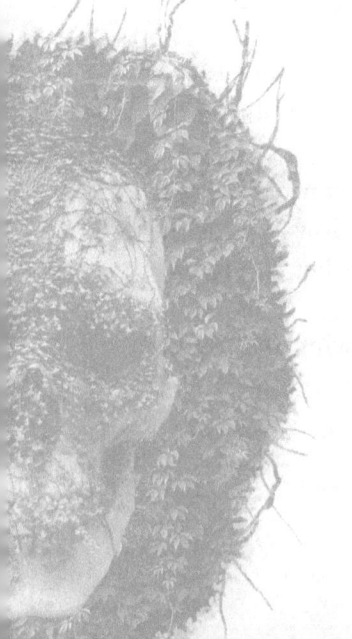

CHAPTER 16

"And many why we shouldn't."
~K. DeSalvo~

"'We need to talk,' you said. We are here. Talk," Vistrus gets straight to the point as the two sit in his museum office.

"Is it safe?" Sylvia asks. "I don't feel comfortable talking unless it's safe. I need to know it's safe."

He answers with a nod.

"What have you told them?" she asks.

"Told who?" he asks, unsure why they are having this conversation.

"The children. Our children. The ones in The Nation," she answers.

"About what?" He gets a little annoyed at her lack of specificity.

"The murders. The abductions. Everything that's been happening and uprooting their lives." Sylvia's anger grows at his playing dumb on the matter.

"You are not on the council. It is not…"

Sylvia snaps in an interruption. "Not yet, and yes, it is my concern," she says, mocking him. "It's become my concern. This is not just my family being attacked. It is me. I am taking the hits! All of them! At least currently. The DeSalvos and the Taylors took hits, and look what happened to them."

She grabs a face wipe from her purse and begins removing the concealer and foundation to reveal new bruises on top of old ones, all that were well concealed beyond what little showed through. Her face is a veritable Jackson Pollack of various blues, yellows, and purples.

"Why have you not come to me yet?" Vistrus asks, feeling the blame for her attacks.

"I have. Before I was attacked. I came forward when that damned parchment was found. I said something should be done. But did anyone listen? No. Sylvia couldn't possibly have anything of value." The volume in her voice rises.

"Why not after the attack?" he presses.

"Because you and the council still would have done nothing! I have to find out who is involved from a teenager! Not from an adult and definitely not a council member! That would have been too much work!" she says in full anger.

"What do you want us to do about it now? What can we do for you?" he asks.

She knows the question comes from the right place but also a place tainted by the poison of politics.

"It doesn't matter what I say. You and The Council will do nothing. And that is why I will never be on it. It's not that I'm not qualified; it's that I won't be complacent like you and the rest of those lackeys—too afraid to do what is needed because of diplomatic measures or some other reason. All of which are just excuses to hide behind, but no one will ever admit it. That might make you look like you don't always have the answers. No one believes it anymore," she says in defeat.

His face contorts in anger, and his lips part to speak, but he remains silent. He knows the words that Sylvia says are born from pain and frustration. He stays calm, though, because he thinks she might be right. He may have become too complacent about affairs with The Council.

He calms down further before speaking and feels newfound, growing respect for Sylvia.

"We have been looking into the murders. There is nothing that tells us the bigger picture behind them. The only lead we have is that the supplies came from the hospital," Vistrus offers up.

"Have you been back since? Have you found the mole? Has anything been done, or is The Council sitting on that information for a more convenient time?" Sylvia asks.

"Things were done," he starts with no hope in his voice. "The Doctor left for an extended business trip. No way to reach him."

"When did he leave for this trip?" Sylvia asks.

"Too long ago," he replies.

"Something is off. Doesn't something feel off? Feels off to me," she rambles.

He nods as the wheels are already turning in his head.

"How much do the kids know?" he asks.

"I'm not sure. At this point, I think just suspicions. What do you know they know?" She evades telling him the extent of what Scarlett told her.

"Jack knows, which I assume means the rest, too, know what he remembers from the abduction. Machines, injections, the blond man that he eliminated, the police..." Vistrus trails off.

"I know about the police. Everyone knows about the police. What do we do?" Sylvia asks, as her anger starts subsiding.

"Precisely why we have not found whoever killed the two families. We cannot risk going to law enforcement when one of them is against us," Vistrus warns. "We also know the hospital. But from those points, all our leads have dried up," Vistrus says, with a tinge of discouragement in his voice. "I do not know what to do anymore. The Council will not move without a solid lead. 'Any compromise to our cover is a compromise to our safety as a whole,' they say."

"These attacks on me..." Sylvia tries to suppress the vivid memories that well up tears, "...I don't think all of them were by the same man."

"What would make you say that?" Vistrus is intrigued by her theory.

"Most of them, all but one really; he wore a mask and scrubs," she says. "He would scream things about becoming one of us or just like us, some child-of-the-night baloney. Silly notions of a fanboy who's read too many comics and watched too many horror movies. Crazy kid, I say, but what does that matter? No one listens to little ol' Sylvia."

"Stop," Vistrus commands.

Sylvia snaps out of her distracted rant. "What?"

"If he is talking about becoming a 'child of the night,' that means he knows, or he is crazy," Vistrus postulates.

"That's what I was trying to say. If we don't know which it is, then we can't really do anything about it. Sometimes I feel like I have to spell everything out for you." Sylvia taps the side of her head. "Lack of picking up on subtext can be really annoying."

"So can babbling," he deadpans, looking her square in the eye.

She shuts up and looks down at his desk.

"So, what do we do?" she whispers.

Vistrus purses his lips in thought. He glances at an old picture of Inessa, as if to divine an answer.

"Until we know who he is, nothing," Vistrus replies.

A light bulb goes off in his head. A little smile crosses his lips. "You said he wore scrubs?"

"Yeah," Sylvia confirms. "Generic blue scrubs. I did see a tattoo on him. On his neck. It was one of those flu-de-flu things."

"Flu-de-flu?" Vistrus asks.

"Yeah. Those things that look like spearheads that curve outward. They put them on walls and clothes for decorations.

"Ah, the flu-de-flu, more commonly known as the fleur-de-lis," he chuckles.

And with that, an image flashes in his mind□the vision of the hospital worker in blue scrubs with a slight limp, his injured hands twirling his pendant. It has to be him. The intruder in Sylvia's home has to have supplied the people who tortured the DeSalvos and the Taylors.

"I know who he is. He is the leak! I was talking to him!" the anger in his voice rises. "I could have had him!"

Sylvia puts a hand on the desk. "We'll get him."

Vistrus does not take her hand in comfort, though he does inhale a deep breath to calm down.

Sylvia pulls her hand back. "So, what now?"

"What now, indeed? Keep yourself safe. The Council and I have much to discuss," Vistrus says to a less-than-satisfied Sylvia.

"Do we need to go in circles on this topic again?" she asks.

"No," he says with a specific authority that means business, "they will listen."

CHAPTER 17

"No matter what move you make,
ensure you can retreat, if needed,
and keep The Nation hidden."
~N. DeSalvo~

The closed window shades, drawn curtains, and yellow-hued lightbulb from the table lamps give Scarlett and Connor's house a look more akin to a secret meeting place than a house where people live, eat, and sleep. But the shadows cast on the walls and the little shards of moonlight that sneak in between the shades and curtains make sure the ominous look keeps in character with tonight's event. Scarlett and Allison sit on the couch across the coffee table from Duncan, who has pulled up a dining room chair.

The table is littered with loose-leaf paper held together to form a six-by-six, pieced-together monstrosity of clear tape and paper. The black pen scribbles are interrupted by the tape holding the battle plans together. A generic outline of a house and street is the main focus. The surrounding homes are an even more generic square, with a little room left over for the yard and fences.

Allison starts drawing their places for the assault on the map as the doorbell rings. She stops and looks at the other two in the room.

Duncan stands. "I invited someone."

Scarlett's eyes grow big. "This isn't exactly legal. Who are you dragging into this?"

Duncan opens the door to see Brianna in a baby blue sundress, her hair done up in something reminiscent of the 1950s. She waves to the group, still standing outside.

Scarlett scrunches her lips, as she waves her left hand out in front of her. "Come on in." The sound of disbelief at Duncan's invitation is evident in her voice.

The tone is not lost on Brianna. "If it's not okay, I can come back later."

As Scarlett looks at Allison, the de facto leader of this rebellion, she sees a sort of yearning in her eyes, as she stares at Brianna instead of her usual stern look of defiance. The kind of longing a puppy dog has when they are patiently waiting to be told they can eat the precariously balanced treat on their nose.

Scarlett shakes her head and looks back to the door. "Nope. I think you'll be needed. Just know what is said here tonight cannot leave this room. Is that understood, Duncan?"

He laughs. "Yeah, but I thought you'll need my peeps. No?"

"When that time comes, you can carefully choose your words. Until then, not a word. Understood?" Scarlett warns.

Duncan throws up his hands. "Loud and clear."

Brianna's innocence shines as she pulls a chair up to the coffee table turned battle board. "So, like, are we planning a surprise party or something?"

Allison chuckles. "Something like that, yeah. A surprise for sure."

Scarlett pipes up, "Bri, you're more than welcome here, but what we are planning … it's not all exactly…"

Allison takes the floor. "Legal. We're planning a sort of assault on a cop and a teacher. But they're bad people. Like, bad as bad comes."

Duncan chimes in with a creepy, rickety voice, "They make you rub the lotion on the skin! Wah-ha-ha!"

"What lotion?" Bri asks.

Duncan returns his voice to normal. "Just … never mind. They're not the good cops you run to when in trouble or the teacher you seek out when you need something."

Bri looks at Duncan, unsure if coming here was the best decision. He returns with a slight nod.

"You're sure?" she asks him.

He nods again.

Brianna takes a deep breath, trying to hold back the words she knows she is about to say. "Cool. I'm in."

Allison smiles at her, a friendly smile that Brianna has not seen in the last few years. "This is something that can affect the rest of our lives," Allison says to Bri.

"Just another in a long list of recent events," Bri snarks.

"Let's get to it." Allison claps. "Assuming this doesn't land us in jail or worse, Scarlett and I think it's best to make sure whatever homework we are assigned to do over winter break is finished before break begins. Yes, that means a lot of work leading up till then, since we might not get a chance to do it during break."

"But if we end up in prison or juvie, won't having done all that work be pointless?" Duncan illuminates a seemingly valid point.

"This is for the 'if we come out clean'," Scarlett answers.

Duncan and Brianna nod.

"Where's Jack?" Brianna looks around the room.

Duncan puts his hand on her leg and gives a few quick, slight shakes of his head.

"Sorry," Brianna whispers.

"We're doing this for him. But he doesn't need to know," Scarlett tells the group.

"So, what's the plan?" Duncan rubs his hands together.

Allison uses the pen and points to the streets in front of the house. "There are big oak trees on the properties between the street and the sidewalk. You and your guys will be here, providing lookout."

"Lookout? That's all?" Duncan sounds like he's been relegated to toilet duty.

"It's more important than you know. The house is a cop's house. He's married to the teacher. They are both involved in some bad stuff," Scarlett illuminates again.

"But lookout?" Duncan repeats in an almost petulant return.

"Yeah. Breaking into a cop's house can almost certainly bring more cops. And lucky for you and your disdain for authority, bad cops bring bad cops. The kind you like to tussle with," Scarlett explains further. "Your and your friends' job is to keep any authority figure from entering the house."

A smile crosses his face. "I think I can do that. But if it comes to that, it doesn't matter how much homework I'm ahead on; graduation will be off the table."

"What about us?" Bri asks, as if she is some badass character from a Guy Ritchie film.

"We go in," Allison continues. "You and Scarlett will knock on the front door. When she answers, say whatever it takes, do whatever it takes, to get inside. Getting inside is the most important part."

"Why?" Brianna asks, still mentally getting up to speed with the plan.

"'Cause while you two are getting in through the front door, I'll be sneaking in the basement," Allison smirks.

Duncan chimes in with a hint of excitement, "What happens once you're all inside?"

Allison and Scarlett both look at each other. This part of the plan they have yet to clearly hammer out. They both look silently while Bri and Duncan stare with cocked heads, like dogs trying to understand what their owners are saying to them.

Duncan lets out a laugh. "You two have no idea, do you?"

Allison pipes up, "Well, not exactly. Just different ideas of what we think should happen."

"Oh, that's great!" Duncan laughs. "You have this genius plan to break into two corrupt authority figures' house, and what, see what happens?"

"We like to say, play it by ear," Scarlett interjects.

Duncan laughs again. "Do you know who showed up and played it by ear? Napoleon. Napoleon showed up and just waited to see what happened. He played it by ear. Look how well that worked out for him."

"Didn't he die at Waterloo?" Allison asks.

Duncan shakes his head. "He was defeated there and died in exile on the island of St. Helena."

"So, what do you think we should do?" Scarlett proposes.

"What exactly did these two do that you can't just call the police on them?" Duncan asks.

"Kidnapped and killed Jack's family and almost killed Jack," Allison admits.

Duncan throws up his hands, waving them around. "Woah. Wait. Wait one second. Just hold on. You want to break into not only a cop's house but a murderer cop and his murdering wife's house while I stand outside and watch? Do you want to get yourself killed?"

Bri looks at the girls. "He still doesn't know."

Allison looks at Duncan. "Duncan, are you in?"

Duncan sits for a moment, shaking his head at the audacity and boldness of their plan. "Am I in? Man, this is deep. Like really deep. The Mariana Trench is shallow compared to this. Wow. Yeah. Fuck it. I'm in, but I'm going in with you. My guys will stand watch and do what needs done, but I'm going in with you."

"I'm not sure that's the best idea … you going in. Don't you think it's a bad idea, Bri?" Scarlett tries to steer her answer.

"I'm not sure any of us should be going in," Bri admits. "This night just took a serious turn to crazy town. Are we all sure this is what needs to be done?"

Scarlett and Allison both nod their heads. Duncan sits there, chuckling to himself at the ludicrousness of the situation. Brianna tosses glances between the other three, trying to figure out if this is all some sort of joke or prank or something.

Allison sits a little straighter in her chair. "The so-called authorities can't, or plain won't, do anything about it. Our Declaration of Independence even states that ... and I'm sure what I am saying is pretty damn close ... whenever a government becomes destructive, it's up to the people to do something about it, make it right so as they seem safe and happy."

All of them just stare at her, shocked at the recall function of her memory at the moment.

After a long silent minute or two of being stared at, Allison urges a response from the rest. "Well?"

"Never in a million would I ever have thought my helping you for your course last year would have stuck with you. I'm so proud of you right now." Scarlett waves off the tears she's holding back like a proud mother.

"Damn, Allison," Duncan smiles. "That was inspiring."

"Yeah," Allison says, as if she knows this already, "we had some pretty bad mofos who were pissed off at England a long time ago."

Bri shakes her head, laughing at the situation before them. "Fine. Duncan, you're in with us. But no matter what happens in there, no matter what you see, you say nothing to anyone but us three. Or you will never touch this body again." She points to herself with both index fingers.

Not wanting to make light of a serious situation, Duncan keeps cute quips to himself. "So, when exactly is this all going down then?" he asks.

"December 30th. Make sure your boys' calendars are cleared that day. Shit's about to get real," Allison declares.

CHAPTER 18

"Sometimes, your cup will runneth over.
Don't drown in the overflow."
~E. DeSalvo~

The weeks that fill between their plan of approach to the execution of their assault are anything but a soothing calm before the storm for Allison, which in turn, makes them stormy as well for Scarlett. Connor's uncharacteristic distance from his girlfriend and his family, the dwindling text messages and calls—from good morning, beautiful and good night, sleepy head to skipped days to being almost nil—all slowly start eating away at Allison. Allison desperately clings to the belief that he is still the same old Connor they all remember from a few months ago and not this changed person who pushed away his hometown the moment he left.

Right now, though, minutes before her school day begins, in the middle of the hall while hunched in her locker, none of that matters. Allison needs calm, needs a moment of serenity where her mind isn't filled by all the nagging thoughts that usually reside there. She opens an opaque red water bottle and drinks a long-needed, throat-burning drink of whatever long-forgotten alcohol she filled it with last. A soothing stream of liquid to wash away all those bitter thoughts and bring a sense of calm.

The concealment by the stream of students and the ten-inch deep walls of her locker and locker door is all she needs to keep her secret safe.

As the burn works its way through her mouth and down her throat, she can feel the sting of Connor's absence drifting away. She can feel the numbing agents diligently doing their job as she mentally pre-pares herself for the upcoming event, the event that hasn't been spoken of since the night at Scarlett's. She can feel all cares of what might happen to her in the future slip away, as she finishes the remains of the water bottle before tucking it back into its hiding place.

She hopes she can still pass for sober in these high school halls.

Allison strolls the hallway to the girl's locker room to change for gym class. She walks down the stairwell to the first floor with surgeon-like precision, a sign that, perhaps, the remains of her water bottle were a bit too much for the moment. But she feels good, of clear mind and soul. Or at least of clear soul. Her mind, on the other hand, quickly becomes clouded.

After successfully descending the stairs, she con-tinues down the long hallway to the locker room. She laughs to herself in amusement at how much time students spend going from hall to hall just to get in and out of one locker or another all year long.

Before that thought has any time to manifest into a semblance of an existential crisis for Allison, she sees Duncan standing at the corner of the hall talking with his crew.

She saunters on up, hoping she looks far more casual than she imagines. In her mind, she wants to come across as cool and collected—a runway model with calm confidence. She feels she might be coming across more as a drunken pirate holding a jug of rum. Not the image she wants any of her teachers to see.

"Well, hello there, Duncan," she says. A little bit of pirate creeps out in her voice as the thought overtakes her speech.

Duncan, arms crossed, and his friends all turn to her. The crowd of students in the halls starts to dwindle. But there are still those around, those who can't be seen as they walk the side halls closer to where Allison, Duncan, and the rest stand. One such person walking in their direction is Linda Espinoza. Of all the people who aren't supposed to hear what might be said next, Linda is top of that list.

"Allison," Duncan says, with a head tilt and slightly amused smile, "these are some of my friends."

She turns to them and gives a sloppy wave. "What's up, guys?"

Duncan leans in but is no quieter. "Late night?"

Allison laughs at his question. "No, no, no." She changes to a whisper, "Long morning."

Duncan raises a brow and uncrosses his arms. "Everything good?"

"Perfect." she forces out a smile. "So?"

"So, I was just telling them about our plans," he whispers, slightly softer than his normal speaking voice.

The footsteps around the corner caught the last of his sentence. Nothing that sounds sinister but enough to catch the attention of someone with something sinister to hide. Linda stops and turns an ear in their direction.

"Ah, yes. The plans. Doomsday is coming, boys. Don't let the sweet face of this girl fool ya!" Allison points at her face and then at them. "Christmas Day might be all roasted chestnuts and sleigh bells, but a few days later … well, that day will not be forgotten soon."

Duncan pipes up, "You never told me who it was. Which teacher did all those things? I can't look at any of them without wonderin' what they hide behind their smiles."

"Don't forget the cop," Allison adds.

One of the other boys laughs. "Damn blue-badge tweakers. This sounds like a fun time."

"The 30th, we get payback on that bitch and her husband for Connor and Jack," Allison says with a clenched fist.

From around the corner, Linda turns back to head in the direction from which she was walking. Her pace is anything but casual. She has a sense of urgency in her step that warns she will not be stopped for anything.

But to the kids around the other corner of this hall, it is business as usual. "I gotta change for gym. See you soon, Duncan," Allison says, sauntering off.

The toe of her shoe catches on the ground as she turns the corner. This little misstep causes her to look down to see what almost caused her to trip. As Allison looks back up, she sees, only in a glance, who she thinks is Linda turning into the short hall that leads to a stairwell that rises to all three floors and has an exit to the teacher's lounge on this floor.

Allison turns the opposite direction into the locker room a few yards short of the stairwell Linda ducked into. As she changes into her speckled blue gym uniform T-shirt and solid blue basketball shorts, the image of the glance, the smile that Allison thinks she saw planted on teacher Espinoza's face, lingers. A wry smile that hints at something more than pleasantries, a sinister hue beneath the top layers of rose-gilded kindness.

Allison and Scarlett sit eating lunch among the other students, eager to finish this last day of school before winter break.

Scarlett picks a fry up off her tray. "Why are you in your gym uniform?"

Allison tosses a chicken nugget into her mouth, "'Cause stupid-ass gym coach insisted on doing a final."

Scarlett swallows her fry and chomps down on another. "A final for gym? That's so ridiculous!"

"Yup." Allison sips on a fountain soda.

"I just like the fact the cafeteria is open today for anyone who has breaks between finals," Scarlett observes.

But Allison is lost in thought as she looks around at all the other students eating, chatting, and goofing off with each other.

"Everyone is so excited for winter break. I bet Connor doesn't come home," Allison notes while staring off into space.

Scarlett takes a deep breath to ready herself for the conversation ahead.

"He's been on break since Thanksgiving and nothing. He's forgotten all about his family, his friends, his girlfriend." Allison's voice grows unconsciously louder and louder.

Scarlett extends her hand to calm her down. "Look around, Al. Look at all these people."

Allison tries to look past the surface to see what lies beneath as she grabs Scarlett's hand.

"They are all going home for the holidays. Time to be with family and friends we consider family. But even while they are doing all that, they still have their own issues. Issues no one outside their select few in their circle know about." Scarlett squeezes Allison's hand.

"I don't see it. I try, but I don't. I see everyone else having fun while I sit here not," Allison admits in self-defeat.

"They don't see your budding conflict with being what we are. And we don't see the kid struggling with whatever it is they are struggling with. But they have fun. Try to make the most of what they can." Scarlett tries in vain to cheer her up.

"I know. I just feel that with the things we are finding out, that getting out of West Haven might actually never happen," Allison admits.

"I don't get it. Connor's out ... for at least the school year," Scarlett observes.

"Yeah, and he's way out. Like radio silence out. Amnesia of who and what he left behind." Allison's words are grim.

Scarlett sits back in her seat because she knows that Allison has a point. Her cousin hasn't exactly been around, either literally or metaphorically, since school began. She knows deep down that she can make all the excuses for him that she wants, but he is the one who has seemingly cut them out. Connor is the one who made a mess of his relationship. Scarlett is the one left to clean it up, time and time again.

CHAPTER 19

Christmas Day

"Moments of joy are sparse these days.
Enjoy them when you can."

~B. Scott~

The elder DeSalvo residence is modestly decorated for the holiday celebration. A tree with various colored lights and a mix of whimsy and sentimental ornaments stands watch over a large picture window. The lights add a warm glow to the festive decorations around the room. A few presents under the tree are addressed to the various people here this evening, as well as to one who has been absent for a while.

A small tray of select cheeses and meats sits on the coffee table, and a platter piled high with Russian Tea Cookies is on the dining room table. Allison fills a small paper plate with a dozen cookies. On the kitchen counter rests a pot roast cooked to a perfect medium-rare, along with potato salad, green bean casserole, and various grilled vegetables.

Everyone is gathered in the living room as Allison enters with her plate of cookies and takes a seat next to Jack and Scarlett.

"Jack," Eleanor starts, "thank you for taking us up on the invitation to join us. I hope you are enjoying yourself."

Jack nods his head. "Thank you, ma'am. It's nice to, uh, have a place to be ... on such a night." His voice speeds and slows as his pitch fluctuates. "I apologize about not, well, bringing a gift or a bottle ... or a gift bottle."

Eleanor smiles. "It's okay, young man."

The doorbell rings.

Allison points with her finger as she counts the people in the room, trying to figure out who could be at the door. "Me, Dad, Scar, Jack, Grams. Connor coming?"

Vistrus stands up. "I will get the door."

Eleanor smiles. "I figured with renewed friendships come renewed traditions."

"So, no Connor," Allison laments.

"Sorry, dear," Eleanor apologizes. "He's stuck at school. Some team thing or another. Just never know with kids nowadays."

"Is Gramps gonna be here? I haven't seen him in, like, forever," Scarlett asks.

Eleanor continues smiling. "He, unfortunately, can't be here. He's away on business. But he said he made it up to all of you under the tree."

Vistrus opens the door to see Sylvia and Brianna holding a plate of brownies.

"Merry Christmas, Mr. Petrovsky." Brianna hands him the plate of brownies.

"A happy holiday to you as well, young Waldgrave," he replies.

They enter and shake off the cold.

Sylvia follows Vistrus to the dining room table as he sets the brownies down.

Eleanor looks at Scarlett, Allison, and Jack. "I thought it would be nice since rumor has it you are all friends again."

Allison huffs in amusement. "Rumor has it."

"Hey, Bri, Merry Christmas," Scarlett says with a smile.

"Where's Connor?" Bri asks innocently enough.

Allison's tense face warns Bri not to push the question further.

"We're not talking about that right now," Scarlett cautions in a friendly tone.

Allison shakes her head. "I've been wondering what it will take to get him home for a weekend or even a day."

Eleanor interjects, "He needs his space. It can be difficult adjusting to a new environment. I know you all understand how hard change can be."

"But Grams, he's not even here for Christmas. That's not right." Scarlett takes Allison's side.

"Until we know why, we mustn't judge," Eleanor advises. She stands up from her chair. "Excuse me while I go say hello to your mother, Brianna."

Eleanor makes her way to Vistrus, who now stands at the dining room table, laying out the brownies around the Russian Tea Cakes.

Eleanor whispers, "We should talk."

Vistrus looks around the house. "The den."

Sylvia follows Vistrus as he walks off. Eleanor snatches a few Russian Tea Cookies for herself before leaving the table.

They take a seat away from the young adults in the other room. Some things are not meant for their ears.

"The Council is lost," Eleanor says in hushed tones too quiet for Normal ears.

Vistrus raises a brow. "Nothing more on the prophecy?"

Eleanor shakes her head.

In the other room, Allison picks up hints of whispers from the adults. She bends her ear to them.

Scarlett notices Allison trying to eavesdrop but doesn't stop her. She is interested in what Al hears.

Jack and Brianna, however, seem to not notice and continue eating the cheese and meats in front of them.

Allison motions to Scarlett and silently excuses herself to the kitchen.

Jack looks up at Allison, but Scarlett is the one who responds. "Grabbing sodas for everyone."

That said, he nods and turns back to his cubes of cheese.

Allison creeps into the kitchen, closer to the den's other entrance but stays out of the adult's sight, who are too engaged in their conversation to notice.

Eleanor continues, "With the death of Tracy and her unborn child…"

Before Eleanor can finish the sentence, Allison shouts in shock and disbelief, "Mrs. DeSalvo was pregnant!"

All eyes in the house now point toward the kitchen. From the living room, Scarlett shoots to a standing position. "Aunt Tracy was pregnant!"

Brianna and Jack, unsure of how to react, sit stunned. They stop chewing the meat and cheese in their mouths and let them rest for the moment while the reality of the situation sets in.

Vistrus takes a deep breath, realizing that perhaps a more significant distance was needed, but also that his daughter's intrusion was on the disrespectful side.

Eleanor hangs her head, knowing it was only a matter of time.

Sylvia, ever the apt one in uncomfortable situations, stands up and walks to the kitchen. "I need a martini. Have any Vermouth?"

Without thinking, Eleanor responds, "Cabinet above the sink." She turns to Vistrus. "I don't think all is lost."

"Why would you say that?" Vistrus asks with a heavy heart.

"I do not believe a prophecy written so long ago could be defeated so easily," Eleanor grins. "Assuming it holds any water."

A weak smile crosses Vistrus's lips in hopes she is correct.

Scarlett races into the den. "I was going to have a little cousin? Tiny socks and feet and all?"

"Yes, my dear," Eleanor responds, "but we were not at liberty to say anything until it was no longer possible to hide."

"Why would you have to hide a baby?" Allison asks.

Brianna and Jack are both still sitting uncomfortably in the other room. They slowly start chewing their mouthfuls of cheese and meat again, as if the noise could be distracting or if they shouldn't be chewing in the first place.

"Take a seat, children," Eleanor says.

Scarlett and Allison sit on the carpeted floor facing the three adults.

"There is a prophecy, written long ago, of a Legend. One that will unite the Legends with the Normals. So that we can live as we are without fear of persecution, without fear of hate, or prejudice. A Legend born, a once thought to be extinct Legend, the Grey Fairy." Eleanor pauses and looks at the young women sitting before her. Their eyes locked onto the elder. "The genetics of which split long ago to form two fairy Legends. The Light and The Dark."

Allison throws up her hands. "Wait a second. Are you talking like a good and evil split? That sounds a bit crazy, even for us."

"No, my child. Good and evil is a matter of perspective. Light and Dark, as in different traits," Eleanor begins to explain. Brianna walks into the den with Jack. They take a seat next to Allison and Scarlett, respectively.

"A Dark Fairy will have skin like a tree, earth-like features to distinguish their Legendary form. A Light Fairy is something more akin to a ghost, transparent in their true form."

"Then why not, like, you know, call them, uh, ghosts." Jack's tone is his usual timid nature.

265

Eleanor smiles. "The world is a much more complicated place than you know."

Allison thinks back to that day—the blood, the chaos, the mess, and the carnage. She pictures the bodies in her head, the mutilations, and all the grotesque images ingrained in her mind.

"Her stomach wasn't cut," Allison says.

"We know," Eleanor says in a gentle voice.

Vistrus chimes in, "The Council does not think the person who killed them knew she was pregnant."

"Is this the same person who's been attacking Sylvia?" Scarlett asks.

Shattering glass and spilling liquids on the floor echo in the kitchen.

"Mom?! You've been attacked! More than once!" Brianna finally speaks up.

"We will talk about this later! I have to clean this mess up." Sylvia shuts down that topic.

"We do not think so," Vistrus answers.

"Dad, we need more than that. We are adults now and have figured out a lot of what you all have been trying to hide," Allison demands. "I think it's time to fill us in."

Vistrus wants to smile because he sees his daughter growing up in front of his eyes, but he knows she is still so young, and with youth comes youthful naivety and reactionary behavior. He knows that he cannot hide the world from her forever.

"We believe the person who has assaulted Sylvia was the same person who gave the supplies to the blond man and the officer who kidnapped and tortured Jack and his parents," Vistrus says.

"And killed them and the DeSalvos," Allison says, anger seething in her words.

"Yes," Vistrus confirms, "but what The Council and we do not understand is why we are being attacked."

"Hunted is more like it," Allison blurts out.

"To cure us," Jack mutters.

"What was that, dear?" Eleanor says, trying to get him to speak up.

"To cure us," Jack repeats at a louder volume.

"Death is not a cure," Sylvia interjects from the kitchen.

"We fought back," Jack says. "He wanted samples to study, then he was going to kill us anyway. We were his samples, his guinea pigs." Tears start falling from his eyes as he relives the horrific event in his head.

"I think they have it," Sylvia says, as the sound of broken glass falling into the garbage can is heard.

"The man who attacked me, one time he transitioned. He didn't the other two times," Sylvia informs them.

"Oh my God, Mom! How many times have you been assaulted?!" Brianna shouts in disbelief.

"Three! Three times! I didn't tell you because I was trying to keep you safe." Sylvia's stern words attempt to carry the group conversation forward.

"But if Ms. Walgrave is right and they have the cure, or at least a way to level the battlefield, then why keep attacking us?" Scarlett asks.

"They are hunting the Grey Fairy," Brianna says in a moment of clarity.

All their heads in the room turn to Brianna.

"Explain," Vistrus urges.

"The attacks started when Mrs. DeSalvo was hiding her pregnancy, right? So, that means as much as, whoever these people are, didn't know or acted like they didn't know we all exist, they did. And they probably knew about the prophecy of the Grey Fairy. So, they find a way to make them like us, which is just so not cool; then they start hunting down the one thing that would actually create a level playing field," Brianna explains.

Scarlett pipes up, "It's a classic power struggle. They, again, whoever they are, are trying to keep an upper hand over us because of fear that if we somehow gain control, they will be under us instead of even with us."

"Intelligent words from young mouths," Eleanor notes.

"Fuck that!" Allison shouts. "Excuse my language, Father. But if these people are hunting us because of who we are, then we should take them out. Especially since they killed a pregnant woman! A whole family wiped out because they are different?! Not cool. Not cool at all!"

"What would you expect us to do?" Vistrus postulates.

"Nothing, Dad. We got this," she snortles.

Vistrus tries to explain. "This is not Sparta, Allison. You cannot just eye for an eye everything wrong that happens to you."

Jack sits with thoughts racing through his mind, making him second-guess where he stands on all the issues he thought he had sorted out. "Letting sleeping dogs lie means, well, uh, they will still wake up. And once they are, uh, awake, who knows what they will do."

Scarlett stands up. "Stop! Everyone!"

They all turn their attention to her.

"Let me make sure I understand this. A group of unknown individuals is hunting Legends to cure us, but we think that cure is actually giving Normals our Legendary abilities. And they are really doing this to stop a prophecy from happening, which might not be able to be stopped because it's a prophecy, in order to maintain some sort of hierarchical control over the population in fear of losing said control. All because they are afraid that if we gain control, we will treat them like they treat us instead of as equals?"

The group sits with tilted heads, trying to take in the seeming absurdity of the situation at hand, all while realizing that, as absurd as it sounds, people have died because of the apparent line of thinking.

"Yes?" Eleanor questions her response. "Putting it in those words does make it seem rather ludicrous."

"This is heavy," Allison sighs.

"So not cool," Brianna thinks out loud.

Jack raises his hand, "So, um, what do we, well, do?"

"What do we do, indeed," Vistrus ponders.

But while the adults wonder what can be done diplomatically, Scarlett, Allison, and Brianna all toss each other wry smiles, knowing what they plan to do.

CHAPTER 20

"Loss never gets easy."
~D. Childers~

Scarlett stands in front of her bathroom mirror. She tries to apply a deep red shade of lipstick while smiling ear to ear. She can't stop thinking about the night ahead—date night with Jack, the first in a long time and a welcome distraction from the planned siege in a few days. There is a part of her that feels guilty over the fact that Connor still hasn't come home for break, and Allison will be left to her own devices after she gets off work tonight. But for whatever guilt she feels, the thought of the theater seats, extra buttery popcorn, a large, sugary soda, gummy bears, and being with Jack creates excited butterflies in her tummy that far outweigh anything else. Adding to her butterflies is the fact that Jack was kind enough to let her gawk at Jason Mamoa for two and a half hours.

Scarlett again tries to apply the red lip color while smiling, but she can't stop. Her phone buzzes as it sits on the counter next to the sink faucet. Her already wide smile tries to expand even further as she sees a text come through.

[Jack: Hopping in the shower now. Be there in about half-hour.]

[Scarlett: K. Love you.]

A simple reply that reads so much. A two-word message says all he needs to know about how she feels. And, of course, one letter that lets him know she got his text in the first place. But it is the latter two words that bring a smile to her face—the thought of someone to share herself with in every way: her thoughts, her dreams, her desires, and yes, herself too.

Scarlett checks the time as she closes the messenger app—8:00 p.m. More than enough time to pick her up, grab a quick bite to eat, and get to the 11:30 p.m. showing.

She stares at herself in the mirror, looks at her smile, and lets the butterflies float through her. Scarlett can feel her heart pounding in her chest. She might see Jack every day, but nights out like tonight, when it is just the two of them, are few and far between. She does not resent Allison for it, though. They are best friends and always welcome, but Scarlett is finding out that as relationships grow, so does the need for time with just your partner.

Her excitement for the evening keeps swelling inside her. She finally gets the lipstick applied to her smile and moves on to finish the look off with some mascara, except she notices that her face is looking pale. She steps back from the mirror and takes another look. She looks like herself—her deep red lips are still the same red as a moment ago, but her skin is a touch paler. She looks at the light bulbs that shine down on the mirror to see if something is amiss with them. But everything seems normal, except her suddenly pale skin.

Her heart races more.

Her skin all over her neck, torso, and arms suddenly feels like a thousand tiny, red ants are chomping down and embedding microscopic shards of glass all over. She looks at her skin in the mirror and sees nothing. She turns to herself and starts scratching at the nothing that is there.

Her heart pounds harder.

Scarlett leaves behind tiny, red streaks up and down her arms, as she scratches at whatever is causing the pain. She scratches uncontrollably for countless seconds as the pain and itch intensify. The seconds turn to minutes as the red streaks deepen, and tiny red dots of blood pool on the surface of her arms.

She takes a deep breath in to try and control the pain. Her heart starts to slow, and she takes another deep breath. She can feel the itching and stinging sensations begin to slowly subside. Deep breath after deep breath, she stands in front of the mirror with her eyes closed. Deep breath after deep breath, she feels her adrenaline calm as the itch and burn get softer and softer.

The sensation has passed. The invisible ants have retreated to their colony, and the tiny shards of glass have been cleaned out. The only remnants are the red scratch marks accented by the tiny blood droplets on the surface.

CHAPTER 20

Scarlett finishes applying her mascara and looks down at her phone. 8:52. How long had she scratched? How long had she breathed slowly in and out? Apparently much longer than she thought. It seemed like only moments ago that she read Jack's text. She opens her phone and the messaging app to see if she somehow missed a text from him. Nothing. No notifications across the top of her phone. She checks her missed calls log but again comes up empty. She knows that even if Jack showed up now, they would have more than enough time for dinner before the movie. His tardiness is what has her concerned. She shoots him a quick text.

[Allison: Where you at?]

And shuts down her screen and double-checks her makeup.

She grabs her phone off the sink counter and plops down on the couch, flipping her legs lengthwise. She swipes the screen to access her phone and notices still no response from Jack. She touches his name to call him.

Her chest has a sinking feeling that something is just not right. She starts to think that maybe Jack got pulled over, and it is taking a while for some reason. Then she thinks, *What if it was Officer Max who pulled him over?* Now her heart starts beating harder. She can feel it in her chest, more aware of its presence. The thoughts continue: thoughts of Jack having slipped, fallen, and cracked his head, thoughts of him lying in a ditch somewhere.

The phone rings once. Not a big deal if he doesn't pick up after one ring. No one ever really does.

The phone rings twice. Scarlett is sure he'll answer and make some corny joke about running late. But he doesn't answer.

The phone rings a third time. Maybe he left it in his bedroom, and he has to run from another room to get it. No worries. He'll answer.

Fourth ring. All previous morbid thoughts fly out of her head. She is going to pick him up, but she has to tell Allison what's going on.

Voicemail. The dreaded conclusion to an unanswered call. The greeting that, while it sounds pleasant to her, means whatever is going on will be anything but.

She hangs up the call and dials Allison, as she hops off the couch and puts on her shoes.

Allison picks up as if she is waiting for a call.

"You still at work?" Scarlett asks with a shaky voice.

"What's going on? You sound like something's wrong." Allison notices the strain in Scarlett's voice.

"Jack was supposed to be here like half an hour ago. He's not picking up, not returning my texts. I gotta get to his house." The speed of Scarlett's speech increases with each word spoken.

Scarlett can hear Allison say something to someone close by on her end. Though the person's response is just a whisper, the tone sounded good. "I'm coming to get you. Be outside."

Scarlett paces the sidewalk outside her house for a good five minutes until she hears the screeching tires of Vistrus's Solstice turn the corner. As soon as Allison pulls up, Scarlett hops in, and they are off.

They arrive at Jack's house to see his car is still in the driveway. Allison barely puts the car in park before the two are out their doors.

As they approach the house, they hear nothing. An eerie silence thickens as they make their way to the front door. Despite the interior lights that seep out of the drawn shades and blinds and the porch light on, Scarlett is immediately thrown back to prom night last year—the darkness that overtook everything she saw, the unsettling, nauseating feeling in her gut that kept poking at her to dry heave. All those feelings are back. They hear nothing coming from inside. No footsteps racing to the door. But then again, they didn't ring the doorbell. The girls didn't honk the car horn.

They turn the knob to find it unlocked. Scarlett creaks open the door. They peek inside and are immediately overtaken by the chaos. Blood splattered everywhere grips their attention. Overturned furniture and bookshelves litter the floor. A giant hole is torn into the wall where a bookshelf once stood. The debris of the drywall is scattered everywhere but is almost lost amongst the rest of the rubble. A small vial that seems out of place, and is unfamiliar to Scarlett, lay overturned on the ground. Scarlett and Allison stand shocked, unable to move in the violent silence that envelops them.

While frozen in the sheer terror of the sights before them, they hear a faint cough from Jack's bedroom. The path there shows signs of the struggle—smeared, bloody handprints on the walls, torn and broken walls, broken pictures, and destroyed memories of the lives that once lived here. There is no time for the girls to linger in the hall or be held back by the fright of what might lie ahead. They heard a cough; they must get to Jack.

Inside his bedroom, they find everything in disarray. Jack, in full Legendary form, lies in a puddle of his own blood, still flowing from his wounds. His long, blood-matted hair conceals the gouged injuries beneath. Blood stains his fangs. Surrounded by strewn papers, video games, and DVDs, his eyes cry for help. His 24" flat screen television lay broken on the floor, not far from him. His bed and dresser are the only things left that haven't been destroyed.

Jack looks at Scarlett with sullen, desperate eyes. A mix of blood and saliva seeps out of his mouth. There is no attempt at a smile. Both girls rush to his side, unsure of what to do.

Scarlett cradles Jack in her arms. She watches as he struggles to catch each breath. Each moment becomes more difficult for him to stay within this mortal coil.

"I'm here, Jack. Stay with me, my love," Scarlett whispers to him.

The reality of the situation sinks in for Scarlett. Tears stream down her face as she holds her boyfriend. Jack looks into her eyes with a failing hope that something can be done to save him. Scarlett's eyes don't leave his, afraid to see the extent of the damage done to him. She doesn't want to know; she wants to be here with him. Scarlett wants Jack to know she loves him and will be with him till the end.

Jack musters up the strength to try and speak but is met with a cough that sprays Scarlett with specks of his blood. She doesn't flinch at the cough or the blood and continues holding him.

Jack, again, struggles to take a breath in but manages to hold it without coughing. "She said ... doomsday's... come early."

The energy it took to speak those words sends him into a coughing spasm. Blood and sputum spray from his mouth as Scarlett strokes his hair, trying to calm him down.

Allison snaps out of her horrified daze and pulls out her cell phone. She dials.

"Daddy! Come to Jack's!" Allison cries into her phone. "Hurry!" she cries as she hangs up her phone. The panic in her voice leaves no room for doubt in her father's mind. He has to drop everything and get to Jack's house.

Scarlett frantically combs her fingers through his hair, trying to coax more out of Jack as she whispers words of encouragement. The signs of life fade fast from the young man. His last words echo in her mind, "Doomsday's come early."

Words that hold a vague familiarity for Allison. Then it hits her, words that were spoken at school. In a private conversation.

Allison knows it was Linda who did this. A teacher, a person of authority, and someone who is supposed to be a role model for the youth of today. Someone granted a certain amount of trust for merely being in their position betrays everything that being a teacher stands for.

Allison breaks into hysterics as the image of Linda's cryptic smile as she disappeared into the side hallway creeps back into her mind, an image that her subconscious forces on her. In this moment, surrounded by the chaos of death, she knows why Linda smiled that smile. She heard, and this was the teacher's response.

The girls sit with Jack as the last light of life leaves his eyes. The only sounds they hear are their own cries and tears dripping into the puddles around them.

Scarlett and Allison slow their tears and calm down for the moment. The silence consumes them. They feel trapped and unable to move. The grotesque nature of their immediate surroundings is too surreal to comprehend.

From outside the bedroom door, they hear the main door open. Allison's father's loud, worried voice calls out to them as he enters the carnage.

Vistrus surveys the scene. A scene that is all too familiar to a Legend and all too common as of late. He spots among the debris of the struggle a small, 21-gram vial, uncorked and empty. An overwhelming sadness takes over him. He picks up the cork that lay nearby and closes the bottle. He holds it in his hand when he hears his daughter's voice.

"Daddy!" Allison cries out.

Vistrus strides to the sound of his daughter and finds the girls frozen in disbelief at their ever-shrinking world. He sees Scarlett still clutching her lifeless Jack. His little Allison stares blankly, stripped of any last remaining innocence she may have been holding onto.

Scarlett looks at her friend's father and sees the vial gripped tight in his hand. "Why are you taking that?" The sound in her voice is distant, as if she says the words but isn't in her mind to have spoken them. A detached body that still functions but has no thoughts to accompany it.

Vistrus looks down at his hand, then at Jack. He searches carefully for words more delicate than he is used to. "These vials. They hold our 21 grams. They are what keep us alive."

Scarlett stares past him as he speaks, her words not hearing what he says. Background noise in an otherwise silent world.

Vistrus looks at his daughter as she stares at Jack and Scarlett.

"Daddy!" she calls out again. He is unsure if she is aware he is there or if she needs him to hold her. So, he does. He holds on tight to the vial while embracing his daughter. Allison collapses in his arms as she falls back to the reality surrounding her.

Vistrus embraces his daughter while he looks toward Scarlett. "I am very sorry for your loss."

Vistrus allows the girls to cry until they are too tired to cry any longer. He sits with them, surrounded by the chaos from the night's earlier events, as the sounds of young girls' agony fill his ears. He sits as the emotions surrounding him build and swell like vicious waves pounding against them all. But like all storms, they eventually calm and then end, leaving the three of them sitting with Jack, keeping their departed company a little longer.

Scarlett stares blankly at Vistrus. She doesn't need to say anything, as even he knows the blank expression on her face is asking what they need to do next.

"It is not healthy to stay here. We need to go back to our house and make arrangements," Vistrus says in a gentle yet nudging voice.

The girls stand as if automated to do so. This is not the first time each of them has had to abandon the bodies of those they cared for. They take empty steps away from Jack, leaving all emotions they feel in the room with him. They do not like this life that is being thrust upon them. And for the tiniest fraction of a second, Allison feels jealous of Jack's release. Then the guilt floods in. A deluge of voices in her head telling her she is wrong and that to be envious of the dead serves no good. The immediate guilt starts eating at her from the inside. A stinging sensation in her stomach causes her to vomit as she steps. A flow of bile and fast food spewing forth, landing in front of her on the bloodstained carpet in Jack's bedroom. She turns to her father.

"We should clean this up," Allison states in a sedated voice.

His father nods. "I shall take care of it later. You need to get home." He puts his arm around her shoulder.

Allison nods in defeat as Vistrus walks her out. The stinging sensation is more subtle than a moment ago but building back up. She makes it outside without any further incidents.

Vistrus gets Allison situated in his car without a fuss. Her complacency makes easy work of things. He belts her in, as she is still in shock and unresponsive to her surroundings for the moment.

Outside the car, he pulls out his cell phone. He dials a number and waits. His eyes dart around his surroundings.

"We need an immediate, total cleanse at the Taylor residence." Vistrus's tone is serious yet solemn. "We are leaving now."

Now he must get Scarlett.

He heads back into the house of horror to find Scarlett still standing in the same spot she rose from a few moments ago. Her gaze is fixed on Jack, unwilling to let go of the moment or leave her love.

Vistrus stands in the doorway to Jack's bedroom. He watches as Scarlett stares at Jack's body, looking at the long, blood-matted hair covering his body. Scarlett looks into his eyes, hoping for some sign of life. That this is all some super elaborate and tremendously ill-conceived joke, but it is not. A part of her knows it is not, and he is gone. It is that part that keeps her stuck here, the part that knows he has unwillingly left his friends and his loved ones behind to be one with the universe again. A feeling grows in Scarlett's stomach, too. A sense that burns and boils. A tiny fireball waits patiently to unleash its fury on whoever the soul is that did this to her man. Allison's desire to eliminate the murderers of the first set of killings is now matched by Scarlett's rage. A rage that burns white-hot in her mind.

"Scarlett," Vistrus calls to her, still standing in the open doorway.

The rage inside Scarlett quiets its voice. It calms down enough that she can hide her desires, momentary or otherwise, from the elder in front of her. She turns to him.

"We need to leave. I have people on the way to be with him. He will not be alone," Vistrus assures her.

He puts his arm around Scarlett's shoulder as she walks to him. He feels the tenseness from the weight that she burdens. He says nothing but knows the feeling. He worries how someone her age will be able to handle what he struggles with at a much more experienced age. But for now, he remains silent.

Scarlett settles into the car next to Allison. They stay silent but stare at each other, sharing their pain and anger.

Vistrus starts the car and pulls out into the street. In the rearview mirror, he sees a white cargo van turn onto the road. A sad smile crosses his face as he now awaits the nightly news.

Later, as the morning sun rises, turning that dreadful night into day, the girls sit on the couch at Allison's house. The morning news drones on the television in front of them, but they aren't really paying attention.

"Is that what it was like?" Scarlett asks while staring forward.

"Was what 'what it was like?'" Allison responds while also staring straight past the screen of the television.

"When you found Aunt Tracy and Uncle Ken." Scarlett's answer is without emotion.

"What was it like when you went to Jack's after prom?" Allison volleys back.

Vistrus hangs up his cell phone as he enters the living room. "Arrangements have already been made for a service."

Scarlett looks at Vistrus. "But there was so much hair."

"It will be a closed casket. No one will see him," Vistrus replies with soft words.

"So that's it. I never get to see Jack again," Scarlett notes aloud.

Before Vistrus can respond, the newscaster catches the girls' attention. "In West Haven this morning, a fire has completely engulfed a residence on the Northwest side. We're live on the scene with Summer Winds. Summer?"

The screen cuts to a live feed of a female reporter standing outside the Taylor residence as a firetruck attempts to douse the flames that leap from the roof and windows.

"Thank you, Rose. I'm standing here as…" Summer begins. But the girls' attention fades from the television and shifts to Vistrus.

"Dad, what's going on?" Allison asks.

"Someone's house is on fire. Sad news," he replies.

Neither girl buys his answer.

"I know that's Jack's house. We were there just a few hours ago, and all of a sudden, it's burning to the ground," Allison says as a realization hits her. "Is that what you meant when you said you'd clean up my throw-up later?!"

Vistrus walks over to the television and shuts it off. With tight lips, he looks at the girls. A thought forms in his head.

"The news reports what it knows but, more importantly, what it wants. A way to convey a message to the people to keep them calm. A house fire with a tragic loss keeps the masses calm. A house fire of a family murdered over several occasions because their genetic disposition frightens those who are different causes panic," he explains.

Now he looks into their eyes while the wheels turn in their heads. Memories of past events that they've seen play out on the news, all losing the validity they once held.

"So, everything we see on the news is just some cover-up?" Scarlett asks.

"Not everything. That is just it, though. The cover-up gets lost in the mix. No one is ever the wiser," Vistrus says.

The girls fall back into their seats. Scarlett takes a deep breath and blinks a few times. "I have to work tonight. I should get some sleep."

Allison snaps out of her distant thoughts and looks at Scarlett. "Me too. Can Scarlett crash here, Dad?" Allison asks.

Vistrus nods his head as the girls walk off to get some sleep. Vistrus only hopes they are able to sleep after the night they had.

CHAPTER 21

"Grief only changes shape.
It never leaves."

~R. Chandler~

T he still air in the West Haven cemetery sits heavy on the backs of the living here today. The cold, damp air chills them to the bone. A sorrowful tribute paid by Mother Nature as she takes back one of her own. Jack's casket hovers above its final resting place, waiting for the ropes to lower him down. Scarlett stands at a podium behind the coffin, looking out over the crowd of friends from school, former team-mates, and unknown faces standing by her family, all gathered today. A large turnout for someone with no remaining living family.

Scarlett looks in the distance at her family's burial plot. She whispers to herself, "One day." She turns her attention to the crowd at hand after a moment of silent reverie. "Jack didn't have any blood relatives left alive, but looking out at the people gathered here, he had a much larger family than even he realized." She watches as many of the crowd nods in agreement. No cheers or shouts at this mournful time. Just quiet reflection. "He was different. From the way he held himself in a shy, almost playfully self-deprecating way to the way he talked." The teammates and class-mates solemnly laugh to themselves. "But it was those things that made him so disarming, so easily loveable."

She stops for a moment and holds back the tears she finds starting to collect in her eyes. The cold, still air keeps them from falling. She wipes them away. She looks out and wonders how many knew Jack as she did. How many out there harbor secrets they are too afraid to tell anyone about? How many would have rejected him if they knew what he looked like when he passed? How many would have embraced him? How many would have been there to help him understand what was going on?

She sees Connor work his way to his grand-mother's side. An unexpected sight, given his actions as of late.

"He had a timid voice, unsure of the words that came out of his mouth. But he found inner strength. And it is that inner strength that I shall try and carry on for him, take from him, and make my own." She looks out and makes eye contact with Vistrus, Grandma Eleanor, and Sylvia Waldgrave. "With that strength, I shall not be afraid to be myself. I shall learn to not hide who I am. As no one here should be afraid of themselves. No one here should hide who they are out of fear of others." She stops and takes a deep breath of cold air to help calm her. She realizes the rant she was about to embark on, a tirade that is uncalled for here. "It is that idealism we should all take from Jack Taylor. I love you, and we miss you."

She steps down from the podium and stands at his casket. The crowd slowly disperses, though a few say their silent condolences to the deceased. The coffin begins to lower as the crowd further thins out. Scarlett has been joined by Allison and Connor as the casket makes its final descent into the earth. The coffin comes to rest before Scarlett turns to her cousin.

"Nice to know this is what it takes to get you back home," she jabs at him.

"Low blow, cuz'." His reply comes flat.

Scarlett doesn't seem to acknowledge his response as she starts off walking. Allison follows behind her, effectively shunning her boyfriend.

Connor follows the girls as they trek to her parents' tombstones. The cold nips at his nose, a reminder of his treatment toward his friends.

"I'm only in for the night." Timid words at a sober time.

"Of course. We wouldn't expect anything from the wayward DeSalvo." Scarlett stabs him with her words.

"I have classes. College doesn't care about your life. It's the real world. Don't you get it? The world doesn't care about any of this. The world keeps moving, and if I can't put aside what's happening in my personal life to get done what I need to get done, I'll get left behind." His words sound stone cold, even in the winter weather, but neither girl reacts. They are made of harder stone than any words he throws. "It's not like I've been having the time of my life up there." His tone turns defensive.

Scarlett ignores him as she tries to spend some quiet time with her parents at their gravestones.

Allison looks in his direction but not at him, a half-hearted attempt at her passive-aggressiveness. She doesn't want to be angry. She wants to jump into his arms, or at least she wants to want to jump into his arms. Even if she did want that, now is neither the time nor the place. She knows that even if they were back in the warmth of his house, she still would not want to be in his arms. Allison would be screaming at Connor, giving him her what-for and all.

"What personal life?" Allison asks with a scowl.

"I know I haven't really been in touch lately. College is not exactly this wondrous place with excitement around every corner. It kinda sucks," Connor continues.

"This might take a minute, Mom and Dad," Scarlett says to the stones. She turns to Connor. "We wouldn't know. We haven't heard any actual thoughts from you since you left. Every conversation we have is short in both your words and time. You have pulled yourself so far away from us we weren't sure you'd be home for the funeral since you might have a team retreat, or team meeting, or team outing, or team sleepover."

"This hasn't exactly been easy for me, Scarlett," he starts back up. "I've been struggling day in and day out. Trying to hold myself together. All I want is to be able to talk with my dad again. One more time. Hell, a hundred more times. One more 'I love you' from my mom. I've been scouring over every memory I have with them, every conversation I can remember trying to figure out what I missed. What life lessons they were trying to teach me so I can be better. So I can deal with the loss. Do you have any idea how lonely it is up there?"

"No, we don't, Con," Allison cuts in. "You stand here and lecture us on how you've been struggling to deal, but you have no idea how what you did affects us. How it makes us feel like leftover consolations from a former life. Now that your parents are gone, just phase out anything associated with memories from that era. Next. Time to move on. That is how we feel, like dogs taken to the shelter. I call and call and text but nothing. Not even a good night anymore."

Scarlett chimes in, "Have you even listened to the tapes? Huh, have you? Have you taken the time to figure out the why behind all this madness?"

Connor hangs his head. "I'm sorry. I didn't realize what I did … how it came across to you."

"The whole slacker thing might have been a cool, edgy front for a high school persona, but it sucks, just a bit, to use on your family," Scarlett jabs her words.

Connor nods his head. "I know. Now I know."

"Yeah, well, now it's too late. At least for Jack. When was the last time you spoke with him? Huh, Connor?" Allison scorns.

Connor doesn't answer. He looks back at his friend as they pile dirt on top of him.

"I have listened, over and over and over again. Do you know what I've had to listen to countless times in some half-baked pursuit of vigilante justice? Do you? The sounds of my parents being tortured and killed! I've had to rewind and listen so many times to my mother begging for her life and my father begging for his that I have their final words memorized. I will forever know the agony of what they felt, the pain in their voices as they clung to life until it was stripped away. The unfathomable sound of my father choking, gasping for air. That is what is on those tapes. I have not forgotten about you and Allison or moved on from West Haven. I've been trying to survive being away, trying to figure out how to make this pursuit not so half-baked. And that's why I listened over and over and over. Because I think I got some stuff. The cure. It's why the blond man did what he did. He was gathering blood samples," Connor finishes.

The stone-cold demeanor of the girls has softened as they realize what he has been enduring and why.

"We've known. From what we can tell, whoever they are, are trying to weaponize us. Find a way to make Normals Legendary," Scarlett interjects.

"No..." Connor shakes his head, "...from what I can gather, they want to inhibit our transitions, a sort of neutering of our abilities. The guy on the tape was able to stop them for a short time. I got that much. I think he was working on a permanent solution."

"He's dead, though. So..." Allison leads Connor's thoughts along.

"He was just a pawn, a field guy, muscle to get what they needed. He makes vague references over and over in the recordings, but they are all pronouns," Connor says. "That's all I could gather."

"Well, it's a little more than we had before." Allison turns his head with her finger on his jaw. She looks him in the eyes. "None of us are having a grand ole' time right now. I didn't realize, and I think Scarlett didn't realize what was also on those tapes. We didn't. But you didn't have to experience that all those times alone. We would have been there for you. Superheroes do things alone. You don't have to be a superhero. We have strength enough for that. We need each other's shoulders to lean on."

Connor nods his head in understanding. "You need to fill me in on what you know about what happened to Jack."

Scarlett turns back to her parents' tombstones. "Well, I apologize about the short visit. I will come back soon. I love you guys." She turns to her cousin. "Don't think everything is all hunky-dory between us. I'm still pissed you didn't think to come to us with all that earlier but come on, we'll fill you in."

The three of them start walking back to their cars as the girls fill him in not only with the details of what they know about Jack's death but also with their plan to hold Linda and Max Espinoza accountable. While the tension between them might not have wholly lifted, it has eased, at least for the moment.

As Scarlett and Connor arrive at their grandmother's house, along with Allison, they see that a few people who attended the funeral have gathered there for food and consolation.

They enter the kitchen to see what is available to eat. Grandma Eleanor turns to them. "Come eat!

Don't be sad that he is gone but be glad that he was once here." She throws open her arms, and all three grab her for a comforting group hug.

After grabbing plates of finger sandwiches, they make their way into the living room to find Brianna on the couch next to Duncan. They are engaged in a quiet conversation that ends as they notice the three of them enter.

Allison hears Jack say the word *doomsday* in her mind. A word she used that Duncan heard. Anger swells, knowing that somehow the two incidents are related. She blames him.

In a blinding show of speed, Allison rushes to the couch and grabs Duncan by the back of the neck. The strength of her grip belies her tiny frame. Duncan finds Allison's grip paralyzing as he tries to move away from her.

The others close by fidget at her actions, not wanting to draw unwanted attention but still wanting to show their disapproval. Allison looks around to make sure her father and others aren't taking notice.

"Doomsday," she whispers with a menacing sneer.

Brianna, Scarlett, and Connor watch in shock and horror as Allison holds her painfully tight grip around Duncan's neck. The three of them look toward the adults and try not to draw unwanted attention.

Panic starts to show on Duncan's face. He is still greeted by a solid grip each time he attempts to move.

Eleanor glances in their direction from the kitchen to see Duncan squirm in Allison's grasp but doesn't seem too alarmed, or she is merely staying willfully ignorant.

"Yeah, tonight. Please let go," Duncan pleads.

"He said it," Allison continues. "It was his last words."

Her grip remains resilient.

Duncan's eyes go wide. "Woah. I didn't kill him. Why the hell would I kill Jack? He was a cool cat."

Allison's anger starts to calm down. She looks at Scarlett.

Scarlett tilts her head, wondering why Allison is so enraged. "Al, Duncan would probably not be able to be so casual if he saw *Jack's massive amount of chest hair.*"

Duncan shoots her an unsure look frosted with panic.

Allison loosens her grip. She takes a deep breath as Duncan slides out of her reach.

Eleanor looks to the children once more. "Is everything all right, young man?"

Duncan nods at Eleanor while rubbing his neck. "Yeah, she was working out a kink in my neck. Didn't help much, though."

With that, Eleanor turns her attention back to the adults' conversation.

Duncan looks at Brianna. "Tell your girl to calm herself."

Allison's face goes big. "That bitch heard us! When I went to the locker room, I thought I saw her. I must've." She squints at Duncan like a dog who knows she misbehaved. "I'm... my bad. She must've been listening in just around the corner."

"Who?" Duncan asks.

"Mrs. Espinoza," Allison answers.

"No way. I had her last year. AP Bio," he responds back. "That's heavy."

Brianna leans in and whispers, "Are we seriously still going through with this, then?"

Scarlett stares her dead in the eye and nods.

"Well, all right," Duncan joins in. "I have a few friends who can help keep watch. You said that was our job."

"It is," Allison chimes in. "I know you are coming in with us. Just know that we are more capable than we look."

Duncan rubs his neck. "Yeah. I can tell."

Allison offers an apologetic smile. She knows that Duncan is still missing a significant portion of the picture, but from what he can see, she knows he knows they are strong enough. At least, they all hope.

"Do we have all the details worked out?" Brianna asks.

"Not anymore," Allison says with a sense of disappointment. "It *was* supposed to go down tonight. Now, I'm not sure."

Scarlett takes the helm for a moment. "After a funeral is not the best time to launch an assault. I don't think any of us are in the right frame of mind."

Duncan bobs his head. "Cool, cool. So when, then?"

Brianna chimes in, "How about we all just stay ready? Like in the movies when they all are on, like, permanent alert to do what they need at a moment's notice."

Allison smiles. "I like that idea."

"Then it's settled," Scarlett begins, turning to Duncan. "Will your guys be okay with that?"

"We might lose one or two cats, but yeah, most should be fine with that," he answers with a sly smile.

"Then we need a code phrase or something," Brianna interjects. "Like 'Operation Tacos' or 'Burrito Express.'"

"One, Burrito Express is an actual place, and two, Operation Tacos? That's your brilliant name?" Scarlett tries not to laugh.

"What?" Brianna shrugs. "I'm still, like, really hungry."

Duncan gestures toward the kitchen and the dining room table. "Go grab some more food."

Brianna nods in agreement and heads to the Russian Tea Cookies.

"Operation Die Hard," Duncan offers up.

"No," Scarlett interjects. "I know you love your *Brooklyn 99* and Bruce Willis, but no. We aren't calling this Operation Die Hard."

"Okay, what name do you got?" Duncan throws back.

"Operation … Gogurt?" Scarlett squeaks out.

Allison lets out a full-belly laugh. "No way in hell. If we are all doing this, the last thing I say before we launch is 'Operation Gogurt is a go.' Plus, didn't you just rag on Bri for her food-themed names?"

"Okay, Einstein, then what do you have?" Scarlett puts her on the spot.

"Operation Cobra Kai," Connor offers with an ear-to-ear smile.

Duncan points his finger at him. "Yes! That is it!"

"Seriously?! That's what gets the juices flowing? Operation Cobra Kai?!" Scarlett says.

"It's better than Gogurt, and it was the theme of the Halloween party last year when Jack was missing, and well, he's missing again," Connor says in true mic-drop fashion.

Scarlett laughs in spite of herself. "Fine. Operation Cobra Kai it is." She hunches low as Brianna makes it back to them with a ludicrous amount of cookies. "So, Con, you'll be at college, but the rest of you, if you get a text that says, 'No mercy,' then it's a go. Then the address will follow. Duncan, you must text your guys. Get them to the location."

Duncan nods in affirmation. "Yo, so what do we do in the meantime, with everything that has just happened, I mean? Do we do this soon or no?"

Scarlett shakes her head. "Not soon. We lay low for a while." Scarlett shoots an evil eye toward Allison. "No one talks about it at school, home, or anywhere else." She turns back to everyone. "We need to make the teacher think we've forgotten about it all. That we have no leads anymore. That we were wrong in the first place and in over our heads."

"That last part might be true," Brianna chirps.

"It might be," Scarlett affirms, "but we've come this far and lost so many. We need to make sure their deaths have meaning."

"Radio silence. Sleeper status." Duncan nods, making sure the others are on the same page.

After an extended pause, they are all locked into each other's eyes—a confirming stare of solidarity that they all are in this to the bitter end.

"We got this," Allison states her confidence.

CHAPTER 21

"No mercy," Connor says.

They all look at each other and repeat the phrase, "No mercy."

CHAPTER 22

"Even the best-laid plans fail.
But I'm just paraphrasing,
I could be wrong."
~T. DeSalvo~

Vistrus sits at his desk in his home office with Inessa's diaries strewn about as he rifles through them. The Bluetooth device wrapped around his ear keeps him more distracted than he would like.

He keeps switching between two diaries, flipping their pages, seemingly at random. "I do not care what you do with Scarlett's little tutoring program. There are so many larger things in motion."

Something in one of the diaries catches his eye.

It is all a game of chess. If only Vistrus learned to play too.

"Sylvia, when you and Inessa got together, did she ever talk about games?" He keeps it vague.

"I don't understand. Like board games? We never talked about board games. We had more adult things to talk about. Why would you ask such a strange question?" Sylvia babbles.

Vistrus shakes his head. "It is nothing. Just a curiosity."

To Vistrus, though, it is more than curiosity. Chess is a game that he played, a game that he and Inessa played together so many times back in Russia. What is he missing? Is this some sort of message he can't decipher, or nothing more than the ramblings of a woman gone mad?

"She wants her name attached to the program. Which is all fine and dandy for the next five or so decades, but what about in a century when she is still running around West Haven?" Sylvia rattles on.

Vistrus is listening, but not much. His mind is still caught in his wife's diaries.

"Uh-huh," Vistrus responds, his attention far from Sylvia. "I have to go."

He clicks the side of his earpiece to hang up the phone as he picks up the diary, leaning back in the chair and settling in for a good read.

He notices that by the time Inessa had started writing these entries, she had forgone the custom of dating each one. The only thing that indicates to him the separation of entries is spacing and the subtle changes in handwriting as her moods shifted.

Chess is about protecting the king, but it is not. No. Never. Behind every good man lies a better woman. No different in

> chess. All about the piece that can do the most. If that piece is taken, the king is most vulnerable. I am no Bobby Fischer. Vistrus doesn't understand. I can't make him understand.

Vistrus flips the page to her next writings.

> Sacrifice. Sacrifice. Sacred vice. Scared of life. No one understands. They don't understand. Hard to be so alone, surrounded by love. Hard to feel love, surrounded by alone. So rounded by a home. So grounded on a phone.

A tear falls down his cheek. He remembers her decline as if it was still happening. While he reads, it is happening all over again.

> Good Steve McQueen. Faoi Dhó Duine. The Mind. God Steve. He won't get it. I am done. I am dumb. Why did I do this? The Mind matters. The Mind is all that matters. I have mine. I have mine. No one believes me. No one understands. I have the Mind. But it is empty now. Nothing left in the Mind. Only the Faoi Dhó Duine and white. Save McQueen. Vistrus, love. Falling away. Can't explain. Hidden. Must hide. Secrets die. Can't share. Not secret. God Save The Queen.

Reliving the downfall of his beloved is not making for the feel-good read of the year for him. And while the words he read were few, the time it took him to make it through those words was much longer than simply seeing each letter.

The sound of the front door slamming shut downstairs interrupts his reading.

"Sorry, Dad!" Allison shouts out. "Wind took it a bit!"

He smiles at his daughter's subtlety in the moment. He closes all the diaries and stacks them neatly on his desk. A task for another time.

"It's New Year's Eve. I thought you were going to Connor's to celebrate?" her father shouts to her as he stares at the pile of diaries.

"Scarlett's!" she corrects, as if it's a different house from her room, as she changes clothes. "Connor's at school again! We're just chillin' there! Gonna watch the ball drop!"

"Just remember, school starts back on Wednesday. No excuses about being too tired from tonight. You will have a full day of rest tomorrow," he finishes shouting his fatherly duty for the moment.

Allison laughs to herself at her father. "I'll be fine! I work tomorrow night, anyway!" She mutters under her breath, "Can't get too schwasty."

Scarlett and Allison sit on the couch, sipping glasses of sparkling wine. The television plays out the lives the station thinks everyone wishes they had on this day: limousines, champagne and caviar, countless friends laughing and partying the night away.

"It'd be so cool to be there ... at Times Square." A wistful sigh escapes Allison. "We should go one year."

"Sure, Al." Scarlett sips on her drink. "Next year, we'll trek across the country to surround ourselves with drunk strangers."

Allison nods. "Maybe Connor will be around to go with us."

Scarlett turns to her friend, oblivious to the subtle sarcasm of actually going. "I was joking."

But it's too late. Allison is off in her own world planning the theoretical trip. "And Bri could come too. Duncan. It'll be a group trip!"

"We'll play it by ear," Scarlett drones. "Who knows what the next year holds."

Allison falls out of her cloud, plummeting to Earth. "We'll probably just sit here again. Someone will disappear from our lives, giving us another reason to mourn."

Scarlett backhands Allison's shoulder. "Not cool, Al. Not cool."

The Earth metaphorically meets Allison with terminal velocity. "I'm just saying. A year ago, I was wanting out of this town 'cause it's too dull. Now, we need out to save ourselves. It's been a strange year."

Scarlett gestures to the television. "And tonight, we put the year behind us. We move into tomorrow and the new year with fresh eyes, refreshed attitudes, and an optimistic, or slightly less pessimistic, look at the future."

"Ookaay, Ms. Brightside. What's got you all excited for 2019?" Allison chugs half her glass.

Scarlett lifts the bottle of cheap, fruit-flavored beverage and tops Allison off. "Nothing. Just trying to stay positive myself. This thing has been itching that I just can't scratch."

Allison sets down her drink. "I'll scratch it. Where's it?"

Scarlett chuckles. "Not literally. I mean. Okay, a while ago, I saw something in a teacher's notebook. Then she said something I said sounded poetic, and she said it was Poe."

"Like Edgar Allan Poe?" Allison tries to clarify.

"I assume. But that made me remember the notebook," Scarlett continues. "It means something. I just don't know what."

Allison pulls out her phone. "What did this mysterious teacher say?"

"Something about 'putting out starlight.' But I think there's more to it," Scarlett continues. "She stopped and was, like, waiting for me to respond with something."

"With what?" Allison inches up in her seat as she types the paraphrased words into the search engine.

"That's the thing. I don't know." Scarlett scratches her temple.

"All I'm getting is stuff about radiation and cosmic mumbo jumbo." Allison sounds defeated.

"Add Poe to the search parameters," Scarlett suggests.

And with that simple addition to the search, the top result is a poetry link to Fairy-Land by Edgar Allen Poe. The girls read through it and shortly find the phrase Scarlett struggled to remember.

"What does it mean?" Allison ponders out loud.

"That's what we need to find out," Scarlett answers.

The sound of the television catches the girls' attention. "Ten! Nine! Eight!" The crowd cheers.

"This crowd is going wild!" A caffeine-and-alcohol-laced, excited newscaster states the obvious.

"Five! Four!" The crowd continues.

Scarlett and Allison lift their glasses. "Three! Two! One! Happy New Year!"

Allison's phone rings, breaking Scarlett's thought.

"Happy New Year, babe!" Allison beams. She points to her phone and tells Scarlett, "It's Connor!"

Scarlett chuckles to herself at Allison's excitement. "Happy New Year, cuz."

"No, we're having a quiet but fun night at your place. Talking about poetry, of all things!" Allison beams with excitement.

They clink their glasses in a toast and sip to whatever lies ahead. But in Scarlett's mind, she knows that The Nation has something to do with Edgar Allen Poe; she is just not sure what or why.

CHAPTER 23

"Not everything we wait for is good.
Never mistake coincidence for causality."
~J. Taylor~

The first period of their first day back at school for the last semester of their high school careers: Western Civilization 1920-Present. Allison, Scarlett, Brianna, and Duncan all sit for a final course in mandated social studies to fulfill their requirements to get into college. A class that every senior tries to get into because of who teaches it—Mr. Parlett. A man who treats his students more like adults than any other teacher. A man who has been to more rock concerts than any other teacher admits. A man who knows more about the past than most know about the present. The man who teaches the coveted senior-only class stands at the blackboard, drawing a circle as he brushes his hair back with his free hand.

"What's this?" he asks in a gruff voice reminiscent of Sam Elliot or Jeff Bridges. His timbre lets whoever hears it know he has earned every premature wrinkle forming on his face. A voice gritty enough to grate hard cheese and a smile wide enough to disarm any ill intent.

The class doesn't bother raising hands before calling out, "A circle!"

"Four years of high school education." Mr. Parlett shakes his head at their on-the-nose answer. "At least the geometry teachers did something right." He turns to the circle. "Correct. But more precisely, it is our history and all the possibilities that could have happened." He accents his words by dotting the center of the circle. "Someone tell me a major event in history." He scans the class and calls on a football player decked out in his jersey.

"Columbus discovering the new world," he says with pride.

"How about remembering the name of the class ends with 1920 to present, right?" He points to another student. "Duncan."

"Dub dub two," Duncan spouts off.

"While dub dub does save you a whole four syllables, we use whole words in this class, Mr. Elias. Our conversations outside this class have proven your intelligence to be far higher; don't prove me wrong." Mr. Parlett writes World War II around the outside of the circle as the class chuckles at Duncan's expense.

Duncan's defenses rise. "The evolution of language is an ever-changing occurrence. As someone in higher education, you should be well aware of these things. Especially someone who understands rebellion as you clearly do." Duncan points to the Pink

Floyd and Metallica posters snuck between historical replicas on the walls.

Mr. Parlett turns his attention to Duncan. "And if this were a linguistics course, I would entertain your argument, as it is well stated for something thought up on the fly. But this is a history class, and as much as language and its evolution are entwined in it, we will focus on the course title and your chosen topic. Plus, what's wrong with a little rebellion?" Duncan gives the teacher an approving nod. Mr. Parlett turns back to the board. "This circle represents what we will discuss for the remainder of your high school careers. So, if you are a fan, thank Duncan over there. If not, you're in for a long ride."

A girl raises her hand. "What's inside the circle, then?

"Good question," the teacher responds. "Inside the circle is everything, and I do mean everything involved with World War II. Not just the countries and the invasion of Poland and Belgium. I mean everything. And this is what we will be exploring— all the possible variables that contributed to this war. All the possible outcomes and why it played out the way it did."

He draws a line separating the circle from the rest of the board. "What we need to find is the center of the circle. The lynchpin, if you will, that put every- thing into motion for the war to happen."

The class starts spouting off the usual appease- ment factors that the Allies allowed Hitler, their energy and excitement grow with each response. A few people rattle off the United States policy of non-involvement for the first part of the war. And various others, all of which get listed on the opposite side of the line, leaving the circle still untouched.

"All of these are great answers, which belong in the circle. Are there any other ideas that you have that I should jot down?" Mr. Parlett asks.

"World War I," Scarlett calls out.

The teacher writes it down. "Why World War I … Scarlett, is it?"

"Yes," she confirms. "Because Hitler fought in World War 1 and was injured in battle almost immediately. It helped fuel his anger."

"Okay. That's specific. Where did you learn that?" Mr. Parlett writes her idea in the list of things to go in the circle.

"Mr. Huft's class sophomore year." Scarlett smiles back.

"Well, if we blame it on him being injured, then write syphilis on that list," Duncan counterpoints.

"Explain your reasoning," Mr. Parlett suggests to Duncan, as he waits for a good reason to write the word.

"Because I read a bunch of stuff about the guy. The internet is good for that. Historians say end-stage syphilis caused his megalomania. Well, could have," Duncan defends his suggestion. "Supposedly."

"Sounds good. Syphilis it is." The teacher moves to the circle. "And your internet sources are credible?"

Duncan nods.

"Wait," Brianna pipes up.

"Yes … Sorry, Anna?" Mr. Parlett questions his knowledge of her name.

"Brianna, or Bri. Not Anna. No one calls me Anna," she starts to babble.

"What was your reason for shouting out for me to wait?" he urges her along.

"If we are going to blame a disease, then we blame the person who gave it to him," she states, as if it should be obvious.

"Why?" the teacher pushes.

"Well, we have to assume he did something," she starts before being interrupted by another kid interjecting, "or someone." "Or someone," she reiterates, "for him to get the disease. Risky behavior that ended in bad results."

"Why is that pertinent to this discussion?" Mr. Parlett prods further.

Duncan chimes in, "Because if he had never gotten syphilis, then his brain wouldn't have been chewed upon by the viruses or bacteria or whatever. His brain wouldn't have been damaged, causing the megalomania. Maybe getting injured in the first war wouldn't have made him so angry that he felt the need to go all *Pinky and The Brain*. He could have been just a normal guy."

The teacher gives a half-smile while shaking his head. "Not the most popular theory among certain crowds, I'm sure. But it makes sense." He writes *Syphilis* in the center of the circle. "To further add to why you think it goes to the person responsible for his syphilis, we do not know exactly how he became infected. Just that he was. So, we start with him."

Scarlett raises her hand but doesn't wait to be called upon. "So, the entire class is conjecture, except we can't conject or whatever about the person who gave him syphilis? That seems arbitrary."

The teacher looks out at the students to see if someone has a response. He spots Duncan with a crooked smile. "Duncan, thoughts?"

"If we start with who gave him syphilis, then we need to know who gave that person syphilis, and it becomes too much," Duncan rebuttals.

Allison raises her hand.

"Yes?" the teacher points to her.

"So, that's it? World War II was started 'cause Hitler had syphilis? That can't be right. Aren't you supposed to tell us all this?" Allison asks, lost and frustrated.

He puts down the chalk, wiping his hands as he turns to face the class. "That is what this class is about. You have spent your entire lives in an educational system that tells you all the answers. World War II can be read about in countless books, periodicals, encyclopedias, and internet search results and watched about in just as many movies. But the truth about life is that things get overlooked, lost in the shuffle and chaos of the moment. We are here in this course to teach you how to think critically. To think outside the confines of what we know to find a deeper truth, or at least a deeper possible truth, to why things happened the way they did."

He points to the center of the circle. "From this point of having syphilis, we will look at how things transpired and how they could have transpired if each variable was slightly different. So, for now, we assume that he has this STD. We assume that like historians have speculated, he got the disease from a prostitute in his early 20s."

A kid raises his hand. "Couldn't this have been caused by the same disease that Churchill had?"

Mr. Parlett stops. "Care to elaborate?"

"Well, Randolph Churchill had dementia paralytica, and historians theorize that Hitler could have had that, and not *ter-ti-ary* stage," he clarifies in a snotty tone and cocky smile like he just won a court case.

Duncan looks back at the kid. "Don't defend him, brah. That kind of dementia was linked to *ter-ti-ary* stage syphilis, which is why I said it."

The other kid slumps in defeat.

Scarlett looks at Duncan. "Why did I have to tutor you?"

Duncan smiles. "You didn't in history."

The bell rings. The students hastily pack their things.

"This is the basis for our class. I shall see you all tomorrow. Duncan, may I see you?" Mr. Parlett says, while looking in his planner.

The students shuffle out of the class, leaving their conversation lost in the noise. Brianna waits by the door for him.

"Interesting setup for the semester," the teacher begins.

"Thank you, sir."

Mr. Parlett chuckles. "Not everyone here will agree with your ideas." He watches Duncan nod. "Don't let that dissuade you from thinking. I have a feeling you are far more intelligent than your grades, GPA, and our out-of-class conversations lead me and other people to believe." He pulls out a pad and scribbles on it.

Duncan nods his head, unsure how to react.

"I look forward to a lively end to your high school career." He hands Duncan a hall pass to his next class. "See you tomorrow."

Duncan and Bri walk down the hall. Students flow around them, going about their day.

"Why do you know so much about such an evil man?" Brianna's tone indicates she might not want to know the answer.

"No one thinks they're evil. No one actually sits around twirling their mustache, or whatever, devising plans they think are evil just to be evil," Duncan offers.

"I never would have thought someone like you sided with him," she whispers.

Duncan laughs. "I never said that." He pauses for a moment, searching for the right words. "If you want to know what made evil acts happen, like the events that led up to it, you have to understand the mindset of the person or people who perpetrated the events."

"So…" Brianna responds, still a bit confused.

"To study the evil stuff mankind has done will give me a better understanding of my enemies. Like when boxers study their opponent's old fights," Duncan tries to clarify.

"Yeah, you lost me with the boxing thing. But, like, I think I understand," Brianna smiles as they stop at her locker.

"Let's step back from the world for a moment," Mrs. Hsu advises an antsy Allison. "Close your eyes."

Instead of closing them, Allison gives Mrs. Hsu a raised brow of disbelief.

"You came to me. Have some trust." Mrs. Hsu pauses to let those words sink into Allison's mind. "Now close your eyes."

Allison takes a deep breath and then closes her eyes. She sits upright in the cloth upholstered office chair.

"Relax. All you have to do is listen to me. This isn't some meditation exercise where I count backward from ten. All I am trying to do is calm your nervous energy down a bit."

Allison gives a soft nod. A smile crosses Mrs. Hsu's face, unsure if the nod was in understanding or just a nod of Allison trying to hold still.

"It's been a few months since I've seen you in my office. And that is okay. I am a safe spot. You know I am here." Mrs. Hsu pauses again. She lets the words of safety flow through Allison's ears. "Something brought you back here. Let that reason float to the front of your mind. Don't force it. Don't even think about it. Just be in the moment. When I count to three, you will open your eyes, and we will talk. *One.* There will be no snapping of my fingers. You are of your own volition. *Two.* Your world is safe in here. Anything you say is privileged. *Three.*"

Allison opens her eyes, not in a slow, fluttery fashion or even a sudden jolt. Just a nondescript opening of her eyes, lacking any fanfare.

Mrs. Hsu waits in silence for Allison to talk.

Allison's brow furrows. Her mouth tightens, and her lips pucker out a little as she swallows a build-up of saliva.

"People keep dying. Not just people in the world but people I know. People that are as close to me as anyone is, ya know. And it's not like I am too dumb to realize that people die. I didn't ever think that people didn't die. But so much so soon. And people my age. Like, everyone knows old people die. You get old, your body stops working, or your mind goes to goop, and you slow down and die. Hell, even the celebrities that died young at least had lived a full life. It's one of those things that people think, 'It can never happen to me,' except it can, and it is happening over and over. And then you think about how everyone you care about is dying, and the death starts creeping down to your age, then it's your best friend's boyfriend.

"You find yourself at a cemetery putting someone your own age six feet under, and it hits you. Like we were friends, but we weren't BFFs, ya know. So, my mind starts wandering, thinking about all the things I've been angry about. Wondering why I've been angry. And it hits me. I wasn't mad that we grew apart. I was mad I never told … the person how I felt. I was angry I never admitted to myself that I could feel the way I do for someone like that. But I do. I realize that now."

Allison stops for a moment and stares at Mrs. Hsu to make sure she is still paying attention. Mrs. Hsu's gaze on Allison is wholly attentive. Her pen scribbles in her pad without her even so much as glancing downward.

"I have these dreams. These vivid dreams. And I know they are just dreams, but I found out my mom used to have them. I never knew because she died when I was young and all, but she had them. And I have them. These dreams that seem so real, like I was there in the dream. Not just asleep. But then I think, and I know they are just dreams. But these dreams … where was I going?" Allison waves her left hand in the air, trying to shoo away any distracting thoughts. "But anyways, the dreams are sometimes about death."

With that, Mrs. Hsu straightens herself up as if to interrupt, a gesture that does not go unnoticed by Allison.

"I don't kill anyone. I'm not a murderer, and I have no intentions or thoughts about killing anyone. Don't worry about that. But these dreams make me realize that the people I'm losing aren't the closest people to me. Not yet. And if I lose them, I'd be totally alone. Lost."

Allison takes a deep breath. The air filling her lungs feels refreshing. As if this is the first breath she's had since launching into the verbal explosion of her carbonated and shaken thoughts that were just uncapped.

"But that's just it. The dreams make me realize that the time lost to anger and holding onto what I perceived as being pushed away instead of simply

315

growing apart for a while was wasted. I could have been finding ways to tell this person how I feel, felt, whatever. I could have admitted to myself that I felt this way a long time ago. Not denied myself of who I really am inside, or whatever crap I'm supposed to say when I make a realization."

Mrs. Hsu chuckles a little.

"What?" Allison gets a little defensive.

"You make great leaps after not seeing me. You make these self-realizations that, well, maybe you didn't just make today, may have admitted out loud for the first time, or told someone for the first time. Which is great. Wonderful to realize these things about yourself. But then you dismiss everything you just told me about by calling it crap. You didn't just get cut out of a coloring book. You aren't a carbon copy of someone that already exists. You aren't a statistic in a textbook. Nothing you feel is crap. Nothing you realize about yourself, life, or your existence is crap. Don't dismiss things so easily." Mrs. Hsu returns to write something on her yellow pad.

"Fine," Allison admits in defeat. "Maybe it's not crap, but it's hard to admit I may have been wrong all these years. Wrong about myself. Wrong about my friends. I don't like being wrong. No one does."

"But admitting you are wrong..." Mrs. Hsu interjects, "...means you have the capacity and willingness to be better and change what you realize is wrong."

Allison scratches her head for a moment as she tries to collect her thoughts.

"So, then what do I say to the one I love? How do I admit these feelings I have for someone else when I have the same feelings for the one I am with?" Allison slumps back in her chair.

"Marie-Antoinette is often quoted as saying, 'Let them eat cake!'" Mrs. Hsu starts.

"Yeah. I've heard that phrase before," Allison affirms.

"But did you know that the cake she referred to was not the sugary confection we enjoy at birthdays?" Mrs. Hsu continues.

Allison shakes her head.

"She was referring to the sediment of yeast, barley, malt, hops, and whatever else settles to the bottom of the kegs as the beer is brewed. A thick, cake-like substance," Mrs. Hsu explains.

"Why would anyone eat that? And why would anyone think to eat that?" Allison asks with a contorted disgust on her face.

"The peasants were out of bread—the most basic of food components—and the queen, wanting to further the gap between the rich and poor, said they should eat cake."

"What the hell does that have to do with me?" Allison asks, utterly confused.

"Well, the misinterpretation of the phrase is where I want to start. Relationships can be tricky. The traditional thoughts of monogamy are being questioned and challenged every day and are on the edge of being antiquated. So, given your newfound feelings, or new admittance of feelings, perhaps telling your current partner how you feel and what you want to do about it may open doors that you didn't know were there. It may open some for him or her as well. And thus the misinterpreted cake," Mrs. Hsu offers up.

"But I don't want to lose him. We already went through hard times, and I don't want to lose what we have on the chance he'll be down for becoming poly," Allison refutes.

"It's a chance you will have to take if you think it will make you happier than you currently are. But that's a call you'll have to make. If you approach him with this idea and he says no, you are left with just this other person and nothing you and your current person have built together. I am assuming by the conversation today that this other person doesn't know yet how you feel?" Mrs. Hsu throws out a saving grace.

Allison shakes her head no.

"Then you might want to decide how you approach that situation first. Otherwise, you could end up with nothing, thus the actual cake. And that is not what you want," Mrs. Hsu finishes.

"So, what do I do? How do I approach this and not end up eating yeast pie?" Allison asks with a hint of desperation in her voice.

"There's the rub." Mrs. Hsu taps the side of her nose. "I can't tell you how to handle your life. I, and any social worker, therapist, or anyone in our field, will never be able to tell you how to handle yourself. Only you can do that. So, take the time to make sure you figure things out to handle them properly. So that way, when you do bite into your problems, you taste the right kind of cake."

"Is any of that stuff about cake true? Would the queen actually want people to eat that?" Allison inquires.

"Doesn't matter. The moral of the story stands," Mrs. Hsu smiles.

Scarlett sits at a desk in an otherwise empty classroom, using her last free period of the day to talk to Ms. Waldgrave about her passion project one more time.

Scarlett spends the time alone in this room to think about her Uncle Ken and, in the few moments she has to herself until Ms. Waldgrave enters, everything he taught her. Hard work goes beyond the initial approach. It extends all the way to the finish line. He tried to teach her the little things when attempting to succeed—the subtle, sublime details that unconsciously sway people's minds. Wearing red in the right amount shows power and passion. Too much red shows "the other" type of passion. "After all, it is the color of war and love," he would say. Don't wear anything that has sparkles or sequins or glitter if the occasion doesn't call for it. It takes years or decades off your credibility in the wrong setting, turning a grown, respectable individual into a child. Pants over skirts when debating.

He also taught her that those little things have to happen now, so when she wins and is given a position to change those things, she can. But more than that, in his time with the city council and all her years of childish questions that grew into more adult and intellectual questions, he tried to teach her grace and humility.

Of all the life lessons he taught her, she wonders how many she will never hear. How many he still had to teach her that he will never.

Her thoughts are cut short as Ms. Waldgrave enters the room. "Sorry I'm late. Ran into another teacher and had to take care of some business real quick."

"It's okay, Ms. Waldgrave. I'm free this period. No class to miss," Scarlett replies with a down-to-business demeanor.

Sylvia stops at her desk and smiles at Scarlett, while pulling out a folder from a satchel. "Well, all right then. Down to business, it is." She takes a seat at her desk and opens the folder. "I met with the administration ... again ... about your program."

Scarlett can feel it in her bones, a shiver that indicates something else needs to change. Another great compromise in her grand initiative. But she remains calm. She shows the faintest hint of a smile. One just enough that Ms. Waldgrave realizes Scarlett knows what is coming.

"First of all, they agree to elective credit. They wanted to give half-credit, which would have meant a full year for a semester's worth of work," Sylvia stresses, but she can see the pain growing in Scarlett's face; another blow to her grand plan. "*However*, I convinced them otherwise. Tutors will get a full semester of elective credit for each semester tutored. All classes of students will be eligible to be a tutor, assuming they are selected by the committee."

A smile grows on Scarlett. She senses her smile escaping her control and overtaking her entire face. A caricature of who she was a moment ago. She grabs reign of her runaway smile and reels it in. A more eloquent approach to the excitement.

"They are willing to start the program this year while you are still around to help oversee the selection process now for when you are no longer around." Sylvia pulls out a few sheets of paper from the folder.

"Thank you. This all sounds wonderful." Scarlett tries to contain her swelling joy.

"There is one small caveat. A little provision that must happen, or the whole thing changes from go to no," Sylvia says.

Like all things that swell, they must eventually fall. Scarlett's joy is that thing that falls right now. The swell of excitement dies, falling back to the sea from whence it came, a lifeless shell of what it was just a moment ago.

Scarlett presses her lips together, taking a deep breath. She speaks with gritted teeth, "What … might … that … be?"

"Your name cannot be attached to the program." Sylvia demolishes the last thing that made this Scarlett's. The last, little detail Scarlett didn't think she would have to compromise has to be compromised.

"So, my program, which was supposed to have a subsidy, is now going to have credit so the school officials can buy themselves a new desk or make sure their sports teams can bring home another trophy, can't even have my name on it?" Composure is being thrown out the window. Scarlett rises from her desk.

"Now I know that credit is just as good as money. Hell, classes cost money, so if you can get the credit in exchange for work, then why not? But it's bull, and you know it. Having to take my name off the program I created. Why? So some big shot on the board can put his name on it instead and take credit for everything that I put my time and effort into? Ms. Waldgrave, this sucks, and you know it!" She slams her fists on the desk and falls back into her chair.

Sylvia's tilted head smiles at Scarlett. "My dear, those were some passionate words. A fire in you that will serve you for years to come. However, I propose this to you. Einstein once said, 'It's amazing what can be accomplished if you don't care who gets the credit.' It was a belief that Mr. Kennedy carried with him, which is why he said it. He wanted people to not be so worried about the recognition of their work but the outcome of the work they did and how it affected the world around them."

Scarlett raises a skeptical eyebrow at Ms. Waldgrave. She is sure she just used two different people in that one reference.

"What are you saying?" Scarlett sighs.

"I'm not saying anything. President Harry S. Truman was saying that if you feel like what you are accomplishing is worth accomplishing, then give the credit to anyone, even if it's not yourself, because the accomplishment should be worth more than the person who was credited for it," Sylvia finishes.

Scarlett scrunches her face. She knows that humility was a lesson taught to her at one point. She just never realized until now how humility and being humiliated go hand in hand.

"Fine," Scarlett concedes. "This sucks, though. This was my brainchild. *My* baby."

"Yes. You birthed it. You gave it life. And like a mother who realizes she is too young or incapable or insert-reason-here to care for a child, she lets the adoptive family take credit for the child by giving the baby their surname. You are simply doing the same since you only have a limited time left in this institution." Sylvia tries to quell the anger and frustration in Scarlett.

"I understand your point. I understand your reasoning. Just because I get it doesn't mean it doesn't suck big time," Scarlett so eloquently points out. "And yes, I will be okay with this. Yes, it is more about the program than myself. But that cheesy quote is partially wrong. People do appreciate being recognized for their work. It is in recognition of their efforts that make the hard work worth doing. Otherwise, they feel useless."

"Trust me, I understand." Sylvia flips the papers around on her desk. "If this is what you want. If you are truly going to be okay with everything that you compromised on. If this is still your baby, then sign here." Sylvia points to a dotted line at the bottom of page one. She extends a pen in Scarlett's direction.

Scarlett approaches the desk and takes the pen out of Ms. Waldgrave's hand, signing her name at the bottom.

Sylvia flips a few pages and points to another line. "Here."

Again, Scarlett signs the paper.

"And one more time here." Sylvia flips yet another page.

Scarlett once more reluctantly signs away the skeleton of what was once her baby.

"I know right now it feels like you ended up with something that is nothing like what you first set out to create," Sylvia whispers.

Scarlett shakes her head. "It doesn't. At all."

"I promise you it is. At the very least, in spirit, the program will be what you want. Compensated tutoring for those that can't otherwise afford it. If the administration didn't think it was an idea worth pursuing, then they wouldn't have moved forward with it."

Scarlett sits in her dejection, trying to feel comfortable. Trying to find solace in the abomination she just signed off on. She knows that it is not an absolute abomination, that compensation is still there. That there are powers at work in the school board that she can't control. But it doesn't feel like a win to her; it feels like a great compromise.

"At the end of it all, just remember what President Reagan once said, 'It's amazing what can be accomplished if you don't care who gets the credit,'" Sylvia says with a smile.

"Okay. Seriously! You just quoted like four different people for saying the same quote! Who actually said it?!" Scarlett blurts out with a little laugh.

"If you have to ask that question, then you are still missing the point." Sylvia smiles as she packs up her satchel.

"Seriously! You aren't going to tell me?" Scarlett's tone hints at abjection.

Sylvia doesn't turn back but leaves the classroom, shaking her head in self-amusement.

Scarlett is left alone in the room to bathe in her thoughts.

CHAPTER 24

*"To change the playing field,
one must first level it."*
~K. DeSalvo~

"Has the prophecy been declared dead?" Eleanor laughs. "There's a question I never thought I would hear you ask." She takes a bite of homemade apple pie.

Vistrus sits across from Eleanor in her kitchen, a slice of uneaten pie in front of him. He crosses his arms in silent frustration.

"The great thing about prophecies is that they can never truly die. They only get delayed a while. If they are even delayed at all." Eleanor smiles at him.

"You can be insufferable sometimes, old woman, with your vague answers. They do not mean anything," Vistrus replies with a sly smile. He uncrosses his arms, biting into his pie. He savors it, relishing the flavor. "This..." he points with his fork, "...this is *good* pie."

"Thank you. Trying out a new recipe. Found it on the online." Eleanor accepts his praise with grace.

"I think it is just online. Not *the* online," Vistrus offers for future reference.

She waves her hand at him, standing up and heading to the fridge. "It's all mumbo jumbo to me, anyhow."

He shovels another bite of pie into his mouth, "So, if the prophecy is not declared dead, then what?"

She shrugs.

He raises a brow at her noncommittal reply. "My daughter suggested going through Inessa's diaries. It brings back many memories." The tone of his voice grows reminiscent. "It has not seemed to lead anywhere."

"Why do you need to relive these painful memories? What happened that you feel the need to do so?" Eleanor asks, as she rummages through her fridge.

She turns to him before he can answer, holding a can of whipped cream to top off the remainder of her pie.

He nods as she extends it to him. "Only a little, thank you." He takes a bite and swallows. "I am not sure. It may be nothing. The prophecy spoke of the Grey Fairy."

He looks at her, waiting for some sort of affirmation of what he already knows. She responds by staring at him from the fridge while waiting for him to continue.

"Have you ever heard of something called a Faoi Dhó Duine?"

She closes the door and takes a seat. "Can't say it rings a bell, but at my age, a lot of things get lost in the shuffle."

Their conversation is interrupted by the laughter of Allison and Scarlett entering through the front door.

"So, syphilis caused his brain injury, which is why he was evil?" Allison asks while giggling.

They prance into the kitchen. Scarlett gives her grandmother an obligatory hug.

"We're like a month past that, Al. It started with syphilis, but we've moved on to his scapegoating of the Jewish people. Now we're trying to figure out how much of his political ambition was clouded by his disease," Scarlett explains.

"Whatever it is, we're going to need a few late-night study sessions. I'm gonna need a ton of help to pass this course," Allison says, shaking her head in amusement.

"What are you girls talking about?" Vistrus asks.

"Hey, Dad." Allison wraps her arms around her father and gives him a hug. "Our Western Civilization class. Hitler and the rise of the Third Reich all due to his raging syphilis."

"I don't understand," Eleanor chimes in.

Scarlett steals a slice of apple pie for each of them. "It's a really cool class. So, the whole point of the class is to try and study variables that would not normally be taken into account."

"Yeah," Allison jumps in. "World War II was picked as the topic, and then we all had to try and figure out how and why the war started. And it's because of syphilis, apparently."

"I am missing something," Vistrus says, still a little confused.

Scarlett shovels a massive bite of pie into her mouth. "The teacher says it's about seeing things from a different view. Finding a deeper truth. Not a false truth but a possible deeper one. And so far, we've come to realize that his brain-eating syphilis most likely caused the war."

"One more time," Vistrus reiterates.

"It's about finding the causes that caused the factors that started the war. Digging deeper into the ... what's it called ... the beginning of it all."

"Interesting. What is this teacher's name taking such a bold, historical approach?" Vistrus inquires while finishing off his pie.

"Mr. Parlett. He only teaches this class to seniors. Says it's his way of getting us to think critically," Scarlett says, gulping down another bite.

"By trying to find the absolute start of it all. That is interesting." Vistrus stands from the table. "Thank you for your hospitality, Eleanor. We shall continue this soon."

Eleanor waves him off with a smile. She turns to the girls. "What is it that blesses me with your presence today?"

"Actually, Grams, I just came by to tell you I cleaned this week, so you don't have to come by. Already done," Scarlett says.

"Yeah, the pie was just a bonus," Allison adds, taking another bite.

"It's always nice to see my granddaughter." Eleanor chuckles. "Do you want another slice, Allison?"

Allison wipes the crumbs away from her mouth as she finishes off the piece. "No thanks. Connor is taking me out for my birthday."

"Oh, I didn't realize that was today. Happy birthday." Eleanor takes a seat.

"Thanks. It's actually Tuesday, but he will be at school, so we are going out tonight." Allison rises from her seat and grabs a glass of water.

"What time is he picking you up?" Scarlett asks.

"About 8:00 or so. I'm not sure where he's taking me, though," Allison admits.

"I'll be at work tonight if you guys want to stop by for dessert or something. It'd be nice to see my cousin," Scarlett adds.

Scarlett taps the touch screen computer at work, punching in her employee number that will end her shift for the night. She grabs her coat from the back of the restaurant and says cursory goodbyes to the other employees. As she opens the door to leave, Connor and Allison stroll through, holding hands.

"Hey, Scar, hope we aren't too late for dessert." Allison smiles.

"Cell phone's on me all night. Text to say you were on your way would've been nice. I was about to leave," Scarlett says, annoyed.

"No harm, no foul, though. Right?" Connor tries to lighten the mood.

"I guess. Let's go grab a booth in the bar." Scarlett snatches up a couple of dessert menus and heads to the bar.

They all settle into a rather large booth for only three people. Scarlett stretches out on one side while Allison and Connor cuddle on the other.

"Something's been stuck in my head, like a song you can't seem to get rid of," Scarlett starts.

"What song?" Allison asks.

"No, not a song. Stuck in my head *like* a song," Scarlett repeats.

Connor shakes his head. "What's got you so stuck?"

Scarlett looks at both of them and leans in as their server approaches, pen and pad in hand. "Hey, Scarlett. You guys eating or just hanging out?"

Scarlett glances at Connor and Allison. "Desserts, or have you not eaten yet?"

"Desserts," Connor clarifies.

Scarlett turns to the server. "A piece of cheesecake, extra strawberries, and a chocolate death."

"Any drinks?" the server asks.

"Oh yeah. Coke for me," Scarlett finishes.

"Same," Allison adds.

"Me too," Connor says, raising a finger to ensure his order is included.

The server nods and walks away.

Scarlett leans back into Allison and Connor, whispering, "So, I asked someone if they were in…"

"That's still on your mind?" Allison interjects.

"Yes," Scarlett says, shutting up Allison. "The way they responded was rehearsed. Like it's how that person was supposed to respond. With Poe."

Connor throws up a hand. "I might know why."

Scarlett's eyes grow wide. "Why?!"

Connor leans in as well. The three sit hunched over the bar booth table as if villains from a 1920s movie hatching some evil scheme or planning a bank heist.

"At graduation, Grams gave me a card and told me how to respond," Connor whispers.

"How!" Scarlett whispers back with excitement.

"If asked, I am to say," the volume of his voice lowers even further, "I am in because of his age and his cunning."

"Oh. That's so cool!" Allison adds.

"See!" Scarlett points to him. "That sounds poetic too!"

"Wait. There's more," Connor notes.

"More!?" Scarlett asks, enthusiasm beginning to boil over.

"Yes, Scarlett, more! If you act now, you'll get a paring knife for just shipping and handling!" Allison jests.

Scarlett's sharp eyes cut Allison's bit short. Connor shakes his head with a short laugh. "Paring knife, that's funny."

Allison nods her head at his approval.

"More. If that's how they respond, if I'm the one who asks, I am to say, 'Because of his gripe and his paw.'"

"What the hell does that mean?" Scarlett ponders.

Connor leans back a bit. "I took a poetry course last semester. The athletic association wants us to take courses that won't hinder our athletic obligations."

"Bring it around, cuz'." Scarlett urges.

"It's a line from Kipling's *The Law For The Wolves.* If whoever you asked responded with Poe, and I'm supposed to respond with Kipling, then maybe that's the thing. Poets," Connor hypothesizes.

"Okay, but what do the different poets mean? Age, age upon discovery, level within The Nation?" Scarlett starts tossing out guesses.

"Level within The Nation? What the hell does that mean?" Allison asks.

But before Scarlett can clarify, the server returns with their sodas. "Desserts will be out in a few." She drops straws to go with the drinks and leaves.

"I mean, like…" Scarlett pauses while gathering her thoughts and takes a sip without using the straw, "…civilian, government level, on The Council, I don't know. I'm just spitballing here."

Connor taps the straw on the table to free it from the wrapper. "Any of those could be it." He puts the straw in his drink and takes a large gulp. "What are you supposed to say, Alli?"

Allison gives him a blank look as the desserts hit the table. Scarlett turns to her coworker. "Thanks! Just the check, then. We'll be out of your hair soon."

The server smiles and shakes her head as she walks away.

"I haven't been told what to say. Maybe we should go find out after we finish dessert," Allison notes.

"So, put aside all the cool theories of why we say what we say aside. Why do we have to say anything at all?" Connor thinks out loud.

"Whaddya mean?" Allison says through a mouthful of chocolate.

"I mean, why." Connor shoves strawberries into his mouth. "I mean, why not just say 'yes' if asked the question? Why a whole secret code? Or even if a secret code is used to keep people from just saying 'yes,' why a different phrase for whatever reason different phrases exist?"

Scarlett pontificates as she swallows some cheesecake. "Maybe we don't know the reasons why and won't know why until we understand why there are different phrases in the first place."

They all look at each other, a moment of calm with a satisfactory response. Allison puts up a finger as she shovels an oversized bite of chocolate mixed with cheesecake into her mouth.

After chewing and swallowing enough to talk, she continues. "You know who would know? My father."

The other two nod in agreement. Everyone exchanges glances like dessert needs to end sooner than later.

Connor pulls out some cash as the waitress drops off the check. They each rise and take one last bite before heading out the door.

"Here's what I'm wonderin', though," Connor says, as they walk to the front door. "When we found out about all this, and they told us the importance of the question, how come no one told us right away how to respond."

Scarlett stops in her tracks for a second and scratches the back of her neck. "Yeah, you would think a detail like that would have been addressed."

Allison hops up and down in excitement. "Oh. Oh! Unless that's what we're supposed to figure out. Or, like we just thought, that they have to figure out our place." She rubs her hands together. "This is kinda exciting."

As they enter Allison's house, the soft, distant, but distinct sounds of Bach's *Bourrée in E minor* can be heard playing from the basement. The three young adults stroll their way to Allison's father.

"Is there an instrument your dad can't play?" Connor asks.

Allison shakes her head. "Not really. As long as it has strings or keys, he's solid."

"What about the saxophone or the French horn?" Scarlett asks as they approach the basement stairwell.

"Nothing he has to blow into. Never got into those," Allison says, while they descend the steps.

At the bottom of the stairs, they are greeted by a room whose walls are decorated with various stringed instruments: classical, acoustic, and electric guitars— some six and some 12 string, dulcimers, violins, violas, basses, one Hardanger fiddle, two banjos, and a bala-laika from his old country. The floor houses a harpsi-chord, a cello, and an upright bass in their own stand.

"Holy shit!" Connor exasperates. "I've never been down here."

Vistrus looks up from his guitar but doesn't stop playing. "And you never will be unless I am down here. I hope your birthday outing was fun, Allison."

She smiles, giving her dad a hug as he finishes the piece. "It was. We actually were all out having dessert and, well..." she looks back to her friends, "...we need to talk to you."

Vistrus lets the last chord ring out as he stands and hangs his guitar back on the wall in its spot. "All three of you have a peculiar look. What is going on?"

"What do Poe and Kipling have to do with the question? *The* question," Allison asks, taking a seat at the harpsichord.

Vistrus's face shrinks to its center as he recalls thoughts from that fateful night eight months ago. "The devil is in the details. Do you remember what I told you that night?"

The other three exchange glances, but all are hesitant to say anything. Connor takes a long, deep breath as he turns to Vistrus.

"Bits and pieces. It's all a blur, not exactly a night I want to remember, not that I have a choice about certain moments." Connor finds comfort on a padded stool.

"We might be Legends. We might be viewed as extraordinary. But we are still human, with families and inadequacies to handle difficult situations. For that, I apologize," Vistrus offers up.

"Apologize for what, Dad?"

"Not telling you about the Societies," Vistrus smiles.

"Societies?" Scarlet parrots from the floor.

"Societies. You asked about Poe and Kipling. Each society is named after the poet from which their response is derived," Vistrus starts. "I know, for example, that Connor was told his response at graduation. That he 'is in because of his age and his cunning.'"

Connor jumps in, "And I because of his gripe and his paw."

"So is that it? If we are in The Nation, we respond back with, 'because of his gripe and his paw?'" Allison asks.

Vistrus shakes his head. "Only if you are in the Kipling society. You only respond if you are in the same society and only if you feel comfortable enough to respond."

"Why can't we just be like, 'I'm a werewolf' if someone asks the question?" Connor throws out.

Vistrus takes a frustrated breath. "Because you are not actually a werewolf, for starters. And also, because the phrase gives us a way to communicate in public without giving away the truth to Normals."

Scarlett starts to raise her hand. "Is there a third?"

Vistrus gives a cocked smile. "Because it sounds cool. In all seriousness, I should have told you sooner, Allison, but some things are hard for a father to deal with. Even a father such as myself." He looks his child square in the eye. "You are in a night chilly and dark. Now you say it."

Allison glances at her friends, almost embarrassed to say the phrase. Vistrus steadies her head and fixes her gaze on him.

"Are we even sure that I am actually a vampire or whatever? Can't this all just be a misunderstanding?" Allison denies her true self.

"Nope. I've seen you start to change or transition or whatever." Scarlett is quick to catch her wording.

"You need to learn the phrase. It is your way." Vistrus again looks her in the eye.

Allison's eyes wander as she summons the courage to speak the words. "I am in a night chilly and dark."

Her father looks at her., grabbing her hands. "The night may be chilly, but not dark."

She pulls away from her father's hands. "What does that mean?"

"It is your response back if you so choose." He offers a slight smile.

"The night may be chilly, but not dark?" Allison asks.

Vistrus nods. "We are part of the Coleridge society."

"What about me?" Scarlett asks.

Vistrus takes a moment of his trademark stoicism to contemplate his response. He puts the inside of his thumb and index finger over his upper lip and rubs his face while he thinks.

"Until we know what society you are a part of, we will not know how you should respond," he offers lightly.

"And when will I find out if I'm a Legend or not?" Scarlett asks with growing disappointment.

"When you first transition," Vistrus offers his less-than-satisfactory response.

"Okay, Dad, well, what about the others? Bri said something to us that wasn't that and Scarlett talked to someone who quoted Poe." Allison's denial was growing.

"That is for them to tell," Vistrus says.

And with that, the moment dies. The youths are marinating in an awkward silence of life and adulthood, pounding them from a surreal side. Vistrus stands up and heads to the stairwell, where he stops and waits for the kids to go first.

"Apologies, I overlooked such an important detail that night those months ago." He holds out a hand for them all to leave the basement.

Connor hops off his stool. "Well, that will give me something to chew on while I drive back to college."

"Aren't you staying the weekend?" Allison asks with a puppy dog stare.

Connor starts up the stairs, followed by the others. "Doubleheader tomorrow and one on Sunday. I have to be up early and still…"

"Have a four-hour drive ahead," Allison finishes for him. "It just sucks sometimes."

"I know, baby. It's hard on me too," Connor responds from the top of the stairs.

They walk to the front door and embrace in a warm hug that will have to last until the next time they see each other. Vistrus strolls past, leaving them to their moment together. "Drive safe, young man."

"Always," Connor says, resting his forehead on Allison's.

Once Vistrus has cleared sight, they give each other a deep kiss that lets the other know their distance is nothing to worry about. Only a matter of time until they meet again.

CHAPTER 25

"Life isn't a series of maxims.
So grow up quickly."
~R. Chandler~

"I s it just me, or do all the bands that play here sound the same?" Scarlett shouts over the pop-punk band playing on stage at The Attic this Saturday night.

"I think, like, this is the same band from your birthday," Brianna shouts back with uncertainty in her voice.

"Even if it's not, they could be," Allison jests. "Do you think we'll all still be hanging out together here in ten years?"

Brianna's face twists in disgust at the thought. "God, I hope not."

Scarlett and Allison toss each other looks that are mortally offended; it does not go unnoticed by Brianna.

"No. I mean, I hope we are still friends, and we get to hang out and see each other. I just hope by then we have moved onto bigger and better things," Bri clarifies.

"Come on, Bri," Scarlett laughs as the song dies. "You don't think hanging out here on a Saturday night at almost 30 years old is a banging idea of fun?"

"Lol. Yes, I said, lol. And no, that would be so not ... rad," Bri ends with a questioning uptick.

"Bringing back rad? I can dig it," Allison approves with a nod.

"Thanks," Bri nods back. "I mean, if a really good band plays here or if there's, like, nothing else going on, or whatever, yeah. Come here, have a drink, but every Saturday when we're pushing 30? No way."

"I hear ya on that. It's like, I want to get out of West Haven so bad but feel like I'm destined to be stuck here," Allison drones.

"No bringing down the mood. We passed on Girl's Choice Valentine's weekend to have a girl's night out. A sense of growth and the fact that the dance doesn't seem..." Scarlett gets lost, searching for words.

Brianna chimes in, "I know what you mean. With everything that's been going on this year with our ... ya know, it seems like we are too ... mature for Girl's Choice."

Scarlett does a quick head tilt to the side in surprising agreement with her. "I was trying to find a way to mention Jack and Connor's absences, but you are right. Nice elegance."

"Thanks," Bri beams. "My mother taught me some things."

"Something going on at home, Bri?" Allison inquires.

The music starts up again.

"Nothing more than usual. She's dealing with Duncan and me but still doesn't trust him. Just so annoying," Bri pouts.

"Speaking of, how'd he take the news that you weren't going this year?" Scarlett looks at the band while bending an ear toward Bri.

"He was cool. He is the coolest, though," Bri says with dreamy eyes.

"Does he know?" Scarlett asks, a bit surprised.

"Know what?" Bri is oblivious.

"That you're in?" Scarlett fills in the blank.

"Oh, God, no. I told him that with everything that's been going on, especially like..." she lowers her voice and hunches down, "...Operation Cobra Kai and stuff that the dance didn't feel appropriate. He shrugged and immediately moved on."

Allison has a moment of inward reflection. The look in Brianna's eyes as she talks about Duncan makes Allison wonder what she could have done differently in the past to have Bri talking like that about her. Of course, Allison wonders if Brianna could ever fall for a girl like her or a girl in general. So, she just watches Bri and tries not to dwell on the past.

"Duncan seems to be a good ally," Scarlett tells Brianna.

"Ally? What does that mean?" Bri asks back.

Scarlett is taken aback for a moment. "Um, an ally is a friend. Someone on your side but isn't..."

"I know what an ally is. I meant, what do you mean by *he's* an ally," Bri clarifies.

Scarlett laughs at her misunderstanding. "I mean, he's not *in*, but he seems to be on our side. He helped get my program launched. Saved Al from getting arrested. Willing to help our cause on you-know-who. He's loyal and pretty damn cool."

Brianna smiles and nods.

"Yeah, he is. He's a lucky guy," Allison adds.

The girls sit back and look around The Attic at the people dancing, drinking, and enjoying the music.

"So, this is it. Our final Girl's Choice dance. Our final year of high school. And this is what we are doing. Some would say this is sad," Brianna observes.

"Who cares?" Scarlett blurts. "We're doing what we do. All others can suck it. If this is what we want to do, then so be it. If no one else wants to be here, then whatever. We are surrounded by strangers who had the same idea for tonight."

"Then maybe this is our calm," Allison mutters.

"What?" Scarlett hears her under the music.

Allison turns to Scarlett, taking her eyes off Brianna for a moment. "Our calm. The calm before the storm. Like when a big storm is coming. There is always that calm before it strikes. A moment where you think that everything will turn out okay and nothing will happen. No rain, no wind, no damage. Just a peaceful calm. Maybe this is ours."

"If this is the calm, then the storm is either going to be really mild or extremely deadly. Either way, the eerie and ominous dread I am feeling will play out." Scarlett stares off into the crowd. She wonders if anyone else is going through the same thing. But how can they? How can anyone going through this much death, this much loss, have the urge or energy to dance? All she can muster up is sitting here when she should be at her last Girl's Choice dance, wondering what the near future holds.

CHAPTER 26

*"When you have nothing important left to say,
think of something pithy.
It may fool whoever's listening."*
~J. Taylor~

Scarlett sits on her couch, remote in one hand, flipping through television channels, and cell phone in her other as she texts Allison. The first day of her final spring break seems to be nothing more than a mundane Monday.

Allison's thoughts about the calm before the storm might appear proven correct. The weeks since the Valentine's Day Girl's Choice dance have been unnoteworthy, mellow, and inconsequential. Bri, Duncan, and his friends have been mum about Operation Cobra Kai. Even Linda Espinoza has been lying low: no snide, veiled comments about her biases, and no students have gone missing. Nothing. Just classes, gossip about the latest rumor floating around, and homework. No sign of anything brewing. The calm before the storm, if ever there was one—if there is a storm brewing somewhere.

Scarlett sends a text message to Allison saying she should come over, as the front door to the house starts to unlock. Scarlett scoots to the far side of the couch; no company was expected so soon after her text. Her grandmother came by yesterday to help clean the house, making this person a complete surprise. She stares at the knob as it turns. She holds the remote behind her ear, ready to throw it at the would-be intruder. But the door opens, and Connor, not a strange robber, is the one walking through.

He wheels a suitcase behind him in one hand, his backpack slung over the opposite shoulder. His low-hung head does not hide his red face, which is clearly visible from the couch.

Scarlett hops up and runs to her cousin. Frustration, anger, and disappointment shine across his face in blinding expressions.

"What are you doing home? What's going on?" Scarlett asks, as she takes the backpack from him. She sets it down. He takes his jacket off, tossing it on the floor next to the closet door. Scarlett leads him to the couch.

He plops down, rests his elbows on his knees, and buries his face in his hands.

"Say something, Cuz'. What happened?" she urges.

He just shakes his buried head. "I'm done."

She sits, the urge to say something welling inside her, wanting to burst forth, but she holds back.

He lifts his head just enough to turn an eye on her. "Over. Done. The college experience has ended."

"I don't understand," Scarlett says. But it's a lie. The words he speaks aren't hard to comprehend. To her, they are not words that need to be looked up in a dictionary. The why behind them is what she doesn't get. "What happened?"

"All those games that I played. Preseason. Nothing that counted. Basically, practice," Connor explains.

"Yeah, I know what preseason is." Scarlett nods.

"But that's not even it, Scar. It's everything. I was gone. Far away and Jack … he died. I can't help but wonder … if I was here … if Jack decided to go to college, would things be different? If I had stayed back home, could he still be alive? Would we both be dead? Could we have stopped our parents' killers before they killed Jack? So many questions run through my head every day, all day long. Then this happens. The only thing I had going for my future stripped out from under me for something I didn't even do." With the last words, he takes a deep breath and falls back into the couch. With each breath he takes in the silence between them, he sinks further into the couch cushions.

Scarlett leans back as well, using the remote to turn off the distraction of the television. They sit in silence, staring forward at the room before them. Neither one says anything, as both just exist in the moment. The moments after Connor's outpour fills the room with the weight of the words he spoke, a weight that keeps either of them from moving or speaking.

Like all moments, they must come to an end. A moment where Scarlett realizes Connor can't sit here forever, and she cannot help. But she knows someone who can.

She pulls out her cell phone and dials.

A few rings go by. Nothing unusual. Finally, someone picks up. "Grandpa. Just the person I needed. Can you come over?"

Her stare moves to her cousin as she asks for a visit from her grandparent. Connor doesn't move. His stare is resolved to face forward into the passing moment of the empty room.

"See you soon. Love you." Scarlett hangs up the phone and rises from the couch.

She walks to the kitchen and pours two glasses of ice water. She hands one to Connor without exchanging words and leaves the other on the table for her grandfather.

As soon as she sets the water down, the door opens. Allison enters and beams with immediate excitement at the sight of her boyfriend. He does not return her outward enthusiasm. He turns to her, then faces forward again to stare at the emptiness in front of him.

Scarlett hastily steps to Allison and leads her outside. Allison's head is fixed on Connor even as the door closes behind them.

"What's wrong?" Allison stares through the closed door, as if she is still looking at him.

The brisk mid-30s temperatures bite at Scarlett. "I'll let him tell you, but he needs time." Scarlett wraps her arm around Allison for comfort as much as warmth.

Allison finally turns to her best friend. "Did he cheat on me? Did he come all the way home to tell me he met someone else?"

Scarlett shakes her head. "No. I promise it's not that; it's not about you at all. But it's not my place to say."

"You need a coat," Allison observes. "It's not exactly BBQ weather nice yet."

"I'll be fine," Scarlett assures. "We should go somewhere. Give him space."

A car stops on the street. A silver-haired man with a captivating and disarming smile exits the vehicle. An immediate sense of calm washes over Scarlett, who watches her grandfather's hair whip in the wind as he walks up the driveway.

Scarlett meets him halfway. "I am so glad you were home. He needs you, Grandpa Nick."

Nick embraces his granddaughter in a patronly hug. "Things have been a little unusual around here this past year."

"They certainly have," she confirms as shivers set in.

"I suspect they aren't going to get any less interesting anytime soon," he says to her. He turns to Allison. "Hello, young lady."

Allison waves. "Hi."

"He's inside, I presume?" Nick asks.

Scarlett nods. "I poured you some ice water, too."

He gives a satisfied smile. "You need a jacket. It's cold, in case you haven't noticed." He takes off his Vintage World War II brown leather bomber jacket, wrapping it around Scarlett before heading inside.

Nick smiles as his granddaughter and Allison run off to their car. A cold wind whips, causing Nick to wrap his arms around himself for a quick moment before heading indoors to his grandson.

Connor is still slumped on the couch, his vacant eyes staring straight ahead. The weight of the past couple years' events pushes down, making movement seem impossible.

Nick sits next to Connor. The elder puts a hand on Connor's knee, giving it a subtle shake, then a that-a-boy slap. "I think I have some things to explain."

Connor's head falls toward his grandfather. His eyes shift enough to see Nick's face.

"Everything's gone. I worked my whole life for this. It was what I wanted. It was my ticket out of here. To a good life," Connor sighs.

Nick tightens his face. "What was wrong with the life your parents provided? Was the life they gave you less than adequate?"

Connor is quick to straighten up in his seat, all weight lifted off in the challenge of his grandfather's words.

"No. They did great. But isn't the point of parents to want a better life for their children than they had? For the children to want a better life as an adult than they had growing up?" Connor turns to Nick.

Nick shakes his head. "The words you speak miss the intention behind them." He pauses for a moment. The circumstances surrounding Connor are strenuous, so Nick wants to tread lightly. "What is it you want?"

"From you or in general?"

"Out of your life."

"To play baseball. To be back at college. To know that I am doing something more," Connor confesses.

Nick cracks a smile. "Those are very vague desires. They lack tactile definition. Why do you want to play baseball? Why do you want to be back at college? What is that something more that you want to be doing? What is so wrong with looking through the *TV Guide* and having a nice, relaxed life?"

Connor sits, no real answers flow to the front of his mind. No solid idea of what can be said to answer the proposed questions.

Nick notices the wheels turning in the young DeSalvo's head. "No need to answer those right now. Think. Ponder. Let the possibilities flow. So, tell me, what happened at school?"

"All the preseason games went great. Classes were good. Everything seemed ... in place. But as spring break approached, they started random drug testing on the players," Connor starts. He notices a grimace on Nick's face. A sign that his grandfather knows where the story is headed and why. "And I was tested. But Grandpa, I don't do drugs!"

Nick nods in acknowledgment. "I know you don't. I know you would never. But the result of the test is not because you do drugs; it is because of who you are."

"Who I am?" Connor asks, more than a bit confused.

"Yes. Because of your condition. Normals have no idea what we are. Remember, we are Legends, myths, stories told by those gathered around campfires and romanticized about in movies. We are not real to them. But we are. And our conditions hint at the Normal world in strange and, sometimes, unfortunate ways.

In your instance, it shows as a false positive on certain drug tests."

The tense look locked on Connor's face doesn't seem to loosen. "My situation? Not all werewolves register false positives on drug tests? Just me, who wants to play baseball?" Connor asks, sinking back into the cushions of the couch.

A small laugh escapes Nick. "Not just you. All werewolves. Not everything about being a Legend is wine and roses, young man."

"I need something more than what you're giving me, Grandpa. Some light at the end of this tunnel. And a light that isn't a train charging toward me," Connor pleads.

"I have something that might ease the burden of your wanting a better life," Nick starts as he drinks his glass of water.

Connor looks up at him but doesn't say anything.

"Your parents had a little life insurance policy. It stays in trust until you are 21." Nick takes a long, slow drink, forcing a reaction from Connor.

"I don't want their money; I want to make a future for myself, not be a trust-fund baby living off the life insurance payout of his dead parents. That's why I wanted baseball," Connor's voice rises in volume as the frustration mounts again.

"Those are the cards you were dealt. The money will be enough to do anything you want, but it is not enough to do nothing. Baseball might be out, but you said you wanted a better life than this. This money will allow you to figure that out and make it happen." The tone in Nick's voice changes from a nurturing paternal figure to a slightly grizzled, deal-with-it forceful intonation.

Connor raises a brow and bobs his head. "I guess that's something. But you know I would trade all the money, however much it is, to have them back, right?"

Nick relaxes his posture and rubs his grandson's head, messing up his hair. "I know, Connor. I know. Here's the why of why I needed to come over and not Grandma; we need to talk about your future."

"I thought we kinda were." Connor finally takes a drink of his water.

"Why do you want out of West Haven?"

"I dunno. Just want something more, I guess," Connor resigns.

"What if West Haven could offer you more?" Nick asks, clearly baiting Connor.

"Like what?" Connor says, taking the bait.

"The better life you want. The ability to, as you put it, do something more?"

"Depends on what that 'something more' is." Connor's face lights up with a look of playful skepticism. "Wait, you aren't about to tell me about how sometimes when one door closes, another opens, are you?"

Nick chuckles a good belly laugh. "No. Though sometimes maxims can be true, I try not to use such cliches. There are things in the works, things within The Nation. And I think you have the potential to find a place within."

Connor's face drops—the weight of realization pulling it down. "Can I ask you something? It's about The Nation."

"Always."

"How many of us are there? Is almost all West Haven Legends or Legendary or whatever?" Connor asks in meek tones.

Nick's eyes look toward the ceiling, his head tilting from left to right as he searches for the answer. "The best answer I can give is that our true numbers are unknown. There are those of us who will not answer to 'Are you in?' when asked because we might not feel safe. Some might not have transitioned yet or choose not to be involved in The Nation and keep their condition in check, living a Normal life. But I can tell you this ... West Haven has a high enough concentration that a council was put into place here. That should say something."

Connor drinks more water as thoughts swirl through his head. "And you think I might have a place somewhere involved with that?"

Nick smiles and nods. "I do."

"So, you won't tell me what happened? Nothing at all?" Allison whines while looking through a row of CDs.

"We've been talking in circles since we left my house. Now stop! It's not my place," Scarlett reprimands. She, too, thumbs through rows of CDs, hoping for something to catch her eye.

"Fine." Allison forfeits her fight. She pulls her flask out of her back pocket and takes a swig. "Then what about the other thing?"

Scarlett doesn't look up to notice Allison's drinking. "What other thing?"

"The operation?" Allison's voice lowers, as if her words could spill government secrets.

Scarlett stops thumbing the CDs and turns her attention to Allison. "As I said at Christmas, we have to make them think we have put it all behind us." She looks around the store for any ears pointed their direction. "All in good time. I have not forgotten."

"Are we doing prom this year?" Allison's abrupt and begrudging change of subject pleases Scarlett.

"Actually, we are, and Bri is planning out the whole thing for all of us." Scarlett smiles.

"What does that mean? I'm not finding anything I absolutely need right now," Allison sidenotes.

"Me too. Or neither. Whatever. I'm finding nothing." Scarlett starts walking toward the exit. "I mean, Bri is renting the limo. She is paying and reserving the hotel. She's getting us a suite!"

"A sweet suite!" Allison puns.

"I'll give you that one; it will be sweet. I just hope the rest of the school year is uneventful. We need a break," Scarlett notes.

"As I said, the calm before the storm."

CHAPTER 27

Prom

"Bite me."
~S. Waldgrave~

Allison and her father sit at the kitchen table enjoying, what Vistrus considers, a late breakfast. A fatherly smile across his face as he watches his daughter scarf down chocolate waffles and bacon. A glass of red wine next to his plate that Allison eyes with curiosity.

"Dad, the red wine … that you always drink … is it wine?" Allison tiptoes around the real question she wants to ask.

"As opposed to?" He lets the sentence trail off.

"Blood. I mean, we are vampires. Am I going to have to start drinking blood? I mean, I don't even like rare meat." Allison starts to ramble.

Vistrus holds up a fork to stop her talking and extends the cup with the other. "It is wine. If you do not believe me, have a sip."

"Wine and chocolate waffles don't sound like the best combination, but thanks for promoting underage drinking," Allison jokes.

"We have porphyria. Specifically, EPP, which means we need heme. So, yes, we need outside blood. But there are no West Haven vampire blood-drinking orgies or the like. Those notions are romanticized. Motion picture production company musings paint false pictures to grab money out of moviegoers' pockets," he explains.

Allison stops eating for a moment. "But we see those movies. We've seen tons of them."

"I never said they were not fun and amusing to watch. I love those movies. That is what is so great about them. They allow our imaginations to take over and remove us from life's problems for a while. But to the point, rare steak, raw meats, and fish. But never raw chicken. We can still get sick, remember. We just will not die from it. Even without the fear of death, illness is no less miserable." He tears into a strip of bacon, playing up the blood-hungry vampire for a quick laugh with his child.

Allison laughs along with her father. She picks up a strip of bacon and is about to mimic him, but she decides against it. Something inside her isn't ready to admit her true self just yet.

"Prom is tonight, correct?"

"Yes, Dad. Bri is picking us up in the limo, then we are all staying at … some hotel. I've told you this before," she reminds him.

"I know. Just making sure. The school year is almost over. Your classes are all going well, I assume?"

"Yes. All five of my classes are going swimmingly." Allison gives her father a wry smile.

"Quick rundown, please—grades and high points," he politely orders.

"Working backward. Gym class, I cannot play volleyball. Way too short. Otherwise, kinda cool," she says with a casualness reserved for teenage apathy. "Free period before that where I finished whatever work I didn't finish in my other free period. Sixth-period English class, Film Studies. We just watched *Citizen Kane*. Revolutionary for its time. Didn't age well. Let's see." She counts backward on her schedule, figuring out where she's at. "Lunch ... always a favorite. Geology. Fun times. Rocks, stones, tectonic plates. It rocks." She pauses, thinking about what comes next but stops when her father chuckles. "What?"

"Geology rocks?" he repeats her pun.

"Yeah. It is a little more interesting than I thought it would be," she admits, still missing her pun." Finding her place again, "Art. Fun class. Can't draw. And history, Western Civilization."

Vistrus jumps in, "Ah, yes. If I recall, syphilis and the downfall of the axis powers."

Allison's eyes light up with a particular enthusiasm for this class that she hasn't shown for any other. "I know it seems strange, but the teacher is fascinating and knows his stuff. The class isn't actually about syphilis."

Vistrus slows down his chewing to give more attention to his daughter and her growing excitement about this course.

"It traces the events in Hitler's life that unfolded to lead up to World War II. It makes us look at history and examine, contemplate, percolate …wait, no … postulate … whatever, if any variables changed, if the war might have not started, started differently, or ended differently," she pauses, making sure her father is still listening.

Vistrus swallows a bite of food. "Please go on."

"Every World War II history class starts with Hitler's rise to power. His invasion of Poland and all the usual stuff. We look deeper. To see if all of that might have been avoidable."

"World peace through better parenting and STD testing?" he ponders.

"Sorta. Mr. Parlett said it was like a disease, the war, not syphilis. I mean, yeah. Syphilis is a disease, but the analogy or metaphor here is that the symptoms that caused the war were laid by other factors. We try to look at earlier signs to see if anything could have alerted them to the disease that would rage on the world stage. His words, not mine," she finishes her argument on the benefits of the class, unsure if her father is swayed.

"Interesting course. Instead of late-stage symptoms, your teacher has you trying to identify early symptoms that mostly go unnoticed. I like his thinking." And just like that, he is lost in thought. His mind has wandered far from home. A look on his face of content curiosity seems to be all he needs at the moment.

Allison finishes her chocolate waffles and kisses her dad on the cheek before running off to start her beauty regimen for the night's event.

A black stretched limousine pulls up to the Rosemont convention center, the venue for this year's senior prom, stopping at the designated curbside drop-off. The driver steps out and opens the passenger door. First to step out is Duncan, dressed in a tailed, black tuxedo vest, tuxedo shirt—the sleeves of which have been torn off—pants and shoes to match. As he turns around to help the ladies out of the limo, he dons a black golfer's cap to match his rudded take on a formal outfit.

Next out is Connor, dressed in a more traditional tuxedo. He also dons the same golfer's cap in group solidarity.

Duncan's fingerless gloved hands extend to offer leverage to the ladies. Brianna exits the limo, grasping Duncan with her baby blue satin-gloved hand, exuding all the elegance of a true lady. She bows her head to her gentleman as she eases on out. Duncan continues on to help Scarlett out of the limo. She emerges in a dark red dress, long and flowing. Fitted sleeves ending in flowing cuffs and a low-cut back with an elegant and slightly modest front give her a classic look.

Connor reaches out and is met by Allison's dark-gloved hand. A satin glove with full fingers but a vented palm. Allison dresses in her favorite formal look—black lace overlaid on the skirt that fades to white as it works its way up her top.

The five of them make a grand entrance, side by side, into the venue. The lobby has an overly large chandelier hanging from the ceiling. The diamonds that make up the fixture reflect light throughout the large entranceway.

After a short escalator ride up, the group finds themselves outside the door to the prom hall. Balloons decorate both archways into the room. A sign outside welcomes the senior class of 2019, complete with the class picture. Not that any student would be able to pick themselves out of a group photo of over 600. It is still a beautiful, finishing touch.

They open the doors, and music blares out at them. A throwback to the 1980s. A time before they were born, yet the music lives on. A fun, danceable tune about bustin' a move pounds out of the speakers as the soon-to-be-graduates dance about.

The five shimmy their way to the punch bowl and grab a glass. Standing guard over the virgin beverages, and ensuring they stay that way, is none other than Linda Espinoza. Allison turns to the group and gives them a dead stare that tells them to play it cool.

"Hiya, Ms. Espinoza! Great dance, huh?!" Allison bluffs in an almost-too-cheerful voice.

"You kiddies have any fun plans later tonight?" Linda's voice sounds innocent enough.

"Staying at some hotel. Usual prom stuff! Have fun!" That said, Allison skips off.

Linda doesn't say anything but nods and forces out a small smile. She glances down at her watch and pulls out her cell phone. The teens try not to stare as Linda checks a text message or email.

The group finds a table. Connor and Duncan remain standing while all the girls take a seat. The young men keep a lookout while the girls hike up their dresses to pull flasks out of their garter belts. They each pour some random alcohol into their drinks and do the same for the boys. After which, they replace them in their garter belts.

The flavor of the alcohol is of little importance tonight. Tonight, for the girls at least, it is about saying goodbye to the past. A four-year run of ups and downs. A chapter in their lives that even those in the group would not believe had happened had it not happened to them.

The group dances and laughs the next few hours away, listening to the music that helped shape who they have become. They reminisce about times that can be reminisced about in public. Allison and Connor exchange glances that are hoping for privacy later.

Allison tries to keep her thoughts on Connor, though she can't help but notice Brianna. The way her smile has relaxed—all the fake facade of popularity has faded away. The natural, almost open mouth, parted teeth smile is something that Allison wishes Brianna had somewhere for her.

It is a look on Allison's face that does not go unnoticed by Connor. "What's that look for, love? Something happen between you two?"

Allison snaps back to the moment as the last sentence resonates through her ears. "What? Something happen? Between Bri and me? No?" She laughs a nervous laugh. "What would make you think something happened between us? Nothing happened."

Connor shrugs off his notion. "You had this look. Like you either wanted to kiss her or kill her."

Again, Allison laughs nervously. "Kiss her? God no! Why would I want…"

"I was thinking the 'kill her' part might be the more worrisome of the two," Connor interjects.

"Oh." Allison realizes his take on the stare is not the same as her own. "Nope. Everything is fine. Just kinda glad we are friends again."

Scarlett looks around the hall at her hallway-friends of the past four years. She knows they will stay connected on Facebook and possibly Instagram or Twitter. She can't help but wonder how many she will end up keeping in touch with. How many will fall victim to becoming nothing more than people that share memes every so often and hit like buttons to show that they still remember the other person? She can't help but wonder how long that will go on before the day comes when she is scrolling her friends list, and her memory has faded to where half her class is nothing more than strangers she wouldn't recognize in person.

She tries to pull herself out of future ruminations, but one last thought pushes its way to the front of her mind, waving its hand like a fan trying to touch a basketball player as they make their way to the court. A thought that makes her wonder how many of these people would shun her, or worse, if they found out who she really was. Like so many people who can't hide what society has not fully come to accept about them, she, too, wonders who would not accept her. How many classmates would unfriend her for something that has no effect on their lives whatsoever?

No matter, though, the tap on her shoulder from Allison brings her back to shore from the sea of her thoughts. "We're gonna head to the hotel."

Scarlett looks at her friends, gathering their belongings that made their way tableside throughout the night. The rest of the prom rages on, but for these young adults, the time has come to cap off the bookend to their high school careers.

As they make their way in the limo and begin to pull away, Allison spots Linda Espinoza leaving the facility earlier than a chaperone should. Or at least sooner than Allison thinks a chaperone should. Before she can say anything to the group, Duncan holds a flask in front of her face.

"Still a bit left. Yours if ya want it." Duncan shakes the container.

Allison takes it and downs the last of what she can only guess is isopropyl rubbing alcohol by the taste of it.

"What the hell was that?" She rubs the dribble from her chin.

Duncan gives a maniacal laugh. "Spirytus Rekufuktem. I can't pronounce it."

"Rectumfuktu? It tastes like crap," Allison says, still wiping the taste from her tongue.

"It's some Polish liquor. Like 95% alcohol. I watered it down a bit, though. Didn't want us blacking out at prom," Duncan notes.

They arrive at the hotel a little worse for wear. They all feel a little happier than perhaps they should, as the last of the alcohol has hit their heads. They stroll on up to the hotel clerk with goofy grins across their faces.

"R'm f'r Wal' grave," Brianna mumbles.

The middle-aged hotel clerk eyes her suspiciously as he types into the hotel computer. After searching, he looks at Brianna. "The reservation shows two occupants. I see five of you."

Brianna throws up her arms, pulling her chin to her neck. "C'mon..." Brianna pauses to read his nametag, "...Burt. Like, we're not actually going to be doing any sleeping. Let it slide."

Burt takes a deep breath, pressing his lips together. "The extra people will be another $75.00."

"That's bullshit. The number of people doesn't mean we want a bigger room. Just give us the damn key." Duncan starts getting a little belligerent.

Burt turns his attention to Duncan. "And I'll need Sylvia's driver's license. I assume she is with you tonight. She was the one that rented the room, after all."

Allison's face contorts at Burt's snotty, holier-than-thou tone. "Listen here, Burt. No, Sylvia isn't with us. It's prom night. Just give us the damn key!"

"And no. Please leave the hotel," Burt says with his power of hourly employment.

"What? Ernie not putting out?" Allison digs at him.

Burt doesn't respond but picks up the phone and dials a number. "Can you please kindly escort the youths at my counter out of the building? Thank you." He hangs up the phone and smiles smugly at the group.

Duncan starts walking away. The rest of the group follows before any more scene plays out. As he exits the building, Duncan flips Burt the bird.

"I'm just glad I t'ld the driver to wait'll we had the room b'fore I signed," Brianna smiles.

They all pile back into the limo.

"T' my place, Argyle. Looks like we're headed home," Bri instructs.

The limo driver nods his cap to her and pulls away.

The drive home is a bit more silent than the ride to the hotel. A feeling settling into everyone's minds that the night is over—that high school is over. A notion in the group that any more activity tonight would not end well, or at the very least, would be forced fun to prolong a night that ended at the convention center. A feeling that does not go unnoticed by Argyle.

The driver rolls down the divide and talks while glancing at them in the rearview mirror. "Quite the shift in mood. Anything I can do to help?"

"Drive," Allison flatly says.

"Hey, hey," Argyle says, trying to lift the mood, "this is not my first day, ya know. Just trying to fulfill my driverly duties."

"Nothing, honestly," Connor says, a bit dejected. "Not unless you can give us back the last two years."

"I can't do that, my friend, but if you don't mind, a little unasked tidbit of wisdom…" he trails off, waiting for some sort of response.

Connor sees Argyle check the rearview mirror and gives him a nod to continue.

"Now, I don't know what y'all been through for a two-year period that you want a mulligan, but I do know that it's not what you go through; it's how you deal with the experience. But don't take me too seriously; I'm just your driver for the night," he smiles at them through the rearview. "*Aaand* we have arrived."

The street outside the Waldgrave residence is darker than usual. The streetlight that illuminates the portion of the road right outside their house has burnt out, giving a slightly more ominous feeling. From inside the limo, the group notices a cop car parked on the street right outside the house. No lights are on, headlight or cherries, and the vehicle is turned off. Nothing unusual, except no police officer lives in the area.

They exit the limo and sign him off for the night with a generous tip. No porch light stands as a beacon, just shadows on the front door. The curtains are closed on the dark house. Even the tree in the front yard casts an ever-darker shadow on the house.

Connor glances at the squad car parked out front. He read the number 51 on its side. A sobering reminder of past events.

"Hey, guys!" Connor shouts in a whisper. "I think Operation Cobra Kai needs to happen now!" He points to the car.

Allison and Scarlett look at each other, a silent understanding of things about to go down. Allison leans an ear toward the house. Movement. Lots of it.

Allison points to the house. "Lots of noise in there."

"Wait. I thought Operation Cobra Kai was gonna be at the cop's place?" Duncan asks.

"Change of plans," Connor cuts off Duncan's line of thinking. "It's happening now."

Duncan pats himself down, looking for his phone. "I'll call my...shit! My phone is in the limo!"

"Looks like we're the operation," Connor observes.

They all look around at each other, then at Duncan. A silent conversation among themselves about what to do with Duncan.

Brianna turns to her man with a smile. "Dear, so, all those things that we told you about why Operation ... Cobra Kai is happening." She shakes her head at the name. "They're all true, but there's more to it and no time to explain. You know I love you, right?" Brianna instructs him.

Duncan nods. "Of course. And I love you."

"I know. We have to get in there. You may see things. You can't tell anyone, and I mean anyone, what you see. Understood?" Brianna instructs him.

"Is your mom, like, Walter White or something?" Duncan asks, extremely confused about the situation.

"Something, but ways away from anything like that." Brianna plants a kiss on his cheek.

At the front door, the commotion inside is now audible to everyone. The group bursts through the

door like angry, well-dressed Kool-Aid mascots —
arms waving, screaming loudly.

The scene inside halts them in their tracks. The
commotion they heard was not the beginning of the
struggle but the end. Sylvia is slumped on the floor, a
bloody heap. Her eyes shift to the youths, screaming
for help though her mouth is silent. Her skin is scaled
in a thick, brownish-grey bark where it hasn't been
torn clean off. The missing patches reveal blood and
muscle beneath. Towering over the helpless Sylvia is
Linda, machete in hand; her eyes are wild, her smile
without care of right or wrong.

Across the room, a young man the kids have never
seen before lies face down and motionless. Blood cakes
his hospital scrubs. A chain with a fleur-de-lis pendant
lay broken next to him.

Officer Max Espinoza leans against a wall streaked
with his own blood. He squats, trying to hold himself
up. Tufts of hair grow over his arms, hands, and face.
A surprise to the youths.

Duncan stands in shock, unable to move at the
carnage before him. Bri runs to her mother, tears
already streaming down her face.

Linda sees Bri charging in her general direction and lifts her machete, ready to strike down on
the grieving daughter. Allison's fury grows. Allison
begins charging, transitioning in the process as Linda
lifts the blade into the air.

In the ten or so feet to Linda, Allison's transition is complete—thinned lips and protruding veins
throughout her entire body, her nose withered and
recessed, hair thin and wispy, muscles enough to

challenge even the most adept UFC fighter, blood and teeth pouring out her mouth.

Before Linda can swing the machete down on Bri, Allison tramples Linda, toppling her to the ground. Allison knocks the machete loose, causing it to go sliding across the floor in the opposite direction of Max.

As if taken over by an alien entity, Allison begins pummeling Linda. The first hit shatters her nose, sending blood flying everywhere. Linda tries to crawl out from underneath Allison.

"Why did you do this?!" screams Allison.

She doesn't wait for a response but continues the onslaught of hammer fists to the face. Linda struggles against the beating and starts to forfeit her efforts.

"You think you can hurt the mother of the girl I love and get away with it!" The words fly out of her mouth without any filter or forethought as to who might hear them.

A snapping sound resonates as another fist connects below the eye. Her friends stand behind her, stunned at the words they hear and the actions she takes, but their clothes at the moment and stillness make them look more like high society viewing a gladiatorial death match than teenagers who just finished prom.

"You can't take them away from me! Stop taking everyone away!" Allison pounds more fists into the pulpy mess becoming Linda's face. Her body lays limp beneath Allison.

"You think you can keep coming, and we'll just sit back?! We won't let this happen?!" Blood spews forth from Linda's mouth as fist after furious fist connects.

Allison grabs hold of Linda's hair and bashes her head into the floor, the pooling blood beneath spatters around.

Connor steps to Allison and tries to grab her. As if with no effort at all, Allison throws Connor off her. She turns to her friends to see the look of shock and horror etched onto all their faces.

"I'm so sorry, Bri," Allison cries.

Allison turns her attention to Max, who clutches his side, blood seeping out between his fingers. He sits on the floor, struggling for each breath.

Allison lurches to the injured officer. "Is this what you want?! Is this why you took Jack?!"

Max, no tears left to shed, looks at Allison. "I didn't know. I was told they could cure me. I was told this was for the greater good. Convinced me that our kind was evil." His pale face struggles to catch air between his words.

Allison points to his deceased wife and Sylvia. "Are they the greater good? Dead people? Is death the greater good? Violence? What exactly is the greater good here?! How are we the evil ones when all you bring is death?! How?! How?!" She grabs his throat, trying to force out a response.

"He found me. Told me it was a disease. That he had a cure," Max gasps out. "He said that we were less than human and evil by nature. That our conditions made us inferior. That I could be better if I was cured. I could be good."

Allison tightens her grip. "What made you think there is a simple solution to the thoughts you feel? Did you really think that an injection could take away your wicked thoughts? Look around! Did you?!"

He uses his other hand to try and loosen her grip around his throat while coughing out a little blood, "I couldn't control it. I wasn't like your friends. I was wild. I couldn't contain myself. I didn't know. He said we were all beasts. He said when I changed, I was evil. He would cure me if I helped him cure others. Please. He painted such a bad picture of who I was. I ate up every lie."

She lets go of his throat, dropping him down a few inches. She returns to the rest of the group, who are a little jumpy. She looks at Duncan, standing slack-jawed and unblinking at the scene before him.

"You okay, Duncan?" She waves a hand in front of his face and snaps her fingers a few times, finally getting him to blink and look at her.

"What ... are ... you?" Duncan stammers out.

Allison doesn't answer his question but instead turns to the others. "So what do we do?"

Scarlett and Bri stare at Allison, unsure if she realizes the self-revelation she had while bludgeoning Linda was aired out loud. Connor decides to look past it and tend to the situation at hand.

"Let's see what he can tell us. You need to calm down. Go to another room. Take a breather. Call your father," Connor forcefully suggests.

Allison pulls herself out of her rage, nods her head, and walks out of the room.

"So, you guys can just ... Hulk out?" Duncan asks.

Connor puts a hand up to Duncan in a universal "now is not the time" gesture.

Connor slowly and cautiously approaches Max.

"You look hurt." Connor gets down on one knee next to Max, like a football coach having a one-on-one with a player.

"I need help," Max pleads.

"Tit for tat, you'll get your help. We aren't like you. We are not killers," Connor starts.

Max looks in the direction of Allison but doesn't dare say anything.

"Special circumstances, if ever there were," Connor answers Max's unspoken question. "Who is it you work for?"

"I don't know exactly," Max cries.

Connor looks around at the carnage. "Not knowing is not looking real good for you right now. I could call my girl back in here."

Max's breathing quickens. "No, please. Look. I don't know who. I was approached by a guy at my station. He said he knew what I was."

"What is his name?" Connor urges.

"Never told me. Never needed it. He's dead now, anyway. Your friend killed him," Max says.

"You mean Jack?! Who *you* killed!" Connor shouts.

"It wasn't just me who killed him. I didn't want to. After what happened last year, I didn't know. I was trapped," Max frantically explains.

"You were trapped? As in, you were given no choice but to kill my family, my best friend's family, and my best friend?" Connor's disbelief in Max's words is evident in his voice.

Max feverishly nods his head.

"And tonight?" Connor tilts his head at Max.

"All we needed were samples. No one was supposed to die," Max whimpers.

Connor gestures to the face-down body in scrubs. "Who is that? A casualty of war?"

Max shakes his head. "He was used by my handler, the blond man. He was told he could become one of us. When my handler died, I tried to tell him that's not how this works. But his mind was already set. He was used for hospital supplies and a watchdog for Legends."

"So that guy ratted out the people he wanted to be like? Why?" Connor continues.

"So, whoever it is that I am working for can study them. This is all about the cure. To make me Normal. No more turning into a monster. Just being normal. Please, I need help!"

Connor shakes his head. "So did my parents. So did her mother." He points at Bri, who is still holding her mom.

"I don't want any of this anymore. I was wrong. I know I was wrong. I am so sorry," Max offers.

"Sorry? And that is going to make everything better?" Connor laughs.

Allison slowly shuffles into the room, silent tears flowing down her face, holding a cell phone in her left hand. She looks at the phone. "He'll be here soon. He shouldn't have to clean up any more messes." Her stare turns to Max. "He shouldn't have had to clean up any."

Max starts to shake and cry at the calm that is Allison. "Please! I just want to disappear. Get away from this place."

"What about the people you work for? What are they going to do? Just let you walk? You still haven't told us who they are," Connor reminds.

"I told you I don't know. They worked with my handler. They sent me instructions, missions, whatever, in the mail. My wife worked with them. She hunted down potential Legends and tested them. It's how we got your friend. If you let me go, I'll have to run. Leave this town. You'll never see me again." Max tries to convince them.

"How do I know you won't stay? How do I know all of this isn't a lie so you can kill us another time?" Connor asks.

"He won't. His eyes," Allison whispers. "We can't kill him."

A visible sign of relief is seen washing over Max.

"If we kill him, then we are no better than him or his wife or his handler. And trust me, you don't want that burden on your shoulders..." she glances at Linda's corpse. "I know too soon."

Bri looks back at Allison. "So we just let him walk? After what he did?"

"Yes. If he survives the wound, he won't be in town because if we see him even so much as buy freezer waffles, we will end him." Allison ensures he understands her terms.

"What about whoever it is he works for?" Scarlett chimes in.

"We will deal with that as it comes," Allison responds, still creepy calm.

A car door slams shut outside. A moment later, Vistrus walks through the door. He immediately stops at the sight of his daughter's bloodied fists. Seeing Linda's face and quickly putting two and two together, he walks to his daughter and embraces her in a tight hug. She stands there, arms at her side, held by her father.

"I am sorry for your loss, Brianna," Vistrus offers condolences.

Brianna nods in acceptance of his words.

"You can stay with us while your house is taken care of if you would like," Vistrus offers.

Duncan wants to speak, but the words stay locked inside. Scarlett speaks up, "You can stay with me as well. I don't think Connor will mind."

Bri smiles in acknowledgment before turning back to her mother.

Vistrus lets go of his daughter and runs his right hand through his hair over and over as he tries to figure everything out.

"You should all go back to my house. Clean yourselves up. I will take it from here," Vistrus suggests in a tone that is anything but a suggestion. He pulls out his cell phone and dials a number. A moment later, all he says is, "I need a taxi service. One passenger, out-of-state fare. A tow truck for a remodel. And lastly, one deep cleaning. Trace my GPS." Vistrus hangs up and looks at his daughter, who is starting to collapse under the weight of her actions. Vistrus tosses

Connor the keys to his car. "Take everyone back. Get the blood off my daughter. I have to stay here. I will get a lift back."

CHAPTER 28

*"My job is not to simply protect you
from the world, but also
prepare you for it."*
~V. DeSalvo~

Allison's eyes flutter as she tosses and turns in her sleep. The shadows cast from the outside world dance about her room as if to tease her in her unrest.

"I'm sorry," she mutters in a pained voice.

Her legs kick at anything they can before settling into a runner's rhythm.

Her voice cries louder and louder. "No! I didn't mean it! I'm sorry! I'm sorry!"

The crescendo stops. All becomes silent and still. Even the shadows seem to have stopped dancing on the walls. Allison lays on her side, at peace for the moment. She pulls her pillow in tight, squeezing it into her.

Her heart starts racing, pounding against her ribs in an attempt to break out of its flesh-and-bone prison.

Sweat beads along her brow and neck. Her face goes flush for a moment, then all color drains away.

She shoots up in bed, eyes wide and on high alert. "Daddy!" she screams with the intensity of a person trapped and helpless, as they hang single-handedly from a branch that is slowly starting to crack off the side of a cliff.

The sound of fast-approaching footsteps halts at her door as it swings open and her lights switch on.

"Allison, what happened?" Vistrus says, wiping the sleep out of his eyes.

She stares past him, unable to focus her sight or thoughts on him. She sits upright, breathing in and out, trying to understand the subconscious conse-quences of her actions.

"Three nights in a row. You have barely gotten any sleep." Vistrus sits next to his daughter, running his hand over her head.

She turns to him, a tear falling down her face, but still, she says nothing.

Allison walks down the high school halls, staring at the ground, oblivious to her surroundings, except for the whispers. She hears them as she passes by.

"Did you hear what happened?"

"Mrs. Espinoza and Ms. Waldgrave were killed. Some home invasion."

"So sad."

"She was such a great teacher."

"I heard it was a guy hopped up on some new Russian drug."

"Mrs. Espinoza taught me so much. She was always so kind."

"Man, Ms. Waldgrave was the coolest teacher."

"I heard that Bri and her group found them after prom."

"I thought that they caught the guy and killed him themselves."

And the whispers go on and on, but Allison doesn't lift her head. She doesn't want to see anyone. She doesn't want to be there hearing the whispers and feeling the staring eyes cut into her like slivers under fingernails. She knows what she did, and every stare, no matter its intent, feels to Allison like it knows as well. The judging eyes see that she is a killer. A murderer. They are all just too afraid to say anything, too scared they might be next. Even though she knows they don't know, the thought that they might is what keeps her head down.

Trashcans line the hallways for the senior class to empty out their lockers. Allison grabs one and sets it next to her locker. She opens it up and starts throwing out every little thing that has built up over the year. Scraps, photos that decorate the inside door, and a random flask still holding some alcohol. Without checking for teachers, hall monitors, or security, she opens it, downing whatever was left in it. After shaking out the last drop, she tosses it in the garbage, just another disposable piece of junk. She continues emptying it until the only things left are her backpack and textbooks to be returned. No folders with class-work, no bottles of old soda too flat to drink, nothing. She slings the backpack around her shoulder, takes the combination lock out of the handle, and slams the door shut. She walks down the hall toward the first final of her second semester. As she passes a garbage can, she tosses in the lock.

"It all means nothing," she whispers.

As she walks into her final exam, she can feel the eyes upon her. She stops and takes a deep breath. She focuses her ears on her surroundings. Nothing. No racing hearts, no fast breathing. Nothing that signals to her anyone knows her deed. All she can feel in this room is the stress of the exam. It helps instill a sense of calm at the moment. She takes her seat and waits for the starting bell. But for a brief moment, she is calm.

The teacher looks at her watch. "In three, two, one, go."

Vistrus sits at the hardwood desk in his home office. Soft classical music carries in from another room. A stack of his wife's diaries lay open in front of him while his phone distracts him from research.

"No. I already talked with her today. I am not coming in. I am taking a personal day."

He pauses as the other person buzzes unwanted words in his ear.

Vistrus's frustration mounts. "You are more than capable of taking care of it from this point out. Just finish it up. I will be back the day after tomorrow."

He lets out a sigh of relief at the following words he hears.

"If any emergencies arise, call me. Otherwise, I trust your judgment. If I did not, you would not be working with me." Vistrus pauses for a quick response on the other end. "Thank you. See you soon."

He hangs up the phone, setting it in the drawer to keep unwanted distractions away.

Turning back to the diaries, he flips through the pages without paying attention. "There has to be something in here. Something that will help me help Allison. I cannot fail my daughter now."

He sets that diary volume aside and grabs the one before it. He opens to the first page.

> Too late. They are gone. The Mind is clear. Not to figure out why I had to clear it. I have to keep a clear mind. Time and space never-ending. Must remember it all. Safety first! Safety first!

The memories of his wife flood back. "The Mind," the random phrase she would utter that, to her, seemed perfectly normal—like he should know what she meant. He thinks that maybe he was supposed to know. Even in her diaries, she made notes, time and time again, of getting him to understand. He wonders what he can do now, years after her death, to understand what she meant and how it all started. It hits him like a ton of bricks across his chest. A sudden, powerful beating of his heart, a shot of adrenaline, and tenseness in his muscles let him know his daughter is much brighter than she lets on. The conversation they had about her class ... about looking to the root of it all. Looking for the early symptoms, the variables that no one noticed, that, if noticed, could have possibly saved her life.

He goes back to the beginning of her diaries, the first volume she started, hoping that the reason she began will be the overlooked variable he needs right now.

My new mission started. The beauty of the swirling green-and-black walls were indescribable. The vision of them stays etched in my mind, despite the task at hand. Maybe that's what it is. A mind of sorts. The Mind is black-and-green marble.

He lets go of the book. His breathing stops being voluntary. The realization of the reference to the green-and-black walls. The Mind is the old council chambers. She was there, inside those slanted walls decades before Vistrus. She never told him, but why? What mission was started? What was she involved in that he didn't know about?

He gasps for breath, returning his autonomic function to normal. He starts scanning the pages of the first volume. Most of the entries are vague, talking of her husband and the feelings of hiding her objective from him. She writes about the inner frustration of lying, even for the greater good. The guilt she feels and has felt for years.

His mind starts to question how well he actually knew Inessa. He wonders what was real. But a little solace is taken in that she wrote about the guilt and the pain she felt from keeping it. As she noted, though, it was the price for what she did.

The rest of the volume seems to be her feelings and insignificant writing about the council chambers. Vistrus did notice that numerous entries were headed with various random letters—all capital. Some entries had more than others but never less than two. And all entries only used the same groupings, no matter how few—BSOTMLPW.

Vistrus takes out a piece of scratch paper and begins going back through this volume, noting the different groupings used: BSOTMLPW, BSOT, BSOTML, BSOTPW, BSMLPW, BS, BSML, BSPW. The intrigue in the letters occupies him for a while as he ponders their meaning and significance. He wonders if it could be a coded counting system akin to Roman numerals or something else.

But an entry catches his eye, an entry that sets aside his fascination with that strange sequence of letters. One that takes a sudden turn from her previous entries by mentioning people she calls Sentinels.

The silent ones who observe. Never interfering, like documentarians. I was approached. We talked, or at least I think we did. He never spoke a word. Neither did his female companion. But still, we spoke. I knew what they were saying as if holding a conversation with a house cat. People make up their cat's response, but yet it feels so real. And they responded to my inner dialogue as if they placed it there. They spoke of something they called "The Legend of the Faoi Dhó' Duine," after which they handed me the parchment.

Vistrus looks around. A sudden, eerie feeling that he is being watched. He closes the diaries before him and slows his breath. He listens to the world around him. Nothing. Not even another heartbeat on this floor of the house. Just paranoia from his readings. He must hide the diaries, put them in a safe. Somewhere that no one, not even Allison, can get to or find. He must hide them and the parchment.

He grabs the collection of diaries and tucks them under his arm. Even in the safety of his own home, he is extra careful to avoid windows or any way someone might peer inside and see him. He collects the rolled-up parchment and heads to his music room.

He closes and locks the door behind him as he begins his descent down the stairs. At the bottom, he closes and locks that one as well. A double measure against any prying eyes. He knows he is alone in his house, but time has taught him never to assume anything. So, he looks around the room, behind the chairs, and into the engineering room that houses his soundboard for recording. All empty.

Feeling a little more secure in his isolation, he rolls his harpsichord off the area rug it rests on. The carpet rolls up, revealing nothing unusual, just the same hardwood floor throughout the room. He knocks on a few boards in a couple of different spots, listening carefully for a change in sound. Once he hears it, he presses down on one side of the plank, lifting the opposite side. He grabs the high end and slides it out. He removes a few surrounding boards and sets them aside, exposing a safe hidden below.

He enters the combination, and it opens. He places the diaries inside. He grabs the parchment, taking one last look at the impossible drawing that had been charcoaled out so many decades ago, shaking his head. He rolls it back up and places it inside. He puts everything back precisely as it was. Until he can figure out what the legend of the Faoi Dhó Duine entails, he must do everything he can to keep the identity a secret. Also, what this has to do with Inessa that these Sentinels, as she called them, entrusted her with such secrets.

The years of his wife's mental decline, she was trying to reach out, gripped in what he could only imagine being paranoia unimaginably more intense than he felt moments ago. A feeling gripped her day in and day out, tightening its grip as time marched on. A sense that, in part, shut down her ability to communicate. He must get to the bottom of what haunted his wife and how they relate to her decline: her dreams. The last thing he wants to see is his daughter slide down the same slope.

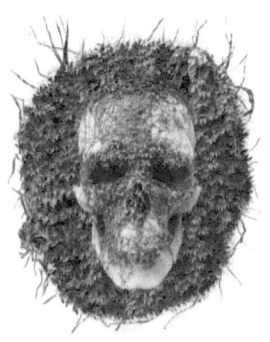

CHAPTER 29

"Remember what they say
about all good things."
~B. DeSalvo~

Students, seated in folding chairs facing the main graduation stage, once again fill the football stadium. Joyous parents watching their young ones grow up before their eyes overrun the bleachers. The warm breeze and cloudless sky signal Mother Nature shines down on the day.

Standing on stage behind the microphone at this moment is Brianna. With a saddened smile, she looks out to her fellow graduating class of 2019. She sees the smiles on their faces and the hopeful look in their eyes as they put to rest the past four years to move on to bigger and better things.

But three students in the crowd are not smiling. No hopeful twinkle in their eye. No wandering minds filled with excitement, looking forward to next year studying or partying away in some dormitory. No, the thoughts of Scarlett, Allison, and Duncan are still caught in the moment those eight nights ago. The night they saw their friend's mother die right before their eyes. A night that Allison lost all control of her emotions and not only transitioned in front of someone who was not in The Nation, but in a fit of anger and vengeance, brutally killed a teacher at this very school.

Duncan sits, his mind still there too. The image of his friend, Allison, looking the way she did, the transition to her other self etched into his mind. He knows he cannot tell anyone so the image just festers, wanting to be spoken about, wanting to escape, but he knows it must stay there—or at least within the group.

Scarlett sits staring forward, memories in her mind of the cover-up when Jack died. Memories of prom night. A little selfish yearning within that wanted nothing more than a regular prom. A tiny voice in her head that wanted nothing more than a typical end to her high school career. But she knows normal is not something she can have. If only she fully knew why.

Allison sits in the middle of the crowd, a few rows back from Scarlett. She stares ahead at the girl on stage she unknowingly confessed her feelings for while slaughtering another. Allison stares at the girl on stage who, even after watching her kill another person, gave her a hug for trying to save her mother and saving the rest of them. But this moment is not for daydreaming about the girl she can't have. Anxiety fills this moment about how the deaths of Mrs. Espinoza and Ms. Waldgrave will be covered up. Allison wonders because of the rumors that were whispered, the stories that, after a week, still haven't died. In an age where things are forgotten as quickly as they came, what rumor will become the truth?

"Today we look back..." Brianna looks out to the crowd, "...but not to yearn. Not to wish that we were still freshmen with four years ahead or to repeat any of what transpired. We look back to remember what we learned inside the classroom and out. If we think about the first day of our freshman year compared to the last day of our senior, we notice a difference. You would notice the bright light of eagerness; the shiny newness has dulled down, yellowed a bit. And that is okay because you can still remember what it was like to look down the long halls for the first time. You can still remember the agony of navigating the three floors and all the wings, trying to make it from one end to your locker and to the other, within the impossibly short three minutes they gave us between classes.

"But we did it. We made it work. It started with something small, like time management in three-minute increments, but it became so much more. It became reports, and homework, and tests, and finals, and homework, and still more homework. That turned into late nights and early mornings, and somehow, between all that, we made time for sports and choir and band and dances and dating for the first time and a first kiss. Which, of course, led to heartbreak. But we learned to deal. We learned to deal with what high school threw at us. But we learned something greater. We learned that life didn't stop for high school. It didn't pause while we were here. Friends moved away. Children were born."

Brianna stops for a moment. She looks down at the speech in front of her. She knows the next line. She's practiced it countless times over the past few days, but it is still hard. A tear falls from her eye.

"Children are born. People…" she struggles for a moment, trying to pull herself together. "People … and people die. People we love. People who have helped shape us to become who we are today. They die. And there's no way to thank them for everything they did. No last chance to say goodbye or I love … Mom … or thank you for raising me."

Brianna looks out at the crowd and makes eye contact with Allison. "But in that darkness, you find a light. A shoulder to lean on. An old friend." She looks up, trying to find Duncan. "An unsuspecting romance. Perhaps a guiding light whose moral compass always points north when yours is slightly off. All these things that life throws at you to help you remember that bad things happen, but good will always be around."

Brianna looks back down at her speech and turns the page. She sniffles into the microphone as she prepares herself for the next part.

"We are becoming adults. It is not an instantaneous event that occurs on your 18th birthday. Sure, in the eyes of the law, it is, but in reality, it takes time. So, as we move forward, we must move forward onto each new chapter of our lives, not with the dulled shine of our last day but with the newness of our first. For it is in that light that we see the good in things that we will come to overlook later. It is within the good that we can fall back on when times get tough, and we need someone to lean on. We do not know what the future holds. We can only try to imagine. But don't. Let it come to you as it will. It might be better than anything you can possibly dream of.

"I leave you now with a short video that the staff put together so that we can remember all the things that those who have gone before us did to help shape our lives."

The screen behind Brianna lights up as she walks away. Some inspirational music more apt for a Facebook video than a memorial video plays as images of Sylvia and Linda slideshow for the students to watch.

All the students are filled with memories over the past four years of the kind nature that Linda projected herself to be. The fun, carefree teacher that boys smiled at and girls wanted to be like. Images of Linda teaching class, laughing during some school trip she chaperoned, and eating popcorn at the homecoming football games over her tenure. All photos make her out to be a saint.

Images of the same vein are displayed for Sylvia. Pictures show her spinning clay on a wheel covered in wet, gray gook. Images of her in front of a canvas showing her class painting techniques. Pep rally photos of her eyeballing misbehaving kids, which garnished a few chuckles. But all images show her best side.

They are the consequences of Allison's actions. The cover-up that keeps The Nation and the Legends within hidden. The price to pay for staying safe and away from discrimination and persecution. The cost of making a sinner look like a saint. The side of her personality that will forever be hidden from society to protect the greater good.

Allison knows what she did was wrong on a fundamental level. She deals with the pain and the guilt every day since. She knew there would be a cover-up. The death of Jack brought that into harsh light. Her price to pay, for the moment, is watching two women become memorialized and remembered as upstanding members of society, the cream of the crop, the people we should all aspire to be. One of which was an okay mother and a great teacher. A flawed individual who couldn't change her ways, set in stone but regretful of her actions. The other is Linda Espinoza— teacher and killer, presented in slideshow fashion alongside the woman she killed.

The greater price Allison has to pay is living with it.

BOOK CLUB QUESTIONS

1. Did you think the first sentence of the book was effective? Why do you think the author started with that sentence?

2. Which part of the book resonated emotionally with you?

3. Why do you think the author chose this particular book title?

4. If you could pick a different title for the book, what would it be and why?

5. Was there symbolism present? If so, what did you think of the message the author was trying to convey?

6. Did the characters seem believable to you? Did they remind you of anyone?

7. Which character in the book would you most like to meet?

8. Share a favorite quote from the book. Why did this quote stand out?

9. What other books by this author have you read? How did they compare to this book?

10. If you got the chance to ask the author of this book one question, what would it be?

ABOUT AUTHOR

N ick Savage is an award-winning and Amazon best-selling author. He lives in the greater Orlando, Florida area with his wife and two cats. He is an avid video game nerd, artist, and musician.

Other books by Nick Savage:

Other books in *The West Haven Undead* series:
Us Of Legendary Gods
The West Haven Undead

The Fairlane Incidents
The Fortunate Finn Fairlane
The Fragile Finn Fairlane

Coming Soon:
World Whore, D

More books from
4 Horsemen Publications

Paranormal & Urban Fantasy

Amanda Fasciano
Waking Up Dead
Dead Vessel

Beau Lake
The Beast Beside Me
The Beast Within Me
Taming the Beast: Novella
The Beast After Me
Charming the Beast: Novella
The Beast Like Me
An Eye for Emeralds
Swimming in Sapphires
Pining for Pearls

Chelsea Burton Dunn
By Moonlight

J.M. Paquette
Call Me Forth
Invite Me In
Keep Me Close

Jessica Salina
Not My Time

Kait Disney-Leugers
Antique Magic

Lyra R. Saenz
Prelude
Falsetto in the Woods: Novella
Ragtime Swing
Sonata
Song of the Sea
The Devil's Trill
Bercuese
To Heal a Songbird
Ghost March
Nocturne

Megan Mackie
The Saint Liars
The Devil's Day
The Finder of the Lucky Devil

Paige Lavoie
I'm in Love with Mothman

Robert J. Lewis
Shadow Guardian and the
Three Bears

Valerie Willis
Cedric: The Demonic Knight
Romasanta: Father of
Werewolves

The Oracle: Keeper of the
Gaea's Gate

Artemis: Eye of Gaea
King Incubus: A New Reign

SciFi

BRANDON HILL &
TERENCE PEGASUS
Between the Devil and the Dark
Wrath & Redemption

C.K. WESTBROOK
The Shooting
The Collision

NICK SAVAGE
Us of Legendary Gods

PC NOTTINGHAM
Mummified Moon

T.S. SIMONS
Antipodes
The Liminal Space
Ouroboros
Caim
Sessrúmnir
The 45th Parallel

TY CARLSON
The Bench
The Favorite
The Shadowless

YOUNG ADULT FANTASY

BLAISE RAMSAY
Through The Black Mirror
The City of Nightmares
The Astral Tower
The Lost Book of
the Old Blood
Shadow of the Dark Witch
Chamber of the Dead God

C.R. RICE
Denial
Anger
Bargaining
Depression
Acceptance
Broken Beginnings:
Story of Thane
Shattered Start: Story of Sera
Sins of The Father:
Story of Silas

Honorable Darkness: Story of
Hex and Snip
A Love Lost: Story of Radnar

LESLIE &
JANICE SOMMERS
Brighde Reborn

M.E. BATT

The Syphon's Daughter

VALERIE WILLIS
Rebirth
Judgment
Death

DISCOVER MORE AT
4HorsemenPublications.com